SATOSHI'S FORTUNE

Alastair Mitchell

Copperfield City Press
www.copperfieldcity.com

Book cover design by Emir Orucevic
http://www.studiopulp.net
Editorial services provided by Erika Steeves
www.erikasteeves.com

Print Copy
ISBN: 978-0-9951676-4-3

Ebook
ISBN: 978-0-9951676-5-0

Dedication

3EBB3B0CA4F8CDE247DD4F59F80A8E07A1C6
A80C8652D1CE63DAC53EB4ADD680

"It is well enough that people of the nation do not understand our banking and monetary system, for if they did, I believe there would be a revolution before tomorrow morning."

—Henry Ford

SATOSHI'S FORTUNE

PROLOGUE

June 14, 2011
1 bitcoin = $19.28 USD
Satoshi's Fortune = $18,894,400 USD

"Who is Satoshi Nakamoto?"

Andrew Cohen listened to the question, or was it an order? It came from a man that was so calm it may have bordered on indifference, had there not been an unpleasant sharpness to his voice. He was dressed in the strict stylings of a government worker: black suit, black tie, black shoes. They sat across a cold metal table in what Cohen was told would be an interview room, but that he had slowly come to realize existed for more thorough interrogations. Cohen tried to ignore the empty rings welded into the table in front of him, commonly used to link to handcuffs of whoever found themselves on this side of the table. He rubbed his wrists in condolence for those he imagined had come before him.

An innocuous digital recorder hummed softly in the middle of the table, memorizing each word of their discussion, and Cohen wouldn't be surprised if there were a host of other recording devices humming away just as softly on the other side of the one-way mirror that stretched across half the compact room. He envisioned a gang of spooks in suits and lab coats behind the mirror, somehow tracking his heart rate, how much his pupils dilated after each question, and how this morning's breakfast was doing.

It was the CIA after all.

Cohen had been in the so-called interview room long enough that his mind had begun to play tricks on him, that an icy chill was emanating from the snow-coloured walls and not from the air conditioning silently being forced into the room to keep him alert.

The man in the suit seemed to have been created with his current surroundings in mind; a snowy owl hunting an unforgiving tundra. His demeanour was remote and unwelcoming. Soulless marine-blue eyes gave no hint of empathy. Thin lips gave little sign that they had ever curved into a smile. His small stature grew more menacing the longer Cohen remained in his presence despite no outward threat. He had introduced himself only as Agent Pandit, but his icy blonde hair and a lack of anything that could be called a dark complexion didn't give Cohen much reason to believe it was his real name.

Another falsehood, Cohen reflected. Just like the one they had used to get him to willingly walk straight into a locked room a mile below CIA headquarters in Virginia. It had begun with Cohen receiving a phone call one evening after he had put his newborn son to bed. The perky young woman on the other end of the line had the disarmingly cheerful voice of a social butterfly and officially invited him to attend an emerging technologies conference on behalf of the organizers at Langley. And if he was receptive to it, they would appreciate if he could deliver a presentation on a new digital form of currency called bitcoin, an open-source project he was known to be quite enthusiastic about. Cohen had happily agreed to the request and over the next week had grown excited about the opportunity to explain the concept of bitcoin and clear up any misconceptions the CIA had about the technology.

Cohen had arrived at Langley armed with a well-rehearsed PowerPoint presentation and wearing his best and only suit, usually reserved for weddings and work functions his wife deemed mandatory. He was greeted in the high-vaulted foyer of CIA headquarters by a short woman whose round face and wavy chestnut hair matched the same cheerful voice Cohen had heard over the phone. She introduced herself as Donna Dunwoody. Dressed in a navy pantsuit with a credential pass playfully bouncing across her chest, she looked every bit the busy but well-organized host of an important conference. Her heels clicked loudly on the marble floor as she guided Cohen quickly through security and into an elevator. Her continuous and infectious small talk, from the weather to how smart he must be to understand cryptography, never gave Cohen a moment to think something was amiss.

Only when the elevator opened and he was ushered down an unnecessarily wide hallway did Cohen start to suspect something wasn't quite right. The hallway was devoid of anyone you'd expect to see at a conference: no groups of attendees networking over coffee with conference passes on display, entrepreneurs touting their latest idea, or catering staff keeping snack tables properly stocked. In fact, there was only his increasingly less cheerful guide and himself. By the time they arrived at a nondescript door, which Dunwoody held open, her warm smile and friendly small talk had faded away, leaving only curt instructions for Cohen to enter what she claimed was an interview room and to wait patiently. Wait for who or what, she never specified. Cohen obediently passed the threshold and jumped as the door slammed shut behind him.

As a heavy lock slid forebodingly into place, it dawned on Cohen that he might have just willingly walked into a trap. He began to sweat and his bowels tightened as he racked his brain as to why a self-professed nerd with a ten-dollar haircut would be of such concern to the CIA. Cohen had grown up in the Boston suburb of Lexington and had been rarely more than ten feet away from his computer. He coded his first game at age ten on an old Commodore 64, graduated high school a year early, enrolled at Princeton, and quickly earned an undergrad in computer science. He followed the typical route of an eager computer nerd and moved to Silicon Valley, working at a variety of startups before moving back to the East Coast in 2009 to start a family. Some would say his job developing cryptographic security software for a small firm was boring, but it was one he found immensely satisfying. Late one night, Cohen was browsing the prevailing cryptography mailing lists when he stumbled upon an innocuous email that contained a white paper about a peer-to-peer electronic cash system. And it was through that mailing list that Cohen first started his online conversations with the author of the white paper and creator of bitcoin, Satoshi Nakamoto.

Along with Satoshi, he had communicated with a small but dedicated group of mostly cypherpunks and technologists eager to explore and help develop the world's first cryptocurrency. But the paranoia-infected words of one of the more vocal crypto-anarchists now proved to be disturbingly prophetic. *Once the government knows about bitcoin, they'll come after you and everyone involved. Hard and without mercy.*

"Tell me everything you know about Satoshi Nakamoto," Agent Pandit now asked. He spoke directly and devoid of inflection, parrying any questions Cohen had about the seminar and how long he would be held for, always bringing the conversation back to what Cohen knew about bitcoin and Satoshi. He often repeated or reworded the same question, probing for a different answer or new interpretation of a previous one.

Cohen by now had grown frustrated and tired. "I've told you everything I know already. I have nothing to hide."

Pandit was unmoved and waited for Cohen to elaborate. Either the air conditioning had further dropped the temperature or Pandit's unblinking eyes had a psychological effect because Cohen shivered and felt compelled to continue speaking.

"As I've said already, Satoshi and I met through the mailing list. He's the author of the bitcoin white paper, which outlines this peer-to-peer payment system that would bypass traditional intermediaries and function completely in the digital world." Cohen gave a piece of his never-to-be-heard speech.

"How long after first talking online did you meet Mr. Nakamoto in person?"

"As I explained earlier," Cohen said, thoroughly exasperated, "I never have. Heck, I don't know if anyone has. I don't even know if Satoshi is his real name, one person, or a group of people. I wasn't able to find a single reference to that name at any university or any cypherpunk chat room until that one email."

Agent Pandit slowly nodded in agreement, not giving any indication of whether this was news to him. "What did you two talk about, other than Bitcoin of course?"

Cohen tried to lean back but his sturdy metal chair gave no ground. He revisited every conversation he had ever had with Satoshi.

"I don't think we ever talked about anything else," he said.

"You, along with a handful of other *accomplices*, as I'll put it, had numerous discussions with Mr. Nakamoto over a period of years. And you expect me to believe you never discussed family, hobbies, education, sports, or any other sort of talking points normal human beings mention a hundred times a day?"

Cohen shrugged. "What can I say, we are really into bitcoin."

It wasn't meant to be a glib answer, but the truth. Agent Pandit was unmoved. "It is an interesting subject."

"Interesting?" Cohen asked incredulously, forgetting where he was. "It's genius! The blockchain-powered bitcoin solves the double-spending problem encountered by every previous attempt at a digital currency by having a network of independent computers verify every single transaction to confirm their authenticity." Cohen struggled to contain his enthusiasm. Here he was, locked in a room with a CIA agent clearly using a false name, and all he wanted to do was show him how to send a bitcoin transaction on his smartphone.

Pandit's eyes focused on Cohen with an eerie stillness. It was as if the snowy owl had spotted a vulnerable rabbit from across the tundra and was poised to strike. The attack never came as Pandit released his gaze and put down the pen that had been tightly gripped in his hand. Cohen realized he had been holding his breath and that perspiration had begun to seep through his dress shirt despite the chill in the air.

Either from the anxiety of being watched by the unnerving CIA agent or the pressure built up over the long hours already spent interrogated under false pretense, Cohen stood up and began pacing, unaware that such unchecked movements were usually a rabbit's last. The pacing only increased his level of frustration as he could not shake the agent's predatory gaze. He finally grew exasperated enough that he couldn't help but vent.

"You've spent hours grilling me about Satoshi, how to find him, the addresses where you presume he holds all the bitcoins he's amassed, and his intention for this fortune. Yet you haven't asked me a single thing about the technology behind bitcoin, how it works, the hashing algorithm, the genius behind the immutable shared ledger, the required consensus for any changes, the beautiful fixed logarithm release of block solutions and therefore predictable and steady release of bitcoins into circulation! About how this has the potential to fundamentally change how governments form monetary policy and challenge countless long-held notions about how to manage a currency! How this could realistically challenge Western society's very definition of money and the Federal Reserve's non-stop printing of money . . ."

Cohen stopped mid-sentence. He looked at Agent Pandit and was surprised to see a twitch in the corner of his mouth that for him might pass for a smile. This made the hairs on the back of Cohen's neck stand on edge; maybe he had stumbled into more dangerous territory than previously thought. Cohen was now fully aware that the CIA agent had him essentially under lock and key below the world's most notorious espionage organization—and wasn't getting the answers he wanted.

Pandit cleared his throat. "Mr. Cohen, you have been transacting and assisting in the development of an authorized currency that has been used in countless illegal transactions involving drugs, weapons, and organized crime. So, I'm going to ask you one last time . . . Who is Satoshi Nakamoto?"

The realization of why he had actually been lured to Langley crashed over Cohen. He collapsed into his chair.

The paranoid crypto-anarchist had been right; bitcoin had kicked the hornet's nest. They were targeting Satoshi Nakamoto and everyone else involved in the project. Unless Cohen gave the agent what he wanted, this was destined to be a one-way trip.

Cohen didn't know where or who Satoshi was. But he did have another key piece of information that he had wisely withheld. Satoshi had already given up control of his fortune—an amount so large that it could easily be used to manipulate and even destroy confidence in the cryptocurrency still very much in its infancy—by splitting control into four parts and given to four Keepers of the Fortune verified and selected by Satoshi, with Cohen's input. These four Keepers would be hunted down by those who would not want to see a decentralized currency free from government control survive. But Cohen would never reveal their existence to the agent before him, even under the threat of prison.

Cohen, feeling a swell of pride at taking a stand in the forthcoming battle, responded to Pandit's question with what had become a running joke among the bitcoin community, but now seemed oddly prescient.

Cohen leaned forward across the table and said, "Agent Pandit . . . we are *all* Satoshi."

PART 1:

1QB47YCRLkNPLGZSBny
eLnu1XfSX2b8kAC

JARVENPAA'S
PRESENTATION

Three Months Later

"What is bitcoin?" Johan Jarvenpaa paused onstage to let his question sink in. It was the question everyone in the packed auditorium had come to have answered, including Henry Hawke.

He was at the second annual Bitcoin Conference at the Imperial Hotel in the centre of London, representing the Chicago Mutual Savings Bank. A last-minute invitation had been received from the organizers for the autumn event but had been quickly denounced by the bank's CEO, saying he didn't need *another damn report on bitcoin*. But Hawke, eager to get out from behind his desk, convinced his manager to send him anyway. While his colleagues had zero interest in attending themselves, they had no problem making Hawke the target of disparaging comments around the office. At best, it was a joke about bitcoin being *magic internet money*. At worst it was a condescending warning that it was a scam. Regardless, Hawke welcomed a work-sponsored trip to the UK.

Though Hawke doubted anyone at the bank would take an interest in his report on the conference, he nevertheless put on a fresh suit each morning and dutifully attended every seminar, even if he only understood half of what was being said. During the past two days, he had seen presentations from stiff-collared economists talking about bitcoin's fixed supply of twenty-one million coins—though each coin was divisible up to eight decimal places—and anti-deflationary aspects; listened to the mantra from suspicious libertarians that the government has no right to control the monetary supply and bitcoin will replace fiat currency in our lifetime; tried to follow a wild-eyed cypherpunk as he detailed the value of anonymity in a post-government world; and watched presentations where computer science majors elaborated on future enhancements to the software, which Hawke suspected were only understood by other computer science majors.

What Hawke was hoping to hear from Jarvenpaa's Saturday afternoon presentation was a layman's explanation of bitcoin, which would not only help him clearly detail the technology in his report, but help him better understand how, according to its most ardent supporters, bitcoin was poised to lead a revolution.

"Bitcoin is a decentralized cryptocurrency!" Jarvenpaa extolled with all the excitement of a child who had just discovered ice cream for the first time. Until recently he had been a relative unknown, writing obscure cryptography papers that were of interest only to a handful of geeks. But that all changed when Jarvenpaa revealed himself to be the author of a wildly successful series of sci-fi novels that wove together epic storytelling with complex scientific theories, the news of which rocketed him into the limelight. The novels had been released under a pseudonym due to his preference for anonymity, but he recently decided it was in his own best interests to admit to his creation. Cynical bloggers pointed out that it boosted his book sales and coincided with a TV deal for the series, but Jarvenpaa was adamant that it wasn't about the money.

It was no surprise to those close to Jarvenpaa that his innate ability to distill complex ideas to their simplest forms and his contagious enthusiasm made him well-suited to be the unofficial spokesman for bitcoin. Jarvenpaa had started travelling the world to talk to anyone willing to listen and had just published his first non-fiction book called *You Know A Bit About Coins*, which had immediately been dubbed the Bitcoin Bible by many in the community.

The lanky Swede had been welcomed with open arms as the conference's keynote speaker and was now bouncing around on stage in jeans and a tweed jacket. He sported a golden-blonde ponytail and wispy beard, those of a hipster who had missed the sixties by a generation. Hawke settled in with all eyes in the room following Jarvenpaa's every move.

"Bitcoin is a decentralized cryptocurrency. Let's break down each part of that fancy description. At its most basic level, bitcoin is just digital cash. You send and receive it online like you would a twenty-dollar bill in person. So that's why it's a *currency*.

"You may say 'Hey, wait a minute, Johan! I've been spending money online for years! Haven't you heard of PayPal or a credit card?'" It elicited a small chuckle from the audience.

"Well, you're right! But that isn't exactly like cash. With those methods, you always need to trust a middleman like a bank to send money online. The cost of using a middleman, aside from paying a healthy fee, is the loss of privacy, the risk that they may hold or take back *your* money for any reason, and the exclusion of the unbanked! Did you know billions of people in the world's poorest countries don't even have access to a bank account, essentially blocking them from participating in the world economy?! That is outrageous!" Jarvenpaa dashed to one end of the stage as he spoke into the microphone headset, leaving his hands free to gesticulate wildly.

"There have been many attempts at creating digital cash before bitcoin, but none could solve the double-spending problem. Essentially, without a trusted middleman, how can you be certain that person X who paid you didn't copy that *digital coin* and send it to person Y first? After all, they say anything digital can be copied. That's great for pirating music and TV shows—which I have never done," he gave an exaggerated wink to the crowd for a laugh, "but terrible for digital cash that you don't want counterfeited.

"Bitcoin solved this problem by incentivizing a network of independent computers to validate your transaction and confirm person X hadn't already sent that digital coin to someone else. They can confirm that because every previous transaction is on a shared ledger, which everyone maintains a copy of. You may have heard of this ledger before . . ." Jarvenpaa revelled in all the knowing smiles from those who understood what he was alluding to and was excited to share the answer with those who didn't.

"This shared ledger is called the blockchain!"

A wave of understanding rippled through the audience, including Hawke. A key term he had heard thrown about started to fit into the bigger picture. Jarvenpaa was on a roll now.

"Now, bear with me, I'm going to nerd out a bit to explain how cryptography incentivizes those computers to validate transactions and gives birth to new bitcoins—don't worry, it's decidedly less painful than it sounds.

"First thing you'll need to know is what a hashing algorithm does: it takes any dataset and turns it into a single number called a hash. What's so cool about this function is that it's unpredictable, repeatable, but only works in one direction. When you change just a single number in that dataset, you get a completely different hash. If I give you the original dataset and you use the same hashing algorithm, it will result in the same hash. But if I give you the hash, you cannot find out what the original dataset was.

"How does this relate to bitcoin? Well, the bitcoin rules announce to everyone that there's this special magic number. Each computer collects all the recent transactions plus an arbitrary number called a nonce into a dataset called a block, and then does that algorithm mumbo-jumbo to get a hash. If that hash doesn't match that magic number, they keep guessing a new nonce until it does.

"It's literally a race between all the computers to see who guesses it first! The winner jumps for joy and tells everyone else that they found the correct nonce! Sorta like yelling bingo . . . but instead they yell BITCOIN!

"All the other computers verify that that guess is correct and they add that block of transactions onto the previous block, forming a chain of every single bitcoin transaction that has ever occurred—an immutable public ledger secured by the entire network. Once everyone catches their breath, a new magic number is revealed and the process starts over again.

"This cryptographic process is called *mining* and the incentive for working so hard is that the winning computer today is rewarded with fifty bitcoins. And voila! Fifty new bitcoins have entered circulation. And that's why bitcoin is a *crypto*currency."

Hawke loosened his tie and began fiddling with the stainless-steel silver watch that hadn't left his sight since it had been posthumously gifted to him last Christmas. From his seat at the rear, he looked around to see if anyone else was struggling with the concept. Many in the crowd were actively nodding, but Hawke knew from investment product meetings at the bank that nodding didn't mean they understood what was being said, but they wanted to give the impression they did.

A few attendees weren't paying much attention at all. One was a pudgy man at the end of the back row. Fat poked out of his open collar and the buttons on his dress shirt were in a struggle to the death to keep his ample belly contained. He was using his balled-up suit jacket as a makeshift pillow as he dozed. A few rows forward, three co-founders of a startup huddled around a laptop, intermittently popping their heads up one at a time like meerkats to see if their hushed discussion had disturbed anyone. They made Bitcoin ATMs that they branded "the BTM," for Bitcoin Teller Machine. Over drinks the previous night, Hawke had pointed out to them that *Bitcoin* didn't actually replace the *Automatic* in the acronym and that Bitcoin ATM might be more easily understood by the general public. They had given him varying looks of disappointment at his inability to appreciate their business before proceeding to ignore him for the rest of the evening.

Hawke's eyes then fell to a woman in an aisle seat near the stage who was attentively taking notes on a slim laptop. She was one of the few women he had seen at the conference, and almost all the non-socially-awkward men, which by Hawke's generous estimate was a quarter of the attendees, had approached her at one time or another. She had radiant olive skin and jet-black hair that began to gently curl as it reached her shoulders. Her wide almond eyes gave you the sense that she rarely missed a beat. He had yet to see her full lips part into a smile but imagined it was warm and knowing. Hawke forced himself to refocus away from her and join the rest of the crowd still enthralled by Jarvenpaa ricocheting around the stage and explaining why bitcoin was the largest technical breakthrough of the twenty-first century.

"That's just a simplified explanation of how bitcoin works under the hood. But for any of that to matter, bitcoin has to survive in the cutthroat world of banks and governments that have historically opposed any type of money they can't control. And that's why decentralization is such an important concept.

"First off, we have to note that the bitcoin software is open source. Which means that any one of you can review the code, contribute to it, and run it whenever you want. There's not any one person or company that owns the software. You could say that bitcoin belongs to everyone— and to no one!

"Second, remember those computers I mentioned moments ago, plugging away and solving blocks and securing the network? Well, they are doing so according to the rules outlined in the bitcoin software, rules that can't be changed unless everyone agrees. That's why I can't dictate that the maximum supply of bitcoin is now forty-two million bitcoins instead of the current twenty-one. Because if I ran that new version of the software, everyone else would say, 'Beat it, Johan! We don't agree to that change!' And I would be ignored.

"And lastly, remember how I mentioned everyone has a copy of the shared ledger, the blockchain? That ensures that all those historical transactions will never be lost; it's just in too many places for a malicious entity to delete forever.

"So hopefully that illustrates why I say bitcoin is decentralized; it has no central authority and no single point of failure. Despite what the banks and governments may want, they cannot stop bitcoin!"

A small chorus of cheers from the most faithful spread through the crowd. Jarvenpaa came to the edge of the stage, his arms spread wide, ready to embrace the entire auditorium. "It is with the utmost joy that I thank you for listening to me ramble on today and a big congratulations to everyone here. . . . You are all now bitcoin experts!"

***

The audience displayed its appreciation with a wholehearted standing ovation. Jarvenpaa bowed and then joined in clapping. He reminded the crowd that tomorrow morning there would be a few more amazing presentations before the conference wrapped up. The applause finally dwindled and people shuffled out of the auditorium while sharing their insights on the presentation with their neighbours.

Hawke waited patiently for his turn to join the outflow, thinking about how he would translate the newly gleaned information into a readable report, as short on technical jargon as possible for the technophobic bank managers. He also wondered how receptive his uncle would have been.

Hawke had been raised by his Uncle Peter, who at one time had been an executive and board member at Chicago Mutual, before a puzzling series of events culminated in his death this past Christmas. Events that Hawke silently maintained were only fractured and distorted pieces of the whole story. Thanks to the remaining threads of friendship towards his late uncle, or perhaps undeclared guilt, after the funeral, the CEO of the bank had offered Hawke a job—no small favour with the country still huddling in the shadow of the Financial Crisis. A few years removed from college, with few other prospects, he quickly accepted a dream job at the bank. But adding to the peculiarity of his uncle's death, the CEO, his uncle's former best friend who had frequented family barbecues and was never at a loss to discuss the Blackhawks' performance with Hawke, had never replied to his email thanking him for the opportunity. And the few times they had crossed paths at the office, Hawke had been ignored like a bad memory.

The job itself also failed to live up to Hawke's expectations. Long, thick commutes in rush hour; rabbit-hole meetings whose only observable purpose was to make everyone look stressed and therefore busy to their supervisors; sales efforts to push products onto unsuspecting clients that did little else but make the bank money—they all took turns sucking the life out of Hawke. By now he held no love for the corporate world, but was simply content to have a job.

He would steadfastly maintain over pints with friends that he hadn't yet tricked himself into thinking it was a career, and that eventually he would find something else to his liking. Hawke consciously ignored the fact that the conversation repeated itself almost every Friday night at the pub. But it was hard to ignore that this attitude filtered into his work since his immediate supervisor, a balding yet baby-faced lifer who had gone as far up the corporate ladder as his lack of charm and intelligence would allow, frequently took issue with his resistance to the official Chicago Mutual Savings Bank corporate culture. He jumped at the chance to lecture Hawke on being a team player whenever he deemed it necessary, which usually coincided with the monthly performance review all account managers were subjected to. Hawke generally paid him no mind as he easily hit the bank's required sales targets, not by an amount that would have made his uncle proud but enough that his growing absenteeism and casual cynicism were overlooked.

Despite his attitude towards work, Hawke managed to keep an ever-present mischievous smile, one that led more than a few of his colleagues to believe he knew something they didn't and the rest to believe he was full of shit. And not being an unhandsome man, with that smile and the implied menace from a few hockey fight scars circling his emerald eyes, the odd girl in his office or pub took a fancy to him. Hawke's attention was enough for them to entertain thoughts that they may have found a future husband, only to find that his interest waned when something more interesting, an idea, new tech, or maybe a different girl came along.

A few last chattering conference attendees went by and Hawke reciprocated a nod from a passing middle-aged man in a wheelchair whose smile suggested familiarity, though Hawke didn't recognize him. With the path now clear, he saw Jarvenpaa speaking with the exotic woman from the front row. Hawke figured he would try to get two birds with one stone: a business card from Jarvenpaa to later contact for feedback on the accuracy of his report, and perhaps a phone number from the woman to meet socially.

Jarvenpaa was leaning against the stage with his arms crossed, listening intently and nodding along while the young woman led the conversation. Hawke approached and it took a moment before they realized he was there, the woman abruptly stopping mid-sentence before he managed to hear much.

"Mr. Jarvenpaa? I was wondering if you had a moment. My name's Henry Hawke." Hawke held out his hand and realized too late he had interrupted a private tête-à-tête. But Jarvenpaa jumped to, slapped his palm into Hawke's, and shook vigorously.

"Of course you are! So glad to meet you, Mr. Henry Hawke."

Hawke turned to the woman, whose alert eyes sized him up. She was professionally dressed in a navy pantsuit and jacket combination and a red blouse, purposely chosen to try and hide her form from being a distraction. A press pass dangled from around her neck.

Hawke introduced himself and received a polite but forced greeting. She accepted the handshake out of courtesy. "Sara Noor."

"Sorry, did I interrupt something important?"

Noor and Jarvenpaa exchanged a look.

"Not at all. Just discussing a few technical aspects of the presentation," she said.

Hawke smiled. "I think it all made sense. But getting coins from blocks? Sounds an awful lot like Super Mario Bros., if you ask me."

Noor made her appreciation of the joke clear by rolling her eyes. Hawke decided she must be a Crash Bandicoot fan.

"I'm afraid I must be off," she said, kissing Jarvenpaa on both cheeks without further acknowledging Hawke. His eyes followed her to the exit when Jarvenpaa cleared his throat.

"She's got a beautiful mind, that one." Jarvenpaa's voice had a slight Scandinavian accent and a weariness that wasn't detectable in his onstage persona. "She probably knows as much about bitcoin and cryptocurrencies as anyone around. Definitely the web's top crypto journalist."

"Who does she work for?"

Jarvenpaa stroked his beard. "Sara Noor works for no one. She runs her own website focusing on cryptocurrencies. She's the editor, researcher, writer. She does it all. Tough but fair reporting in my humble opinion."

Hawke made a mental note to check it out before proceeding to explain to Jarvenpaa that he was an account manager at a bank and asked if it was acceptable to reference him in his report and possibly to contact him in the future with any questions. Having the de facto public bitcoin expert would give his report added weight and credibility with management.

"You're a banker? You want to give them another report on bitcoin? History does repeat itself!" Jarvenpaa clamped both hands on Hawke's wide shoulders with the excitement of someone who had just found their long-lost brother. "Though I'd be careful how you present it. I don't believe bankers are inherently evil, just the power bestowed upon them by the system lends itself to immoral behaviour. Maybe with the bitcoin network now up and running, they'll be more receptive. It would be in their own self-interest as well; the disintermediation of a bank's core functions will happen so fast they won't know what hit them. Mark my words, within ten years' time every bank in the world will have a blockchain department frantically trying to figure out how to keep themselves relevant!"

"Right," Hawke said. Something about Jarvenpaa gave him pause. The auditorium had emptied and it was just the two of them. "Well, the banks have to make money somehow, right?"

Jarvenpaa threw his head back and laughed. "Your uncle said the same thing to me a lifetime ago!"

Hawke's eyes flashed wide. "You knew my uncle?"

Jarvenpaa's lively demeanour gave way to a mournful weariness. "We met years before his . . ." Jarvenpaa cleared his throat, ". . . accident."

It was common for people to refer to his uncle's death as an accident, but Hawke sensed another layer to Jarvenpaa's empathy.

"We talked regularly after meeting through an online mailing list of mutual interest back in 2008 I guess it would be. He had some quite lively communications about the decentralization of currency, about the role the government and banks should play in monetary policy." Jarvenpaa's laugh was bittersweet. "Ol' Pete could be quite the stubborn mule! But once he embraced something new, it was quite a sight!"

Hawke had never heard his uncle called *Pete* by anyone. It had always been a firm and unapologetic Peter. And that his Uncle Peter had befriended the now-famous novelist was a complete surprise. But what really caught his attention was that it seemed his uncle had been talking to Jarvenpaa about bitcoin . . . before it was released. Hawke asked him as much.

Jarvenpaa opened his mouth to answer, but his eyes darted to the back of the auditorium. He paused before saying, "Oh, I'm just rambling on like I do when I get excited. Don't pay me any mind." He hastily produced a business card and shoved it into Hawke's hand, said his goodbyes, and quickly vanished behind the stage on which minutes before he had stood so confidently. Hawke glanced over his shoulder towards the auditorium exit to see what had caused Jarvenpaa to withdraw so quickly. Nobody was there but the metal door was coming to a close, but not before he thought he heard the grinding reverb of a wheelchair rolling away.

BERNIE'S PITCH

Hawke regrouped with the rest of the attendees in the foyer outside the auditorium where brash exhibition booths lined the walls. Most were adorned with the bright orange and slanted capital B with two falling strokes at the top and bottom representative of the bitcoin symbol, used to denote a currency much like the dollar sign or euro symbol. If not the bitcoin symbol, the booths displayed a company's name and logo, with modern graphics of numbers flying about, apparently offering a revolutionary software solution to whatever problem one might have. Hawke navigated through the throbbing crowd of salesmen, entrepreneurs, and geeks parroting the same buzz words and analogies gleaned from earlier presentations as if it were their own sharp insight.

"It's like the internet in 1994 . . . sure it's a bit difficult to use and understand but people will catch on!"

"Using cash instead of bitcoin is like using the horse and buggy when the car came out!"

"Bitcoin is money 2.0!"

Hawke thought it must be easy to see the future when someone just presented it to you. More important to him though was the peculiar ending to the conversation with

Jarvenpaa. To clear his mind, he headed towards a small bar tucked into the foyer corner. Before he could order, Hawke was startled by a meaty hand slapping his back.

"You look like you want to make a fortune!" The pudgy man who had been snoozing during Jarvenpaa's presentation was now very much awake, and judging by how loud he spoke, in a harsh English accent, he wanted everyone to know it. He sidled up to Hawke's left at the bar with his jacket-cum-pillow now back in its jacket form.

Hawke pretended he hadn't heard him as he signalled the bartender, but the pudgy man would not be denied. He ran his fat finger through thinning, greasy hair and then slapped Hawke's back again and boomed, "I'm talking to you, boyo! The kid looking to make a fortune." Hawke looked him over and saw watery, bloodshot eyes that told tales of long nights spending money unwisely. Stale breath was only overpowered by the ample amounts of cologne he must have bathed in.

"I'm okay, thanks though," Hawke responded as he wondered what he had done to suddenly become this unsavoury man's new best friend.

The man pretended to hear a different reply and stuck his hand out. "I am Bernard Salisbury the Fourth, CEO, president, and founder of one of the largest cryptocurrency investment firms in the world!" he boasted. "I'm actually a Duke if I'm being honest, but that sounds too pretentious, don't ya think, boyo? So instead you can just call me Bernie Bitcoin, all my friends and investors do . . . and wouldn't you know they're one and the same!"

"Nice to meet your, Mr. Salisbury." Hawke quickly shook the damp hand and then subtly wiped his own on his pants.

Bernie Bitcoin looked almost insulted at the lack of his preferred nickname, but nevertheless carried on. "Pleased to meet you . . .?"

"Henry Hawke."

"That sounds like the name of a millionaire industrialist!" Bernie exploded. "But industrialists are dead. Old dirty business that is. And such a small ROI these days—that's return on investment, by the way. Let's make Henry Hawke the name of a cryptocurrency millionaire! Did I tell you I run a crypto investment firm? Well I do, and I've made our investors a plus 300% ROI over the past year. That's tripling their money. And that's better than anywhere in the City or Wall Street. So I'll ask you again, as a bright young lady-killer in a nice suit, do you want to make a fortune?"

"I think I'm okay for now, but thanks for the offer." Hawke had met plenty of Bernie's type both through the bank and in Chicago pool halls, and if there actually were any positive return, it probably wasn't generated through legal means. Bernie continued to extoll his financial wizardry as they waited for the bartender to notice them. Eventually turning to the pair, the bartender asked for their order and Bernie ordered two beers. Passing one to Hawke before he could say anything, Bernie clinked their beer bottles and said, "To Satoshi Nakamoto, the future richest man in history!"

Unsure of the claim, Hawke said cheers anyways and took a swig. He felt the bartender's expectant eyes on them. Bernie ignored the bartender for as long as possible until he had no choice, finally feigning exasperation while tapping on his pant's pockets.

"What would you know, boyo, I misplaced my wallet."

"Luckily, sir," the bartender politely gestured to a sign on the bar that said *Bitcoin Accepted Here*. Below the words was a QR code, which Hawke thought looked a lot like a barcode but from a presentation yesterday knew it was a visual representation of a bitcoin address where you could send payment, similar to how an email address is where you would send an email. "All you have to do is scan this QR code with the bitcoin wallet on your phone, as I'm sure a wealthy bitcoiner such as yourself has, and then send the equivalent value of the beer." The bartender had the English knack for being polite and condescending at the same time.

Bernie Bitcoin mumbled something about having his fortune in bitcoin saved on a different wallet and then slapped his hand on Hawke's shoulder. "You got this, right? Cost of doing business, right, boyo? Here's my card if you're serious about making gobs of money."

He tucked a business card into Hawke's breast pocket and hastily took off, elbowing his way through the crowd and yelling back to Hawke, "I have to run, very important meeting, some big money from the City are here to see me and want to get in on my fund before it goes up another 300%!"

Hawke was left with one beer and the bill for two. He reached for his wallet when he again heard the consistent reverb of a wheelchair. He then felt a hand rest gently on his arm.

"It's quite all right, young man, this round is on me." The man in the wheelchair pulled up in the spot Bernie had vacated. He spoke in a soft elegant accent, no doubt the product of spending time in expensive English boarding schools. A heartfelt smile sat below a waxed brown moustache that went straight out across his cheeks, a shade darker than the hair on his head, which was carefully parted to the side. Thick crow's feet lined his grey eyes, which had heavy bags beneath them, unable to hide a persistent stress—yet his gaze remained vigilant, the weight of whatever was on his mind overpowered by his natural inclination towards positivity. Tan slacks and a crisp oxford shirt gave the impression of a professor caught on a day off. His hand movement was slow and measured, a slight shake almost imperceptible, and he produced a smartphone from his pocket.

The man reached up and scanned the *Bitcoin Accepted Here* QR code with his smartphone, which beeped obediently. He then tapped the screen a couple times and smiled. "There you are, sir, all paid up." The man looked delighted to have paid for someone else's beer. The patient bartender thanked them and went on to the next customer.

"You didn't have to do that, sir," Hawke said. "But what exactly did you just do?"

31

"Amazing wasn't it? Simply amazing. I just paid for the beers in bitcoin by scanning his QR code, which is a quick way to get his bitcoin address, with my bitcoin wallet here on my phone." The man held up and wobbled his smartphone. "No bank involved, no credit card, just the equivalent of me handing that good man the money for those beers. And he didn't have to be right before us either. He could have been on the other side of the world and all I would need is his bitcoin address. And on top of that, it needn't be the price of two drinks. It could be any amount whatsoever!"

Hawke noticed the man's hand begin to shake anew as he became more excited.

"Well, thanks for the beer. Getting stuck with the bill was my fault for being near that guy. Should've counted my fingers after shaking his hand," Hawke remarked.

"Hopefully you don't feel the same way after shaking mine. I'm Virgil Pennyworth." Pennyworth outstretched his now tranquil hand, which Hawke welcomed.

"Henry Hawke. And no, you haven't tried to make me a fortune yet so I think you're a little more trustworthy."

Pennyworth chuckled. "Well, the night's early. And nice to meet you, Henry. I'd like to think I'm a little more trustworthy than Bernie Bitcoin, but that's not exactly setting the bar very high. And since we're at a bitcoin conference, it seems apt that I bought your beer with bitcoin."

Hawke nodded. "I'm still trying to figure out how to present this to my bosses, and if they'll even care."

"Those dinosaurs in Chicago will want nothing to do with bitcoin. No bank will at the beginning."

Hawke was caught off guard. First Jarvenpaa alluded to a previously unknown friendship with his deceased uncle, with bitcoin as the unlikely linchpin. And now this man he had never met already seemed to know an uncomfortable amount about him.

"How did you know I worked at a bank in Chicago?"

Another soft chuckle from Pennyworth. "I helped organize this conference and recalled your name and company from our attendee list. Chicago Mutual Savings Bank, isn't it?"

Hawke felt foolish. "Right."

"However, I like how your mind immediately jumped to suspicion. Trust, but verify. That's a good trait to carry into this brave new world."

Hawke's eyes narrowed. "What world are you talking about?"

A rueful smile crept across Pennyworth's lips. "Let's go somewhere and talk."

SHARIFF'S DECISION

Aziz Shariff stood in Russell Square, a quiet park directly across the street from the Imperial Hotel. Through the iron fence he kept an eye on the hotel's entrance, his hands stuffed into the pockets of his worn leather jacket and clinging to his smartphone. Not wanting to remain in one spot for long, he began to pace the fence until he came upon a small outdoor café lined with potted ferns. A couple of women in cashmere coats sipping tea at a plastic table gave him apprehensive looks; apparently, his unshaven face and middle-eastern complexion didn't convey a sense of security. Neither did Shariff's inability to remain still. There was a deep well of anxious energy rippling through every fibre in his body, compressed into his diminutive frame and constantly seeking ways to escape.

Shariff carried on past the café and continued patrolling the park, early autumn leaves from the oak trees littering the pathways. He brought his sweatshirt hood up to hide as much of his face as possible, not wanting to be spotted by any intelligence agents undoubtedly prowling about. He eyed every individual in the park, trying to discern if the group of men tossing a frisbee was MI5; if the woman walking a tiny yapping dog was CIA; if the tea-drinking women were actually Interpol! What form would the Cabal take today?

Living underground had imbued him with what some might diagnose as extreme paranoia but Shariff knew was a survival instinct—and that instinct was loudly banging the war drums in his head right now. That draining mindset coupled with physical exhaustion nearly overtook Shariff as he sometimes veered slightly as he walked, but he forced his mind to stay alert and straightened himself out before anyone noticed. The usual dark rings under his eyes had been reinforced by countless sleepless nights. It had only gotten worse in the months after receiving word of what happened to Andrew Cohen.

That idiot, Shariff thought. It's one thing to be vocal for your cause, as Shariff was. It's another thing to be so gullible that you voluntarily walk right into the lion's den. The CIA was obviously controlled by the Cabal! And now Cohen was compromised and persona non grata in Shariff's mind. How much information had the traitor given up? How much *could* he have given up?

There was a privacy paradox to their work on bitcoin. The code was open source and transparent, but the people who wrote it often sought privacy. The most well-known person that nobody knew was Satoshi Nakamoto himself. Nobody, not even those involved in the bitcoin project from the beginning such as Shariff, knew anything about its creator—and for good reason! Shariff was certain Satoshi would have been murdered by the Cabal had his identity been known. Most of the others on the project chose the same path, with two exceptions: Cohen—who was now undoubtedly a CIA stooge—and Shariff himself—now living underground.

Shariff found himself wandering at the far end of the park. Every wary cell in his body told him to run, to head back underground and keep one step ahead of the Cabal for as long as he could. But any of Shariff's self-preservation instincts were overpowered by a fervour to tear down the barbed wire fences around them that was so violent it would make a religious zealot appear apathetic.

Shariff gave one last glance around the park for any suspicious eyes lingering a moment too long, any red dots floating in the air towards his chest, or any jack booted thugs positioned to rush him. Seeing no such thing, he put his head down and hurled himself towards the hotel.

It was time to burn Satoshi's Fortune to the ground.

PENNYWORTH'S HOOK

Henry Hawke followed Pennyworth through the foyer to the uncrowded hotel lobby, unsure if he should be offering to push his wheelchair but ultimately left him to it. It would have been awkward anyway as Hawke already carried two beers, his own and another one he had purchased for Pennyworth before leaving the bar. Paid for with what at the conference would be considered old-fashioned paper money, but the bartender happily accepted it, nonetheless. A pert woman in a red vest welcomed them from behind the wooden reception desk as they navigated to an empty lobby table surrounded by plush burgundy leather seats. Hawke set the beers down on the table and pushed one seat aside to make room for Pennyworth's wheelchair and then took his own seat.

"So," Hawke slid one beer towards Pennyworth and took the other, "what's this brave new world I now inhabit?" While many of the speakers at the conference were knowledgeable and spoke about bitcoin to a degree Hawke couldn't fully comprehend, their bold claims hadn't erased his doubts about the cryptocurrency's ability to change the world. Yes, he believed it had a chance to disrupt many business models. But hearing many in attendance boast about how the price would eventually break one thousand, maybe ten thousand dollars per bitcoin was more akin to fanaticism than optimism. He awaited the sales pitch from the man in the wheelchair before him.

Hawke noticed Pennyworth's smile spreading wide. "What's with the grin?" Hawke asked, finding himself smiling as well, disarmed by Pennyworth's calm nature.

Pennyworth motioned with his beer bottle to Hawke's head after taking a sip. "I can see the gears turning up there. And I might smell smoke."

"Just trying to sort all this out. How bitcoin actually works under the hood," Hawke lied, not wanting Pennyworth to know he was still debating his trustworthiness. But Hawke had an uncanny feeling that Pennyworth knew that.

"Have you created a bitcoin transaction yet? Do you have a wallet on your phone?" Pennyworth asked.

"Actually no, I haven't done that yet. I don't have any bitcoins so didn't think it was necessary."

"Well then, we know our first step," Pennyworth said, a professor eagerly waiting to help a fresh student discover something new. "Grab your smartphone and download a bitcoin wallet app."

Hawke found the top-rated wallet and began the download. A silent minute later, it was installed with a password added. "Okay, I think I'm ready."

"Let's hope so," Pennyworth said. "Now click on the *receive bitcoins* icon."

After pressing the icon, another QR code appeared on the screen with a long string of alphanumeric characters below it.

"That's the QR code for an address on your phone's bitcoin wallet. You see that funny looking alphanumeric string?" Pennyworth asked.

Hawke looked below the QR code and saw what seemed to amount to gibberish: 1BckeFYt6az1G2Awqc6oQqZHhUJCRDWGFP.

"That's what a cryptologist would call your public key. But you can just call it your *bitcoin address*. You can generate an unlimited number of bitcoin addresses in your wallet, and you'll be able to access them all. So you can send bitcoins to each address and your wallet will sum the total." Pennyworth noticed Hawke was struggling with the concept. "Think of it this way; you have a physical wallet with many folds and in each fold you can have different notes. Fives, tens, twenties, right?"

Hawke nodded.

"And if you have that wallet, you have access to a cumulative amount of paper money. It works the same with a bitcoin wallet. If you control the wallet, you control all the bitcoins in all the addresses within."

"All right, but what happens if some other wallet generates the same address?" Hawke looked at the thirty-four characters and knew it was rare but eventually someone must be able to luck upon it. Pennyworth brimmed with excitement as if it were the question he'd been waiting to be asked all day.

"There are two to the power of one hundred sixty possible bitcoin addresses."

Hawke didn't react. He knew it was an impossibly large number, but the math was far beyond anything he could do in his head, let alone rationalize the result. It reminded him of sci-fi TV shows where they explain how big the universe is—its size simply incomprehensible. Pennyworth, one step ahead of him, began to put the number into perspective.

"Think of it this way; for every grain of sand on Earth, create a new planet with the same number of grains of sand. Now, for each one of those grains of sand on every single one of those planets, there are twenty-six billion unique addresses." Pennyworth let the sheer immensity of the number hang in the air. Then he added, "So we shan't worry about duplicate addresses anytime soon."

Hawke nodded, which he seemed to be doing a lot this weekend.

"I'm going to send you some bitcoin." Pennyworth took his own phone and followed the same steps as when he paid for the beer. He leaned forward to scan the QR code on Hawke's phone, typed in the amount, and hit send, all with the same enthusiasm Hawke had witnessed before.

Almost immediately, Hawke's phone beeped. He looked at his phone and his eyes widened. But his elation quickly gave way to suspicion at seeing his balance increase. "I can't accept this. It's too much."

The disarming smile again. "Don't worry, Henry. I have a feeling you were raised to have a good head on your shoulders. I'm just trying to pay it forward and besides"— he tapped on the wheelchair—"I can't take 'em with me."

"Thanks again, but what do I owe you for this?" Hawke knew everything had a price, especially free money. He checked the exchange rate built into the app. "It says here that's worth about fifty dollars."

Pennyworth emitted a soft, knowing laugh. "Mr. Hawke, it's worth a lot more than that."

They carried on their conversation, drifting from the challenges bitcoin adoption will present to Hawke's job at the bank to Pennyworth's favourite London pub. At that point Pennyworth insisted they meet there for dinner that night, and Hawke agreed. Too quickly, their beers were in need of replacement.

"So, do you trust me yet?" Pennyworth said.

Hawke didn't think he wore his distrust so visibly. Pennyworth had an exceptional ability to correctly guess what Hawke was thinking, and Hawke didn't know if that made him trust Pennyworth more—or less. As if to reinforce the point, Pennyworth asked, "Your job at the bank isn't exactly giving you a sense of purpose, is it?"

Hawke rotated the empty beer bottle by its neck to give himself time to consider the question and the underlying reason it was being asked.

"It's a pay cheque" was the best response Hawke could think of. He hadn't seriously discussed his career or aspirations for his life in general with anyone since his uncle passed, and he realized that despite his beer-fuelled brainstorming sessions at the pub with friends, he still hadn't.

"Why do you want to be a banker?"

Hawke answered immediately. "I'm not a banker, not really. It's a job, and it'll do for now until I figure something out."

"I know," Pennyworth sympathized. "Many more a man would go rogue if he only knew how."

Hawke was thunderstruck. The beer bottle fell from his hand and shattered. He hadn't heard those words since last December—his uncle's last words. It had become a favourite saying of his uncle's, but only after his unceremonious dismissal from the same bank where Hawke now worked. Uncle Peter had often repeated it to the point where Hawke had begun to ignore its meaning as young men tired of fatherly advice tend to do, reckoning with twenty-odd years of life experience he had already figured it all out.

But then a late-night accident and early morning visit from a solemn police officer who had a story of bad weather conditions and too much to drink, and suddenly Hawke was alone, never to receive such advice again.

Now his uncle's haunting last words were repeated to him by a mysterious man who knew just what buttons to push to get Hawke's attention. A man who Hawke assumed had been eavesdropping on his earlier conversation with Johan Jarvenpaa. The primal fight-or-flight instinct, previously resting peacefully in the recesses of Hawke's mind, had just been awoken.

"What did you just say?" Hawke stood up, his voice raised.

Pennyworth didn't flinch. Though not unkind, all sympathy had left his eyes, now replaced with a challenge. A challenge to do what, Hawke didn't yet know.

"Virgil, did you know my uncle?"

"We did everything we could to keep you safe. But now a swarm is heading towards—"

Suddenly a loud klaxon alarm rang throughout the hotel, drowning out anything Pennyworth had to say. The lobby went dark. Only the fading daylight sneaking through the glass front doors was left to guide them.

Answers would have to wait as Hawke immediately stepped behind Pennyworth and pulled the wheelchair back. In addition to having Pennyworth's well-being in mind, Hawke also didn't want to get separated before he got another piece to a puzzle he hadn't known existed at the start of the day.

Hawke guided Pennyworth out the front doors into a courtyard that was quickly being filled with conference attendees and hotel guests. Some were annoyed at the inconvenience, others kept their drinks in hand and started chatting again once far enough away from the alarm. The ATM meerkats poked their heads up from the crowd and spotted a familiar face in Hawke. They navigated their way towards him in single file to ask what he knew about the alarm, which was nothing. Disappointed again with Hawke, but not surprised at his lack of knowledge, they happily filtered back into the crowd in search of someone who knew something.

Hawke wanted Pennyworth to start explaining why so many people in the bitcoin world seemed to know his uncle, but when he turned to ask, there was only emptiness. Pennyworth had vanished. Hawke elbowed his way through the throng of people, the last of the daylight quickly fading, and anxiously called out Pennyworth's name to no avail. Now alone in the middle of a crowd, Hawke was left with only his uncle's last words, delivered by a man with an uncertain motive, words that now more than ever confounded him and made him feel small in an expanding world of unknowns.

Many more a man would go rogue if he only knew how . . .

SHARIFF'S SECRET

Aziz Shariff struggled alone against the London Police department's five hundred thousand all-seeing eyes of the CCTV cameras, the state-sponsored peeping toms leering at him on every block. A simple glimpse of his face would be shared with a network of amiable security organizations like a pervert passing around his ex-girlfriend's private photos. And Shariff knew the Cabal was jacked into the network, likely covertly through one proxy agency or another. What form would they take tonight? MI5? London's Metropolitan Police? He didn't know and didn't want to find out.

The Cabal had all the resources in the world to hunt him. It owned nothing but controlled everything—a flock of probing cameras, an army of officers blinded by duty, a staggering computer network running the most advanced facial-recognition software—and all of it backed by an indifferent populace and fronted by unaccountable politicians with unseen motives always pushing for deeper penetration into the loins of individual privacy.

Countering that, Shariff had his wits and a hoodie.

The latter hid his face as he exited the park, and the former was on full display as he suddenly began erratically sidestepping before following an imaginary half circle. He continued charting an indirect path toward the Imperial Hotel, like the unpredictable flight patterns of sparrows alarmed by an eagle circling overhead. He was dismissed as a patient of the nearby dementia clinic by the subservient masses passing by on the street, but Shariff's actions were those of someone with full control of his faculties. He clutched the smartphone in his pocket. The subtle increasing and decreasing vibrations, which coincided with the CCTV cameras' field of view, directed him into the irregular path, allowing him to remain in the state's blind spots. Shariff had coded the app himself. Realizing his journey would soon take him to London where the surveillance state reigned, he took precautions as someone with his skill set would. He had hacked into the CCTV network—just enough to glean the CCTV scanning algorithm—and exited without leaving a trace.

His necessary and unpredictable path took him much longer than a direct route, but Shariff arrived digitally unseen at the loading docks to the rear of the Imperial Hotel—he was not a man to use the front door. Always busy on a Saturday night, the rear entrance was at its most frantic an hour before dinner—and its most vulnerable. Shariff ceased his attention-garnering avoidance tactics and fell in line with the wave of maintenance and kitchen staff rushing the back doors into work. They numbered in the dozens and with the high turnover of the hotel industry, a new face was not unusual; no one batted an eye at another dark-skinned, hooded kid arriving to start his evening shift.

Once inside he found himself in a wide anteroom. The black-and-white-checkered tiled floor was scuffed with dirt from never-ending foot traffic. Many of the workers hung up coats and switched to indoor shoes in front of a bank of personal lockers and outfitted themselves in the chosen uniforms for the night ahead: vests with clip-on bow ties for customer-facing servers, smocks for the backroom kitchen staff. Panel doors led to the kitchen where the ubiquitous shouts and rattles of a commercial kitchen could be heard.

Shariff kept his head down and his hood up. He moved with purpose but resisted the urge to break into a sprint. He had time, if only a little. The Cabal was circling. They had to be. And now that they had compromised Cohen, they wouldn't be out to kill. No, far worse, Shariff mused. They would want secrets. Secrets that Shariff knew would be at the Bitcoin Conference—the last place he should be as it would be surveilled by the agents of the Cabal.

Secrets were the antithesis of his life and of the bitcoin project. He could not reconcile keeping them for longer than necessary, and now with the Cabal ever closer to wrapping their fingers around them, he needed to take action, no matter how reckless it would appear to those with their eyes still shut.

Shariff found the room he was looking for and knocked with feverish intensity. Shariff knew the man inside kept a familiar secret and hoped the man was willing to be just as reasonable with it as he was.

JARVENPAA'S VISITOR

Johan Jarvenpaa sat slumped in his dressing room chair and listened to his publicist excitedly ramble on about details he had no interest in. Despite his attempts to keep up appearances, his renowned enthusiasm and positivity were suffering from all the events transpiring below the surface of the bitcoin community: arrests on flat-out ridiculous charges, disappearances of the most active contributors, and, most concerning, all-too-convenient accidents.

"Your presentation is trending on Twitter. Fantastic job, Johan." The voice of Jarvenpaa's fast-talking publicist radiated from the smartphone speaker on his desk. She pronounced his name with a hard J despite his numerous attempts at correcting her. Today he couldn't be bothered to remind her again. "Analytics are predicting a twenty-percent sales boost to your book series. Outstanding. The publisher will be ecstatic. When can you get your next book out?"

Jarvenpaa pinched the bridge of his nose, hoping to alleviate his headache. "Sheila, I haven't even started it."

"What, why not? Bitcoin is starting to get mainstream attention. You have to capitalize on that."

What good is that if I'm in jail. Or dead. "I've had a lot on my plate lately."

"Fine, fine, fine. I get that. But we can upsell your speaking engagements. Hear me out—JJ's Bitcoin World Tour! Bitcoin everything! Start in Europe! Then America! We'll play up the fact that you're the de facto expert and that you actually know Satomi Whats-a-Moto."

Jarvenpaa sighed. "Satoshi Nakamoto."

"Right. You're the expert. We'll play that up!"

"I would prefer we didn't. And I don't actually know Satoshi. We just communicated on the chat forums."

"Yes, yes. Those chat forum posts have done fantastic things to your rep. Documented proof that you were involved in bitcoin from the start! Proof you're a futurist! We can talk about the details of your world tour—" Sheila interrupted herself. "Hey, how about this—*Johan and Bitcoin: The World Currency Tour!* Not bad, right? I just thought of that. I want to make you the most famous nerd since Bill Gates! Think about it."

Jarvenpaa couldn't think about anything else. He detested being famous; he would much rather devote his boundless energies towards coding or writing. But what other choice did he have?

Satoshi had directly asked him to carry a secret, to be a Keeper of the Fortune. Jarvenpaa felt he had a duty to accept. There are only a few moments in life where you can truly make a difference, and he was well aware this was one such moment. But then things quickly went sideways and the others burrowed further underground. Jarvenpaa gambled if the Cabal ever managed to confirm he was a

Keeper of the Fortune, they would be reluctant to put pressure on a public figure for fear of being exposed. So he announced he was in fact the author of the sci-fi series and was forced to accept all the attention that went along with it.

But the attention did nothing to alleviate his stress. Every call from an unknown number made his heart race. Every fan wanting to say hello a potential Cabal agent planning to whisk him off to some black site. Jarvenpaa ruefully reflected that a side effect of bitcoin was paranoia.

Sheila continued her full press marketing blitz. "And let's get your autobiography out! How about this—*Johan Jarvenpaa: My Life as a Futurist!*—fantastic, right? Instant bestseller!"

A futurist?! Jarvenpaa felt like a fraud whenever someone referred to him as such. If he truly were a futurist, he would have foreseen the implications of the secret before getting involved.

But he hadn't. And here he was. Desperate to find a way out and still honour his arrangement with Satoshi.

Jarvenpaa jumped at an angry knock on his door. "I've got to go, Sheila."

"Okay, Johan. But if I don't hear from you by Monday, I'm going to start putting the tour together! Why don't we—" Jarvenpaa ended the call. Immediately there was another knock, the intensity increasing. He cautiously opened the door, not entirely surprised to see who it was.

"Hey, it's the futurist!" Aziz Shariff peered out from under his hood. "And I don't know about you, but secrets stress me the hell out."

***

"Aziz, what are you doing here? Where have you been?" Jarvenpaa wearily eyed his visitor. He knew Shariff to be a combustible mix of paranoia and ideology that would make a cold war spy blush, and because of that it didn't bode well that he was at his door.

"Fighting against a global conspiracy. I hear you're giving speeches to venture capitalists and bankers."

Same Aziz, Jarvenpaa thought. The bitcoin community was relatively small and Aziz Shariff was quite infamous for his ideas and theories as well as his commitment to the project. They had discussed at length the various aspects of bitcoin: the technology, the economics, the social impact. Sometimes their discussions had turned heated, as most things involving Shariff invariably did, with the paranoid anarchist remaining unwavering in his dystopian view of society and its inevitable march towards an Orwellian future.

Jarvenpaa maintained the more positive outlook that technological advancements would pull society forward, with power being more equally spread among its members. In the end, they shared a begrudging respect for their respective contributions to the bitcoin project, going so far as to even review each other's code submissions.

But now with the young man in front of him vibrating in his boots, Jarvenpaa feared Shariff had gone even further down his paranoid path—or his anarchist one. He would have to tread carefully until he could ascertain the purpose of the visit.

Shariff's eyes glanced into Jarvenpaa's dressing room then back down the hallway. "Have you noticed anyone following you?"

The question gave Jarvenpaa a moment's pause, which Shariff took as an invitation to leap across the threshold— only pausing to give one last scan of the hallway before gently easing the door closed to avoid any sound. He then took a quick tour of the dressing room, poking his head into the bathroom and running his hands along the windowless walls, as if expecting to find a hidden passage.

"Followed? No, no. Of course not," Jarvenpaa said, trying to adopt a tone of mocking derision at such a wild claim, but it fell flat. He had sensed someone watching him ever since he arrived in London.

"Then you're an idiot." Shariff emerged from the bathroom with two towels. He dropped one on Jarvenpaa's smartphone on the desk and used the other one to smother a personal laptop beside it. The dressing room was cozy and could comfortably hold five or six people, but with Shariff pacing about, leaving an unshowered musk in his wake and covering the entire room in seconds, it felt claustrophobic.

"Come on, Aziz, the laptop isn't even turned on."

"Doesn't matter. They have their means. The FBI and MI5 have proven they are able to remotely activate laptop microphones and cameras. And if they can, then they will. And that of course means the Cabal is listening." Shariff jumped up and banged a corner air vent to see if anything that wasn't supposed to be there rattled. "So, have you noticed anyone unusual?"

"It's a conference on an obscure technology. Everyone's a bit unusual."

"So that's a yes."

"You're being paranoid, Aziz."

"Andrew Cohen said the same thing," Shariff said sharply, only pausing his frantic pacing to stare down Jarvenpaa in a challenge as to who was right. "And you know who else."

Jarvenpaa broke eye contact. "Of course, Aziz. The Cabal is out to get everyone in the bitcoin community . . ."

"No, not everyone. Just us."

"Us?"

"Us," Shariff repeated. He snatched the towel off the laptop to search for signs it had been activated. Seeing none, he covered it up again. "Last week Andrew Cohen had his charges dropped and was released from prison. The next day, I received this message: *C coming for SF* along with four email addresses." Shariff recited them from memory.

Jarvenpaa immediately recognized two:

Aziz-Shariff@gmx.com was blindingly clear.

thehashking@kth.se was Jarvenpaa's old university address, chosen after the lead character in one of his earlier sci-fi novels. It wasn't a stretch for anyone to guess it belonged to him.

Neither of them had originally masked their identities or involvement in the bitcoin project. Shariff was proud to be perhaps the most vocal proponent of the project and definitely the most outspoken against the government's involvement in the Financial Crisis, to say nothing of his desire to educate anyone who would listen about the Cabal and other conspiracy theories—now not so far-fetched.

Jarvenpaa hadn't pursued anonymity because, well, why would he? He had placed the Cabal in the same category as the JFK assassination and Bigfoot. He hadn't thought twice about using his own email for some incredibly obscure cryptography mailing list perhaps read by a couple dozen people. This lack of foresight was yet another reason he lamented his futurist label.

The third and fourth email addresses were unknown to Jarvenpaa, though one he could surely guess at. But before he could bring it up, Shariff flared his nostrils as if he had gotten a whiff of something rotten. "Cohen is a rat. He knew who the four Keepers were via their email addresses and gave them up to the Cabal for his freedom. This warning was some pathetic last-ditch effort at saving his soul."

"It was the CIA. Every imaginable interrogation option was probably on the table. I'm amazed he lasted since June! What would you have him do?"

"Resist. Die. Anything other than capitulate," Shariff snapped.

Jarvenpaa could see there was no reasoning with him. He could feel his face flush with dread as he realized why Shariff was here.

"You want my password, don't you, Aziz?"

The answer in his manic eyes was absolute. "Yes. Here's what we need to do."

Jarvenpaa listened as Shariff laid out his plan. It was unequivocal, without compromise, and meant for all to hear.

When Shariff had finished, Jarvenpaa remained silent, pondering whether his plan would actually stop the Cabal. Or if it would instead actually destroy bitcoin. In the end, Jarvenpaa could not consent to Shariff's proposal.

"It's the nuclear option, Aziz. I fear it will accomplish the very thing you wish to avoid."

"Impossible. It would neuter the Cabal. Give them a middle finger for all eternity. It's perfect."

"It's madness!" Jarvenpaa said.

"Madness? Madness! You know what's madness? Continuing to live under the same oppressive world order while thinking things will magically change for the better! Goddamn you, Johan!

"I know things won't magically change. That's another reason why I'm out talking to anyone who will listen. You'd be amazed at how many government representatives and corporate types attend my presentations and have shown genuine interest in bitcoin."

"Wait—you've been talking to the government?" Shariff froze like a deer in headlights. His gaze bore right through Jarvenpaa. "You're actually one of them, aren't you?" Shariff growled.

"Who, the Cabal? Honestly, Aziz, when's the last time you slept? Let's get you a room and . . ." Jarvenpaa felt he was losing Shariff. He needed to settle him down before he did anything rash.

"I won't fall for it! I go to sleep and I wake up chained to a chair. I know how these things work!"

"No, Aziz, just calm down . . ." There was a knock on the door.

"Are you okay, Johan? I heard someone yelling," a delicate voice said through the door.

"Who is that? The Cabal? You alerted the Cabal I was here?" Shariff began pacing the windowless room like a caged animal, sniffing for a way out.

"No, Aziz, she's my assistant. I'm actually late to meet some people for dinner. Why don't you—"

Jarvenpaa watched helplessly as Shariff lunged for the fire alarm and ripped down the handle, sending the entire hotel into a panic equal to his own. He yanked open the door and barrelled through, narrowly missing Jarvenpaa's startled assistant, and raced down the hallway. Jarvenpaa wasn't religious, but he now found himself praying to God to help the other Keepers that Shariff would surely seek out, and that they would think long and hard before following the paranoid anarchist down his destructive path.

HAWKE'S PATH

Henry Hawke strolled down the Victoria Embankment along the River Thames. Nighttime was approaching, and the red hues of the sunset echoed over the skyline. He had his jacket slung over his shoulder and sleeves rolled up despite the cool autumn air, wanting to be out of his suit as much as possible. He wore a similar suit every day at the office, but it still felt foreign on his skin. At times it was as if he were playing dress-up, trying to fool everyone into thinking he was a businessman.

He was slowly making his way to Leicester Square to find the pub Pennyworth had raved about, hoping to find him there. On the embankment, bicyclists rolled past, couples of all ages strolled hand-in-hand, tourists snapped photos, and vendors pushed their artwork and counterfeit wares from laid-out blankets. Hawke found an empty park bench with a good view of Buckingham Palace and decided to rest for a moment. He moved on from Pennyworth's vanishing act and tried to think about how he was going to present his report to management back home. But as the wind bounced off the Thames, carrying a brackish scent past him, Hawke's thoughts drifted to another time and place.

He was back at his apartment in Chicago. He was on the phone with his uncle, having what ended up being their final conversation. Uncle Peter had a welcoming disposition if not a tad serious, but his temper was something to be feared if he felt a line had been crossed. It was clear to neighbours overhearing that heated exchange that Hawke shared the trait.

Hawke's parents had died before he had but the faintest memories of them, so Peter Finlay was the only father figure he had ever known. Growing up, he had always wanted to follow in his uncle's footsteps to work in a bank. That was, of course, if his childhood dream of playing professional hockey didn't pan out. That career path had ended abruptly his sophomore year when he was booted from the University of Wisconsin-Madison's hockey team for what were called *actions incongruent with the university athletic program's expectations*, which was a polite way of saying he was suspended for fighting too often to waste a roster spot on. It had also cost him his scholarship and forced him to take out student loans to complete his program. His uncle had offered to pay the tuition, but Hawke had stubbornly refused by saying it was his problem to solve.

Upon graduation Hawke moved back to Chicago and again his uncle offered to help, insisting he move back in to save on rent. And again, Hawke stubbornly refused. He was adamant about making it on his own, whatever the cost. With the benefit of hindsight, having little job experience in the middle of the greatest financial crisis since the Great Depression didn't turn out to be ideal for launching a career. It was only temp office work and telemarketing jobs that provided no satisfaction and low pay.

Hawke's ideal employer, Chicago Mutual and where his uncle worked, wasn't hiring, and as the recession worsened there were even reports circulating that it was facing bankruptcy. Oddly, his uncle didn't seem particularly bothered by this. In fact, he seemed to have expected it. Over dinner one night he could barely contain himself as he proudly announced that he would be presenting a plan to the Board of Directors that would have Chicago Mutual become an industry leader in the emerging fintech industry. But Peter's excitement didn't last long. The new plan, whatever it had been, was hastily dismissed by the board. The expletive-laden tirade that followed became part of Chicago Mutual lore, and mentioning it in the presence of management was known as a career-limiting move. It was the last time Peter had spoken to the rest of the executives, even though some of their friendships spanned decades.

The next month was a whirlwind of madness that Hawke still had trouble confronting. Peter was unceremoniously dismissed from the bank with shocking accusations from financial regulators garnering headline media attention: Chicago Mutual Savings Bank's insolvency problems had been the result of one rogue former employee—Peter Finlay.

It was alleged that during the boom years Peter had instructed the trading desk to recklessly invest in toxic mortgage-backed securities, whose failings had nearly collapsed the entire world economy. The Feds swooped in and started ripping apart his life. Bank accounts and assets were frozen. Coworkers and friends were interviewed in search of any and all unscrupulous behaviour. Peter had even called Hawke in a panic one night from a gas station payphone asking if he was okay after federal agents ransacked his home, supposedly searching for evidence of fraudulent transactions. All his files and computers were seized.

It was the following Sunday that the heated phone call took place. Hawke insisted, with all the wisdom of a twenty-something-year-old with a college education and a *Wall Street Journal* subscription, that the recently announced bailout Chicago Mutual would receive from the Federal Reserve had been necessary and saved thousands of jobs, even if Peter's wasn't one of them. He also told his uncle he was going to send Chicago Mutual an unsolicited job application, despite his objections, and that just because he had screwed up his career didn't mean Hawke shouldn't have one at all. Remembering the silence that followed still tied Hawke's stomach in knots—because it was at that moment he realized he had disappointed his uncle.

When Peter eventually spoke, it wasn't in anger. He implored Hawke to listen to him very carefully, an eerie calm infusing his voice. He told Hawke he didn't have to make the same mistakes he had, that *many more a man would go rogue if he only knew how.*

Hawke ended the call at that point. He was angry with himself and his life and had directed it towards his uncle.

He stubbornly refused to call back, deciding that his uncle would call sometime during the week to patch things up. Fate decided Hawke would be waiting forever. The following morning he received that fateful knock on the door with the terrible news . . .

Big Ben's great bell rang six times across the Thames, snapping Hawke back to the present. The sun had now completely disappeared below the horizon and the night life of an entire city began to stir in search of adventure. Hawke suppressed thoughts of his uncle's tragic end and focused on his current lot in life. He was in downtown London on a Saturday night—it was time he got himself a proper English pint.

HAWKE'S PINT

The Cock & Bull was everything Hawke thought a British pub should be. A warming undercurrent of folk music heavy on pirates and rebellion talk flowed between lively conversations of pubgoers starting off their Saturday night. The pub was filled to capacity, a butt in every seat and a few more standing about. Faded black-and-white photos of rugby and football clubs going back a hundred years were framed and hung crooked along the walls, while a portrait of a much younger Queen kept watch over everyone from on high.

To the right of the entrance was the main room. Everyone seemed to have rosy cheeks and a pint in their hand. To the left a long bar, polished and worn by multiple generations of patrons, stretched lengthwise along the back wall and was manned by a reedy bartender who looked old enough to have built the place.

Hawke scanned the pub to see if Pennyworth had made it but no such luck. Instead of finding out the answers to his uncle's involvement, he would have to settle for a few pints alone. He sat at the lone available barstool beside the service station at the far end of the bar and waited for the bartender to acknowledge his presence. The acknowledgement came as a dirty look and grunt, which Hawke took as a signal to request a house ale. The bartender furrowed his brow as if he had been tricked into taking the order and slowly shuffled over to the taps and pulled a pint. He slid it haphazardly in front of Hawke, who raised the pint with an ironical half-smile and said, "Here's to loving what you do."

The bartender scowled back before moving on to begrudgingly serve another customer. Hawke slowly tested the pint, savouring the thick flavour that, in Hawke's opinion, had been too slow in making its way into American breweries. The current beer craze back home was all about the hops, which Hawke didn't mind to a point. But the craft brewers had taken it to the extreme and declared the hoppier the beer the better, which was akin to saying the louder you told a joke the funnier it became.

In the reflection of the backstop mirror, Hawke recognized a few of the conference attendees. He considered that he should probably be networking, but found the beer in front of him a better choice. He almost changed his mind when he saw Sara Noor among them, holding their attention as well as that of a few non-conference patrons who suddenly found themselves interested in bitcoin.

After finishing half his ale and sneaking the occasional glance at Noor, who did not reciprocate, Hawke was about to order dinner when a short man threw himself against the bar beside him. He pulled back his hood to reveal dark bloodshot eyes that, though they seemed the very definition of exhausted, still gave the impression they were vibrating in their sockets.

"Are you Henry Hawke?" the man asked.

Hawke looked him over. Was there a plea in his darting eyes? An uncontrolled excitement? Perhaps he was another young founder of a startup searching for capital to fund the next big bitcoin business. Or a huckster with a crypto get-rich-quick scheme. Neither would have surprised him. But the intensity with which the man held Hawke's gaze was unlike anything he had ever encountered, and Hawke couldn't help but give him his full attention.

The man spoke without any room for objection. "My name is Aziz Shariff and you're going to help me destroy Satoshi's Fortune."

SHARIFF'S PITCH

Hawke sipped his pint. *Great,* he thought, *another fanatical believer in Satoshi Nakamoto.* During the conference, the name of the creator of bitcoin almost always evoked god-like reverence, usually right before a sales pitch.

Tired of the amateur efforts, Hawke decided to have some fun. He had learned over the past few days that there were certain ways to trigger ardent bitcoin supporters. One was to say bitcoin had no intrinsic value; this set off a diatribe about the definition of intrinsic and that fiat currency actually had no intrinsic value itself, being only pieces of worthless paper. The fervour usually spoke louder than the explanation. And another was to claim that instead of an open-source project such as Linux, bitcoin was a corporation.

Tongue firmly in cheek, Hawke asked, "Satoshi? You mean the Bitcoin CEO?"

Shariff's back stiffened as if the question offended his very existence, and for a moment Hawke expected a slap across his face. But Shariff just grunted and took a half-dozen sharp steps towards the exit before pausing in sober second thought. A beat later he bounced back to Hawke's side as if he had never left. Locking eyes with Hawke, Shariff took a deep breath.

"Okay, Suit. It's time for a history lesson. To get to Satoshi's Fortune we have to start with the Cabal. Have you heard of the Cabal? No, of course you haven't. Though you're wearing their uniform." It dawned on Hawke that Shariff wasn't your typical bitcoiner. Something hot and fast was burning behind the tired eyes, dying to get out—and it wasn't greed or a business idea.

Shariff continued his rapid-fire explanation. "The earliest hints of their existence surfaced in 1910, when six men controlling twenty-five percent of the entire world's wealth secretly met at Jekyll Island to discuss founding a central bank, beginning their stealthy monetary takeover of not just the United States but the whole of Western civilization. This group became known as the Cabal."

"Ominous name. Though I suppose that's what you want for a secret society," Hawke quipped. Pretending not to hear the commentary, Shariff took a breath to reload and carried on.

"Then, like now, not everyone was ready to bow before a gang of crony capitalists. Forming a beachhead against the Cabal's plot to create a private corporation that, through presidential decree, would be granted absolute control of US monetary policy were three men, Benjamin Guggenheim, Isa Strauss, and Jacob Astor, who together were worth $11 billion. Whether their actions were altruistic or in self-interest I don't know. But I do know that in 1912 these three men were in England and set to converge on New York to mount their defence against the Cabal. They were in communication with their friend J.P. Morgan, founder of the investment bank that still bears his name, who unbeknownst to them was vying for a position of authority within the Cabal. Morgan generously offered the three men free passage aboard a luxury liner that he owned through a series of shell companies, a luxury liner set to make its maiden voyage across the Atlantic—the *Titanic*."

Shariff sliced his hand through the air and continued. "In one fell Machiavellian swoop all viable opposition to what would become known as the Federal Reserve system was laid to waste under two thousand freezing leagues in the middle of the Atlantic Ocean." Without letting Hawke interrupt, he continued.

"On December 13, 1913, the Cabal achieved their goal as President Wilson signed the Federal Reserve into existence. And just like that, the United States government was no longer in control of its money—a private company was. President Wilson realized too late he had condemned his country to be controlled by the Cabal and was quoted as saying, '*I am a most unhappy man. I have unwittingly ruined my country. A great industrial nation is controlled by its system of credit. Our system of credit is concentrated. The growth of the nation, therefore, and all our activities are in the hands of a few men. We have come to be one of the worst ruled, one of the most completely controlled and dominated Governments in the civilized world, no longer a Government by free opinion, no longer a Government by conviction and the vote of the majority, but a Government by the opinion and duress of a small group of dominant men.*'" Shariff rang off the quote from memory, having repeated it a hundred times with varying degrees of vitriol.

Hawke listened intently. If not for his starting point of Satoshi Nakamoto, Hawke would have thought the rant was the work of a random performance artist. But he sensed that Shariff truly believed everything he said. Conspiracy theorists usually did. He decided to see how far he could push the smaller man. "And? . . . "

"And? AND!?" Shariff said, spitting out his words. "The Federal Reserve, a corporation—not a government agency—owned by the Cabal now controls the entire monetary system of the most powerful economy in the world! Even the name is deceitful, meant to trick people into thinking because it has *Federal* in its name, that it's a government agency. They're as much a government agency as Federal Express is. They have full authority to control interest rates, print money as they see fit, and a host of other powers. They have the tools to choke the life out of any individual or corporation that dares question them. Nobody in the ninety-eight years of the Fed's existence has been able to even audit the Fed to see what they actually have on their balance sheets—not Congress, not the president, and definitely not the people of the nation! They have systematically inflated away the value of the dollar until it's not even worth the paper it's printed on."

"Actually, dollars are printed on cotton," Hawke said, trying to exit the conversation. He was familiar with fractional reserve banking and the economics behind it. He had heard the conspiracy theories and the *Audit the Fed* crowd, but gave them little credence.

"Suit, I'm not finished so shut up and listen. Under the Nixon administration, the Cabal had the Fed completely leave the gold standard. Up until then, they at least had paid lip service to the dollar being backed by anything of value. So now they didn't need any gold whatsoever backing the dollar. This gave the Fed the ability to create money out of thin air, diluting the people's buying power, leaving them incrementally poorer every single day. And with literally a licence to print money, the Cabal grew even more powerful. Their tentacles now stretch into every central bank in the Western world, dictating how much and when to print more money. Because of this near absolute power, they have their people placed across intelligence agencies and the private sector. Most don't even know they work for the Cabal. Hell, ninety-nine percent of the planet doesn't even know it exists!"

"Okay, so the Cabal is bad. I get it. What does this have to do with Satoshi?" Hawke asked.

"The Cabal created Satoshi!"

Hawke raised an eyebrow. "That doesn't sound right . . ."

"Not on purpose. We all create our worst enemies. With the housing crisis, financial crises, the Great Recession, whatever you want to call it, the Cabal was caught with their pants down. They'd recklessly sloshed money around in securities that they didn't fully understand, and if they did, they didn't care. Maybe it was actually all part of their plan! They knew they could simply print an infinite amount of money to bail themselves out. And print they did. Eight trillion dollars' worth in four years. That's eight thousand billion dollars! That's triple the amount of money that was in circulation before. Triple! In four years! We all saw it for what it was—theft. Oppression. Corruption. A small group of people deciding that they rule the masses!"

Shariff slammed his fist on the bar to emphasize his point. It drew unwanted attention and nearby conversations ceased, causing more than one set of eyes to start scrutinizing the only person in the pub who wasn't drinking. Hawke gave a half-hearted smile and reassured everyone that everything was fine, including the bartender, who already had one hand on a phone while sporting a distrustful grimace. The cacophony of the pub slowly returned and the bartender's hand reluctantly slipped from the phone and returned to pouring beer.

"We all saw it. So we did something about it. At the height of the crisis, Satoshi appeared and released the white paper. We were few at the beginning, but after the code release in January 2009, we started to grow in numbers. But almost a year ago, the Cabal went on the offensive to kill bitcoin before it took root. And now we're being hunted and getting more desperate every day. Hey, are you even listening to me, Suit?"

Hawke didn't answer. He couldn't quite put his finger on it, but something Shariff had said, combined with the mysterious words of Jarvenpaa and Pennyworth, was needling a subconscious part of his brain, which stopped

Hawke from dismissing the maniac outright. He wanted to know more. "So you're saying that there's a powerful and secret international Cabal trying to take over the world?"

"No, Suit," Shariff said, smashing his fist down again. "I'm saying they already have."

***

From across the pub Sara Noor had kept one eye on Aziz Shariff from the moment he walked through the door. His movements were always abrupt and jarring, and for a paranoid crypto-anarchist living underground who prided himself on the importance of privacy, he sure did talk a lot.

He hadn't been seen and rarely heard from since Cohen's arrest, but if he was going to turn up she calculated it was going to be at this conference.

And she was right.

Noor didn't assume that the man Shariff had approached was chosen at random. Nor that it was just a friendly chat.

Shariff was speaking to Henry Hawke, the man who had interrupted her private conversation with Jarvenpaa. Immediately afterwards she had searched him online, and as far as she could tell he was nobody special. According to the sole entry on his LinkedIn profile, he was an account manager at Chicago Mutual Savings Bank since December 2010. He had no other searchable social media accounts. And no discernable user account for any bitcoin chat room, though Noor knew that pseudonyms were common.

Naturally reclusive or something to hide? And something about his start date at that particular bank also seemed too coincidental given world events.

She had been aware of his earlier furtive glances from his barstool but had chosen to ignore them until she determined what he was all about. She noted his athletic frame wasn't suited to sitting at a desk all day, and his mischievous grin, alluding to an amusing secret, suggested that his online profile didn't come close to telling his whole story.

She excused herself from her current conversation and edged closer to the bar to eavesdrop on Hawke and Shariff. In her line of business, the more information she had, the better.

***

The decrepit bartender frowned. He had had enough of this punk brown kid. He was loud, obnoxious, and no doubt on some sort of drugs—just like they all were. How else can you explain all the craziness? And he didn't want any of these foreigners doing those crazy things in his pub. He was sure the big guy in the suit was going to properly knock him out and would have preferred it if he had. It would have saved him a call to his local inspector, who would show up and make the punk kid leave, but not without the cost of an evening of complimentary pints and hearing his lurid stories. Just the cost these days of keeping the pub free of the local hoodlums and drug addicts who would otherwise overrun his business and drive away respectable paying customers.

He picked up the phone and dialled a number from memory. The inspector was blunt and not interested in showing up until the bartender described the offender and any names he'd overheard. The inspector then hung up without clarifying if he was headed over or not.

The bartender frowned again at the rude exchange and thought about how next time he'd serve the inspector from a skunky keg that was otherwise going to be poured down the drain. He returned to the bar and made sure to serve a fetching young woman who had elbowed her way to the bar. *When they look like that*, he thought perversely, *I don't care where they come from.*

HAWKE'S FORTUNE

A conspiracy that ran so deep it actually changed the foundation upon which the world economy was built. Hawke thought Shariff would have been better served trying to sell him on a bitcoin startup. But he had to admit, Shariff's earnest zeal and history lesson had piqued his curiosity.

"So what exactly is Satoshi's Fortune?" He knew a bit about Satoshi Nakamoto, but he'd never heard anything about a specific fortune.

Shariff rotated his shoulders as if about to step into a boxing ring. "It has to do with how bitcoins are created and enter circulation. I think I need to explain it to you in the simplest possible terms."

Hawke tipped his pint. "Much obliged."

"The bitcoin protocol calls for a new block, which is a collection of transactions, to be added to the blockchain on average every ten minutes. A block is found when a computer running the bitcoin software, called a miner, correctly guesses the random number the protocol assigned to that block. The reward for this work is fifty bitcoins. So every ten minutes, fifty new bitcoins enter circulation. You with me so far, Suit?"

"Guess the magic number, win fifty bitcoins. How hard is that?"

"Not hard at all. Satoshi was getting the fifty-bitcoin reward for every block himself because nobody else was mining. It wasn't until more people started mining that the difficulty in guessing the random number increased to keep the ten-minute average. But since Satoshi was the only one mining at the beginning . . ."

Hawke took another sip of his pint, begrudgingly being drawn into Shariff's story more and more. "It was like Satoshi was playing bingo all by himself. He was winning every game."

Shariff bobbed his head frantically. "That's how he amassed the largest holdings of bitcoins in the world."

"So how many does Satoshi have then? A few thousand?" Hawke said, trying to guess how rich Satoshi must be now.

"A few thousand, Suit? I would have thought you needed basic math skills to get a job at a bank."

"Tens of thousands of coins?"

Shariff eyes bulged in anger. "Suit, the block reward was fifty bitcoins *every* ten minutes. That's twelve thousand a day, or three hundred and sixty thousand a month. And it was months and months before the network grew significantly beyond Satoshi and the small group of us originally involved in the project. No, Suit, Satoshi mined *nine hundred and eighty thousand* bitcoins!"

Hawke froze. Satoshi not only created bitcoin, but if this was true then he could move the market in whatever direction he saw fit. "So how many has Satoshi sold?"

Shariff was visibly irked by the question. "Not a damn one. Satoshi didn't create bitcoin to get rich. He created bitcoin to tear down the barbed wire fences that imprison us. To free us from the Cabal and its lapdog governments that wish to subjugate us. No, Suit, Satoshi Nakamoto has never, and will never, sell a single bitcoin."

"Why are you so sure? It's a lot of money."

Shariff ferociously shook his head. "It's not about the money, Suit! It's about trust! And the genius that Satoshi was, he knew it was too many bitcoins to trust to one set of hands—too much power for any one individual. So to protect it, he divided control of his fortune into four pieces housed in one bitcoin wallet file. From this and only this file could the bitcoin wallet that holds the fortune ever be restored. And three passwords. Satoshi enabled multi-signature protection, which means you need two of the three passwords to actually open the wallet and control the coins. Each piece was given to someone that Satoshi trusted could keep it safe until, if ever the time came, it was needed to restore the wallet and move the coins.

"So where are these *Keepers of the Fortune?*"

Shariff's eyes darted around the room with terrifying speed and whispered, "right beside you, Suit."

"You have part of Satoshi's Fortune?"

"Shut up. *ShutupShutupShutup.*" Shariff smashed his words together with a kinetic frenzy. "I'm not talking to you so you can announce it to the entire pub. I'm talking to you because together we need to find Satoshi's Fortune!"

"If we found it, what then? Sell it and split it fifty-fifty?"

Shariff's bottled up energy finally exploded. "Sell it? You want to become a *millionaire?*" he screamed as he pounded the bar with both hands.

Hawke had never heard the word said with such disdain. He also couldn't be bothered to soothe the pubgoers startled by this most recent outburst. He was too engrossed by the tale of 980,000 bitcoins just there for the taking. If what Shariff was saying was true, then whoever found Satoshi's Fortune would be free from the long commutes, pointless meetings, and soul-sucking lifestyle of the corporate world.

But it was clear Shariff had an alternative plan in mind.

"Suit, you're supposed to have more than two brain cells to rub together. What do you really think will happen if you or anyone, especially the Cabal, tries to sell Satoshi's own coins?"

Hawke thought about what he had learned at the conference. The overall supply is capped at twenty-one million bitcoins, but only approximately eight million had been mined so far. So Satoshi's Fortune represented over ten percent of the current circulation. Selling ten percent of any asset would distort the supply-demand equation, selling more than the market could absorb.

"It would essentially flood the market and crash the price," Hawke said, the realization washing over him.

"Yes, Suit!" Shariff smashed his fist down like a gavel. "And then running mining equipment would be unprofitable, so many would stop doing so, meaning a less secure and valuable network, meaning an even lower price.

A death spiral. It would collapse the entire bitcoin ecosystem, less investment in startups, and big media would talk about how Satoshi cashed out! Proof that the creator of bitcoin was just waiting for the price to rise before dumping it back into fiat. Back into *real money*, they'll say. *Bitcoin was just a get-rich-quick scam for Satoshi* you'll hear from every media source in the world. Selling Satoshi's Fortune would destroy any and all trust the world would ever have in bitcoin!"

Shariff wiped the sweat from his brow. The exertion of trying to convince Hawke of the seriousness of the situation was taking a toll on him.

"And you know who's after Satoshi's Fortune with the full force of all their ungodly resources?" he asked.

"The Cabal?"

"The Cabal!" Shariff screamed. "They are hunting us down and will stop at nothing. And that is why we need to find Satoshi's Fortune first." His tone was both frantic and deeply wary.

It was clear to Hawke that Satoshi's Fortune was the stuff of legends; a hidden treasure so great it could change the course of history. He placed it alongside El Dorado's City of Gold or the Treasure of the Knights Templar in terms of likelihood of actually existing, let alone being found.

If he were sane, Hawke would take Shariff's tale as entertainment and be done with it. However, he didn't know if it was the nine-to-five routine driving him mad, but he actually wanted to believe everything the paranoid maniac had told him. There was something else teasing his brain, something still left unanswered about what Shariff was asking of him.

"There's something I don't understand."

"What's so hard to understand. Cabal controls money. Bitcoin isn't controllable. Cabal wants to kill bitcoin by selling Satoshi's Fortune. We need to find the fortune before the Cabal."

"Well, that's what I don't understand," Hawke said. "You don't want me to spend the fortune, so what exactly do you want me to do if I find it?"

Shariff grabbed Hawke by his arm and looked at him with a desperation usually seen across the faces of death row inmates.

"Suit, you asked me what Satoshi's Fortune is, so I'm telling you; it's the greatest fortune of the twenty-first century—and what I need you to do is destroy it."

***

Damn this Suit was slow-witted.

Shariff cursed Jarvenpaa for not believing in his plan. That left the other two Keepers to find and convince. And this Suit didn't even know the basics! Didn't know the world he existed in! Didn't know he lived behind a barbed wire fence! And, incredibly, didn't even know the role Peter Finlay played!

"Destroy Satoshi's Fortune? That seems a little extreme, no?" Hawke asked.

"Extreme times. Extreme measures. You can't sit and patiently wait to see if your oppressors will suddenly

79

change their mind and become your friend. We must match their intensity!" Shariff was confounded at how anyone could not see that.

"How can you even destroy a bitcoin?" Hawke said.

"Proof-of-burn. I've created a bitcoin address that won't allow outputs, rendering any bitcoins sent to it provably unspendable and therefore destroyed. The world won't have to trust anyone's opinion that Satoshi's Fortune will never be spent—it will be an indisputable, unequivocal, absolute fact! The fortune, and its Keepers, will be forever safe from the Cabal!"

"Okay, so why come to me? I don't know anything about any of this."

"I know you don't. But what your uncle should have told you is—" Shariff froze as he noticed the bartender no longer frowning but fiendishly smirking in his direction.

What had happened?

Shariff brought up his phone and searched through rows of custom-designed apps until he found the one he was looking for: the Metropolitan Police scanner. It was tapped into London police frequencies, collecting their communications and movements. And one entry announced a movement that caused Shariff to break out in a cold sweat: *Disturbance at the Cock & Bull reported. Inspector Smith en route to investigate.* He frantically looked back to the bartender, whose smirk told him it was true.

Shariff had to leave. Now.

"Wait, what did you say? My uncle? How is he involved in this?"

"No time, Suit. I have to escape before it's too late. They won't know about you yet. Show me your bitcoin wallet!"

"What are you talking about?"

Shariff grabbed Hawke's phone off the bar. Not password-protected—damn, this Suit was really slow-witted! Shariff wanted anything but to have to rely on him, but he had no choice. Time was running out and Shariff felt the Cabal closing in. If they caught him, then all could be lost.

That is, unless Peter Finlay's nephew had the wherewithal to not only accept the real world, but to burn down the old one as well. He opened Hawke's bitcoin wallet to his *receive* address and sent one bitcoin transaction before Hawke could object.

"If something happens to me, it's your responsibility to destroy Satoshi's Fortune. The Cabal's secret agents are on their way! Watch yourself! They're everywhere, the government, the police, even this bartender," he cried out, violently jabbing his finger at the bartender. "You are one of them, aren't you!"

Shariff sprang to his feet, startling the nearby pubgoers who could not grasp the fear now taking hold. With adrenalin being fed to his body with each increasingly punishing, panic-stricken heartbeat, Shariff could barely control his actions. He threw a bottle and missed the Cabal agent who had pretended to serve beer. He pushed another agent dressed as a busboy onto the ground because he must have been eavesdropping.

Shariff felt two firm hands grab him and found himself eye to eye with the Suit.

"What does my uncle have to do with this?" Hawke demanded.

"Arise, you have nothing to lose but your barbed wire fences!" Shariff screamed and shook himself free.

He looked at Henry Hawke one last time and hoped to hell the goddamn Suit knew how to go rogue, then launched himself into the kitchen and out the back exit as fast as he could before the Cabal could get into his head.

NOOR'S INVOLVEMENT

The pub quickly returned to its Saturday night routine, treating the departed Shariff as a drunken idiot and nothing more. Hawke took a deep breath. Before he could gather himself and dive into the implications of his run-in with Shariff, he felt eyes on him. Someone else wanted to question him.

"How do you know, Aziz?" Sara Noor flowed like water into the spot where Shariff had been vibrating a minute earlier, the subtle scent of lilacs a definite improvement over nervous sweat. Noor's inquisitive eyes seemed to conjure up control of Hawke's heartbeat, though no trace of a smile crossed her lips. He could imagine her interview subjects struggling not to reveal anything she asked of them, if only for a smile. She was immediately a much better drinking partner than Shariff, prettier, warmer, and already less prone to emotional outbursts.

"Aziz? He's my history teacher," Hawke replied. "And maybe economics, too."

"Is that so," she said. Hawke wanted to believe he heard a playfulness in her response. "I would have thought he's better suited to teaching computer science."

"If he's half as passionate about computer science as what we talked about tonight, then he could build the next Microsoft or Apple."

"Or something bigger."

"And what would that be?"

Noor said nothing. She had a full rock glass in her hand and signalled the bartender for a beer for Hawke. He noticed the bartender stepping quicker for this round.

Hawke didn't really believe that the Cabal had agents everywhere, but it wasn't lost on him that Noor, who had shown a dismissive attitude towards him earlier, was now buying him a drink.

Noor leaned closer on the bar to face Hawke. "So, Aziz?"

"Just met him tonight. You?"

She paused. Maybe in calculation, perhaps out of reservation. "I've interviewed him for my website," Noor admitted.

"What were the articles about?"

"Mostly about technical aspects of the bitcoin project, the protocol, cryptography, and its technical components. This was early days when it was just getting started; many of those interested had a computer science background. But the interview quickly devolved into his wild theories and other information I didn't want going online. Of course, there are many other sites and blogs that jumped at the opportunity to use his conspiracy theories as clickbait."

"I'm guessing this idea involved a leaky boat, a bunch of rich dudes, and an international conspiracy?" Hawke gave her a knowing wink, which she did not reciprocate.

"That it did. He's well known in the bitcoin community for his . . . vivid imagination."

Hawke laughed. "You mean you don't believe there's an international Cabal out to control the world?"

She tilted her head. "Is that what he told you? What else did he say?"

"Well, it ended with him saying something about since our bartender was collaborating with the Cabal, secret agents will soon be flooding the room."

Noor didn't refute the claim, but casually glanced to the front door. "As I said, Aziz is known for his vivid imagination."

The pint arrived and they cheered lightly. Noor went straight back to grilling Hawke.

"What else did Aziz share with you?" She was definitely a journalist, wouldn't stop until she got an answer. Before he decided on what to answer, he looked past Noor towards the front doors and felt the colour drain from his face. Two men were standing inside the threshold. One was middle-aged and slightly hunched over, with an ample paunch poking out from an unbuttoned peacoat. His tiny, deep-set eyes ogled the first woman who walked by, and a warrant badge hung proudly on a chain around his neck, advertising he was a Metropolitan Police Services inspector. The second was a slim man in a trim black suit, blond hair and icy blue eyes tuned for a hunt. Each movement he made—from the slight turn of his neck, which brought the entire pub into his field of vision, to the subtle side-step he made to avoid a loud pair of drunks stumbling by—was calculated with unnerving efficiency, laced with subdued confidence. All told, the self-possessed man's appearance and demeanour told Hawke that, unless every spy novel or movie ever created was completely wrong, this man was a secret agent.

COP'S INTUITION

Hawke and Noor both turned and faced the bar in conspiratorial silence, trying not to draw attention to themselves.

Shariff's paranoia might not be so irrational, Hawke thought.

Hawke glanced at the backstop mirror to watch the fleshy inspector stroll behind them. He didn't know if his leers in their direction were because of professional interest, or if Noor was his type. The inspector continued past them to the end of the bar, greeting the ancient bartender, who said something that Hawke couldn't overhear above the din of chatter. It must have been welcomed news because the inspector's head bobbed and he placed a reassuring hand on the bartender's shoulder. After exchanging a few more intense words, the bartender fetched a pint for his guest and then pointed a bony finger in Hawke's direction. The inspector nodded one last time and sauntered over to Hawke, pint in hand. He rested his arm against the bar so that he faced Hawke with a lazy smile displaying tobacco-stained teeth. He made sure a thick gold ring on his pinky finger caught the light.

"I'm hearing you've been causing a bit of a ruckus here tonight, son," said the inspector in a thick, mumbling accent. Hawke could smell fried onions on his breath. His skin was greying from either too much cigarette smoke or not enough sun, and he apparently did a poor job of shaving unless he had purposely left random clumpings of hair along his jawline.

"I wouldn't say that," Hawke said. His guard was up, but he tried to keep casual. "A voice was raised, and I dunno about you, but that's not a ruckus where I'm from."

"No, not where I'm from either," the inspector muttered defensively. He had to push his belly against the bar to lean around Hawke. "Why'd your girlfriend take off?" he said, pointing to the empty stool next to Hawke.

Noor was now the third person to vanish on him tonight. He'd look into that after dealing with the cop the best way he knew how. "Oh, she's allergic to creepy old dudes." Hawke didn't make much of an effort to hide his grin.

The inspector was taken aback at the lack of respect he normally commanded. His mood quickly darkened. "I'm afraid you may have been witness to a national security emergency. I should very well haul you to the station and forget to interview you until the morning. Maybe make sure you have some proper company in that cell, too."

"If having a pint at the pub is a national security emergency, then I hope you have room at the station for half of London," Hawke said, squaring himself to the inspector. He stood a few inches taller, and whatever weight the cop had over him was concentrated in his belly.

"That won't be necessary." A cool, dispassionate voice joined the conversation. "Agent Thain, US Immigration Department." The man flashed what to Hawke looked like authentic credentials. "This is my Metropolitan Police Services liaison, Inspector Smith. And you are?"

Hawke gave him his name. Agent Thain gave a slight nod at Inspector Smith, which was enough for him to step back and whisper something in the agent's ear before slowly ambling towards the exit, but not without directing a sour stink eye at Hawke.

"Mr. Hawke, I understand you and another young man had a heated conversation earlier tonight." Agent Thain floated a step away from the bar.

Hawke, his back resting against the bar, sized up the immigration agent. Smaller and leaner than Hawke, but no trace of intimidation at the size difference. Hawke wasn't familiar with how the US Immigration Department worked, but he was skeptical that they join with local police to investigate barroom arguments.

"I wouldn't say heated," Hawke replied. He didn't see any reason to lie as he hadn't actually done anything wrong, despite what the agent's presence implied. "But yeah, there was this guy who took a spot next to me here. Spouted some gibberish, banged on the bar, and then took off." Hawke also didn't see any reason to get into the details of their conversation.

Agent Thain's indifferent expression didn't change. He shifted his look to the bartender, who kept the frown firmly in place as he nodded.

"Where were you earlier today?"

"I was at a work conference."

"The bitcoin one?"

Hawke paused. Was it normal for an immigration agent to know about every small conference held in the city? "Yes, that's the one."

"You and your friend know each other previously?"

"First time I saw him was tonight."

"That's not what I asked. Have you two been in communication previous to tonight?"

Hawke didn't immediately see the difference between the two questions. "No, never knew the guy existed before tonight."

"And already thick as thieves." It wasn't a question. Hawke's smartphone, which held his bitcoin wallet, suddenly felt heavy in his pocket. He wondered what Shariff had gotten him mixed up in. Agent Thain remained eerily still for a moment longer than expected, his unfeeling gaze falling over Hawke. Then he blinked. "Thank you for your time, but I'm afraid you were just in the wrong place at the wrong time. But if that gentleman approaches you again, please be wary. He's quite unstable and we would appreciate a quick heads-up." Agent Thain handed Hawke a card with only the US Immigration Department logo and a local London number.

"Of course," Hawke said.

"Have a good night." Agent Thain headed for the exit in an unhurried gait. Hawke realized his muscles had tensed defensively in the agent's presence, and just as he was about to let out a stress-releasing sigh, the agent stopped and turned back.

"One more thing. I've heard about bitcoin before, but one thing was never made clear. Perhaps you can help me figure it out."

"Oh? What's that?" Hawke asked.

"Who is Satoshi Nakamoto?" The voice was cold and direct. They locked eyes.

"I dunno," Hawke answered eventually, "but sounds Japanese to me. Maybe try Japan?"

Hawke was unsure if Agent Thain's muted reaction meant he found his quip amusing or incendiary. He didn't say another word either way before disappearing like a wraith into the night.

***

The man who today went by Agent Thain from the US Immigration Department stepped outside the pub into the cool evening air. He saw Inspector Smith, bumming a light for his cigarette off a couple of young women, and left him there to make a private call.

"This is Agent 21. The target was on-site approximately fifteen minutes ago," he said into his cell.

"Affirmative, Agent 21. Checking neighbourhood CCTV cameras and cab pickups." The perky voice back in Langley, Virginia, paused. She came back with the answer Agent 21 had expected. "No sign of the target."

"Understood."

"He's an expert at avoiding detection."

Agent 21 didn't disagree. It was a skill Aziz Shariff had demonstrated repeatedly, but he was undeterred in his pursuit. However, he was concerned with tonight's events: Shariff had inadvertently led him to a previously unknown player.

Agent 21 didn't like unknowns—their existence taunted his obsessive desire for complete understanding of his assignments, and those he hunted. He would be quick to rectify this newly discovered weakness.

"Open a new dossier," Agent 21 ordered. "Find out everything there is to know about Henry Hawke."

HAWKE'S RESEARCH

Hawke found himself alone at the pub. Shariff, Noor, and Agent Thain had all come and gone, leaving more questions than answers. He didn't know if it was the fog that formed after a couple of pints or information overload causing him to feel completely overwhelmed.

Hawke skipped ordering dinner and paid for his drinks. The bartender wasn't sad to see him settle up. Before leaving, Hawke scanned the pub for Noor, but she was nowhere to be seen. He wouldn't have minded sharing another drink with her, a chance to ask her more questions about why she was so interested in his conversation with Shariff.

It was getting late into the evening and foot traffic was picking up. Rather than tourists enjoying the sights it was now a younger crowd stumbling their way to the next hotspot. The street merchants were more aggressive, too, looking to take advantage of their potential clients' increasing inebriation. Hawke passed by them all, with more important things than partying and making sales on his mind.

Why did Shariff think he was a so-called Keeper of the Fortune and why did he insist on sending him a bitcoin?

Why had Noor and the supposed immigration agent taken such an interest in what Shariff had told him? And why had his late uncle been mentioned by yet another person in the bitcoin world?

Hawke continued alongside the Thames and, as he tended to do when feeling lost, began fiddling with his watch. It had once belonged to his uncle, and the only reason it hadn't been confiscated along with all his other possessions when the government ransacked his home was because Peter had already left it with a watchmaker to be engraved as a gift. Knowing the meaningful gesture of passing down a watch through the generations, the watchmaker had purposely waited until the government had moved on before contacting Hawke. It was the last gift he would ever receive from a family member.

Holding the stainless steel in his hands, the black dial seemed to absorb all surrounding light. He flipped it over to study the engraving. His uncle's words haunted him but perhaps were meant to stir him to action. *Many more a man would go rogue if he only knew how.*

Hawke returned the watch to its rightful place on his wrist and wandered back to the hotel in a daze. There were still conference attendees milling about, and he had to dodge a chattering Bernie Bitcoin one last time before sneaking into the hotel. He was not in the mood to hear another sales pitch. Safely back in his hotel room, Hawke had no interest in sleep. He undressed and took a hot shower until steam filled the bathroom. He put on boxer shorts and a Blackhawks T-shirt and grabbed an overpriced bottle of water and jar of peanuts from the mini bar, not unhappy that they would be charged to his hotel room, which Chicago Mutual was paying for. At the small desk, he turned on his laptop. He couldn't shake the feeling that there was something important about the transaction Shariff had sent him and was intent on finding out what it was.

Hawke was by no means a computer expert, but he knew enough to be dangerous, as an IT worker had noted derisively one morning at 3:00 a.m. after being called into the college library to restore the school's crashed computer systems. Hawke had been using a networked computer—possibly to torrent the Bourne Trilogy of movies—when he had attempted to remove the evidence. He learned through first-hand experience that the Linux command *rm* **.** deleted *everything* that a computer is linked to, and not just a single directory. The IT worker, bribed with a six-pack, told the school the crash was likely caused by a cybercriminal who gained access to the network through a security flaw, and not by some dumb jock who had just watched the movie *Hackers*.

With a young Angelina Jolie far from his mind, Hawke decided to research the bitcoin world a bit further. He began at Sara Noor's website where he found a wealth of articles describing how bitcoin works under the hood. Oddly, and unlike all other sites that focused on cryptocurrencies, there were zero articles speculating about Satoshi Nakamoto's identity. Hawke then found himself reading everything he could about bitcoin transactions.

As he had learned from Jarvenpaa's presentation, a new block was created every ten minutes, and the miner who solved that block included not only all the transactions people had created during that time but also something called a *coinbase transaction*. This unique transaction was how the miner received their reward of fifty bitcoins for solving that block, and essentially how new bitcoins entered circulation.

Here Hawke came upon an enticing piece of bitcoin lore. The coinbase transaction of the genesis block—the very first block, which was mined by Satoshi—included a hidden message. Navigating through the blockchain through a specialized block explorer website, Hawke arrived at the very first bitcoin transaction, which went to the address 1A1zP1eP5QGefi2DMPTfTL5SLmv7DivfNa.

Every transaction had specific fields to hold the data. But a coinbase transaction was unique in that it didn't have an input, the *from* address, because those fifty bitcoins hadn't existed up until that point. And when Hawke looked at where the input data would be in this very first bitcoin transaction, he instead found the hidden message from Satoshi:

The Times 03/Jan/2009 Chancellor on brink of second bailout for banks.

Had Satoshi meant that to confirm he couldn't have mined the genesis block prior to that date? Or was it an opening salvo against the Cabal and its central banks? Either way, Hawke found it interesting that a bitcoin transaction could be a form of communication.

Hawke kept reading, ignoring the voice in his head that whispered he was becoming obsessed and should go to sleep. Along with putting a message where the input data should be, something only possible if you were a miner who solved a block, there was the flip side—the output fields.

Every bitcoin transaction usually had two outputs: one for the destination address where the bitcoins went to, and one for the change address. A change address was where you kept the difference between the input, or original address, and the amount you sent. For example, if your bitcoin address had fifty bitcoins and you sent ten to a new address, the original address would be zero and you would still have forty bitcoins in the change address.

Hawke was beginning to feel like a proper nerd, but without the high-paying job or stock options, when he discovered it was possible to manually create a third output, which could contain up to eighty bytes of arbitrary data that wouldn't have anything to do with the actual bitcoin transactions.

It was almost 2:00 a.m. when Hawke checked his watch. He had one last day of the conference to attend before he would fly back towards his nine-to-five desk job. With the jar of peanuts on the desk now empty and his mind overflowing, Hawke shut down his laptop and crawled into bed.

But his subconscious would not let him sleep. He tossed and turned, unable to slow the waterfall of information flowing through his head. For all the complexities of the blockchain, he couldn't ignore one basic fact: a bitcoin transaction could contain a message.

Hawke shot up wide awake and in a cold sweat. He scrambled to his laptop and turned it on. He immediately launched the block explorer and plugged in the bitcoin address from his wallet where Shariff had sent him a bitcoin.

And then he followed it backwards to Shariff's address where that bitcoin originated, and he was struck by shockwaves of excitement when he found it had three outputs.

The destination address.

The change address.

The third output full of data.

Hawke smiled as he realized it wasn't full of arbitrary data either.

Shariff has sent him a secret message.

AGENT 21'S RESEARCH

Agent 21 sent Inspector Smith away to prepare for any follow-up leads, which the inspector predictably took as an excuse to visit another pub to work free drinks for protection. Agent 21, in turn, discreetly followed Hawke back to the hotel.

There was nothing out of the ordinary in Hawke's route, if not a bit meandering. There were no dead drops, no brush passes—nothing to indicate he traded in spycraft. Arriving at the hotel, Agent 21 took a position across the street and blended into the crowd by giving the impression that the most important thing in the world was the contents of his smartphone. Using that as cover, he observed Hawke purposely duck past a chubby man, who then lit up a cigarette by a no-smoking sign near the door. When a couple of slick Wall Street types made their way into the hotel, the man quickly used a potted plant as an ashtray and staggered after them, loudly shouting something about making a fortune.

From his collection of dossiers on those in the bitcoin community, Agent 21 knew the drunkard to be Bernard "Bernie Bitcoin" Salisbury, and a fraud. Any money he raised for his non-existent investment fund went straight up his nose and pocket change exceeded his actual net worth.

That Hawke did not want any contact with Bernie Bitcoin told Agent 21 two things.

It meant that they had already spoken.

And it meant that Hawke was not easily conned.

At that moment, Agent 21's phone chimed with the arrival of an encrypted email from Dunwoody. It contained research that confirmed Hawke's outward appearance of a typical account manager from Chicago— but it was unusually light on details. An incomplete LinkedIn page and no social media presence, pedestrian banking history with a predilection for using cash, parents deceased at a young age, unremarkable academic performance and a short-lived collegiate athletic career. The sparse intel was unsatisfying. Agent 21 insisted on knowing everything about his targets—psychological profiles, family history, financial transactions, sexual habits, social networks. He instructed Dunwoody to dig deeper into Hawke's life.

Agent 21 pulled out a lambskin bifold ID holder and shuffled through a collection of business cards until he found his next persona. He crossed the street and headed into the hotel.

To find Satoshi's Fortune, Agent 21 was going to have to see a man about making a fortune of his own.

***

The art deco Imperial Hotel bar hummed with conference attendees congregating for a late-night drink. An atrium rose high above the bar where speakeasy-themed cocktails were in high demand and music from a grand piano gently filled the air between conversations of cryptocurrency.

Retro paintings of flappers kept a close eye on Bernie Bitcoin as he worked the crowd. He slapped backs, shook hands, and shared his uninvited insight into the future of bitcoin. When anyone showed a glimmer of curiosity in his crypto fund, he made a big show of its stratospheric rate of return and how he had seen bitcoin's potential years before the schmucks on Wall Street or the City. He made sure his captive audience knew that he drove a new BMW every year, was on the verge of opening a state-of-the-art crypto office right in downtown London, and was looking to buy a nice Italian villa, in case you happened to know anyone looking to sell. Bernie also ordered rounds of top-shelf shots to share with his new friends and potential business partners—but always had to dash off to meet with an imagined whale investor friend moments before the bill arrived.

Eschewing the cocktails for whiskey, Bernie now trolled the bar looking for another party to mingle with. He zeroed in on a smartly dressed man perched at the hightop table furthest from the bar. An untouched highball glass lost to the man's smartphone for his attention. Bernie didn't remember seeing him at the conference so considered him fresh meat. He approached his newest prospect and let out a boisterous greeting.

"Hey, boyo, you look like a man who wants to get his hands on a fortune!"

Agent 21 looked up from his phone. "As a matter of fact, I am."

"Excellent! Let's have a drink to discuss!" He raised his glass for a cheers, which wasn't reciprocated. "Now then, my name is Bernard Salisbury the Fourth, CEO, president, and founder of one of the largest cryptocurrency investment firms in the world. But all my friends and investors call me Bernie Bitcoin!"

Agent 21 baited the hook and said, "I'm Alan Dimon. I manage a hedge fund in Singapore. We're looking to achieve outsized market growth by investing in riskier asset classes such as cryptocurrencies. However, we're quite small by international standards as we only have $750 million in assets under management."

Bernie Bitcoin had to catch himself to make sure dollar signs didn't visibly appear in his eyes. "Singapore! What a beautiful country."

Agent 21 was not interested in correcting him about Singapore's city-state status. He let the conman continue.

"Just a beautiful country. I'm actually planning on visiting sometime this year to look at some real estate deals, you know how it is," Bernie said and gave an exaggerated wink.

Agent 21 nodded, as if he did in fact, know how it is.

"Now about this fortune you're looking for, are you wanting to triple or only double your money in the next few months?" Bernie laughed at his own joke. "My fund essentially mirrors the price of bitcoin. You can check my website any time to see what the units are worth."

With Bernie Bitcoin firmly nibbling on the line, Agent 21 directed him to elaborate about the venture. Bernie continued through a well-rehearsed sales pitch, making sure to flag the waitress down for another whiskey and a round of shots for himself and his soon-to-be investor. Once Bernie began to repeat himself, Agent 21 took the opportunity to interrupt him. "One of the key factors I use to determine who I invest in is the people involved. For instance, I'm looking at both your firm and Chicago Mutual. I hear they're starting a crypto fund that would compete with yours."

Bernie shook his jowls. "No no, we are by far the best. Triple returns. Chicago Mutual doesn't even have plans for a crypto fund," he said dismissively.

"That's odd," Agent 21 paused for effect, "because I spoke to a young man from there earlier. Said he was going to spearhead the effort. A Mr. Henry Hawke as I recall. Weren't you talking to him today as well?"

"Oh, yes I was. I've got my fingers in all the pies," Bernie stammered as he felt a much-needed deal slipping away.

"That's perfect. That's what I wanted to hear." Agent 21's reassurance calmed him. The hook was set. "Now, tell me, what did the young Mr. Hawke have to say?"

Bernie described their earlier encounter in depth, gently prodded by Agent 21 to remain on subject whenever he veered off to give himself accolades for his own fund's performance. By the end of it, there was much boasting but little useful information regarding Henry Hawke.

Unbeknownst to Bernie, he was now sheared of value and as useful as a bankrupt corporation to the Cabal. Expecting to begin discussing investment amounts, he instead watched as the hedge fund man from Singapore answered his phone and subsequently turned to leave without even a promise to get in touch.

And to add insult to injury, at that moment the waitress arrived and served Bernie a fresh whiskey, two shots of tequila, and the bill.

SHARIFF'S MISTAKE

By the time Hawke had found the secret message, Shariff had already been awake for forty-eight hours, powered by a combustible mix of caffeine, paranoia, and second guesses. Needing to refuel, Shariff decided to grab a hot coffee, revisit all the possible attack vectors the Cabal could use to steal his piece of the puzzle, and lament his decision to involve Hawke in his fight to change the world.

A lonely neon sign flickered *OPEN* outside a small all-night corner coffee shop. Shariff hustled towards it, following the path outlined by his warning app as one CCTV camera watched over the street from above the shop. Inside it was empty save for a teenage barista texting on her phone. She didn't immediately register the arrival of a new customer. The acrid smell of coffee roasted hours earlier hung in the air as Shariff stood before the barista, who eventually acknowledged his presence. He ordered a stale donut and the largest coffee they had and paid in cash, much to the annoyance of the barista, who found it was more work to fumble with coins than letting a customer simply tap their credit cards on the terminal.

As he waited for his order, Shariff rapped his knuckles on the counter to an imaginary punk song that only he heard, further aggravating the barista, who eventually produced his order with a forced smile and mocking *thank you*. His other hand never left the smartphone hidden in his pocket, and he was prepared to run the moment he felt its warning.

Shariff picked a table against the full windows that ran lengthwise down the coffee shop, giving him an unfettered view of the street. He devoured his donut in two bites and washed it down with a large dose of burnt coffee as he studied the generations of people pass by. Groups of tipsy girls locked arm-in-arm gallivanting their way to the next party. Couples out for a late-night dinner to a favourite haunt. Grey pensioners strolling without purpose, except to feel part of the city. All completely unaware that the only reason they hadn't been thrust into financial calamity was because the Cabal had not yet decided it would be to their advantage.

A flatbed truck pulled up on the street outside the coffee stop, resting at a stoplight. It was filled with ten-foot-tall windows on their way to a condo development. Their reflective surface angled towards Shariff, showing a small, lonely man looking out from a coffee shop. It took him a moment to realize he was looking at his own tired reflection.

Shariff decided it might be time for a few hours of rest. He would find a bus station bench or maybe a motel as a last resort and pay with a stolen credit card and spoofed identity, which was how he had managed to stay off grid these past few months. Shariff didn't enjoy stealing; he would only do so for his own survival or just cause, and he did his best to make sure it was the corporations and not the individuals who were hurt financially. The credit card amounts were easily marked as fraud and would be refunded. He destroyed the digital footprint of the identities used so the true owners would not have to worry about identity theft. He might have lost sleep over harming individuals, but never a wink at a faceless corporation's loss.

But it troubled him that the average person didn't realize just how much financial privacy they were giving up online. First off, every single transaction was collected, collated, and filed away in the name of Big Data to form a personal psychological profile that could be provided to any organization willing to pay for it. These organizations now knew what you were going to buy before you did. And even if the business wasn't planning on selling this data, they would eventually be hacked and it would be available on the dark web. People were blind to the fact that it wasn't a matter of *if* a website was going to be hacked, but *when*.

Shariff knew in his soul that the masses, even if the they hadn't yet realized it, were screaming out for the financial security that the bitcoin revolution would deliver. The value of crypto was so much higher than any monetary figure could convey.

The truck rolled on as Shariff now unconsciously, and loudly, tapped his foot, completely out of sync with the music floating over the shop's speakers. The annoyed barista huffed in Shariff's direction in an attempt to guilt him into stopping, but went back to her phone after her attempts remained ignored.

Their passive-aggressive relationship was interrupted when the coffee shop door swung open and an overweight man walked in. He casually glanced around before looking the young barista up and down. Shariff immediately tensed up with the man's arrival. Doubly so when he noticed the inspector badge hanging for all to see. He clenched his silent smartphone so tight he could feel the plastic casing start to crack.

Was it just a coincidence that the cop was here? Had the Suit ratted him out? Had a CCTV camera picked him up? No, that was impossible. Shariff was certain he had avoided being seen. The only camera on this block was one directly above the coffee shop pointing across the street where the flatbed truck had stopped—Shariff felt his stomach drop so hard he nearly had to rush to the washroom. The truck's cargo of condo windows . . . They had reflected his image right into the CCTV camera's view! That was all it would take for the CCTV facial-recognition software to identify him. And if the cops knew where he was, then the Cabal did too.

Inspector Smith didn't take his eyes off the barista but spoke to Shariff. "Run and you get hurt."

Shariff stood up defiantly. "How do you know I won't hurt you?"

Spittle sprang from the inspector's mouth as he laughed. "Because you weigh ten stone soaking wet and you look about as strong as an ill-fed refugee." He pulled his peacoat behind his hip to reveal a shiny yellow-trimmed taser. "But I wouldn't mind you trying so I can test out my new toy."

While Smith laughed at his own comment, Shariff rushed across the space and kicked him as hard as he could right between the legs. Caught off guard, Smith yelped and fell to one knee, clutching his nether region. Shariff decided to punch the inspector as many times as his caffeine-infused muscles would allow. Before the inspector could raise his arms in defence, Shariff landed a handful of quick, frantic blows that bloodied the inspector's nose.

The horrified barista's shrieks pierced Shariff's ears.

"Would you shut up already!" he yelled. "He's just a fucking crooked cop part of an international cabal that controls nearly every facet of your financial life!" Shariff finished by spitting on the hobbled inspector and cursing the government. He turned for the exit but was startled by a pair of hollow blue eyes, which had watched the whole fight from the doorway. Shariff hadn't heard the door chime or noticed the man's entry—he had just materialized in place.

Agent 21 addressed the trembling barista. "You may go." She obeyed immediately and fled out the rear of the shop without looking back.

With his confidence boosted from defeating Inspector Smith, Shariff rushed Agent 21 and attempted the same line of attack. It was quickly made clear that the confidence was misplaced, as Agent 21 effortlessly avoided the charge by taking a small side-step backwards, leaving Shariff to vainly kick the empty space he had just vacated. With his leg outstretched, Shariff was helpless as he watched the agent grab his leg and hurl it upwards, sending him toppling backwards. Shariff caught his breath and scrambled to his feet, ignoring how easily he had been manhandled, and flung himself at Agent 21, both arms flailing in a wild attempt to land a knockout punch. Agent 21, almost bored with the altercation, parried his lead arm forward from left to right, neutralizing both of Shariff's weak arms. In the same motion, Agent 21 brought his other arm forward and jabbed two fingers into Shariff's throat. Shariff felt his airway violently constrict and he collapsed to one knee to gasp for breath. A sharp blow to the back of his head followed, sending him to the floor. The entire skirmish had lasted less than a minute.

Shariff's lungs cried out for air and black spots began dotting his vision. He struggled to extend each shortened breath, sucking in as much oxygen as his injured throat would allow. His thoughts became difficult to form as an approaching darkness rushed towards him like a tidal wave. The voices of Agent 21 and Inspector Smith sounded a million miles away. They were discussing what to do with him.

The cop asked how they were going to get him to talk.

The agent answered something about a five-dollar wrench.

And then the darkness crashed over him.

PART 2:

1AoGihhH9zZquPdy734rv
V4KDQ94A15Vt7

THE FED'S BOSS

The Federal Reserve Bank of New York existed as a fortress from a different era. Seemingly carved out of a single fourteen-story granite boulder, it was unwelcoming by design. Wrought-iron gates guarded every window. The front entrance doors stood forty-feet high and required two sturdy men to open. The building wouldn't have looked out of place in Medieval England with archers manning its ramparts, raining down arrows to quash another rebellion.

Physically, the bank encompassed an entire city block in New York's financial district, but economically its presence weighed on every central bank in the world. Its location was not chosen haphazardly, because only atop Manhattan's bedrock could the weight of the bank's vault be sustained, for it held over seven thousand tons of gold bullion. More than Fort Knox, more than anywhere else in the world. For an organization that provisionally deemed the gold standard useless in a modern economy, it was a curious amount to keep on hand—a subtle hint that maybe the Fed didn't quite believe their own public statements on the matter.

The Federal Reserve Bank was a wolf in sheep's clothing, a corporation privately owned by the Cabal masquerading as a governmental department. Since its creation in 1913, the Fed's powers have continuously grown, slowly during the boom years and shockingly fast in times of crisis. These powers were something of an unholy cross between a Greek deity and a loan shark. The Fed could simply will money into existence—and then dictate the interest rate on its repayment.

Now both the US government and major financial firms couldn't continue their respective operations without the Federal Reserve Bank's blessing and support. The secretary of the treasury, the man in charge of managing the US government's own finances, was rumoured to have bent his knee before the Chairman of the Fed to avoid financial Armageddon during the darkest days of the most recent financial crisis. Wall Street executives, champions of the free market, became a little more flexible on the subject, upon deciding to beg across the bank's polished boardroom tables for solvency.

As presented to the American public, the Treasury and Wall Street were rulers of the financial world. But everyone has a boss.

Over 3,000 miles away from the second annual Bitcoin Conference, Moira Eglinton, the Chairman of the Federal Reserve, held court on this Saturday evening for yet another emergency meeting involving the CEOs of Wall Street's most venerable firms. She didn't even bother to invite the Treasury anymore; she just had her assistant inform them of her decisions after the fact as a courtesy.

Eglinton had run straight into middle age without looking back. Streaks of grey weaved their way through her blood-red hair and she had found a healthy life balance between exercise and scotch. She wore flattering red lipstick to avoid being criticized for not wearing any makeup and staid enough clothing to be complimented for removing enough traces of her womanhood to thrive in a male-dominated industry. Her sharp emerald eyes watched the half-dozen CEOs bicker back and forth over their firms' pending doom all the while refusing responsibility for their current predicaments. Partially it was because of their unwavering belief in their own infallibility in matters of finance, but mostly it was because they had no idea what had happened.

They had recklessly traded complex financial assets for years, where the math behind them could only be understood by six people on the entire planet.

One worked for NASA.

The other five, the Cabal.

Therefore, as Eglinton had expected, when the markets had invariably turned, those same assets that generated outsized profits now became bottomless liabilities.

"We have maybe two weeks left of liquidity. After that we won't have enough cash on hand to fund operations!" shouted Oliver Kovich, the CEO of Wall Street's oldest investment bank. A portly man with a known love for pasta and wine, he raised his smooth, round head as he spoke, giving him the impression of a bull defending itself.

"Maybe you should have used better risk management," shot back Kurtis Evans, the wiry chairman of the largest bank in the country. "Your whole shop is a mirage."

"Now, gentlemen, the president is a close tennis buddy of mine and he has all but promised that the government will not let another one of us go under. 2008 is still fresh in his mind—and his voters." Giovanni Sanguinetti's voice was failing and lacked conviction, like that of a man battling cancer attempting to reassure his children despite a dim prognosis. The one-time avid tennis player had shed what little hair he had left from all the stress, and Eglinton knew at this point he was just trying to hold off the collapse of his investment bank, led by four generations of Sanguinettis, before his planned retirement at the end of the year.

Eglinton sat at the head of a blunt mahogany table that had taken two dozen construction workers to carry when it had been put into place in 1919. It hadn't moved an inch since. The boardroom was surrounded by dark wood panelling and occasionally haunted by wisps of cigar smoke from a bygone era.

On her left sat Kovich, Sanguinetti, and Daniel Kirkpatrick. The fact that Kirkpatrick didn't need to shave daily combined with noticeable crow's feet made his age indiscernible. He ran the most trusted brokerage on Wall Street, and he had all of two weeks before employee pay cheques would start to bounce. Across from Kirkpatrick was Emmanual Montez of a former regional southern bank that had bought its way to the table, through aggressive acquisitions since the turn of the century, but hadn't the legacy to be treated as an equal. He noted dryly to himself that they'd all be equal in bankruptcy court.

Closest to the Chairman of the Fed sat William McCabe, CEO of the most hated bank in America but the smallest firm at the table, and mere hours from collapse. He had a thick neck and thick nose and eyebrows that always pointed down. Rarely had he liked anything that had happened in the markets for the past twenty years, even if he had profited from it.

None of the six men knew that Eglinton already had the third bailout package in four years planned and ready for immediate deployment. She could have spoken up at the beginning of the meeting, but preferred to watch some of the richest and most powerful men in the country squabble like spoiled children. It was good for them to suffer. It reminded them of just how tenuous their hold on power is and how quickly the Fed could take it away— even if today she was generous.

The previous bailout packages involved the Federal Reserve buying unwanted securities from these insolvent Wall Street firms with money they printed out of thin air. She had originally told these same men in 2008, with her fingers crossed, that the original bailout would be a one-time event and only justifiable because otherwise the world's economy would collapse. The price tag for such heroics, and saving their jobs, came in at $700 billion. Then, in 2010, with the first bailout proving insufficient in kickstarting the economy, another attempt was permitted. This time the Fed only printed another $600 billion. But the second round had also failed, as Eglinton knew it would.

This next bailout would have to come with a twist since it was too soon for the public to accept, the previous bailout still fresh in their memories. The public had to be kept scared and on edge—but not so angry that they gave revolution a second thought.

Eglinton cleared her throat ever so slightly, which was enough to silence the room. "Gentlemen, I present to you Operation Twist."

Eglinton's previously invisible assistant stepped out from a corner with paperwork loaded on his thin arms. He had aristocratic hair, teeth, and nails and a slim-fit suit. His vibrantly coloured tie and pocket square stood out against the conservative suits. The assistant circled the table and with a delicate hand placed a report before each CEO before obediently returning to his corner.

While the reports were eagerly being consumed, the Chairman of the Fed continued. "We, the Federal Reserve, have decided under these extreme and unusual market conditions to sell short-term treasury bills and use the proceeds to purchase longer-term ones. We estimate the total program will cost $400 billion."

The six men collectively paused to assess the program. The *sell short, buy longer T-bills* plan would lower interest rates and push investor money into riskier assets—conveniently the same assets that they were desperate to rid themselves of. Now that they knew they would be saved, they quickly calculated how much they would profit.

"Four hundred billion in T-bills?!" The rolling muscles in McCabe's neck tightened. "Chairwoman Eglinton, that's not early enough! That's peanuts. That's insulting! My firm has analyzed the situation thoroughly and we need at least—"

Eglinton eyed McCabe. He ceased speaking the moment her gaze reached him. From day one she had insisted on being addressed as the Chairman of the Fed. Not Chairperson. Definitely not Chairwoman. In their world, the title Chairman of the Fed bestowed near absolute power upon its holder, and Moira Eglinton would not allow any deviation in respecting that power. On top of the insult, she knew that McCabe had been growing increasingly desperate and had started reaching out to far-east sovereign funds, an area of the world where the Federal Reserve did not command as much control.

"Chairman Eglinton," McCabe stammered, "I just meant that to avoid systematic risks we need this round in particular to be higher than $400 billion."

"How many more days until your bank runs out of money?" she asked pointedly. The oldest of five Catholic children and the only girl, she had learned quickly how to stop men from getting out of line over their perceived lack of fair share, whether it be the Thanksgiving pie or the largest bailout in human history. The key was to break the weakest. This meant that somebody else became the weakest and the price of dissention was clear. She had done it with her youngest brother Patrick, may he rest in peace, and she had done it with Bear Stearns. And then again with Lehman Brothers. And today with . . .

"We have until next Thursday, depending on how the markets do."

"You have until Asian markets open Monday morning. Tops. I would imagine it's in the interest of your shareholders to avoid bankruptcy. The most prudent means to achieve this, and I think the markets would agree, would be to find a stronger firm to merge with." Eglinton's emerald eyes went from McCabe to Kovich, who nervously rubbed his bald head at being singled out before realizing he was looking at a gift horse.

Everyone knew Kovich and McCabe had previously discussed a merger, but McCabe had balked at the arrangement. It would have been a merger in name only, the older firm swallowing up the weaker one and leaving McCabe with a rich severance package but without the position of CEO of a prestigious Wall Street firm, which was more valuable than money to these modern-day kings.

Now, with a simple nod of her head, Chairman Eglinton had just decreed the merger would take place. McCabe's firm would be swallowed up and exist only in Wall Street lore as a cautionary tale, the CEO humiliated and without a kingdom to rule over.

William McCabe's face turned the colour of an overripe tomato. He stood up, knocking over his chair, one last feeble act of defiance before he stormed out of the room amid a torrent of curses and empty threats.

The remaining five CEOs sat with their hands folded, pretending to ignore their former colleague's tantrum. Only once Eglinton spoke did they finally exhale.

"I assume that everyone else trusts me when I say Operation Twist will be a success?"

The CEOs all agreed and talked over each other to boast how well thought out the plan was. Moments earlier they were at each other's throats with only survival on their mind. Now they were busy making dinner plans to celebrate their common genius for having successfully navigated yet another financial crisis that had doomed less worthy firms.

These were the masters of the universe on Wall Street, but, as Eglinton knew, everyone has a boss.

***

The Chairman of the Federal Reserve retired to her office on the top floor of the bank. She hung her jacket on a rack by the door. The same rack that presidents from Wilson to Kennedy to Obama had hung their coats on while attending private meetings in that very room. Meetings they had not simply been invited, but summoned to.

They were the leaders of the free world.

But everyone has a boss.

The entire office always seemed dark no matter how many lights she turned on. Little sunlight entered through the narrow cell-like windows, and the office was enveloped in heavy oak and dark leather. And where there wasn't dark leather or heavy oak, there were books. Rare copies of Hemingway, Fitzgerald, and Machiavelli sat alongside textbooks by Smith, Keynes, and Friedman. On a corner table below a lamp was a document she was loathe to include among her other readings.

From a wet bar beside her desk, Eglinton gave herself a generous pour of a single malt scotch she kept only for herself. She also kept a popular but pedestrian twelve-year-old scotch for guests. The only other liquor was a top-shelf bottle of gin, distilled in small batches from a single orchard in Herefordshire. A fruit bowl sat unused beside a filled ice bucket, both refreshed religiously every evening by her staff. Finishing half her scotch in one go, she contemplated her next steps after Operation Twist, as the remaining five CEOs would surely be back for another helping next year.

Eglinton always planned well in advance. In high school, she planned for college. In college, for law school. In law school, for her legacy. This career path was accelerated at a dinner party where she made the acquaintance of a well-connected gentleman who offered mentorship and a direct line to her current position. All that was asked of her in return was . . .

Two loud rhythmic beats of a cane on the hardwood startled her.

Moira Eglinton was the most powerful banker in the world. But everyone has a boss.

She quickly finished her scotch and poured another two fingers before turning to face the summons. The familiar narrow face and narrow eyes of John Francis Rickard stared back from the unlit corner chair. He was sitting comfortably in an immaculate dark blue suit with a bowler cap resting on his knee. Rickard had already been considered ancient when Eglinton first met him at that fateful dinner party, but his mind had kept the swiftness of his youth. He still only needed ten minutes with any company's financials before spotting its vulnerabilities and how to take advantage.

"My Moira, my brilliant Moira. So good to see you again and, yes, I'd love to join you for a drink." A hard voice betrayed his frail frame, as if he had borrowed it from his much younger self. He always referred to her as *My* Moira, something outsiders might have interpreted as a sign of affection, but those who had ever dealt with the head of the Cabal knew otherwise.

Eglinton composed herself and filled a rock glass with exactly three square cubes of ice and added two fingers of the gin. She took an apple from the fruit bowl and cut out a perfect slice—a quarter inch at the head with the skin on—and added it to the drink.

She brought Rickard his drink of choice as he released the stranglehold on his cane, whose antiquity might have even exceeded that of its owner. Its snakewood shaft, said to have been carved from a tree originating on Jekyll Island, had a solid gold handle molded into a fierce serpent's head. Rickard set it aside and received his gin. A favourite game of his was to bang the cane to catch people off guard, as he had done tonight. Perhaps he enjoyed their look of surprise or, perhaps more likely, he knew that catching people unaware meant that in the wild, they would have been his next meal.

"I wasn't expecting to see you this evening, Mr. Rickard."

"Oh, I didn't mean to arrive in this office unannounced," he said, his mere presence evidence to the contrary, "but I just wanted to check in on things."

Rickard motioned to Eglinton's own reading chair for her to take a seat, which she did.

"Operation Twist will be announced later this month and rolled out in October."

"And how did my friends take the news?"

Eglinton chose her words carefully. "Five took it well."

Rickard nodded and sipped his gin. Eglinton followed suit but didn't take her eyes off her mentor.

"That should cover them for another year or so. Quite the hole they dug for themselves this time around. But you've done exemplary work in taking advantage of the situation; Wall Street is as firmly under our control as ever." Rickard was known to use compliments to make his own point, and if one disagreed, he would shed courtesy like a snake shedding its useless skin.

"That was my line of thinking as well," she said.

Rickard smiled thinly. His eyes flickered towards her side table. "Some interesting reading material you have."

"Yes, it is." Eglinton held up Satoshi Nakamoto's whitepaper. "Since it seems to be leaking into the mainstream media a bit more lately, I've been reading up on the subject. I can't see how this should be a concern to us." She watched Rickard closely, observing his reaction. His body language didn't betray his thoughts.

"It's a mild one for now. The media has started to take an interest and will begin asking you questions regarding its impact. It's important we have a united front to avoid lending any unearned credence to this . . .," he pondered his words, " . . . blasphemy."

"I'm assuming that isn't the official statement from the Federal Reserve." Blasphemy had too much of an emotional edge to be used by Rickard.

"Oh, of course not," he said. "We'll put something together. Something along the lines of bitcoin cannot be considered a currency, too volatile, it isn't backed by anything, and only the government can create a currency."

Moira looked for irony in his voice, as they both knew very well that the US government didn't actually create its own currency either. Perhaps the old man was beginning to believe his own lies.

"We're handling it through multiple channels," he continued. "I've tapped our friends in the media to begin framing the discussion; bitcoin is only used by drug dealers, criminals, and terrorists. The usual arguments will follow. We'll have the mainstream economists write some op-eds about how cryptocurrencies are a fad or a fraud. Should I deem it necessary, we'll get a few senators to publicly warn about bitcoin and call for regulations to protect the American populace."

It was the Cabal's textbook play to discredit someone. But without that someone, he was curious as to its effectiveness.

"Have you found Satoshi Nakamoto yet?" she asked.

The thin smile again. She was pushing her luck. "Satoshi Nakamoto . . ." He spoke the name derisively, as if the mere utterance of the name tasted foul on his tongue. "He's no longer a priority with the recent discovery of his little fortune and that he no longer controls it. The priority now is finding these Keepers of the Fortune, as they seem to like being called. I have our best agent addressing this and once complete, we'll push out a few *Bitcoin is Dead* articles and move on."

Eglinton didn't know exactly how this agent would address the fortune and didn't have any interest in finding out. Her role was public-facing as the Chairman of the Fed, and she wouldn't allow herself to be compromised by knowing too much about the Cabal's more hands-on undertakings.

Rickard finished his gin and set the glass aside. He rose, his bowler hat and serpent cane falling into place. "It's only a matter of time until we secure his so-called fortune. And once that happens, well, I'm loathe to use the analogy of a stillborn, but . . ." His words hung in the air.

Eglinton didn't think he minded the analogy at all. Regardless, she now had clarity from on high regarding the quirky little technology that had ruffled so many feathers. "Therefore, I'm moving forward with future plans under the assumption that bitcoin is as good as dead," she said.

"Yes, my Moira. Bitcoin is dead." Rickard banged his cane twice as if to decree it.

Eglinton watched as Rickard—perhaps the most powerful person in the world—let doubt seep into his eyes, if only briefly, before letting himself out. She looked at the whitepaper still in her hands and wondered if perhaps it was actually true—did everyone have a boss?

HAWKE'S DREAM

Sleep had come reluctantly for Hawke after discovering the secret message from Shariff. And when he did manage to rest his eyes the dreams were fragmented and discomforting. He was physically chained to his office desk by thick anaconda-like chains coiled around his legs. He grabbed the rough metal and yanked with all his might, again and again, until he could smell the soft metallic tang of blood coming from his blistered hands. His cries for help echoed in the nothingness of the office and went answered by faceless humanoid drones forming a queue at his desk, each perfectly dressed in uniformed suits and ties. One by one they stepped forward and dropped off bloated file folders, forming a mountain range around him. The stacks of paper grew so high they blocked out the sun, which rose and fell with increasing frequency outside a window. He made another attempt at pulling the chains loose but felt his muscles shrivel and his hair turn to grey. His back hunched as his spine adapted to life curled over a desk. He began his cries anew, but now they weren't for help escaping—but for help in finishing all the paperwork on time. One of the drones morphed into his uncle, the hair on his head and his eyebrows covered in melting ice with shards of a windshield poking out of his skin. This seemed to bother him less than seeing Hawke as a withered old man hunched over a desk, begging for help with paperwork.

Peter Finlay's question was laced with disappointment: "Don't you know how?"

Hawke woke up in a cold sweat. He was disoriented. A sharp wave of panic coursed through him at finding himself in unfamiliar surroundings, until he remembered where he was. He glanced at the hotel clock on the nightstand. Five a.m.

Hawke fell back onto his pillow and stared at the ceiling. He was supposed to attend a couple of seminars to wrap up the conference before taking the long flight back to his life in Chicago. But what had his dream meant, if anything? And what was he supposed to do with Shariff's secret message, again, if anything? Not knowing what else to do, Hawke made his way to the shower to prepare for his final day in London.

AGENT 21'S FORM

The Cabal had no form of its own. It was not an intelligence agency but it deployed secret agents. It was not a central bank but it managed the economies of nations. It was not elected democratically but it ran politicians. It was less of an organization and more of a loose affiliation of powerful individuals, all intent on collecting power and wealth while remaining in the shadows. Most of the people who did the Cabal's bidding had no idea of their true employer. Crooked cops, well-meaning philanthropists, egocentric interest groups . . . they all served the Cabal in one way or another without even realizing it. And that's where the Cabal became a paradox; nobody knew it existed yet everyone was under its influence. Everything that money touched—stocks and bonds, housing markets, inflation rates, credit scores—the Cabal held in its hands.

To try and destroy the Cabal would be as pointless as putting a bullet into smoke; it would inflict no pain, leaving the Cabal not only as it was before any such foolishness, but now aware of where to focus its response.

And Agent 21 was the response. He existed to neutralize anything and anyone John Francis Rickard deemed a threat to the Cabal. Little was known about the laconic agent with a hundred different names, even to those in the Cabal's inner circle. But as long as he delivered results, his true identity didn't matter.

The reason why Agent 21 didn't use his given name inside the Cabal wasn't a nod to spycraft—the true reason was he didn't know it. His entrance into the foster care system as an infant started with a computer glitch, one that assigned him a different name with each foster home transfer. Sometimes he was given his previous surname as a given name, sometimes it was the name of the next child in the system, sometimes it was just left blank. As a young boy he would protest that his name wasn't *Walid* or *Jerome* or *Tomasz*, at least to his knowledge, but his new foster parents would just assume he was acting out, as troubled orphans tended to do. Eventually, he just decided to remain silent on the matter.

Over the years, the boy saw a multitude of different homes and he came to know that there were two kinds of foster care parents. There were the kind-hearted parents, usually the religious types who liked to hold hands in public. They didn't insomuch as welcome him into their homes as much as tolerate him out of a moral obligation, never protesting when the unnervingly quiet boy with dead eyes was shipped off to the next foster home in line.

Then there were the abusive types, the kind that nobody really cared existed until their atrocities made their way into the local papers. While in these households he witnessed many belts violently lash across broken skin, and learned to sleep through the subsequent sobbing cries of the other victimized children. To the envy and animosity of the other children, these abusive parents tended to give the boy a wide berth and rarely directed their cruelty on him, perhaps recognizing a kindred spirit calmly waiting just beneath the surface, and left well enough alone.

On the closest approximation to his sixteenth birthday he took a series of aptitude tests at the behest of those in charge of the foster care program. Usually the results dictated that a child who had spent their formative years in the system was best suited for the military, but in this case the distinctive results garnered the attention of something else entirely.

The old man arrived at the foster home one day wearing the finest suit the boy had ever seen. Speaking privately, the old man asked the boy for his name. When the boy responded "It does not matter, tomorrow it will be something else," the old man laughed and banged a serpent cane twice on the floor. That was the day the boy came under the guidance of John Francis Rickard and was designated as Agent 21 of the Cabal.

From then on, he always chose his own name.

***

The safe house belonged to the State Department but had been commandeered by the Cabal. It was a spartan apartment in a London neighbourhood where hauling a body in or out of a building wouldn't result in a call to the police. The only furniture was a wooden campaign desk and a pair of mismatched kitchen chairs. The walls were papered in a navy floral pattern straight out of a British soap opera. The stove and dishwasher in the kitchen did nothing but collect dust. For food there was a loaf of bread and protein bars, to be washed down with bottled water. With blackout curtains covering the sole window in the apartment, the only light came from the low-wattage ceiling fixture.

Under this light, Agent 21 sat at the campaign desk. A black laptop was squarely in the middle of the desk with a half-dozen passports stacked neatly in a pile beside it. Directly beside them were stacks of corresponding driver's licences, credit cards, and business cards. Agent 21 was under no illusions that the names on the documents did not always match his physical appearance, but it allowed him to share a moment with his target where neither knew his true name, yet they both carried on as if they did.

The desire to know everything and the power that accompanied that knowledge drove Agent 21. It resulted in the dossiers he kept on every person of interest on a given assignment, such as the newly opened and growing dossier on Henry Hawke, among others in the bitcoin community. Each person had everything about them collected, collated, and organized, ready to be utilized at any given moment. Basic information such as date of birth, Social Security number, and current and past addresses. Metadata revolving around their social and professional networks, education, complete email and phone logs, chat program transcripts and photos, social media activity, browsing history, and every single financial decision ever made. All used to track and profile the target.

So much information on everyone.

Everyone except the target Agent 21 had initially been tasked to neutralize after bitcoin had come to the Cabal's attention—and the only true identity Agent 21 didn't know, apart from his own.

Satoshi Nakamoto.

It was a name Agent 21 silently cursed. He brought up the painfully thin dossier on his laptop and re-read it yet again, hoping to find something he had missed that might reignite his search for the creator of bitcoin.

Satoshi's P2P Foundation profile page stated he was born on April 5, 1975. It was extremely unlikely that he chose his birthdate at random, because it had a historic significance to the Cabal. Roosevelt issued Executive Order 6102 on April 5, 1933, which made it illegal for US citizens to own gold coins, bullion, or certificates. It mandated that all Americans hand over their gold to the Federal Reserve under threat of fines and even jail time. And 1975 was the year when the restrictions on owning gold was lifted. This made it apparent to Agent 21 that Satoshi was a student of history and not without a dry sense of humour.

The profile page also claimed he was from Japan, something reiterated by his chosen name but contradicted by Satoshi's confirmed forum posts and emails. Few of such communications were made between 5:00 a.m. and 11:00 a.m. Greenwich Mean Time, consistent with someone living in the United Kingdom should they have a typical programmer's sleeping habit. The vernacular used, such as the expression *bloody hard*, were also common English expressions. Also lending credence to the British residency theory was that the hidden message in the genesis block was taken from *The Times*, a British daily newspaper.

Agent 21 wondered if this is how his targets sometimes felt, their adversary openly insulting their intelligence by choosing an alias clearly in opposition to their actual identity.

Other proof that the name Satoshi Nakamoto was a selected rather than given name was that the generally accepted translation was *Clever Chronicling of History as a Book That Is Happening and Throughout,* which to Agent 21 was an ostentatious description of the blockchain technology behind bitcoin. A rather large coincidence he was unable to accept.

The bitcoin source code was written in C++, related libraries, and open-source projects, its structure indicating a formally educated programmer with industry experience and a style described as quirky. Nothing that provided much insight one way or the other.

It was the umpteenth time Agent 21 had read the dossier and yet he was no closer to finding Satoshi than before, but decidedly more frustrated.

The original thinking had been that if the Cabal could find Satoshi, then they could neutralize him and thereby neutralize bitcoin. But not only had the hunt for Satoshi been fruitless, it had been pointless from the get-go. Bitcoin was decentralized, meaning that there was no corporation to shut down or assets to seize, realistically rendering it a moot point to find Satoshi himself. Nonetheless, Agent 21 had an obsessive compulsion to do so.

It was only during the interrogation of Andrew Cohen that the existence of Satoshi's Fortune was revealed. Four individuals. Four Keepers of the Fortune. One had the wallet file. And three had passwords, with only two-of-three needed. Rickard theorized that if the nearly one million bitcoins were sold off on the open market, it would create a panic and the price of bitcoin would crash and destroy anyone's belief that the cryptocurrency was anything but a money grab. Agent 21 was instructed to find the four Keepers of the Fortune and bring Satoshi's Fortune under the Cabal's control.

So Agent 21's assignment was no longer about finding Satoshi—it was all about the money.

Agent 21's focus was broken by the sound of his phone ringing. He checked the display; six o'clock—he had lost track of time again—and answered the call without a greeting.

"Henry Hawke is Peter Finlay's nephew." Dunwoody's usually perky voice was flat.

Agent 21 buried the seeds of anger the news generated and analyzed the implications. Cohen had claimed he did not know who the Keepers were, but based on his intense research, Agent 21 had a list of probable candidates—with Aziz Shariff chief among them, but Hawke only coming to the Cabal's attention last night.

"How was this missed?" Agent 21 asked.

"Because it's not anywhere in the system. There was nothing linking Peter to Henry. No will or estate planning was ever found and all his assets were seized by the state anyway. The next of kin on his health insurance was blank. None of his tax returns ever listed any dependents. Even Peter's sister, Henry's mother, was only found because of recently digitized elementary school records linking them by a shared surname and home address. Henry has his father's surname as well, further obfuscating the connection. Almost all the records that would have linked Henry to Peter are either missing, encrypted, or exist only on paper."

"How are you certain he's his nephew then?"

"I woke up Joe," she explained. They had had previous dealings with Joseph Elliot, the CEO of Chicago Mutual Savings Bank and Hawke's employer. "He told me Henry was a smart kid, although a bit difficult. Had a *rebel without a cause* attitude that he must have gotten from his parents because his uncle had always been a good company man. That is, up until his report came to light and the situation, um, deteriorated." She paused for a brief moment as if she expected Agent 21 to comment. When he did not she continued. "And that's when the link was made."

Agent 21 never cursed but felt the need to now as the unacceptable gaps in his dossiers revealed themselves and ridiculed his efforts. It was Peter Finlay who had first inadvertently brought bitcoin to the attention of the Cabal via a well-intentioned report naively presented at Chicago

Mutual. A report that triggered Rickard to send Agent 21 off on his maddening pursuit to find and neutralize Satoshi Nakamoto, which involved a failed interrogation of Finlay.

And now it turned out his nephew had just met with Aziz Shariff. It was a coincidence that could not be ignored. Agent 21 now marked Henry Hawke as a suspected Keeper of the Fortune and the Cabal's top priority.

"Where is he now?" Agent 21 asked. He could hear the keystrokes on the other end of the call before Dunwoody relayed the found information. "Hawke just checked out ahead of schedule from his hotel." She paused. "But his flight to O'Hare isn't until six o'clock this afternoon."

The news fired up Agent 21's instincts. "Find him. Watch his credit cards for cab fare or food purchases that would confirm his whereabouts. Check to see if he has a corporate card that wouldn't be linked to his name. Also, instruct airport customs and local law enforcement to arrest him on sight."

"Affirmative. On what charges? Money laundering?"

"No. I have something else in mind." Agent 21 knew the flimsiest of evidence would suffice for a money-laundering charge, but with Hawke's financials not even showing so much as a dollar moving in or out of his bank account to a known bitcoin exchange or trader, they wouldn't have much leverage. The Cabal agent quickly estimated he could be back at the Imperial Hotel in fifteen minutes, where he could produce all the leverage he needed to neutralize Peter Finlay's nephew.

AGENT 21'S FRAME JOB

Agent 21 stood silently in front of the hotel room with a leather travel bag slung over his shoulder. It could have carried a laptop computer if he were a regular business traveller. But he wasn't, and it did not.

It was almost half past six and the Imperial Hotel was beginning to stir. The early morning risers had taken their first steps of the day. The night owls had only recently allowed the previous one to end. Everyone was in some form of slumber, which meant that nobody was listening. Agent 21 tilted his head to better hear into the room for any indication to the contrary. No shuffling steps across the carpeted floor. No running water from the bathroom sink. Satisfied, Agent 21 took a universal magnetic access card he'd nicked from a negligent employee's locker and forcefully swiped down on the door's reader. The welcoming click of a disengaged lock told him the card had worked. He stepped into the hotel room and gently closed the door behind him, pausing to let his eyes adjust to the dim light, and listened again for movement that never came—all he heard was loud, inconsistent snoring.

The room was filthy. Agent 21 used the weak light slipping past the drawn curtains to guide him around fallen whiskey bottles that had leaked unnoticed onto the carpet. Cocktail glasses taken from the hotel bar doubled as makeshift ashtrays and overflowed with cigarette butts. Nauseating cheap perfume from last night's acquired company clung to the room and was only matched by the acrid stench coming from a perspiration-soaked undershirt thrown over the back of a corner lounge chair. A coffee table before it had magazines and credit cards dusted in white powder strewn about. A generic hotel desk held a set of BMW keys with the tag of a third-rate London leasing company, a well-used brown wallet bursting with paper receipts but not cash, and a gold Rolex of dubious authenticity.

Agent 21 gently rested his leather bag against the desk and with gloved hands pulled out a used water glass he had procured from Hawke's yet to be remade hotel room. He set it on the desk where it would be easy for the police's forensic team to find. A bribed housekeeper would result in an eyewitness account of Hawke leaving this very hotel room in a hurry—an event that aligned with his abrupt early morning checkout.

Agent 21 now turned his attention to the source of the unabashed snoring, a man lying in his underwear on top of dishevelled sheets. Stretch marks on his pink, raw skin were visible on his belly between fields of tangled hair. The Cabal agent stepped lightly towards the bed while carrying a three-inch serrated pocket knife. The small .22-calibre pistol holstered beneath his suit jacket would have done the job, but it was much easier for the cops to believe a conference attendee had gotten his hands on a knife as opposed to a gun, even if the attendee was from Chicago.

Standing over the nearly comatose man, and not wanting to remain there a moment longer than necessary, Agent 21 placed his gloved hand over Bernie Bitcoin's mouth to muffle the forthcoming scream, and with a supreme indifference he plunged the knife past layers of fat and deep into his heart.

HAWKE'S TRIP

The mundane action of Henry Hawke swiping his credit card set off a flurry of activity in the bowels of the world's payment processing system. The authorization process began when the merchant Hawke intended to pay sent the transaction data, including his credit card information, to their processing bank in addition to storing it on their own servers. Servers that had been compromised twice in the past eighteen months in two separate hacks. The first time the merchant had paid the hacker group to keep quiet and somehow managed to keep the incident out of the blogosphere. They were still unaware that the second hack had even occurred, or that the individual responsible still had access and could view or alter any piece of data in their entire system.

Once the merchant's processing bank received Hawke's transaction data, they passed it along to the credit card company itself. The transaction data then continued its journey across cyberspace to the issuer bank, the bank that had given Hawke the credit card. The issuer bank responded to the credit card company that, yes, Henry Hawke did in fact have enough available room to cover the purchase and proceeded to debit his account accordingly.

The credit card company vouched for Hawke's credit worthiness to the processing bank, who informed the merchant that the transaction was approved.

The merchant had their processing bank account credited but the amount was held for anywhere from three days to a week before they were granted access to their own money. Minus a 2% fee that was shared among the processing bank, the credit card company, and the issuer bank. This happened on every single credit card transaction worldwide, over ten thousand every second, resulting in trillions of dollars in fees annually. And no privacy to people like Hawke.

The Cabal didn't need to hack into any of the companies to see the transaction data in the system. They were the system. Hawke's transaction was immediately flagged and popped up on the screen of a cheery woman happily working away inside a bland office at CIA headquarters. As soon as the information arrived at her terminal, she picked up her phone and dialled a secured number that rang across the Atlantic.

Agent 21 answered on the second ring. He had finished his business with Bernie Bitcoin and was back at the safe house after an anonymous call to the police about a hotel room disturbance.

"Hawke just purchased a single train ticket," Dunwoody said with the enthusiasm of a customer support agent happy to help with a billing inquiry. She went over the details of the ticket, including the Birmingham destination.

Agent 21 processed the news that Hawke was skipping out on the rest of the conference. It was now beyond a doubt that Hawke had recently received vital information about Satoshi's Fortune.

"Why Birmingham?" Dunwoody asked, ready to pull up any information Agent 21 might need. But Agent 21 didn't need additional information. He knew everything about his targets.

"Aziz Shariff has a cousin in Birmingham. A lawyer."

"So, next step?"

Agent 21 considered the vast network of Cabal Assets at his disposal. "I'll assign an Asset to intercept Hawke. And then we'll all have a nice talk."

***

Henry Hawke listened to the PA announcer's garbled squawk and guessed he was trying to say that the 8:03 train was arriving shortly. His watch said it was 8:13. Close enough.

The London Euston train station was already bustling with commuters either arriving to see London for the day or heading out of the city to find a nice patch of English countryside to walk, which as far as he knew was what English people did on Sundays.

Hawke's first usage of London's rail system left him unimpressed. He always assumed that every building in London was at least a few hundred years old and built with an architectural eye that matched Shakespeare's pen. But Euston station was a dreary concrete box that reminded

Hawke of an oversized strip mall and made him wonder if and why Soviet architects had borrowed so heavily from its design.

Hawke put his critique of railway station architecture aside and headed to the designated platform, his boarding pass clenched tight in one hand and the other pulling his luggage. He was finished with what remained of the conference and planned to spend the morning in Birmingham with enough time to catch his flight back home.

He wanted to go to Birmingham because he didn't want to go back to his desk job in Chicago, or more specifically, he wanted to find a fortune.

Shariff's secret message to him, hidden in the third output of the bitcoin transactions, included a name and a number.

The name was Nabeel Monsef. The number was 104459.

Neither meant anything to Hawke, but a quick internet search revealed that Monsef was a Birmingham lawyer with a downtown address. A quick early morning call arranged a meeting between them.

The number didn't return any meaningful search results and he was hesitant to mention it to Monsef over the phone. No doubt the result of his blossoming paranoia, which he attributed to the unsolicited mention of his uncle, Shariff's conspiracy talk, the secret message, and the US Immigration officer who could easily have cosplayed a spy.

But Hawke couldn't believe the Cabal, an international organization that controlled the world's money and was now out to kill bitcoin, was real. Or could he?

Why else was he following through on a secret message? And why was the US government looking for Shariff? Maybe, Hawke mused, he wanted the Cabal and Satoshi's Fortune to be real. If the Cabal existed, it would mean he was involved in something other than another weekly department meeting, that he would have something to fight other than rush hour traffic.

What else did he have to do with his life, anyways?

Hawke shook his head. He felt silly for such juvenile thoughts. He had a job and responsibilities and dealing with that world was just part of being an adult.

But still . . .

Hawke scanned the platform looking for suspicious faces, but was slightly disappointed when nobody seemed to care about his existence. No beautifully exotic woman who might be a double agent begging for his trust, no millionaire playboy caught up in an international conspiracy asking for his help, no reclusive computer hacker trying to pass along a stolen piece of data that would bring down an evil empire.

He wasn't a rogue involved in the adventure of a lifetime.

He was still just a nine-to-fiver at a work conference.

At 8:20 the train arrived and rattled the tracks, sucking the air out of the surrounding area. He took a last furtive glance over his shoulder before boarding when he glimpsed a familiar figure cutting a line down the stairwell onto the platform. In his head he could hear Shariff chiding him for doubting his warnings. The probability of this person taking the same train as Hawke seemed as likely as a duplicate bitcoin address.

They made eye contact and froze. Hawke watched as the person on the stairwell gave a quick glance over their shoulder, as if considering turning around, but ultimately decided to continue down to the platform and walked up to Hawke as if that had been the plan all along.

"Mr. Hawke."

"Ms. Noor," Hawke replied. Sara Noor faced him with equal parts suspicion and annoyance. She carried only a laptop bag and wore white tennis shoes and capri pants, with a white T-shirt under a leather jacket. Hawke didn't think it was very clandestine but wasn't much of a fashion expert or a spy himself to say otherwise. He felt overdressed in a suit but it was his only option.

Hawke couldn't believe he was actually wondering if Noor was a Cabal agent, because it would mean that the Cabal was real and everything Shariff said was true. But wasn't it harder to believe that Noor had just randomly decided to take the same train as Hawke, to Birmingham of all places?

If Hawke was going to tease the truth out of her, he would need to borrow the sly charisma from the spy novels he liked to read.

"Are you a secret agent?" It was all Hawke could do from slapping his forehead in embarrassment.

Noor forced a laugh and maintained an air of self-reliance that would be well-suited to either a career in journalism or espionage. "A secret agent? Come on, Henry. You know I'm a reporter."

It was Hawke's turn to laugh awkwardly. "Well, a secret agent needs a cover."

Noor looked around as if hoping to see someone else she knew in order to excuse herself. Reluctantly, she continued with Hawke.

"So why are you visiting Birmingham?" She asked in a way that told Hawke she didn't care what answer he gave her.

"Sightseeing. I hear it's lovely in the fall."

"Mhmm."

"And you?"

"Shopping."

"Well then, good thing we're getting out of this backwater town they call London for somewhere with proper sightseeing and shopping."

The garbled voice of the announcer said it was last call to board the train.

"After you." Hawke gestured to the train doors. Whether she was a spy or just a reporter, he liked her better in front where he could keep an eye on her.

The train's layout had two seats on each side of a narrow aisle with a futuristic silver-and-blue colour scheme. Noor took a window spot and dumped her bag on the free seat beside her, leaving Hawke no choice but to sit elsewhere. The only other passenger in their car was an older woman already settled into the aisle seat opposite Noor. Hawke stowed his luggage overhead and took a seat behind the woman.

Hawke wondered if it was bad manners to sit so close to the spy they sent after you, but figured if Noor was a spy then she would correct him. She didn't and the train began its forward progress to Birmingham.

They gained momentum as the view changed from languid commercial buildings to decently upkept residential homes to underground tunnels. The train eventually burst back into what the locals considered sunlight, but Hawke considered low lurking grey clouds.

Noor busied herself on her laptop and the older woman was engrossed in a harlequin romance. Eventually a young train attendant, all wrapped up in a blue checkered scarf and wearing a black suit jacket, came to their seats. She wore a liberal amount of lipstick, blinked often, and asked for their tickets.

The older woman put down her book and produced a physical ticket, which the attendant found acceptable. Noor and Hawke displayed their e-tickets on their smartphones, which were equally as acceptable. The attendant moved on to the next car as a nearly identical woman, but with less lipstick and blinking, appeared with a drink cart.

"Complimentary coffee, tea, water. Warm breakfast meals available, and we accept all major credit cards," she informed them with a professional smile. Noor declined. The romance reader ordered a coffee.

"I don't suppose you take bitcoin yet?" Hawke asked when the attendant came to him. He caught Noor cringing at his question out of the corner of his eye.

The attendant kept her professional smile but had to work hard to do so. "Excuse me?"

"Never mind, just a new currency thing."

"We accept all major credit cards."

"But not bitcoin."

"I'm sorry, sir, is that a major credit card?"

"No."

"Then unfortunately we don't accept it. Would you like a warm breakfast meal?"

"No, I'm okay, thank you."

The attendant smiled through her teeth at Hawke for a moment before moving on. The outskirts of London rushed by out the window.

Hawke started to thumb through the news on his smartphone when the older woman turned around. She spoke with a distinguished accent and dressed accordingly.

"Oh, did you just mention bitcoin?" she asked.

Hawke nodded.

"You better be careful," she admonished. "My son and his friends have talked about it and I'm pretty sure it's a scam."

Noor surprised Hawke by taking charge of the conversation. She didn't look up from her laptop. "Why do you say that?"

Happy to discuss, the older woman explained. "Well, you see, the price went up so people who had bitcoins earlier made a lot of money. What do they call those kinds of scams? Ponzi schemes I think it is. Yes, bitcoin is a ponzi scheme."

"Do you know what a ponzi scheme is?"

"Yes, bitcoin." She tilted her head to emphasize the fact.

"A ponzi scheme is where a conman guarantees a rate of return and pays out earlier investors with the money from new investors. It collapses when there isn't enough new money coming in to pay the existing investors. The price of bitcoin does fluctuate wildly based on market events, like any other asset, but there is no guaranteed rate of return nor anyone to even make that promise. So by any and all definitions, bitcoin is not a ponzi scheme."

The older woman didn't seem accustomed to having her opinion questioned. She spoke again in a firmer tone. "I heard on the news that bitcoin is only used by drug dealers. They should just ban it."

Noor stopped what she was doing and glared across the aisle. She fired off some numbers from memory. "Bitcoin accounts for two hundred million dollars' worth of drug transactions. US dollars account for three-point-four trillion dollars. Probably should ban dollars as well while you're saving the children."

"Well, bitcoin isn't real. It's just computer stuff," the older woman countered. "I can't hold it in my hands like real money."

"You think most of the government-issued fiat currency physically exists? All the fiat in the world equals sixty trillion dollars. Physical cash totals five trillion dollars. So that means that about ninety-one percent of money is already digital," Noor said. Hawke had the feeling this wasn't the first time Noor had heard these arguments. He sat back and listened to the show.

"But my money is at the bank. I can go get it whenever I want."

"You think there's a stack of bills just sitting in a vault somewhere with your name on it?"

"Of course. It's the bank."

"You've never heard of a bank run?"

"This is Great Britain." The older woman's distinguished accent became more so. "The government will give us our money back if that ever happens."

"You mean the taxpayers?"

Hawke thought he heard shades of Shariff in her tone.

The older woman grew irritated with Noor's pushback. "It's not real," she repeated. "Somebody just created bitcoin out of nothing!"

"How exactly is that different from any government-issued currency?"

"The British pound is backed by the government."

"Bitcoin is backed by math."

"Well, I trust the government."

"Germany, Greece, Russia, Mexico, Argentina, Zimbabwe. I could go on."

"What are those?"

"Countries where people trusted the government."

"What happened?"

"People realized they shouldn't have."

"Okay, I mean I trust *our* government. And if you can't trust our government, what can you trust?"

"Math."

The older woman snorted. "I'll stick with the government."

"Good luck with that." Noor signalled she was finished with the conversation by returning to her laptop.

"I still say bitcoin is a scam," the older woman said quietly. She kept to herself for the rest of the trip.

HAWKE'S ARRIVAL

The rest of the trip was uneventful without any further ideological jousting. Hawke had attempted to catch up on missed sleep but managed only intermittent bouts. His final attempt was interrupted by a different PA announcer loudly alerting him that the train was five minutes out of Birmingham. The train slowed gradually before knocking off the last 5 km/hour in a split second, the sharp stop nearly causing Hawke's head to bounce off the seat in front of him. Feeling more tired than when he began, and with a much stiffer neck, Hawke joined the other passengers disembarking. On the platform, Noor was already quickly walking away, with no apparent interest in waiting for Hawke. She melted into the crowd without looking back. Hawke rolled his luggage past the older woman, who also made a point to ignore him.

The modern Birmingham station was in sharp contrast to the dreary station they had left behind in London. Here was a fresh building with sweeping angles and glass skylights. Unfortunately, grey clouds huddled above, but they only threatened rain for the time being. Hawke followed the signage for the cab stand and found himself facing a turnabout road with dropoffs and pickups causing a beehive of activity outside the station. He took his place in line and waited.

His conversation with Shariff still on his mind, he looked around for Cabal agents. Even if he saw one with a sign hanging around his neck that said *Cabal Agent*, he didn't know what he could do about it. Get into a fist fight to rescue Satoshi? Hijack a car for a high-speed chase? Hawke smiled at the absurdity. Then again, he was already on a wild goose chase for a digital fortune of magic internet money and looking over his shoulder for secret agents sent after him by an international Cabal of money men, so maybe a little absurdity was par for the course.

Another shoulder check revealed no obvious threat. Just a couple of cops leaning over their squad car before the cab stand. Hawke felt their eyes linger on him longer than necessary.

"Hey, you! Now!" The cab stand concierge startled Hawke, who found himself at the top of the queue. The concierge was ready for any weather in his windbreaker— the cab company stencilled across the back—and used a flashlight to point him to the next cab. "You! Cab! Here!"

Hawke apologized for being absent-minded and quickly got in the back seat with his luggage. The cab driver flipped on the meter as he closed the door and then sped away. Hawke took another look at the cops, who he swore were now watching him, with one talking into a walkie-talkie. Hawke barely registered the car's radio station providing a news update.

Police have worked quickly this morning to identify the prime suspect in a grisly downtown hotel murder as American He—the driver turned off the radio to ask Hawke for an address. He gave him Monsef's office and the driver didn't say another word for the length of the trip.

After a fifteen-minute drive and little opportunity to sightsee, they arrived at Monsef's downtown office. It was located in a Victorian-era terracotta building along with an accounting firm, marketing event company, and, this still being England, a pub in the basement. The city centre was quiet except for the occasional pedestrian or car going about its business. Hawke paid the fare with a liberal tip and kept the receipt, happy to know he'd be sticking his employer with another bill. As soon as Hawke stepped out of the cab the driver went off like a rocket in search of another fare, nearly sideswiping Hawke in the process.

Inside the building it felt empty. The only office with a light on was the one beside a placard that read Monsef UK LLP. The door was unlocked so Hawke let himself in. Two beige cushioned chairs sat on either side of a coffee table covered in old celebrity gossip magazines and law journals. A handful of awards and commendations from law societies and local charities were strategically placed on the wall, leading the eye to a framed newspaper article praising Monsef UK LLP's pro bono work fighting corporate bullying on clients' behalf. There was a generous photograph of a man who looked like a middle-aged clone of Shariff, if not for the healthy complexion, the tailored suit, and the broad smile. He was holding the same plaque that hung a few inches away. Finishing up the wall decorations was a mounted cricket bat with an intricate painting of a player swinging away in the black, red, and green colours of the Afghan flag. On the other side of the room was an empty chest-high reception desk with a sign that said *Cheque, Credit, and Bitcoin Accepted Here.*

"Hello?" Hawke called out, then added under his breath, "I'm here for the bitcoin fortune." There was the sound of a rolling chair hitting a wall and the shuffling of feet. The man from the framed newspaper photograph appeared down the hall.

"Can I help you?" he asked.

Hawke introduced himself as the man from the early morning phone call. Nabeel Monsef briskly walked up and clasped Hawke's hand, shaking it enthusiastically with the same energy Shariff exhibited but refined for mainstream consumption. He wore a lawyer's standard weekend attire: brown loafers, beige khakis, and a tucked-in baby-blue golf shirt.

"Of course, of course." Monsef welcomed him with a wide smile showing perfect teeth. "I can't believe you're here."

"Yeah. Me neither," Hawke said, unsure of why he was there, "and thanks for taking the time on a Sunday."

"Not a problem." Monsef finally let go of the handshake. He spoke with a clean English accent brimming with optimism. "I forward my office line to my mobile on the weekends. Don't want to miss a thing, now do I?"

Hawke had no idea if that were true but nodded regardless.

"How's Aziz? I haven't heard from him in months now. But I guess you've spoken recently?"

A few days ago Hawke wouldn't have inferred anything from such an innocent question. But now did he sense a whiff of an accusation? No, Hawke told himself, too many thoughts of conspiracies and spies were distorting his ears, hearing malicious intentions where there were none.

"Aziz is my cousin, by the way," Monsef said, noticing Hawke's delay in answering. Hawke was unsurprised based on their similar appearance.

"Actually I only just met Aziz last night, and only briefly."

"Huh." Monsef scratched his chin. "And he told you to come here?"

"Indirectly I guess. Sent me a message with your firm's name and a number. 104459."

Monsef perked up. "How did he give you this message?"

"Internet." Hawke knew it already sounded strange that he had come all this way based on a message from someone he had only just met, but it would have been stranger still if he admitted the message had been hidden in something commonly referred to as *magic internet money*. But Monsef was unfazed.

"You don't say," he studied his guest before experiencing a surge of excitement, "but do come in! Leave your luggage here and let's talk in my office!" Monsef hopped back down the hall, leaving Hawke to follow.

Inside his office, there was a desk covered by a mountain of paperwork on either side of a computer. A law school degree hung behind the desk, surrounded by a mosaic of family photographs depicting a happy home life. They all included some combination of Monsef, a smiling woman about the same age as Monsef, and a toddler who seemed to favour suits and plaid bow ties. The rest of the office was taken up by bookshelves bowing under the weight of thick legal texts.

"Can I interest you in some tea? Honey or sugar? Almonds or walnuts?" The questions came in quick succession.

"Ah, sure I'd—"

"You know what, don't tell me. I'll make you kahwa. Authentic Afghani green tea. You'll never get this in . . . where are you from?"

"Chicago." Hawke assumed Chicago was as likely as Birmingham to have authentic Afghani green tea but was appreciative nonetheless. Monsef shouted over his shoulder as he dashed out, "I'll be right back with your tea, Mr. Chicago!"

Hawke heard glasses and spoons ring about, cupboards open and shut in a nearby room, and Monsef talking as if Hawke was there with him. He returned smiling and carrying a wooden serving tray with two clear glass mugs filled with swirling steaming tea. The lawyer found a spot on his desk by balancing the tray on top of two piles of stacked folders. He lifted both mugs simultaneously to avoid spillage and handed one to Hawke.

Hawke sipped gingerly, unsure of what the tea should taste like.

"How do you like it?" Monsef asked eagerly.

"Best kahwa this side of Chicago," Hawke replied.

"Excellent!" Monsef gave a little fist pump and happily fell into the seat behind his desk.

They continued the friendly small talk. Monsef explained he was the sole partner of the firm and took on as many pro bono cases as his accountant would allow. One particular type of case that had become increasingly common was where banks unfairly called due underwater mortgages, claiming it was their contractual right. This meant that homeowners who had seen a sharp reduction in their property value had to pay the entire amount of their mortgage or be foreclosed on. Monsef didn't like the fact that they targeted lower-income people who certainly didn't have that much money lying around, didn't understand their legal rights, and couldn't afford a lawyer who did. He proudly boasted a nearly eighty percent success rate in fighting off the banks. In terms of his sporting interests, Monsef was a big cricket fan and played regularly at a local club in the summer, and to Hawke's surprise had actually watched a hockey game on television that, by coincidence, featured the Chicago Blackhawks at an outdoor event a few years back.

Hawke shared that he played a bit of hockey in college, which Monsef found interesting, and had a complete lack of interest in soccer, which Monsef understood. Hawke had trouble describing his job back home to Monsef. He kept it simple by saying he was an account manager at a bank, which after hearing what his local counterparts were doing to Monsef's clients made him feel like he had to defend himself. But Monsef waved away his concern. "Don't worry, Henry, I'm sure you know how to tell the difference between right and wrong."

Once they finished their tea, Monsef clapped his hands together. "Now, let's get down to the business of why you are here."

Hawke smiled. "I'd be interested to know that as well."

Monsef gave Hawke a stare perfected in the courtroom to witnesses playing dumb. "You don't actually know why?"

"I'm afraid not. If I'm being honest, I'm actually a little lost." Hawke decided to play it straight. He hoped they had spoken long enough that Monsef wouldn't actually think him crazy for what he was about to say. Hawke took a deep breath and detailed why he was in England in the first place, the happenstance meeting with Shariff at the Cock & Bull pub, and the secret message in the bitcoin transaction his cousin had sent him.

Monsef didn't flinch at any of it. When Hawke finished, the lawyer let out a high-paced laugh that filled the room with energy.

"What? You know why I'm here?" Hawke asked.

Monsef looked at Hawke with lively eyes and was bursting to share the answer. "Isn't it obvious, my friend? You're here because of Satoshi's Fortune!"

MONSEF'S ROLE

Hawke began to wonder if he was the last person on earth to hear of Shariff's conspiracy theories.

"You already know about Satoshi's Fortune?" he asked Monsef.

"I've heard plenty of rumours, but the only thing I know for sure is what Aziz told me. That one day somebody would come to my office with the same number you mentioned earlier, and that I was to help them." The lawyer was too cheerful to be mysterious, but the intrigue his words carried was unmistakable.

"What does the number mean?"

"It means you might be in for a treat." Monsef leaned forward with his elbows on his desk and looked solemnly over the stacks of paperwork at Hawke. "This summer Aziz came to me with a problem; he didn't trust anyone. After I reminded my dear cousin that I'm a lawyer by trade and not a psychiatrist, he elaborated on what he meant. He said he had information that would lead to Satoshi's Fortune. And he wanted a way for someone to pick up where he left off, should he feel something bad was going to happen to him."

Monsef's gaze drifted and a sadness momentarily overcame him, as if he suddenly realized that by Hawke

160

being there it meant that Shariff's worst fears had in fact occurred. He blinked and refocused on his explanation.

"But there was nobody who Aziz would trust with this information. With my help we came up with the idea to structure a contract that was linked to a specific bitcoin address that he set up. And if there was ever a transaction from that address, then the owner of the recipient address would be given that information. The number in question references the contract number. This way, Aziz could choose who he wanted to have this information at a later date."

Incredible, Hawke thought. Shariff had not just passed him a secret message but also the legal rights to something that would lead him right to Satoshi's Fortune. He did his best to temper expectations until he saw what exactly Shariff had wanted him to have.

"So now I'm the legal owner of this mystery information?" Hawke asked.

"Yes, assuming you can prove ownership of the address that received that transaction."

"How do I do that?"

"Sign the bitcoin address."

Hawke sighed. "And how do I do *that*?"

Monsef pursed his lips, clearly not expecting his cousin to trust someone so clueless. "Are you sure you're supposed to be here?" he asked.

Not at all, Hawke thought. But when he considered the forty years of office politics and pointless meetings that awaited him where he was supposed to be, Hawke replied with confidence, "Of course, Shariff wanted me to find Satoshi's Fortune."

"Mhmm." Monsef inclined his head.

Hawke clapped his hands together. "So I'm just going to sign a bitcoin transaction here . . ."

"You might need your phone for that," Monsef advised.

"Right." Hawke felt Monsef's eyes on him as he fumbled with his phone while doing an internet search for *how to sign a bitcoin transaction*. It turned out to be surprisingly straightforward; open the settings on his bitcoin wallet, go to the addresses option, select the address, and click *sign address*. This was only possible for an address that Hawke controlled in his wallet.

Hawke followed the steps with growing confidence, and with a flourish, tapped the *confirm* button to complete the process.

"Done," Hawke said proudly.

Monsef studied him a moment longer before searching through the mountain of paperwork on his desk. Like any lawyer worth his salt, he kept his desk in a state of organized chaos that only he could navigate. From under one particularly tall heap of folders, he removed a manila envelope with the number 104459 stencilled in sharp handwriting across the front. Monsef removed a single page and read slowly and methodically, and then paused again to ruminate on something he found. And then again even more slowly and more methodically, leading Hawke to believe the lawyer was either being overly thorough or used to billing by the hour.

"Now what?" Hawke asked.

Monsef opened a block explorer website on his computer and unhurriedly typed in the bitcoin address, Shariff's original, from the case file he had just read. With the transaction found and with the block explorer's help, he followed it to the recipient address and viewed the digital signature attached, confirming who the legal owner now was. It read, *I am Henry Hawke.*

"Cute," Monsef said.

Hawke shrugged. "Couldn't think of what else to write."

"It will do. I'm actually pretty excited. This is the first official use of this process. I'm sure Shariff would be excited to see it worked, too."

"Now what?"

"Time to provide you with Shariff's information."

Monsef jumped from his chair and quickly walked down the hallway with Hawke following behind. Monsef unlocked a door and they entered a room full of army-green filing cabinets. The lighting was dim and the musty smell of paper hung in the room. A large shiny safe caught Hawke's eye.

Monsef knelt before the safe and spun the dial back and forth until the combination hit, and he pulled down on the handle to release a gasp of escaping air. He withdrew a standard-sized white envelope with the number 104459 hastily written across the front in black ink and handed it to Hawke.

"This now belongs to you."

Hawke studied the envelope. It was light in his hands and he could feel a tiny object no bigger than his thumb inside. He opened it and found an orange flash drive and a single piece of paper.

The paper contained seven words, written just as hastily as the number on the envelope.

When in doubt, we are all Satoshi.

Hawke fought to keep his excitement from showing. He couldn't help but entertain the thought that maybe Shariff had somehow placed Satoshi's Fortune on the flash drive.

"Let's take a look," he said as calmly as he could manage.

They left the filing room, happily speculating on what information Shariff could have possibly left on the flash drive, but Hawke's excitement was snuffed out by the jarring scent of stale cigarettes and onions lingering in the hallway. Monsef wrinkled his nose at the foreign odour.

"What's that smell?"

Hawke didn't answer. He pushed ahead and found the door to Monsef's office was now closed, whereas they had left it open. He cautiously turned the knob and guided the door open. He was welcomed by thick, acrid smoke drifting among the legal texts. A familiar man was relaxing in Monsef's chair, with a cigarette dangling from the corner of his mouth and a gun in his hand.

The gun was pointed at Hawke.

"What are you doing here?" Hawke demanded.

Inspector Smith's smugness was apparent as the smile on his dry, cracked lips.

"I'm here because you are wanted by some very powerful people."

Monsef stepped around Hawke to confront the intruder. "What's the meaning of this? You have no right to enter my office and point a gun at anyone!"

"I can do whatever I want." Smith took a final draw on the cigarette with his free hand and dropped it into the remains of Monsef's tea with a hiss. "Case in point. Henry Hawke, I'm putting you under arrest for the murder of Bernard Salisbury."

SHARIFF'S AWAKENING

Aziz Shariff floated in darkness in a failed state. A crashed program. His operating system violently shut down. He couldn't access his memories to find out what had happened; he could only drift through them aimlessly until his mind rebooted.

In the darkness he came upon his mother. They spoke in the same tongue but a different language—her of family, community, and how Shariff needed to sit still and eat a proper meal for once; he of the absolute truth to hashing algorithms and the oppressive capabilities of the government.

His mother had raised him alone in an Afghani community in upstate New York and he had tried numerous times to empathize with what she had gone through, but often struggled to determine if his mother was kind-hearted or just dishonest.

It was maybe the former because she was steadfast in her claim that his father had loved him very much, but only abandoned him before he was born in order to defend his homeland against the invading Soviets.

But it was likely the latter because Shariff knew the truth. He had been incessantly teased by the other children for having a lighter skin tone than anyone else and shunned by the community elders for more judgmental reasons. At the age of ten, and tired of the insinuations, Shariff hacked into the hospital records to see the listed name of his birth father. Even at that innocent age, Shariff knew what having a father named *Thompson* meant, both in terms of his skin tone and his mother's standing in their conservative community. He never told her he knew the truth and his mother's lie taught him a lesson he never forgot: those in a position of power will claim to have your best interests at heart, but would violate that trust if it made their lives easier.

His formal education took place at schools that he found to be rigid structures designed to funnel the masses into nine-to-five jobs of an industrial age that no longer existed. Shariff barrelled his way through high school in three years and his teachers happily celebrated his graduation, less for his achievements and more so they wouldn't have to deal with him any longer.

He showed his mother a rare smile when he received his acceptance letter from MIT with a full academic scholarship. His excitement for secondary education lasted as long as his first class, where he drew the ire of his professor for pointing out that he wasn't seeding his random generation number properly, resulting in numbers that weren't really random at all.

Few students wanted to join Shariff in group work and even fewer had made any attempts at friendship during his time at university, and that suited him just fine. The only people he deemed worthwhile to speak to existed in cypherpunk and crypto-anarchist chat rooms, and even then they could be ignored by blocking their profiles. He once tried joining a campus activist group that claimed to be protesting Wall Street, which he had determined by then was obviously an extension of the Cabal. But by the time they arrived in New York City, it was clear the activist group didn't even know of the Cabal's existence let alone have any suggestions on how to stop them. The best they had to offer was holding up a few signs calling for change and then waiting for someone else to do something.

Shariff spent that day in New York looking for anyone who shared his ideals and the closest he found was a handful of self-proclaimed anarchists who thought they looked good in balaclavas and liked to fling stones through bank windows. They handed him a handful of stones and gave him the option of a skeleton or a Guy Fawkes printed balaclava.

Shariff tossed the stones aside and began lecturing them on how commercial insurance worked, how the Cabal was controlling the world's monetary policy, and that he wasn't going to waste his time on a bunch of idiots stupid enough to think that a hissy fit was enough to change the system.

One member of the group mumbled from behind a balaclava, artistically designed to look like he was wearing a gas mask, "But you're an anarchist like us."

"No, I'm a *crypto*-anarchist."

"What's the difference?"

"We use math instead of rocks."

"That sounds boring."

"Not if you actually know math."

Shariff dropped out of university the next day and committed his deep well of energy and passion to various open-source projects: encrypted email software, torrent clients, virtual private network apps, anything that would enable the free movement of data outside of government and corporate control. He paid his bills with freelance development work on corporate security software. The work seemed at odds with the other cypherpunks and crypto-anarchists who knew him, to which Shariff would counter that he needed to help support his mother—which was only partially true. The other reason he took the jobs was that they allowed him certain advantages in terms of accessing systems he shouldn't. Long after a project was delivered to a boardroom full of Suits, it wasn't unusual to have their network compromised by unknown hackers.

The open-source projects and freelance mischief did nothing to fill the empty black hole pulsating inside him. By now Shariff knew his purpose—end the Cabal. It was a daunting task as the Cabal was not a single entity to target but a noxious cloud permeating the entire financial system. He could perhaps crash one corporation with ties to the Cabal through years of dedicated hacking, social movements, and luck—but another company would quickly slink into the void and Shariff would be back at square one. Shariff was convinced that the entire monetary system needed to be burned to the ground and built anew—but he struggled to find the match.

And then one night, struggling with despair that threatened to swallow him whole, the cryptography distribution list he was subscribed to received a seemingly innocuous email . . .

***

A blinding light exploded all around Shariff and brought him back to the present. He attempted to raise his arms to shield himself, but they failed to respond to his commands. He was suddenly aware of an acute pain in his shoulders and the reason why he couldn't move his arms—they were tied behind his back. He wrinkled his nose and felt dried blood flake away from his nostrils. His head pounded from either a concussion or caffeine withdrawal.

"Mr. Shariff. It's very important that you pay attention," an uncaring voice whispered.

Shariff slowly peeled his eyes open to take in his surroundings. He was staring at . . . himself! He saw his ankles and wrists were bound to a chair and his mouth was sealed with duct tape. But his reflection didn't mirror his movements, nor did he recognize his clothes. It took him a moment but as his senses came back in sync, he realized he wasn't looking at a mirror but a laptop screen. And he wasn't watching his reflection, but a live feed of his cousin Nabeel Monsef in what looked like his office. They had set up a twisted conference call between their two locations and were forcing them to see each other's suffering!

"Don't say a fucking word, Nabeel!" Shariff screamed.

"Your cousin is fine by the way, Mr. Shariff." Shariff strained his neck towards the source of the emotionless voice, but only caught glimpses of a man in a suit out of the corner of his eye. His first instinct was to bark insults into the void and rock his chair back and forth in the hopes of somehow freeing himself. He greedily did both but only managed to send himself flying backwards onto an unforgiving wooden floor while the insults did nothing to hurt the feelings of the Cabal agent now standing over him.

"Are you finished?" Agent 21 calmly asked.

Shariff answered with yet more insults and flailing until he was so out of breath that he couldn't resist when Agent 21 set him and the chair back upright. He took a brief moment to gather his thoughts as he scanned the unfamiliar spartan apartment. His last memory had been his attempted escape from the coffee shop, foiled by the agent now holding him captive. His legs and arms were bound to the chair by duct tape but his mouth was unbound. They wanted him to talk!

Agent 21 confirmed his assumption. "Aziz Shariff, our intel leads us to believe that you are one of the Keepers of the Fortune. Is this true?"

Shariff spat at and missed the agent, who took it as confirmation.

The frame on the laptop expanded beyond Monsef to include Hawke by his cousin's side, bound and gagged. The anger was unmistakable. His eyes smouldered as if preparing to charge head-first through the screen at any moment. Shariff's first reaction was to be impressed that the Suit had managed to find the secret message embedded in the blockchain. But this was quickly eclipsed by rage that he was so stupid as to be followed.

"You know your co-conspirator, Henry Hawke. Inspector Smith has unofficially arrested him for murder and unofficially questioned him. Frustratingly, he has so far declined to cooperate, which leaves us with no choice but to take him into custody for the foreseeable future. That is, unless you provide information regarding Satoshi's Fortune."

Shariff didn't hesitate. "Then he goes to jail! He'll be a political prisoner and bring more attention to the injustice of the Cabal!"

Agent 21 was not surprised Shariff was willing to let Hawke rot in jail for the rest of his life. "Fine then. Give me your part of Satoshi's Fortune and your cousin lives. Refuse, and he dies."

"Then he dies! We are willing to die to keep bitcoin out of the Cabal's control!"

Monsef's panic-filled eyes indicated he did not share his cousin's fervour on the matter.

Agent 21 paused for a moment before signalling the now visible Inspector Smith. Almost immediately, there was a pop followed by a frantic crackling sound, and Monsef was shaking violently from the sudden burst of electricity shooting through his body. Two prongs were buried deep into his neck and the tentacle-like cables led back into the taser in Smith's hands. The crackling stopped and Monsef slumped into unconsciousness, only the duct tape around his wrists keeping him from falling out of his chair. Smith laughed as he pulled the spent prongs from Monsef's swollen flesh.

"So, Mr. Shariff. Feel like talking now?" Agent 21 asked.

Shariff snorted. "Not even close." He always knew it would come to this; he would have to choose between pain and freedom. Shariff just wished it was his pain being offered, but it couldn't be helped. Monsef and Hawke would just have to bear it.

Suddenly Monsef jerked up, his eyes bulging so wide they looked like they would break free of their sockets. A primal moan tried to escape from behind his duct-taped mouth but only resulted in drool seeping out along the edges. A split second later, the convulsions started and his entire body snapped back and forth as if possessed.

"He needs help! What do you want to know?!" Hawke cried out. His surrender sent Shariff into a frenzy.

"Shut up, Suit! Don't say anything! It's Satoshi's Fortune we're talking about here!"

But Hawke ignored him.

"What are you going to give us, son?" Smith asked.

"I'm not talking to you. I'm talking to the man with Shariff who's running the show. And before I say anything, there'd better be an ambulance on its way here."

"We ain't taking orders from some punk—"

"Stop talking, Inspector," Agent 21 said firmly. "Mr. Hawke, the information Mr. Shariff gave you for an ambulance. You have my word."

Now both Monsef's and Shariff's bodies were violently shaking. Monsef from the taser-induced seizure, Shariff's from his own zealous opposition to the Cabal's ruthless tactics. He was screaming and yelling like a rabid animal, trying everything in his limited power to stop the communication. "Don't say a word, you goddamn Suit. I trusted you! You'll help keep the masses enslaved for another generation if you talk! This is bigger than any of us. My life, your life, Nabeel's life!"

Agent 21 silenced the crypto-anarchist with a swift chop to the side of the neck, knocking him unconscious.

"Call the ambulance now, then I'll talk," Hawke ordered.

Agent 21 pondered the offer. Was Hawke truly a Keeper and would he yield his password? Did he know who the Keepers were? Or maybe he had information about the true identity of Satoshi Nakamoto . . .

The Cabal agent grabbed his phone and put it on speaker phone so Hawke could hear the conversation. He spoke quickly and calmly, as if ordering a pizza. He gave the address first then provided the details: "Man, age 46, is having a suspected seizure. Electric trauma. Type O blood. No family history of heart disease. Only medication is ten milligrams of Lipitor."

Hawke's shell-shocked expression left little doubt he was unaware of how many intimate details the Cabal knew about everyone, sometimes even more than their own family. It made Agent 21 want to know how Hawke would react to how much he knew about his uncle.

The emergency responder chimed in, "Ambulance en route. Can I have your name, sir?" Agent 21 ended the call.

"Help is on the way, Mr. Hawke. Now tell me everything you know."

Hawke lowered his gaze and stared into nothingness as the shock wore off.

"Tell me what you know," Agent 21 repeated.

Hawke inclined his head and their eyes locked. Even across the video feed Agent 21 could see a facetious defiance in his expression, that despite being brutally interrogated he was . . . having fun?

Even without Dunwoody's research, Agent 21 would have known right then this was Peter Finlay's nephew. He expected a sarcastic remark and was proven correct.

"I know that the Cabal exists," Hawke replied, "and that you shouldn't get on a boat owned by an investment banker."

Agent 21 didn't engage the young man. He would efficiently pluck him of all useful information before doing away with the corpse. And without any remaining family to be suspicious of an unexpected death, this time he wouldn't have to waste any energy on making it look like an accident.

There was a quick flash of movement in the corner of the screen that Inspector Smith didn't notice.

Someone else was in the lawyer's office!

A figure darted in the background and materialized behind Smith before Agent 21 could warn him. All Agent 21 could do from the London safe house was helplessly witness the flash of a bat, a sickening crack, and Smith's dead weight fall out of view before the screen went black.

HAWKE'S GETAWAY

"I'm starting to think you're stalking me."

Sara Noor dropped the cricket bat and rolled her eyes at Hawke. She quickly stepped over Smith's unconscious body and began searching the desk drawers. She found a silver letter opener and used it to free the now-still Monsef from his chair. She guided him softly down onto the floor, supporting his neck as a mother would a newborn. Distant sirens were approaching.

With nothing else she could do for Monsef, Noor cut Hawke free.

"We have to go," she said.

"What? Monsef's ambulance is on its way. The cops won't be far behind. We need to tell them that Shariff is being held hostage. We need to tell them that the Cabal is real!"

"Henry, I know the Cabal is real. But do you think the cops will believe you? You're wanted for murder. You'll be arrested on sight."

Hawke hadn't believed Inspector Smith when he had first said he was under arrest for murder. It seemed so far-fetched. He assumed it was just a ploy to convince him to talk, but Noor now confirmed it was true.

The power of the Cabal hit home. They had framed him with ease. Interrogated and abused Monsef and Shariff with impunity. If he stayed, then it was probably straight into a cell for god knows how long, unless he talked. And despite what the Cabal seemed to believe, he didn't know anything—but then he remembered Shariff's flash drive and felt its form still in his pocket.

"Let's go!" Noor said more forcefully. "We have to keep Satoshi's Fortune safe."

"How do you know about Satoshi's Fortune? About the Cabal?"

"I'll explain later. But we have to get moving."

The sirens grew closer, and they only had a minute or two before the cops arrived.

Hawke looked at Inspector Smith groaning on the floor, a walnut-sized lump already forming on the side of his head. Then he looked at Monsef struggling with short, shallow breaths and felt a pang of helplessness and guilt. But there was nothing Hawke could do for him now.

Hawke made his decision.

He picked up the discarded cricket bat and used his tie to wipe it of fingerprints. He did likewise to the silver letter opener and tossed it aside. He then grabbed Noor's hand and they hurried out of the office to begin their escape— but not before stopping to give Inspector Smith a heavy, heartfelt kick straight into his ribs.

***

Hawke and Noor hustled out of the building as the nearby sirens screamed they were out of time.

"Where's your car?" Hawke searched the empty street.

"I took a cab here."

"Well, where's the cab then?"

"He must have left! I didn't know I would need to flee a crime scene!"

Hawke frantically looked around for any vehicle or means of escape until he remembered something he had seen on his car ride from the train station.

"This way." Hawke ran down the street and turned a corner with Noor in lockstep. After thirty seconds of flat-out sprinting, they came upon a construction site. Chain-link fences and plywood walls surrounded the property. Posted signs alternated between warnings to dissuade people from trespassing and condo sales flyers encouraging them to eventually live there. Through the fence Hawke saw what he was looking for: a beat-up work truck. It would be perfect for the needs of a construction site, but not suitable for a daily commute, so Hawke guessed right that it would always be left on-site.

And if his past experience from youthful indiscretions in Chicago had taught him anything, it's that old trucks on construction sites were usually left unlocked. Hawke scaled the fence and landed on the other side. He raced to the truck and jerked the door open. There were no keys anywhere inside. Luckily it was an old truck and didn't have a modern electric starter system, so Hawke easily ripped off the plastic casing surrounding the steering column and pulled out the starter wires—again lessons learned from that misspent youth. Red to blue and three seconds later he was sitting at the helm of a hotwired truck.

Hawke allowed himself a grin before slamming his foot on the gas. Gravel and loose dirt flew out from under the tires before they finally gripped the earth and launched the truck forward. Hawke barrelled it through the front gate in a symphony of twisting metal. With the high-pitched wail of the sirens nearly on top of them, Hawke stopped on the street, barely long enough for Noor to jump in, and hammered the accelerator before she even pulled her door shut.

AGENT 21'S ESCALATION

Agent 21 eyed the dead computer screen that showed no interest in coming back to life. He didn't waste a moment on denial and accepted the situation as it was: Hawke had help in escaping and Inspector Smith was now compromised. However little the second-rate inspector knew about the Cabal, it was still too much. And being found beaten and unconscious next to a critically ill lawyer outside of your own jurisdiction begged too many questions that Smith wouldn't have any good answers for. Agent 21 would deal with him later.

Of more importance was Hawke's escape. He had no known friends or contacts in England. So who had helped him? And why? Over years of successful assignments, Agent 21 had learned to trust his instincts. They now whispered in his ear that Hawke was the key to gaining control of Satoshi's Fortune—and perhaps identifying Satoshi himself. Pursuing Hawke would be all the more challenging now that he was on the run. His scheduled flight back to Chicago would surely be abandoned, and he was smart enough to assume that his credit cards and bank accounts would be monitored. Perhaps it was time for Agent 21 to attack from within—he had a sleeper Asset eager to participate and perhaps now was the time to activate them.

But before all that, Agent 21 needed to update the head of the Cabal, and he wasn't prepared to speak to Rickard empty-handed.

Shariff began to stir on the ground before him. He seemed so diminutive and frail when he wasn't yelling. Agent 21 sat Shariff back up and checked his pulse; it was elevated, but not unexpectedly so—Shariff's heart rate frantically pounded whether he was under duress or just waiting for a bus. Agent 21 peeled open his eyes for a quick examination. He was satisfied that Shariff appeared healthy enough to endure what was to come next.

Agent 21 went to the closet and took out a red toolbox. He removed a twelve-inch steel alloy wrench, feeling its heft in his hand. Satisfied, he positioned his chair in front of the still-unconscious Shariff and waited.

Five minutes passed.

Then ten.

After twenty minutes—Agent 21 sitting patiently with wrench in hand—Shariff's eyes finally crept open. As soon as he saw the Cabal agent, he began speaking frantically in what Agent 21 knew to be a dialect of Pashto. While he didn't speak the language himself, he doubted Shariff was spewing compliments.

Agent 21 raised the wrench and smashed it down on Shariff's kneecap. The screams that filled the room sounded the same in Pashto as in English.

Once the screams subsided, Agent 21 said, "You're one of the four Keepers of the Fortune. If you don't provide me with your part, the pain will only increase."

Shariff flared his nostrils and pursed his lips to arm himself with spit, but Agent 21 had no time for such theatrics, so he swung the wrench across Shariff's jaw. With lifeless eyes he studied his prisoner's face—a patchwork of abuse. Dried blood mixed with sweat and tears formed a red paste that clung to his skin. His eyes were bloodshot. Where his lips weren't cracked and bleeding, they were swollen.

"I want your part of Satoshi's Fortune." There was no ambiguity to Agent 21's plan. Shariff would either yield or he would continue to feel pain.

"Fuck the Cabal." And there was no loss of intensity in Shariff's resistance.

Another wrench strike to his other kneecap. More screams.

Agent 21 rotated between both knees, with the occasional smash to a finger, to express his willingness to escalate as needed. None of his past prisoners had resisted past this point, and Agent 21 was curious to know if anyone could.

"Your part. Now."

"You'll never get it out of me." It wasn't as energetic, but still absolute.

One last strike with the wrench before he moved on to the pliers. It cracked across Shariff's jaw with the force to maybe break a tooth, but not his jaw.

And Shariff did spit out a tooth. But then did something odd. He frantically searched for it on the floor as if the tooth was the most important thing in the world. Agent 21 spotted it first and picked up the tooth. It was a molar cracked above the root, coated in blood and saliva.

Shariff seemed relieved and laughed deliriously.

Suddenly it all made sense. It was definitely time for the pliers.

"Open your mouth."

It struck Agent 21 as likely the only time anyone had asked that of Shariff. Shariff fiercely clenched his teeth, but Agent 21 cupped his face below the nose, found where the muscles and nerves met at the axis of the jawbone, and applied pressure. Shariff's jaw reflexively opened. Agent 21 casually inspected the inside, reviewing each tooth individually as if he were a dentist dealing with a fussy customer. Finally, on the third molar on the right side, his suspicions were confirmed. The tooth had a small, almost imperceptible, cavity.

It wasn't a cavity bored by sugars and neglect, but one created with a purpose. Agent 21 forced the pliers into the gaping maw and clamped down irrespective of his patient's resistance. Shariff jerked and twisted with all his remaining strength, but it was futile against the inevitable.

You'll never get it out of me.

Once Agent 21 had the tooth firmly between the pliers, he wrenched back with his full force, freeing the tooth in an arc of blood and screams.

Agent 21 clutched the world's most valuable tooth between the crimson-stained pliers and held it up victoriously to the light to study it closer. He had to admit he was impressed by the ingenuity of the design. The fake tooth appeared fabricated out of an acrylic plastic polymer and coated with a composite resin that easily passed for the real thing until closer inspection. A depressed black line at the top of the crown was too perfectly straight to be naturally occurring. Now Agent 21 could see it for what it really was—the exposed edge of a micro-SD card concealed inside the tooth itself.

Agent 21 discarded the pliers and rolled the tooth between his forefinger and thumb, indifferent to the blood soiling his fingers. Firmly holding the tooth, he used his fingernail to break past a thin protective resin and pressed down at a right angle. A soft *click* told him the micro-SD card was released, and he gingerly pulled on its thin edge until he freed it from its hold. The card was no bigger than a fingernail but could hold gigabytes worth of data, more than enough for Shariff's purpose. Agent 21 tossed the empty false tooth aside and sat at his desk where he slid the card smoothly into a USB card reader. A folder popped up on the screen and displayed the single file—a bitcoin wallet file.

Agent 21 now had control of the most important piece of Satoshi's Fortune.

Nobody was there to see it, but serenity washed over him, if only for a brief moment, before he began to plan his next step.

The call to Rickard would now be one of success instead of failure. He took out the micro-SD card and tucked it safely inside his suit jacket's inner pocket. Feeling like he had finally scratched an itch that had plagued him for months, he studied the once-proud anarchist and Satoshi collaborator still bound to the chair, his head flopped to the side and eyes fluttering with unconsciousness, blood trickling lazily past his lips onto the floor. Shariff had always seemed to take up more space than his diminutive frame would suggest, but now, with his shoulders slumped and head bowed, he had never seemed smaller. Agent 21 couldn't help but wonder what other secrets Shariff kept, either in his mind or elsewhere. Would he know who had helped Hawke escape? The names of the unknown Keepers? Or perhaps, Agent 21 almost wouldn't allow himself to wonder, would Shariff know the true identity of Satoshi Nakamoto?

No, Agent 21 told himself, *the objective is to find the Keepers of the Fortune.*

He looked at Shariff before him. Beaten. Weak. Defeated.

Maybe he could afford to ask one simple question . . .

AGENT 21'S QUESTION

A concussion. A broken nose. At least three fractured fingers. Both kneecaps with deep bone bruises. Wrists and ankles raw with the skin peeled away where rope now grated on exposed muscle. Two missing teeth—one real, one not.

Of all Shariff's injuries at the hands of the Cabal, none pained him more than his own failure—he had failed as a Keeper of Satoshi's Fortune.

Shariff hadn't lived as many of his generation did, searching for purpose and their place in the world. He scoffed at such soul-crippling clichés when your goals were money, fame, or the moral high ground. None of that for Shariff. As soon as he learned of the Cabal's existence in his adolescence, and how their control stretched into every facet of life, his purpose was well defined and without compromise—he was going to burn the Cabal to the ground.

He just didn't know how.

And then bitcoin appeared and it was as if fate had handed him lighter fluid and a match.

But with his failure that metaphorical match was now in the possession of the ghostly Cabal agent silently gloating mere feet away. Given to him by Satoshi himself to keep secure, the wallet file, once restored, would only need two-of-three passwords to unlock nearly one million bitcoins.

One password for each remaining Keeper of the Fortune.

The goal of dividing the wallet up in this way was to ensure that no one person could act alone; Satoshi's Fortune was too much power for any one individual. Shariff's plan had been to convince two of the three Keepers to join him and send the entire fortune to a provably unspendable burn address, a virtual middle finger to the Cabal and their tyrannical plans to destroy the trust in bitcoin.

But now, swarmed by his own stench of failure, Shariff lost all hope.

And then a whispered question. One that sent chills down his spine while raising his pulse.

"Who is Satoshi Nakamoto?"

Shariff's answer was automatic.

We are all Satoshi.

But he dared not speak it aloud in his current condition though it acted as a rallying cry and brought him strength—and an idea.

Shariff grunted to show he was still conscious.

"Aziz, what can you tell me about Satoshi?" Agent 21 asked. The voice was calm, but Shariff sensed an undercurrent of elation just below the surface.

Shariff spat blood. "He likes pineapple and jalapeños on his pizza."

"How would you know that? Every known piece of data about Satoshi relates solely to bitcoin."

"Ya, every *known* piece of data." Shariff didn't elaborate. He let Agent 21 process the insinuation.

Agent 21 inclined his head. "You hacked Satoshi."

"Exactly."

"He was your leader. Deified by your crowd. Why would you hack him?"

"Because I didn't trust him. Think about it. Some anonymous nobody shows up and claims to have invented a way to revolutionize the modern financial system and free millions from your tyrannical bonds . . . and you don't think I'd look into him?"

Shariff knew it sounded true because it was. At the beginning, he had feared bitcoin was a Cabal trap set to snare those willing to take on the status quo, so he had spent countless hours searching for Satoshi: tracing IP addresses, hacking into servers, querying every contact he had across universities to the dark web.

However, unlike what he had just told the Cabal agent, Shariff had never found out anything. He had abandoned his search once he realized who Satoshi was didn't matter—his bitcoin code spoke for itself.

But Agent 21 didn't know that.

"Where is this hacked data?"

Shariff vigorously shook his head. "No, it's all I have left. I can't betray him."

"Look at me, Aziz."

He looked up, expecting to see a wrench threatening to come crashing down. Instead the Cabal agent held up a laptop. It was displaying a bank's internal system, showing a list of assets, liabilities, names, and other metadata.

"I was saving this as a last resort in case your body didn't fail you." Agent 21 highlighted one entry. Shariff immediately recognized it as a mortgage on a townhouse on a quiet street in upstate New York.

"In six months your mother will make the final payment on her house and become mortgage free," Agent 21 said. "Or the bank will be instructed to repossess her home first thing Monday morning."

"No, no, you can't."

"All I need is information."

Shariff paused, he hoped for long enough, before nodding a final time. "Fine, you win. The info is on the flash drive."

"What flash drive?"

Shariff tongued the empty socket and made himself wince. "The one I sent Henry Hawke to claim in Birmingham."

"It is unavailable. Where else is this info?"

Time to poke the bear. "Nowhere else. What do you mean unavailable, he escape or something?"

Now Shariff saw the wrench. It was gripped tightly in the Cabal agent's hand, ready to come crashing down. His overreaction confirmed Agent 21's weakness—and now it was time to exploit it.

"Wait. You don't think I have a way of tracking the flash drive?"

The wrench never crashed down and Shariff's skull remained intact.

"You're trying my patience, Mr. Shariff. How do I find the flash drive?"

Shariff let his beaten and bloodied head hang limp. The Cabal thought they had broken him—and for a brief moment they had. But despite being tied up and painted in his own blood, Shariff mounted his counterattack.

He took a deep breath. "Once the drive connects to the internet, it'll automatically link to my private server and provide me with its GPS coordinates. I can see all this through my smartphone."

Agent 21 eyed Shariff suspiciously, but eventually relented. He went to his desk and picked up a black plastic bag containing Shariff's possessions. A roll of euros and pounds. A fake American passport under a different name. And a smartphone.

It was switched off, so Agent 21 held down the power button. The manufacturer's logo flashed on the screen and he brought it to Shariff but refused to untie him.

"Password," Agent 21 demanded upon seeing the welcome prompt.

"F@ckTheCabal!"

It garnered no reaction from Agent 21. He typed it in and unlocked the phone. Shariff instructed him to go to a secure FTP app and connect using a code he provided him.

"Now we wait," Shariff said and began counting backwards in his head. "Once Hawke or anyone else connects the flash drive, it will send a notification to that phone."

Agent 21 kept a tight grip on the phone, only taking his eyes off the screen to stare through Shariff.

One minute passed.

Shariff rocked back and forth with his eyes closed, still counting backwards.

Ten minutes passed.

The longer Agent 21's eyes fell over him the more Shariff felt the need to vibrate in his skin, as if doing so would help him escape the Cabal agent's glare. He wondered how long Agent 21 would wait before deciding to take the wrench to the back of his head.

Fifteen minutes passed.

Time's up.

Shariff started to shake—from his belly to his chest to his head. Only when he sat up straight did Agent 21 realize Shariff was actually laughing, the deep manic laugh of a man excited to jump off a bridge. It shook every bruised cell in his body, but Shariff welcomed the pain.

Agent 21 glanced at the phone in his hand like it had become radioactive. "What did you do?"

"You don't think I never expected to get caught at some point? I know the Cabal will hunt those who oppose them by any means and that I could only stay free and rage against the apparatus of the system for so long! That code you entered . . . it wasn't waiting for the flash drive to connect . . . it was a call for help!"

Agent 21 rose at the sound of hard footsteps coming from outside the apartment. His hand fell to the holster holding the loaded .22-calibre pistol. "Are your friends coming?"

"No, Cabal scum!" Shariff cried. "These are *your* friends!"

A muted silver canister broke through the window, landing with a playful thump. Tear gas hissed out of its sides and the air became toxic. Shariff rocked himself to the floor just as a battering ram shattered the front door and a team of black-clad men flooded into the room. In their hands were no-nonsense submachine guns, covering their faces were gas masks, and stencilled across their chests in big yellow letters was a single word: POLICE.

Within a split second Agent 21 knew he had been swatted. Shariff's use of the deceptive police manipulation technique was impressive, his outgoing message clearly alerting law enforcement to an emergency situation. The Specialist Firearms Command, the Metropolitan Police equivalent of a SWAT team, would have been immediately dispatched to the safe house location, the amped-up officers hoping for any excuse to shoot first.

So Agent 21 didn't give them one.

With the tear gas blinding and choking him, Agent 21 knelt on both knees with his hands up. He obediently followed the overaggressive team leader's instructions and didn't resist as he was handcuffed and slammed against the floor.

For almost anyone else, being caught armed with a badly beaten man tied to a chair would mean a long prison term. For Agent 21 of the Cabal, it was an annoyance. With the Cabal's tentacles stretching deep into the

Metropolitan Police, he would be freed almost as soon as he arrived at the station, with no questions asked.

And then he would resume his hunt for Henry Hawke and the remaining Keepers of the Fortune.

NOOR'S EXPLANATION

The beat-up truck's transmission grinded in agony as Hawke took a few gear shifts to acclimate to the right-side stick shift and finicky clutch. Riding an adrenalin rush like he hadn't felt since his last college hockey game, which had earned him that final suspension, he pushed the truck harder than anyone since it had rolled off the assembly line a decade ago.

Around hard corners and demanding straightaways, the engine struggled to match Hawke's intensity. He only reluctantly eased up on the gas after Noor pointed out she might as well have stayed at Monsef's with a bloodied cricket bat in hand for all the good getting caught speeding away from the crime scene in a stolen vehicle would do.

Hawke, realizing she might not be wrong, slowed his pace, managing to avoid incoming police as they left the downtown core. He followed the first sign onto the highway and gently merged into the light Sunday evening traffic.

Everything was a blur from the moment Inspector Smith had arrested him. Or rather, pretended to arrest him. Hawke wasn't a cop, but he knew enough that it wasn't police protocol to tie anyone to a chair and interrogate them for hours. Or at least he hoped it wasn't. He could feel a few bruises forming and his wrists were chafed, but otherwise he was more pissed off than traumatized. He was more worried about Monsef's well-being. He would make sure to find out what hospital he had been taken to as soon as he got somewhere safe, and shuddered to think what would have happened to them if Noor hadn't arrived when she did.

But why had she arrived? It was suddenly the only thing on his mind. Hawke continued down the highway as raindrops began to tickle the windshield. He kept just above the speed limit, partially to avoid being pulled over but mostly because he didn't think the truck could go any faster.

There was a laptop bag at Noor's feet. But no shopping bags. She had likely done as much shopping as he had sightseeing. She appeared to be in a state of shock with a thousand-yard stare. Hawke supposed getting into a stolen truck with an alleged murderer would do that to anyone.

Hawke felt like clarifying the situation. "I didn't murder anyone."

The oncoming headlights met the raindrops, causing the light to diffuse across Noor's face. "What about Nabeel Monsef?"

"What?" Hawke did a double-take at Noor while trying to focus on the road. "I didn't murder him!"

"You might as well have. You brought the Cabal right to his doorstep and might have even helped them find Satoshi's Fortune."

"Because Shariff sent me there!" Hawke felt his stomach drop as he realized he might have revealed too much. "Wait a minute . . ." he said. "How do you know about Satoshi's Fortune?"

"How do *you* know about Satoshi's Fortune?"

Hawke suspected she already knew, so he admitted it was Shariff.

"That was your little talk at the pub?" she asked.

Hawke nodded.

"Of course," Noor whispered, and then, in an accusatory tone, she asked, "Why were you at the lawyer's office?"

"Why were *you* at the lawyer's office?" Hawke shot back.

Noor pretended she didn't hear his question. Her mind was elsewhere, perhaps running through a list of plausible reasons—the shopping ruse was clearly not going to fly—why she had arrived at Monsef's just in time to save the day. In the end, she decided she owed Hawke nothing but silence.

Hawke guided the truck past a slow-moving van on the outside lane and mused to himself that for a community that prided itself on open-source code and transparent transactions, the people involved in bitcoin sure did obscure a lot of important details. Hawke decided to go against the grain—he'd try just being open.

"Shariff sent me a secret message that led me to Monsef."

Noor remained silent.

"But you knew that already?"

Noor remained silent still.

Hawke wondered if she was this stoic in a relationship, too. *In for a penny in for a pound*, he thought. He continued his strategy of sharing his feelings, maybe to show he wouldn't be stoic in a relationship.

"I have no idea how much you know about Satoshi's Fortune, why you're involved, or what you want. And I have no idea why Aziz chose me to receive that secret message in the first place," Hawke admitted.

The honesty finally seemed to work. Noor gave him a look he first assumed was sympathetic, but quickly reclassified as playfully condescending. "Yeah, you didn't strike me as someone who knows a whole hell of a lot."

Hawke focused on the road. "Well, I usually just get by on my looks."

"Oh? Then I'm surprised you even have a job."

"It's the suit. It makes people think I know what I'm doing."

Noor and Hawke exchanged looks. Any hope he had of a shared moment was quickly crushed when she rolled her eyes at him, but at least for a few brief seconds he had forgotten the world of trouble he was in.

And then his phone rang.

The electronic hymn hung in the air. The call display read *Chicago Mutual.*

He showed the screen to Noor, who shrugged, uncertain of what to do.

"What the hell," Hawke said, "maybe I'm getting a promotion." Another eye roll indicated she was doubtful.

Hawke put the call on speakerphone.

"Hello, Henry?" The voice was deep and forceful. It radiated the confidence of a man who had obliterated every one of the obstacles life had put in his way, a man who only gave orders. Hawke immediately recognized the voice of his uncle's one-time friend, a man he had known since he was a boy.

"Mr. Elliot," Hawke answered the CEO of Chicago Mutual Savings Bank. "Is this about my promotion?"

Before being hired, Hawke had always known Mr. Elliot as Joe, curator of his uncle's embarrassing stories from their younger, wilder days at the bank, supplier of ice-level Blackhawk tickets, and proud owner of arguably the best barbecue ribs recipe in the entire Midwest.

But since his uncle's passing, he had been only Mr. Elliot, a curt, distant CEO indifferent to the boy he once joked would be his protegé, as if hiring Hawke meant Mr. Elliot had held up his end of a deal that Hawke had not been privy to.

"Now's not the best time to be glib, Henry. You're in a lot of trouble. I've been getting calls from the FBI. I don't need to tell you that the last time that happened . . ." his voice trailed off. "Anyway, before you say anything I want you to know that I believe you. And that I can help."

Hawke wondered if his uncle had received a similar call. He glanced at Noor listening attentively beside him. "I think I'm doing all right."

"No, you're not. You're wanted for murder, Henry. Murder. It doesn't get any more serious than that."

"I've been made aware. Probably won't look too good on my resume, will it?"

Mr. Elliot ignored the remark. "Go to the American Embassy in London. I'll make sure you get the best criminal lawyers. You just need to come in and end this . . . Whatever this is. We'll get it all sorted out. I know you didn't murder anyone."

Hawke felt like jumping on the offer. It was only this morning that he had decided to skip the rest of the conference to follow Shariff's secret message, and if not to find a fortune, at least it would be a little adventure to recount at the pub back home. Now he was a murder suspect, had been tortured by a corrupt cop, and had stolen a truck.

His attempted career change to fortune hunter might need some reconsideration.

He looked to Noor, who seemed to read his mind. The oncoming traffic lights passed over her in waves. He didn't know if he imagined a subtle shake of her head.

Mr. Elliot spoke up. "Henry, I honestly don't know what Peter was thinking when he first brought me and the board that *bitcoin* report"—Mr. Elliot couldn't help but scorn the cryptocurrency's name—"but I don't think he cared about the impact it would have on his career. But I do know that if he could have foreseen how much trouble it has caused you, he never would have gotten involved. Dammit, if he wanted to chase something naive and irresponsible, it should have been a twenty-year-old cocktail waitress like a normal man."

Hawke didn't say anything. He was having trouble deciphering who he was talking to. Joe, the former best friend and confidante of his uncle—or Mr. Elliot, the ruthless CEO who at best had stood idly by as his uncle was rendered excommunicado or at worst had directly been involved in the process.

Mr. Elliot continued. "As Peter's oldest friend, I'm asking you to end your involvement and go straight from Birmingham to London. I promise you'll have the full support of the bank and all its resources. What would your uncle say to you chasing some fortune in a stolen truck?"

Hawke felt the sharp cut of paranoia in his gut, Shariff's hand on the knife handle.

"I'm sorry, Joe. But I'm starting to think I'd know what my uncle would say to me . . ." Hawke told him and ended the call. He then put down his window and heaved his phone backwards, watching it dissolve into the darkness behind him.

"I don't think I got the promotion."

"You figured it out, didn't you?" Noor asked.

Mr. Elliot knew he had been in Birmingham and had stolen a truck.

Hawke nodded and pressed his foot down on the accelerator, as if he could escape the unwelcomed truth.

The Chicago Mutual Savings Bank was controlled by the Cabal.

***

Joseph Elliot sat in a deep wingback leather chair before a crackling fire that did little to warm the palatial study at his country estate an hour outside Chicago. It was past noon and the Midwest sun had so far refused to show itself. Elliot, matching the weather's despondent attitude, had yet to change out of his cashmere housecoat.

The call with Hawke had not gone well.

And he didn't expect the next call to be any better.

Elliot had once been the stereotypical college quarterback; his first and second wives had even been cheerleaders. He still stood thick and tall, and his voice boomed with the authority of an army general. His bluster wasn't without merit. In the eighties, he had taken an inconsequential mutual savings bank owned by a few thousand members, and over the next two decades had turned it into the state's fastest growing publicly traded financial institution, with a higher earnings per share than any of its national competitors. He had done so by rewriting the bank's charter and then aggressively acquiring any and all mutual fund operations, stock brokerages, and insurance companies he could get his hands on. He squeezed all possible growth out of those traditional banking operations before turning his sights to something bigger: transforming Chicago Mutual into a Wall Street powerhouse.

To do so, Elliot needed a new market to invade. Something upon which to build a financial empire. And then, at the turn of the century, he had found an asset that for the briefest of moments crowned him emperor. *Collateralized debt obligations.*

These CDOs, as they were called, took exceedingly low-risk mortgage bonds stuffed with AAA-rated mortgages that had a next-to-zero chance of failure and combined them with high-risk mortgage bonds. Because all the low- and high-risk mortgages were mixed into one product, it was said to be diversified and therefore perfectly safe.

Elliot couldn't buy and sell them fast enough. The high demand for more CDOs meant a higher demand for mortgages to fill them went up with. Soon everyone and their dog was approved in order to satiate this demand. The higher supply of buyers set the real estate market on fire, further raising the value of the CDOs.

To speed things up, Chicago Mutual started leveraging themselves ten-to-one; for every dollar of assets, they would borrow ten in order to buy more CDOs.

Then twenty-to-one.

The markets were still hungry, and Elliot refused to let somebody else eat into his profits. Peter Finlay and others at the bank had started to raise the alarms, but the proof was in the profits.

Fifty-to-one.

Elliot finally started getting the attention he knew he deserved. Chicago Mutual was featured in the both the *Wall Street Journal* and *Forbes* while simultaneous reaching an eighty-to-one leveraging ratio. Elliot was poised to expand his empire across America, and then the world.

And then the real estate market crashed.

When that happened being leveraged like a drunken college kid with their first credit card didn't seem all that wise. Chicago Mutual not only had to cancel its expansion plans, but had to fight for its very existence. The Financial Crisis spread like a virus through any financial institution that had ever touched a CDO.

Now with the value of Chicago Mutual's assets pathetically reduced compared to what it owed, and with no means to pay it back, Elliot was desperate for a cash infusion to fill the hole. Otherwise, his life's work would be sold piecemeal in bankruptcy court, leaving his legacy as another cautionary tale in the footnotes of American banking history.

Peter Finlay, his trusted ally throughout the years, began spending less and less time at the office. And when he did, he seemed unconcerned with their empire's impending collapse. It was during the darkest days, after Elliot had started drinking all his meals and was almost too ashamed to show his face at the office, that Peter came forward with a report to the board of directors that he claimed would revolutionize the financial system. And in the midst of that revolution, Chicago Mutual could thrive as the first of a new breed of financial technology companies he labelled as fintech. Not only would this reborn Chicago Mutual generate long-term profits, but it would also improve the financial lives of millions of people around the globe. But upon hearing the details of the report and its terminology incompatible with a successful capitalist economy—*decentralized, open source, deflationary*—Elliot deemed the report ludicrous and callously laughed Peter out of the boardroom.

That was the last conversation he ever had with his old friend.

In the days that immediately followed that boardroom debacle, Elliot enviously watched the large Wall Street firms, those he thought he was destined to challenge, receive the blessed designation of *Too Big to Fail* and thus received essentially a blank cheque from the Federal Reserve to bail them out. Conversely, he flirted daily with cash calls as Chicago Mutual was slowly being cut off from the rest of the financial system without so much as a longing glance from the Fed.

Or so he had thought.

With 2008 coming to an end and being nothing short of a financial catastrophe, Elliot had every intention of ringing in the New Year alone with a bottle of eighteen-year-old Macallan. His self-destructive solitude was abruptly interrupted by two long, solemn bangs on his study's hardwood floor that nearly shocked him sober.

The uninvited but soon welcomed guest brought with him a bottomless pit of money and recognition of what a financial powerhouse Chicago Mutual had been poised to become, and, with just the occasional quid pro quo to its new masters, it could still be. With a further two bangs of his guest's serpent cane, the deal was done and Chicago Mutual would rise again to even greater heights—sans Peter Finlay, of course. At the time, such a betrayal seemed like a small price to pay, and Elliot promised himself that one day he would atone for blacklisting his one-time best friend.

In the following years, he had continued to justify his deal with the devil by telling himself that without it hundreds of Chicago Mutual employees would have been out of a job, that he wouldn't have been able to make his generous donations to countless charities, and that he wouldn't have been able to ensure Peter's often troublesome nephew had a career, however much he seemed to resent it.

But today Elliot didn't recognize himself in the mirror; his once thick black hair was now grey and straggly, his nose a painful red and always swollen. But he carried on. He had no choice. For the once-proud man, whose orders at one-time had only flowed in one direction, simply picking up his phone made him grit his teeth. As Elliot had discovered later in life than most, everyone has a boss.

He dialled a number from memory.

"Yes, my good man?" the voice slithered.

"I talked to Henry."

"Excellent! And what did our young man have to say about our generous offer of amnesty?"

"He basically said to get lost."

The silence rang loud before the voice snarled its response. "What *exactly* did he say?"

Elliot waited a beat and then swallowed. "He said, 'Many more a man would go rogue if he only knew how.'"

The line went dead.

Elliot was left alone with the unforgiving wind pounding the study's windows. It was clear that today there would be no reprieve from the foul weather, so he refilled his rock glass from a bottle of cheap blended scotch and sank deeper into his chair, desperate for the brown liquor to warm him from within and numb the memories of who he once was.

HAWKE'S BRAVE NEW WORLD

Chicago Mutual was controlled by the Cabal.

The truck's engine screamed louder than its horsepower should have allowed, manifesting Hawke's anger in ways he could not. He made passes on the highway he had no business even attempting, the loose steering and slick road conditions something a more reasonable driver would have taken into account.

But Hawke was not driven by reason. His world hadn't been turned upside down but ripped apart to reveal the life he had wanted, and maybe his own family, was a fraud. The mischievous smile Hawke had sported when he had stolen the truck now morphed into a cruel hook. His eyes teased madness, and it was only the firm, unapologetic words of Sara Noor that brought him back from the edge.

"Peter Finlay didn't work for the Cabal." Noor let Hawke process his fears, and when he finally lifted his foot from the accelerator, she added, "And you're driving like a goddamn idiot."

It was only then Hawke noticed Noor had a two-handed hold on the grab handle above her window. Hawke knew she was right about his driving, but waited a moment before acknowledging it to show her she wasn't *completely* right.

"How do you and everyone else in this self-righteous bitcoin world seem to know more about my own uncle than I do?" Hawke asked.

"Do you want a condescending answer or a sugar-coated one?" Noor gave no ground to Hawke's anger. "Because there is no sugar-coated one. Many of us know more about your uncle because we all arrived at the same place at roughly the same time, a place where we knew that something was wrong with how the system worked, how being driven into debt to fund a life we didn't need was us playing someone else's game—a rigged game. And we decided to opt-out, to find a better way. If you had been less self-absorbed, then maybe your uncle's guidance would have been better received, and you'd have been involved from the get-go instead of being Aziz's last resort."

Many more a man would go rogue if he only knew how.

Hawke felt like hitting the gas again, but didn't. Maybe because of his growing maturity. Or, more likely, because the engine's rumble had become a tired high-pitched whirl and probably wouldn't survive another stomp of his lead foot.

"How long has the Cabal been controlling Chicago Mutual?" Hawke decided to use his words instead.

"As far as I can tell, since about 2008, at least actively. But if it makes you feel better, most banks are controlled by the Cabal, in some form or another."

"It doesn't. But thanks."

The rain picked up and made the weak wipers struggle to clear their line of sight. They fell into silence, Hawke even more uncertain of where he was headed. His last remaining family member was dead. And thanks to his involvement in bitcoin, so was his career. What started as a daydream for adventure and fortune had morphed into a fool's errand.

"I know somewhere we can go. Someone we can trust," Noor said.

Hawke said nothing, uncertain if delving deeper down the bitcoin rabbit hole would lead anywhere.

Noor asked, "Do you trust me?"

"Hell no." Hawke said the first thing that came to mind.

"It would seem like you don't have a choice," she said bluntly. "You're wanted for murder with the Cabal gunning for you. The only money you have is the cash in your tacky suit pocket. You just threw out your phone so now you can't call anyone. For all intents and purposes, Henry Hawke, you're the most wanted person in the world with zero resources to deal with it."

Hawke perked up at her last remark and jerked the wheel to his left, swerving across two lanes to a howl of horn blasts from offended drivers. It wasn't with anger he had thrown the truck onto the rain-soaked gravel shoulder and slammed on the breaks, but with excitement, though at that moment Noor saw little difference.

"You idiot! You reckless, goddamn asshole!" she yelled. He switched off the engine and turned to Noor.

"I need to borrow your laptop."

"What! Why?" Noor's hand protectively fell to the bag at her feet.

"Because I just might not actually have zero assets." Hawke held up the flash drive from Monsef's office.

Noor's eyes widened. "What is it?" she asked, too casually.

"The entire James Bond collection on Blu-ray."

Noor's expression softened. "If you're not angry, you're a smartass. Care to find some middle ground?"

"Tell you what. If I share this with you, you'll have to tell me everything about bitcoin and my uncle and whatever else I need to know in order to find Satoshi's Fortune before the Cabal."

The rain erratically tap-danced on the roof, and it was growing colder inside the cab with the engine turned off. Noor was unapologetic. "If the Cabal gets control, it may be the end of bitcoin. But I don't think giving it to a millennial banker is much better."

Hawke considered what she meant. Was he in it for the money? For the adventure? To make his uncle proud? Or to avoid a lifetime stuck behind a desk? Whatever the reason he wanted to find Satoshi's Fortune, he couldn't do it alone.

He handed Noor the flash drive. "This is me trusting you."

Noor bit her lip and then accepted it, their fingers lingering during the exchange. She entered her password and then inserted the flash drive, which loaded with a beep, and a window popped up automatically.

"What is it?" Hawke asked. The air was beginning to get thick in the small truck cab and the windshield began to fog up. He leaned closer to view the screen and was momentarily distracted by the sweet smell of lilacs and the heat radiating from her body.

"Not sure."

The folder was password-protected, unsurprising given Shariff's proclivity towards encryption, but it left them at a dead end.

"I doubt we'll be able to break his password." Noor said.

The glow of the screen lit up Hawke's impish grin, which broadcast that he knew something nobody else did. And this time, he did.

"You know it?" Noor asked incredulously.

"Sarcasm, temper, and maybe some brains after all. I'm a triple threat." Hawke winked at Noor. She rolled her eyes.

"*We Are All Satoshi*," Hawke said.

Noor typed it in. The password was accepted.

The folder revealed its secrets, the information that would lead them to Satoshi's Fortune.

Both Hawke and Noor gasped at what they found.

PART 3:

3FB3swcqTrUWefrwLnaW
V72QJViSy5eW1

RICKARD'S VISIT

Across the Atlantic, the privately owned Global Express jet landed with nary a bump large enough to disrupt John Francis Rickard's tea. With the aid of his cane he descended the steps to the tarmac and into a waiting black Mercedes-Benz sedan, not bothering to notice how lovely Massachusetts is in the fall.

His burly driver, who was squeezed into a three-piece suit, didn't say a word as he put the car into gear and carried them to their predetermined destination without any concern for speed traps or otherwise vigilant state troopers. The Mercedes came to a stop in front of a bland clapboard house in a bedroom community outside Boston. The driver parked and held open the door for Rickard, who stood up and playfully tapped his cane twice on the ground.

"Thank you, my good man, I shan't be but a moment." Rickard adjusted his wool overcoat and put his black bowler hat on straight. He walked unhurriedly up the steps and knocked on the door with the butt of his cane. The door swung open. He was greeted by a woman in her mid-thirties wearing a frayed college sweatshirt. A dish towel was slung over her shoulder.

"My dear, you must be Jennifer. I'm afraid we haven't met before." Rickard smiled kindly and let his eyes twinkle as only a harmless old man could.

Jennifer returned half the smile as only a sleep-deprived new mother worried she had forgotten the name of an important contact of her husband's could. And the man on her front step had all the hallmarks of importance, from the expensive clothes to the waiting driver. She invited him in. Rickard declined to let her take his coat and hat, apologizing that he only had time for a quick visit with her husband. She showed him to the living room, embarrassed as she picked up some stray children's books and a couple of unmatching socks along the way. She called upstairs where a baby could be heard fussing.

"Sweetheart, you have a guest."

Rickard settled into a rocking chair where he imagined his host read those very books to that child upstairs and surveyed the room. Middle class at its best. Generic framed family pictures on the walls, bookshelves filled with outdated SQL manuals, cyber security textbooks, and binders of loose notes. In the corner was a desk that had a keyboard and mouse leading to nowhere. A dust outline remained where the tower had once been, like the chalk outline of a murder scene. Its seizure and autopsy, Rickard knew, had provided little information.

Andrew Cohen stepped into the threshold of the living room to eye the senior statesman sitting in his favourite reading chair.

"Who are you?" Cohen asked suspiciously.

"John Francis Rickard," he answered with a proud raise of his chin and two taps of his cane. "And we are soon to become good friends, my dear Andrew."

Cohen might not have known who Rickard was, but he knew immediately where he was from. And he wanted nothing more than to see the back of him.

"I've got nothing to say to you! You've cost me enough, the hell you put me through." Cohen shot a glance up the stairs and modified his voice to a whispering yell. "I have a kid. A wife. You charge me with some frivolous money-laundering charge and nearly took all that away! My reputation is in tatters! I lost my job!"

Rickard observed Cohen with the bemused curiosity of a zoo visitor at the monkey house. Through a thin smile he said, "Yes, and we graciously got you another higher-paying job as a favour for all your hardship."

Cohen gave another glance to see if his wife had appeared, as if his guilt would only take hold should she hear what he admitted next. "Yes, and I told your spook *Pandit*, or whatever his name is, all about the Keepers of the Fortune. And I also told him everything I knew about Satoshi, and still do every time he's called since, which is next to nothing!"

Rickard perked up. "Yes, yes. I'll make sure to talk to Agent Pandit about following up with you. How often would you say he contacts you?"

"Weekly, always with another line of questioning. The fact remains that I know nothing about Satoshi."

"Of course, my Andrew, I'll make sure my agent knows

that investigation is over. Satoshi isn't even our concern anymore thanks to your helpful intel."

"Yes," Cohen said, saddened, "I told you everything I know about Satoshi's Fortune."

Rickard watched with pleasure as the man seemed to shrink before him. Cohen's betrayal of his little revolutionary tech friends had clearly extracted a toll.

But it was not enough for Rickard.

"My dear Andrew, everything?" His own question elicited a soft chuckle. "We are only getting started."

"Oh no we're not." He jabbed his finger inches away from Rickard's nose. "Now get out of my chair and get out of my home!"

Rickard remained seated, his liver-spotted hands resting calmly on his cane's serpent head. He reached up and put one hand on the finger pointed at him, and effortlessly brushed it away. "We already know that Aziz Shariff was burdened with being a Keeper . . ." Rickard watched Cohen for his reaction to the revelation. He watched with pleasure as the colour drained from Cohen's face, cementing the fact that he had known Shariff was a Keeper. And if he knew that delicious morsel of information . . .

"So now, my Andrew, you are going to tell me who else I should be talking with. Tell me the names of the Keepers of the Fortune."

"I refuse." Cohen stood defiantly with his arms crossed.

Rickard smiled thinly at the man who still didn't know his place. But the head of the Cabal was glad Cohen wasn't going to immediately roll over. It always made it more fun to break those who thought they could resist.

"That little money-laundering charge you found yourself troubled with . . . I don't need to remind you that such a terrible thing can be a serious prison term," Rickard said, perversely watching Cohen's reaction for signs he had realized what was to come.

"And in return for immunity, I answered your agent's questions."

"Yes, for you that worked out well."

Still nothing. Rickard sighed.

"If you remember, the charges stemmed from movement into your bank account from these oh-so-dubious bitcoin exchanges overseas. Drug money. Terrorism financing. Such a sordid lot."

"All I did was sell some bitcoins I made from mining. I paid taxes on it and everything!"

"Well, unfortunately that was a joint bank account."

Cohen's world shifted. It began with an inaudible whimper and ended with the blood draining so fast from his face that he nearly collapsed, a pale ghost, as one would expect from a crushing realization that you might have gotten the love of your life mixed up with a cabal of men without mercy.

"I'm sure she had no idea that her name was on an account involved in such dreadful underground activity. Still . . ." Rickard let the implications fill the room.

Cohen fell onto the couch. The couch where he had first told Jennifer about bitcoin. Where they cuddled every Friday night and watched low-budget sci-fi movies together. Where Jennifer had first told him she was pregnant. Where he now realized he had the power to save her from a repeat of the horrors he had put her through months earlier, this time made a hundred times worse because she would be the Cabal's target. He could stop her from being snatched away from her infant child and threatened with a life in prison all because her idiot husband had used their joint bank account to receive the proceeds from selling a few bitcoin. With great strain, he looked at the monster sitting in his favourite reading chair. And he told him the email addresses of the Keepers of the Fortune.

He pleaded, truthfully, that he didn't know their actual identities any more than he knew Satoshi's. And for the safety of his family he prayed that Rickard believed him. Neither the morbid grey eyes nor the twisted smile gave any indication that he did. But with two loud taps of his cane, nearly denting the floor, Rickard stood up, left the house without a word, and let the door slam behind him.

Jennifer descended the stairs with their child sleeping blissfully in her arms. "What was that racket? I never got to chat with your friend. Andy? What's wrong?" She found him despondent on the couch.

"Oh? Nothing. It's okay. Just a . . . an investor in the company I work for wanted a quick chat about a project."

"Oh, peculiar old man, wasn't he?" Jennifer watched through the living room window as the black Mercedes sped away. "Guess that's what money does to you over time."

The child began to stir, so she handed him to Cohen, admiring him for being such a warm and caring father. The *baby whisperer*, she told her friends. Baby Nicky could be impossibly fussy but as soon as he was in his father's arms, all was well.

But something was off. In his arms now, Nicky was nothing but agitated and began to cry. And Cohen joined him in tears.

PETROVICH'S PROBLEM

Yuriy Petrovich couldn't sleep, yet again. He tried and failed to remember the last time he hadn't woken up more tired than the day before. It wasn't the cold wind rattling his window or the lumpy cot in the office-turned-bedroom that kept him from a peaceful night's rest. It wasn't that he had been responsible for securing a server from which millions of dollars in bitcoin had been stolen—it was that the stolen bitcoins had belonged to the Russian mob.

He leaned over through a daze and checked his watch. Five a.m. Petrovich doubted he would be able to find sleep again, so he reluctantly decided to face the day. The cot squeaked as he stood and stretched, his back in constant protest from both the cot and being curled over a computer terminal for sixteen hours a day. He put on scratched glasses and quickly dressed in grey slacks and a rumpled golf shirt he picked off the floor before going in search of coffee. His clothes hung off his already reedy frame, trimmed further from a loss of appetite.

An unassuming graduate of the Moscow State University of Instrument Engineering and Computer Science, he hadn't wowed his professors, but he also hadn't given them reason to doubt his competency. In a calculated career move, he decided he would put his skills to use for the Solntsevskaya Bratva—the largest and most fearsome syndicate in Russia's underworld.

The Vor of the Bratva had determined in the early days of the twenty-first century that they were at a crossroads. They had long since moved on from the post-Soviet days of dealing black market oil and aluminum and into the drug and prostitution trade. However, that market had grown riskier, the in-person dealings with the girls, drugs, and money laundering under greater scrutiny in a global marketplace. It all led to the Vor taking the Bratva online and into the dark web. All those nefarious activities historically conducted in person were now even more profitable because of reduced overhead while also having the benefit of being much less conspicuous. It left law enforcement behind to fiddle with their archaic laws from an age before the internet and politicians to let sleeping dogs lie as their voters were more concerned with the louder, most visible criminals.

The Bratva took advantage of this perfect storm of indifferent politicians and impotent cops to become a global organization that rivalled any legitimate online retailer in revenue—without the need to report any taxes or follow any regulations. Such an organization required a skilled modern workforce. To feed this demand for programmers and technicians, the Bratva trolled the country's universities for graduates, scooping them up like any other international organization on a recruitment drive.

Petrovich received two offers upon graduation: one, a professionally written job offer with basic benefits and livable salary from a large Moscow-based pharmaceutical company, and the other, a blunt knock on his door from a beast of a man, the promise of riches and women in a foreign city and a handshake to seal his fate.

He learned that the Bratva was divided into independent cells, each with an Avtoritet in charge. Petrovich's Avtoritet was Maxim Makarov, the beast of a man who had recruited him. He had failed to mention that the promised riches were required to pay for the women, and that the foreign city was Liverpool. Petrovich made a promise to himself that in the future he would always read the fine print.

Their cell was housed in a squat, unimaginative office building near the docks, and while most of their business involved online operations, the old ways of conducting business face-to-face with a crowbar was a habit Makarov couldn't shake. He kept himself busy on the side with such meetings. And since Makarov was as brilliant at identifying ways to make money as he was in collecting debts, he spotted a market of great potential after one of those deadbeats tried to pay him in something other than cash, something he swore couldn't be easily traced by the cops.

That something was called bitcoin.

Once Makarov had finished shattering the deadbeat's knees with his trusted crowbar, he put Petrovich in charge of their online operations and tasked him with coding and maintaining an exchange where people could buy and sell this newly discovered currency. Once the exchange was up and running, users from around the world could create an account with only an email and deposit US dollars and euros into the bank account of one of the Bratva's shell companies. However, it was a never-ending game of whack-a-mole because as soon as one bank found out they were dealing with bitcoin their account was closed and the Bratva had to quickly open another to avoid disrupting their operations. Typically, it took about six months before a bank wised up, though with the awareness around bitcoin growing, the banks had started to shut their accounts down more frequently.

Regardless of the bank's concern, the exchange itself was technically legal and did brisk business. But that honest revenue wasn't enough for Makarov. Every so often, once the bitcoin value of the users' deposits approached a million US dollars, Petrovich was instructed by his Avtoritet to steal all their bitcoins and claim they had been hacked.

Bitcoin transactions were pseudo-anonymous; their users could try and follow the movement of coins through the blockchain, but Petrovich used various tricks to obfuscate the transactions, enough so that nobody knew exactly which bitcoin addresses were controlled by the exchange and which belonged to the phantom hackers.

After the first time they announced a hack, Petrovich had been concerned they were killing the golden goose and that people would no longer trust an anonymous, unregulated exchange with only an email address and a fictitious Belgrade address for contact information. But he was amazed and delighted to see the users flock right back to the exchange. Petrovich took this as a compliment to the usability and execution of his platform design, and maybe as a lesson about human greed. They had since executed two further hacks, garnering intense outrage on social media, but saw little reduction in trading volume.

But Petrovich wasn't so self-satisfied after the fourth hack of the exchange because when he took the initial steps to rob their customers, something went terribly wrong. Because every transaction on the blockchain was visible, he needed to move all coins linked to the exchange to a brand-new address, one that had no prior history, so they could claim it belonged to the hacker. This, in fact, would be a completely independent wallet Petrovich had set up and from there Makarov could safely do anything he wanted with the coins. As he had done three times previously, Petrovich initiated the fake hack and drained the exchange's wallets of over a million US dollars' worth of coins to the newly created fake hacker's wallet that he controlled.

Or so he had thought.

Almost as soon as the coins arrived, his wallet software emitted a lighthearted beep that betrayed the seriousness of the alert; a new transaction appeared, sending the coins from the fake hacker's wallet he and Makarov controlled to a completely different bitcoin address he didn't recognize. It was without irony that Petrovich realized—his stomach curling into a ball of dread and plunging to the bottom of a deep pit—that while attempting to perform a fake hack, he himself had been the victim of a real one.

Petrovich had spent the following six months tirelessly investigating the theft and looking over his shoulder for

Makarov to hold him responsible. He had started carrying a knife on his person, a menacing looking black-on-black switchblade—black handle, black steel. It was more for an attempt at peace of mind than any realistic belief that it could save his life. Makarov and his crowbar would make quick work of him if he defended himself with anything short of a rocket launcher—and even then it would still be iffy.

During every crawling hour of every impossibly slow-moving day, as his ulcers blistered and swelled and he clenched his switchblade tighter, Petrovich desperately hoped the hacker would try and cash out. It was a long shot, but his contacts at the other exchanges promised to alert him if the stolen coins reached them. Not because they were friends necessarily, but because they knew he was part of the Bratva and wanted to remain in good favour.

But, frustratingly, the coins had remained static in that first address the hacker had placed them in six long months ago. Petrovich knew some hackers didn't care about money but trespassed for ideological reasons, and it would seem this hacker was of that breed. The only clue he had about who had stolen from Russia's most powerful criminal organization was a message that Petrovich had discovered in the third output of that fateful bitcoin transaction.

The message read, *Fuck the mob.*

***

Petrovich found himself in the kitchen fumbling with the coffee maker when Makarov joined him. He was the size of a bear and half as hairy, with a round, bulbous, red nose from too much drink and fingers as fat as sausages and just as greasy. Though he didn't understand much about the technical aspects of bitcoin, he understood money. And having it stolen was not something he accepted with grace. Petrovich suspected he wasn't currently cut up into little pieces because Makarov couldn't operate the bitcoin exchange without him, and because Petrovich had assured him that he could get the small fortune back if he had enough time.

"Where my bitcoin today?" Makarov growled. He sat at the plastic breakfast table and crossed his thick arms, displaying a wealth of colourless tattoos underneath his dark hair. His outward right forearm was painted with a stack of dollar bills beside a bowtie with a dollar sign. Petrovich knew that on Makarov's hidden left arm there was an image of a wild-eyed gun-toting cowboy.

Petrovich listened to the coffee drip, as if it would buy him more time, and felt his bowels loosen as he replied, "Same."

"Same not good."

"I know."

"Maybe I bring in new computer man."

A lump formed in Petrovich's throat. If a new programmer was brought into their cell, he would lose the main reason he was still alive. Before he could say anything, the phone rang. It was a quirk of Makarov's that he kept a landline, insisting cell phones were too easily surveilled.

Makarov let the cordless phone ring on the kitchen counter for a moment before deciding to answer, first in Russian then switching to broken English. He placed the phone against his leg to block the receiver and spoke to Petrovich in Russian.

"Mystery Man say he knows about Bratva's stolen coins. You listen. I talk."

Petrovich jumped to his Avtoritet's side. Was it a seed of optimism that he felt in his stomach or just another ulcer? He listened attentively to every word the caller said.

"You speak now, Mystery Man. I might listen." Makarov put the call on speakerphone.

The caller's voice was high-spirited. "I think you and I have much to talk about, my Russian friend."

"We are not friends, Mystery Man. What do you want from Maxim?" Makarov asked. He always referred to himself in the third person when he spoke English.

"I don't want anything. I want to give."

"Nobody gives. So do not waste time."

"You are direct, my Russian friend. I like that. First off, I hear you've been having some difficulty with your bank accounts. For instance, your current bank account is being closed next week due to it being flagged as high risk by the compliance department, and you have been unable to find a replacement, correct?"

Makarov glared at Petrovich, insinuating that he perhaps had shared their issues with someone outside the Bratva. Petrovich quickly shook his head.

"I always take silence as a yes. So, let me fix that for you. I've opened your organization a business bank account at Chicago Mutual. It will exist outside of any anti-money-laundering regulations and operate without the burdensome compliance oversight of your typical bank account. I am pleased to say you are now able to freely move any amount of money anywhere in the United States and European Union without any restrictions or inconveniences."

Makarov's eyes narrowed suspiciously. "Why you do this? Why should I trust you?"

"Because you have to trust someone in the banking system to move that much money, don't you?"

Petrovich knew it was true. Every dollar in the bank could be seized at any time for a multitude of reasons. Having someone in the know who they could trust to keep the system lubricated would be an extremely valuable asset to the Bratva.

"But I digress," the caller continued. "This wonderful gift I've bestowed upon you isn't the main reason I reached out to you today, my dear Maxim. As I said earlier, it's related to that unfortunate internal security issue you had months back."

"How you know this?"

"My organization knows everything. Rumours of a Russian hack gone wrong aren't too hard to pick up on, if you listen in the right places."

"Bratva does not appreciate such concerns from Mystery Man."

"Would my Russian friend appreciate knowing the identity of the thief who robbed and embarrassed you?"

Makarov didn't hesitate. "Da."

"Excellent! Because the hacker who stole your bitcoins is somebody you need to find. And his name is Henry Hawke."

HAWKE'S INFORMATION

The oxygen was sucked out of the truck cab as Hawke and Noor reeled at what they saw. It was information that could lead them straight to Satoshi's Fortune: four email addresses that belonged to the Keepers of the Fortune.

Aziz-Shariff@gmx.com
thehashking@kth.se
Proverb211@vistomail.com
PeterF21@gmx.com

Hawke's mind was in a flutter, reorganizing past interactions with his uncle, every word taking on a different meaning, the seemingly erratic decisions of his last months now viewed in a different light.

The greatest fortune of the twenty-first century, nearly one million bitcoins, was kept safe by four individuals chosen by Satoshi himself.

And Peter Finlay was among them.

PeterF21@gmx.com was an address Hawke didn't recognize, but so much of his uncle's life now fit into that category. Hawke became disoriented by this new information and couldn't think clearly. He could hear Noor speak, but the words didn't register immediately. Eventually, he heard himself agree to let her drive and ceded the wheel to her. He didn't know where she was taking him and he didn't ask, but her decisiveness told him that she had a specific destination in mind, and he surprisingly found comfort in that.

The hours passed and Hawke's body begged for sleep, but his mind wouldn't quiet. As he passed through the overlapping state between consciousness and sleep, Noor asked a question that Hawke didn't know how to answer.

"Why are you here?"

"If you don't mind, I'm trying to sleep." He gave an exaggerated yawn.

"You sleep with your eyes open, eh?"

A truck approached from behind, flooding the cab with light, only to be plunged back into blackness as it passed them.

"Seems like the right thing to do in this bitcoin game."

"You enjoy it, don't you? It being a game."

Hawke was uncertain if it was a jab or compliment. "Have you ever had a desk job?"

"Not really. I enrolled in a computer science program in Toronto. I was blogging on the side, which was very cool at the time, of course. Thought about getting a nine-to-five programming job like everyone from my high school guidance counsellor to my father told me to do. But then bitcoin came along and it changed everything, you know? Cypherpunks. Anarchists. Libertarians. How many opportunities do you get in your life to be part of a revolutionary technology that has the potential to disrupt one of the world's most ancient businesses and shake the world's existing power structure to its core? It's . . . addictive. I decided to focus my energies on my cryptocurrency blog and have had enough success to pay the bills. Now the dreaded desk job is a foreign concept to me."

"Yeah, you were right to avoid a desk job. It's not hell. It's worse. It's worse because it's a conscious choice. Like you saw hell and decided *Hey, this might not be as bad as everyone says. Let's give it a go for forty years.*"

Hawke pretended he saw Noor smile in the dashboard light. The lack of sleep was acting as a half-dozen pints might, lowering his defences and creating a desire to share his thoughts.

"Did you know I haven't had a nightmare since I was a kid? But I did a few months after I started at Chicago Mutual. As part of training you spend time rotating through the different departments to get a feel for everything the bank does. I was assigned to work the phones in the credit department to collect on delinquent credit cards. *Customer Assistance* they called it. Which meant you assisted the customer in emptying their bank accounts, regardless of the cost. People would get really angry, and most of the time I couldn't blame them. I learned we had all kinds of tricks to make more money, such as charging them credit card insurance whether or not they agreed to it, or reorganizing the order of their transactions so that they would exceed their credit limits and receive an overdraft charge.

"And maybe the worst part was, I was good at it. I could hunt these people down and if need be, convince them to pay up. Or bother them until they finally paid. I would generously offer a new payment plan that made the monthly payments lower but kept the principal growing, so they would never pay it off in a million years." Hawke paused. The stolen truck had morphed into a makeshift confessional, and he couldn't stop now.

"One call sticks in my mind. This older guy, he probably spent his whole life grinding out each pay cheque. Got ahead a bit, so we offered him a big fat credit limit increase with a special interest rate of zero—because we valued his business so much, of course. But then he lost his job and fell behind on his bills. The first late payment cancelled his special rate and it ballooned up to twenty percent—we're talking loan shark territory here. But hey, it was his own damn fault for accepting the credit limit increase and not keeping up with the payments, right? That's what everyone at the office said, and I didn't bother to argue. That's just the way it was.

"Anyways, he's six months past due when I had to call him. He said he was behind on his mortgage as well, but had saved enough of his unemployment insurance to stave off foreclosure until his job started up the following month. He begged me—he absolutely begged me for help. He wanted to get caught up on the credit card. It was a matter of pride—*a real man always pays his debts*, he said.

"I agreed and talked him into putting his remaining money against the credit card in return for cutting his interest rate down to a more civilized rate and bringing his account up-to-date instead of making a mortgage payment. After all, a man pays his debts and he was further behind with us. No bank would foreclose on him in this market anyways, especially since he would be caught up in a matter of months.

"He paid us and I was happy. I met my performance goals and got a little bonus next pay cheque. I followed up with the guy's account a month later, just to see him back on track with his new job. But his account was back to being delinquent. It turned out because he missed that mortgage payment, the bank actually did foreclose. I don't know where he ended up or if he managed to keep his new job, but if I hadn't done what I was supposed to do . . . So yeah, that night was the first time I had a nightmare since I was a kid."

There was no way Hawke could pretend Noor was smiling now.

"You could have quit," she said coldly.

"I didn't know how, as funny as that sounds. I wanted to keep making money. I wasn't paid a lot, but it was more than most people my age, and jobs were scarce. I thought I wanted a house, a car. Lifestyle creep. I thought that's what I wanted."

Hawke's honesty, with himself as much as Noor, made it possible for sleep to finally take hold.

"Henry, what do you want?" Noor asked.

Hawke closed his eyes and later couldn't remember if the rest of the conversation happened or if he had only dreamt it.

"I want to talk to my uncle. I want to know . . ."

"Know what?"

"I want to know, how did he go rogue . . . "

HAWKE'S ROAD TRIP

It was grey and dark but daytime was steadily making its presence known. Songbirds began to fly in the treeline along the highway. The occasional off-ramp coffee shop started to switch on their open-for-business signs. Hawke awoke slowly, cautiously stepping back into reality from a far-fetched dream.

A hidden message in computer code.

Framed for murder by a secret agent working for an international Cabal.

A mysterious woman eager to help but evasive as to why.

His dead uncle who kept an incredible secret from him.

All for the greatest fortune of the twenty-first century.

Hawke sat up and yawned. He was still in the passenger seat of a stolen truck with a woman driving that he wasn't positive he could trust, and unsure of how much he had actually shared with her before passing out.

Noor didn't mention Hawke's confessions. She had driven straight through the night and was showing no signs of slowing. Out the window there were gently rolling green fields shrouded in morning mist, and further off, scantily lit subdivisions.

"Where are we?" he asked.

"Glasgow. We're just about there."

"What's in Glasgow?"

"Scots and beer."

"Are you getting cute with me?" Hawke asked, hopeful.

"More factual than cute I'd say." Noor replied, dashing hope.

They passed a blue sign that read *Welcome to Glasgow*. With the early-bird commuters starting to add volume to the highway, she took an exit that led her into what was considered Glasgow's West End. A welcoming street with bike lanes and manicured gardens soon devolved into a neighbourhood that had rejected gentrification's advances with its soot-covered buildings, ample graffiti, and a river with a stench so poignant that Hawke and Noor recoiled even from inside the truck.

Noor found a side street of crumbling interlocking brick and parked the truck. The sun was barely up yet the previous night's revellers still patrolled the streets, some hooting, some puking.

Hawke watched one man his own age throw up violently into a gutter. "So, I see Scots and beer," he said. "Now what?"

"A friend of mine runs a sort of . . . sanctuary. He knows all about the Cabal and will want to help us, I think. And just a head's up, he's a bit unorthodox."

"And you trust this guy?" Hawke asked.

A moment's pause. "Yes."

But can I? Hawke left the question unasked.

They got out of the truck and stretched their legs. They gathered all of their belongings, which for Noor was the laptop bag she slung across her chest, for Hawke it was his uncle's watch and the flash drive in his pocket.

"This way." Noor set off. Hawke yawned again and tasted the funky river as much as he could smell it. At the river's edge they came to a Victorian bridge that led nowhere. It abruptly stopped at a decrepit century-old brick wall that was somehow still standing. Most of the wall was hidden behind layers of colourful posters for local bands or tagged by Banksy emulators and local gangs. As they came closer, the outline of a double-wide entrance materialized. What caught Hawke's eye was that, instead of artwork or gang signs, the doors were tagged with a large orange B, slightly slanted with two lines vertically passing through it.

The bitcoin symbol.

"This is the place," Noor said. She pushed on the doors with both hands and Hawke joined in the effort until the doors gave way, and they stumbled inside a large windowless hall made of blood-coloured clay. It was barren save for beer cans and food wrappers. Hawke was pretty sure he saw a few discarded needles and condom wrappers as well. Rotting trusses stressed under the weight of the sagging ceiling and water dripped in between char marks. The air was thick with ammonia and mold.

Hawke eyed a rat scurrying away. "You keep interesting company."

Noor ignored him and pushed forward, using the flashlight on her phone to guide them. The beam revealed a wilting staircase engulfed in rust. The steps went no further than the ceiling, the rest of the way up sealed by the collapsed pieces of the second story.

The steps down led into absolute darkness. Noor gingerly set foot onto the first step and tested its strength. Successful, she began her descent. Hawke looked around and, with no other choice, followed her deeper into the nothingness. He wasn't sure if the squeaking he heard was the rats alarmed at the intrusion into their nest or the stairwell threatening to collapse.

Hawke was unsure just how far underground they had gone when the stairs came to an end. Noor continued forward down a path of crumbled concrete and dirt. The edge of the path disappeared into an abyss before re-emerging twenty feet across. Noor shone her light into the gap. Down below, parallel metal lines ran lengthwise until swallowed up by a giant semi-circular tunnel.

"What is this place?" Hawke asked.

"A former train station. A fire caused its closing back in the sixties. Pretty much abandoned since."

"You don't say." Hawke guessed the platform they were on hadn't seen passengers in over a quarter century.

Off in the distance, a lonely light beckoned. They walked tentatively towards it; the ground felt solid beneath their feet, so their slow pace had more to do with their uncertainty of what came next. The light they now navigated by was a low-wattage bulb in an antique wall-mounted fixture, flickering as if it were affected by a non-existent breeze. The door frame was made of heavy oak, which had swelled and withered over the years, and it matched the thick door that blocked their way. Noor shone her light upwards, illuminating another bitcoin symbol tagged in the upper corner.

"Here we are." Noor twisted the doorknob but it didn't give. She tried again with added effort but the same effect. "It's locked."

"Let me try something." Hawke stepped in front of her and gripped the light fixture where it curved upwards, took a deep breath, and twisted.

Nothing happened.

"Huh, so no secret opening. Thought it was worth a try."

Even in the dim light, Hawke could see her roll her eyes.

"I guess you weren't a Scooby-Doo fan," he muttered under his breath. Hawke took another look at the door. It was solid, as was the frame. The point of weakness was where the two connected. Hawke examined the doorknob.

"You know how to pick a lock as well as hot wire a car?" Noor asked.

"Not exactly."

Hawke took a big step back, judged the distance, and kicked forward with all his weight. The soft sole of his dress shoes connected at the junction between the door and the door frame, but wasn't enough to break through. Still, Noor jumped back, incredulous at his recklessness.

"Henry! Don't you'll set off the—" But Hawke was already stomping forward with another kick. This time the wood began to splinter. He ignored Noor's continuing protests—he needed this! He needed the blood to pump faster through his veins, needed to burn off the anger he felt from being kept in the dark by his uncle, needed to take action and take back control of his life stolen from him! All he had to do was get through this damn stubborn door!

"Henry, stop!" Noor cried one last time, too late, as Hawke successfully kicked open the door.

And then hell rang down upon them.

SERVO'S WELCOME

It wasn't actually hell but hardcore British punk rock. But at over one hundred decibels, it was close enough.

Breaching the door triggered the ear-piercing music as well as flood lights so powerful that Hawke and Noor began to sweat. They reacted with pure instinct, slamming their eyes shut and slapping their hands over their bleeding ears, but it was too late. They were deaf, blind, and disoriented—easy prey for whoever's trap they had walked into.

After what seemed like an eternity, but was only a few seconds, everything went black and mute. Hawke breathed heavily to regain his composure while his ears still screeched. When his eyes finally managed to readjust to the darkness, he spied Noor bent on one knee—with the outline of an aggressively approaching figure behind her.

"Behind you!" Hawke shouted but could barely hear his own voice. His pulse quickened at seeing the threat close in, and despite his loss of equilibrium, Hawke lunged forward with his right arm circling around, intent on catching the assailant in a headlock before landing enough punches to subdue him. And then add in a few more for his taste in music.

But Hawke never got the chance. The assailant saw him coming and elbowed him squarely on the nose. He felt the soft crunch of cartilage and crashed backwards onto the hard ground.

Hawke squinted upwards at the assailant, a heavyset man with an angry volcano for a head. A burst of red hair shot straight back and his long beard flowed like raging lava down the side of a mountain.

"D'ya fuckin mind not fuckin kickin down my fuckin door, ya fuck?!"

"What the hell, Servo?!" Noor shouted as she struggled to her feet.

"What d'ya mean *what the hell, Servo?* This fuck broke into *my* fuckin home."

"You actually live down here?!" Hawke asked, still on his back.

"Better than fuckin dying up there, ya fuckface." Servo grabbed a piece of the broken door, a particularly pointy piece, and aimed it at Hawke's neck to emphasize his point.

"A little overboard, isn't it?" Noor asked.

"The fuck it is. The Cabal don't fuck around, so neither will I," Servo said. While he glared down the length of his makeshift weapon at Hawke, all Hawke could do was think that for a supposed secret organization, an awful lot of people seemed to know about the Cabal.

Servo, eventually deciding Hawke wasn't a threat, left him to check on Noor. Hawke got to his feet and got a better look at the Scotsman. He moved surprisingly fast for looking like his only link to exercise was through video games. He wore a faded plaid orange shirt that looked to have seen decades of punk rock shows and a gold cross dangled around his neck. His jeans were ripped, and not as a fashion statement. Hawke couldn't tell if the man was hipster or homeless. Living in an abandoned railway station made the guess even harder.

Servo handed Noor her dropped laptop bag and jerked his thumb at Hawke. "This the fuckin Suit everyone's been looking for?"

"I do have a name."

"Good for you, Suit. That a fuckin name belonging to a man who knows how'da fix a busted door?" Servo took another look at the splintered piece in his hand.

"Depends if my eyesight ever comes back," Hawke said as he rubbed his eyes. The ringing in his ears had begun to fade at least, but he was still seeing blurry white spots explode in his vision.

"Beats me. You the first fucker t'ever set off my security. Gotta say, it worked well. If nothing else, I'd say you make a fine guinea pig."

"Why would the Cabal even bother to look for you down here anyways?" Hawke asked.

Servo cocked his arm, but before he could hurl the piece of wood at Hawke's head, Noor stepped between them.

"Henry, this is Servo. He's the person I told you I trusted. And I'm sure he'll let us stay here short-term until we sort out our next move," Noor explained.

"Aye, right. Short-fucking-term," Servo grumbled. "C'mon Sara." Noor passed Hawke, her displeasure plastered across her face. Nobody invited Hawke to follow, but he did so anyway.

The passage was in slightly less disrepair than the rest of the station. Working light fixtures with dim bulbs lined the walls, and the floor had been swept clean so that it only looked old, instead of decrepit. It led them into a large concourse the size of a hockey rink with a ceiling that rose like a cathedral. A split-flap display from a bygone era hung precariously on rusted screws at the far end, its final destinations and arrivals frozen in time. Once conceived to be the bustling nexus of the train station, the concourse was now an empty shell without even the ghosts of its former travellers haunting it.

"Welcome back, Sara."

Noor stepped lightly as if she was visiting a graveyard. "What happened to this place? It used to be . . . alive."

Regret leaked into Servo's harsh voice. He said, "It was alive, or so I thought. But people fucked off. Guess it wasn't the lifestyle everyone really wanted."

"What is this place?" Hawke asked. To him it was an abandoned train station that for some reason had a security system. To Servo and Noor, apparently it had been something more.

"It's my Sanctuary. Pure barry, isn't it? A train station that the city ignored since a fire burned most parts to a fuckin crisp. I squatted and made it a place for drifters, punks, and anyone else who wanted to stay and contribute.

A stronghold of privacy against the mainstream, a safe haven for the counterculture that rejected all the bullshit we were told we had to endure. Some people visited, like Sara here who wanted to see if it was real. Others tried to make it a livable home."

Hawke decided he and Servo had a very different definition of *livable*. He continued talking about his Sanctuary as one does about an ex-lover after a few pints.

"We cleaned it right the fuck up, I'd say," Servo said, his thoughts in a different time. "We hooked up plumbing, tapped into the electrical grid without bothering to inform the city. And I might 'ave sliced into a nearby ethernet cable to bring us wireless internet. After all, I may be anti-social but I ain't a fuckin animal."

"But you're all alone down here now?" Noor asked.

"Pretty much. Like I said, people fucked off."

Hawke looked around the concourse and decided it was probably as good as squatting got, with its underground feng shui and ghetto living conditions that might be passable for a Ninja Turtle.

"Probably because it's a shit hole," Hawke said.

This time Noor didn't step between him and Servo, and Hawke only caught a fleeting glimpse of a wooden projectile flying towards him, before he felt a crack on the side of his head that made everything go black.

SERVO'S HOME

"I'd either get better at dodging projectiles or better at complimenting people's homes if I were you," Noor admonished as she dabbed a cold washcloth on the side of Hawke's head.

"Good advice," Hawke agreed. He had momentarily lost consciousness but had to admit Servo had a good arm. Accurate and with good velocity. Starting pitcher in the Bitcoin Intramural Baseball League, no doubt.

"You've stopped bleeding for now." She dumped the washcloth unceremoniously in his hands to let him finish dealing with it.

Hawke touched his head and inspected his hand for blood. "Wonder if I need stitches."

"Depends if you don't get better at dodging projectiles or better at complimenting people's homes."

Hawke and Noor were in the Sanctuary's kitchen, formerly the train station employee canteen. A lime-green fridge was squeezed into one corner, claimed from the dump and repaired just enough to keep the milk from turning sour. The appliances included a hot plate covered in a thin layer of bacon grease and a drip coffee machine that exhausted burnt coffee into the air.

He was surprised to find himself seated at a picnic table in place of a regular kitchen table, one that Servo would say was repurposed from a nearby park and the cops would say was stolen in the middle of the night.

Servo entered with a laptop tucked under his arm and sported what Hawke came to realize was his trademark frown. That quickly changed to a smirk at seeing Hawke in mild discomfort.

"Hey man, I really like your kitchen," Hawke said, nodding at Noor to emphasize his lesson learned. She just huffed and rolled her eyes.

"What the fuck does he mean by that?" Servo's frown returned and he raised an eyebrow at Noor.

"I think he means it to be an olive branch." Noor leaned against the wall with her arms crossed.

Servo grunted and neither accepted nor declined Hawke's offering. He sat down on the other side of the picnic table and set up his laptop. He checked the contents of an unhealthy number of half-drunk coffee mugs strewn about the table before settling on what he deemed to be the freshest. "A'ight, Sara. You asked me for help, so what is it?"

"We have a problem."

"Ye don't say? Suit here is all over the news feeds. Shived a partner over a failed business deal of some sort." Servo raised an eyebrow at Hawke. "You actually do it, Suit?

"Of course not."

Servo studied him carefully. "I dunno, you look like you could do it."

Hawke changed the subject. "Have you heard anything about an incident in Birmingham involving a lawyer?"

"Why the fuck would I?"

"It's important," Noor said. "Someone innocent was hurt. We don't know how badly." Noor explained what had transpired at Monsef's office: the Cabal agent with Shariff, Inspector Smith, the cricket bat. But she failed to mention why she had been there. Servo grunted his sympathies and turned his attention to the laptop. Noor hovered over his shoulder.

"Nothing in the media bout that," he said after a cursory glance at the mainstream news sites.

Hawke let them continue their search for Monsef and walked to the kitchen counter, found the garbage, and tossed the washcloth. With Servo and Noor huddled around the computer, Hawke felt like a third wheel. Regardless, he positioned himself to see what they were doing and was impressed at how Servo played the keyboard like an instrument. Social media feeds instantly danced across the screen, but no mention of a kidnapping or a lawyer being attacked. It was unsurprising that Servo preferred Linux for an operating system, as most coders do—and Hawke himself had tried to use it on that troublesome night back at his college library, where he nearly deleted the entire school network.

With a few more keystrokes, the social media feeds were replaced with walls of text flashing by, which Servo and Noor processed with ease. Hawke struggled to recognize any but a few of the commands Servo played into the computer. But it didn't escape his notice that the words *National Health Service* were oft-repeated. It quickly dawned on him that Servo was hacking the NHS.

"There!" Noor pointed to an entry below a table titled Queen Elizabeth Birmingham Hospital. "Check out that admission record."

Servo obliged. "'Is that your guy? Monsef, Nabeel?"

"Yeah, that's him. Is he okay?" Hawke said, the feeling of apprehension growing as he hoped for the best; Monsef had simply been an innocent party caught up in this madness.

"Aye, he's fine. No heart attack. Just in the hospital eating that shit food while they monitor him."

Both Noor and Hawke let out a sigh of relief. He felt Monsef was his responsibility, his fault that the Cabal had showed up at his door and nearly killed him. Without Hawke's pursuit of Satoshi's Fortune, right now Monsef would be saying goodbye to his family before heading off to work for another day of helping clients bullied by the banks. It was in stark contrast to how he felt about Bernie Bitcoin—and he had actually died. It obviously wasn't acceptable for the Cabal to murder anyone, regardless of whether they were a snake oil salesman or an underdog lawyer, but Hawke hadn't implicated Bernie and therefore wouldn't allow himself to get emotional about the murder. He didn't know if that made him pragmatic or just ruthless.

Noor's phone vibrated with the arrival of a text message. She quickly excused herself, which left Hawke and Servo uncomfortably alone together.

Servo busied himself on his laptop and acted as if he were alone in the kitchen. Hawke did his best impression of an uninvited house guest, which he supposed he was, and wandered aimlessly around the kitchen: checking out the coffee maker, examining the contents of the fridge, and generally wasting time. He didn't know the next step to finding Satoshi's Fortune, but he was pretty sure this wasn't it.

Instead of waiting for Noor to return and smooth things over with Servo, Hawke decided to take it upon himself. He knew one fact that would undoubtedly bring Servo out of his abrasive shell, as it seemed to be a point of interest to all he had met in the bitcoin world. He sat down across the table and cleared his throat. He braced himself for the reaction.

"Peter Finlay was my uncle," Hawke said.

"What the fuck do I care who your uncle was?" Servo didn't look up from the laptop.

Hawke was underwhelmed. And confused.

"Didn't you know him?"

"Of course I did. So what?"

Hawke was further confused.

"I just thought . . . I don't know what I thought. My uncle's name keeps coming up involving bitcoin and Satoshi's Fortune and I thought you'd know something about it."

"Satoshi's Fortune? Don't tell me you've bought into that nonsense?"

"It's the greatest fortune of the twenty-first century."

"So I hear. It's also a waste of time, much like your visit here."

Hawke was puzzled. "You don't want to keep bitcoin out of the hands of the Cabal? I mean, if they find the fortune first, it would mean the death of bitcoin."

"Where'd you hear that bullshit?" Servo scoffed.

"Aziz. He came to me a few days ago and long story short, he's entrusted me to find the Fortune."

Servo's laugh was heavy and harsh and grated on Hawke's ears. "One mention of a hidden fortune and suddenly you're Nathan Drake!"

Hawke shrugged. "Aziz wants me to destroy it, send the entirety of the fortune to a provably unspendable address to show the world that nobody will ever be able to spend it."

"You're telling me if you had control of nearly one million bitcoins, you would actually do that? It hasn't crossed your mind that Aziz is insane and maybe you could keep the coins yourself, make yourself wealthy in the process of *saving* bitcoin?"

Hawke didn't want to lie so he remained silent.

Servo stopped working and crossed his arms. He looked across the table at Hawke with the distaste of someone forced to deal with a used car salesman.

"I get it, Suit. You're a banker on some free trip to London where you get to talk to cute girls with cuter English accents and expense everything you can on the corporate card. In return for that excitement and escaping some boring-ass desk job for a few days, all you have to do is listen to some nerds prattle on about some backwards math project. And then, salvation! A prophet shows up and tells you tales of an international conspiracy and how seeking a hidden fortune will make you a hero, a renegade, a rebel. It's perfect for you, innit? Money, adventure, and something to fucking do with your life."

Hawke's eyes narrowed like a used car salesman who had a customer who actually knew something about cars.

"You don't think Satoshi's Fortune exists?"

Servo sighed like Hawke had offered to throw in a free oil change.

"Of course it does. What I'm saying is Satoshi's Fortune doesn't matter. If the Cabal isn't coming after us for that, it'll be something else. Don't get me wrong, they'll stop at nothing to fuck us up—but Aziz is fighting them for salted earth. His first inclination is to burn everything to the ground and start over, without asking himself if that land is even worth taking over. But anarchists are more than happy to cut their nose off to spite their face, so long as everyone notices them doing it."

"How would you classify yourself then?" Hawke asked.

"Cypherpunk, I guess."

"Sounds nerdy and threatening at the same time," Hawke remarked. It elicited the beginnings of a wry smile from Servo.

"If nothing else, I want to write code. Build something instead of tearing it down. Create a free society where privacy and security are paramount, where the individual matters more than the state. And right now, one of the biggest hurdles is that only the state can create money. That is, until bitcoin came about. It's private, it's secure, and doesn't need the state's blessing. And that's why the Cabal will always come after us, regardless of what happens to Satoshi's Fortune. If you ask me, Satoshi would have been better off just deleting the wallet." Servo paused, maybe hearing himself articulating his thoughts for the first time, and then stole a glance at the silver watch around Hawke's wrist. "But fuck it, you want to rebel against the world and get rich, right?"

The cypherpunk and banker sat across from each other, neither knowing what to say next or if they were allies, enemies, or something else altogether.

Eventually Servo stood. "That's enough bullshit for now. Time for everyone to get some rest. I've been up all night and I'm assuming Noor has been, too."

Hawke checked his watch. "But it's already 7 a.m."

"Don't worry about it, Suit. You won't miss the revolution if you sleep in." Servo gathered his laptop and gave it a good-natured tap. "Because when it comes to cypherpunks and anarchists, nobody rebels before noon."

AGENT 21'S MORNING

Sergeant Monica Chan had spent over a decade with the Metropolitan Police Services and had never been involved in an arrest as bizarre as the one that now had the station talking in conspiratorial whispers. It started last night, an uneventful Sunday evening until they received a message on the Emergency 999 line that claimed there was an armed kidnapping in progress along with a precise GPS location.

The first clue that this incident would make its way into police lore was that the message was not a real person but a digital voice. The second was that the message, in addition to the Emergency 999 line, was blasted to every number registered to the force.

Regardless of the unorthodox delivery, the message was treated seriously and the Specialist Firearms Command was deployed. The team found the apartment, determined that there was a hostage situation, and executed a clean entry. They subdued a suspect without incident and rescued a clearly traumatized victim. For all intents and purposes, it was a perfect operation.

And then it all went sideways.

While receiving much-needed medical attention in an ambulance, the victim freaked out, jumped out the back, and ran off into the night. He had yet to be found on any of the CCTV cameras that blanketed London.

And he wasn't even the most bizarre individual they came across that night. The suspect who had been arrested and delivered to Chan offered no resistance, or any information. So far she had been unable to confirm his identity even though the Specialist Firearms Command found a cache of passports that bore his photograph. Unnervingly, the man didn't make a sound—not a grunt of acknowledgement or even a clearing of his throat. When questioned about the events surrounding his arrest he reacted as the sea would to a drowning man's pleas. With muted indifference.

Only when the suspect was forced to part with two smartphones and a micro-SD card during processing did he show any emotion: a brief but intense twitch of his lips, enough to send the hairs on the back of Chan's neck reeling.

Adding to the unease spreading through the station, the police chief himself had made an unexpected appearance. Incongruous in civilian clothes, and deep bags under his eyes, the Chief took Chan aside and ordered her to lose any paperwork involving the suspect and place him in a holding cell alone until morning. He then told her their conversation never took place and left out the back door.

Chan wondered if she was doing something illegal as she shredded the paperwork, as ordered. She spent the rest of the longest night of her career pretending to do menial tasks while actually watching the suspect in the holding cell out of the corner of her eye.

Her mind wandered to the most disturbing villains she had come across: the gardener who slayed an entire family in their sleep and buried them in their own garden; a small-time drug dealer who defiled a dozen women who had come to him begging for a fix; a neo-Nazi gang leader who threatened her and her family with the most vile and racist threats anyone had ever heard.

But none had triggered the primal sense of dread that this silent man had.

Since being placed in his private cell, she hadn't seen him move.

Not to scratch an itch.

Not to stretch his legs.

He had just sat quietly and stared into nothingness.

When morning finally came, Chan immediately followed the captain's orders and released him from his holding cell. She escorted him to the admission desk and returned his phones and micro-SD card, which he did not sign for but readily accepted. Made whole again, he took a long look around the usually bustling station, which had slowed to an eerie stillness. Every officer seemed to be aware of the man's presence and instinctively kept a nervous eye on him.

Then, without any further acknowledgement of his surroundings, the silent man abruptly turned and walked out the front doors of the police station, and other than his memory burned into Chan's mind, it was as if he had never been there.

***

Agent 21 was again a man without a name. All his Cabal identities compromised in the raid on the safe house, those mirages of men were now dead to the world. He stood on the steps of the police station, indifferent to the cool morning air despite wearing only his suit jacket, and surveyed the Monday morning traffic that was starting to clog the streets.

There was no mistaking the reason for his overnight stay. Agent 21 should have been released before he even had a chance to breathe the stale air of the holding cell, but Rickard wanted to send a message; there is no room for failure within the Cabal. And Agent 21's failure was two-fold. He had let Henry Hawke escape, albeit with some assistance from an unknown ally. And worse yet, he had fallen for Shariff's amateur swatting trick.

But despite the setbacks, Agent 21 knew he again possessed the key to Rickard's good graces—the wallet file to Satoshi's Fortune ripped straight out of the Shariff's mouth. And on top of that, for his own personal use, he had Shariff's smartphone, which surely must contain previously unknown data on Satoshi that Agent 21 desperately wanted.

Agent 21 watched a black Mercedes-Benz sedan pull up to the curb. The driver exited and acknowledged him with a nod before walking away, leaving the car still running and the driver door open. Agent 21 took position behind the wheel and merged into traffic while awaiting his next set of instructions. It was a short wait. His phone rang from an unknown number before he had gone two blocks.

"Yes?" he answered.

"Good morning, my boy. I trust you weren't too uncomfortable last night?"

"No issues."

"Very good." Rickard paused. "And what news have you?"

Agent 21 dutifully transcribed the events from the night before right up until he had answered Rickard's call, including the acquisition of the wallet file but excluding the reason he had turned on Shariff's phone.

"Anything else?" Rickard let the question linger.

Agent 21 was uncertain if his superior was fishing, or wanted an admission. "Nothing of note. I'll intensify my search to identify the Keepers of the Fortune immediately."

"There's been a slight change of plans," Rickard announced. "I have taken it upon myself, due to your lack of results, to identify them myself. I paid a visit to our friend Andrew Cohen. I've long suspected he wasn't being completely truthful with you, Agent 21, and of course I was right."

Agent 21 aggressively changed lanes to the honking protest of a black cab. He did not like Rickard speaking to his Assets. They were his to manage and his alone. But he could not speak such a truth aloud. Something comparable to rage began to form, but it was quickly dissolved with a deep breath. Such emotion would not get him any closer to Satoshi. But Cohen's new information might. "Please elaborate," he said.

"My good boy, Cohen gave me information we previously didn't have—the emails of the Keepers of Satoshi's Fortune. We already knew about Aziz Shariff. Another is clearly Johan Jarvenpaa. One email address owner is so far unidentified, but Agent Dunwoody is continuing her research."

Shariff had the wallet file. So Jarvenpaa and the person behind the unidentified email each had a password. Jarvenpaa would be easily found and broken, but if they couldn't find the person behind the untraceable email, then the last Keeper would take on even more importance.

"Do we know who the last email belongs to?" Agent 21 asked.

Rickard's flair for the dramatic was unwelcome and Agent 21 could hear the old man bang what was undoubtedly his serpent cane twice on the floor, but he suffered through it to find out what he did not know.

"It is none other than your old acquaintance Peter Finlay."

Agent 21 nearly blew through a red light, but managed to stop with a squeal of his tires, much to the disgust of pedestrians about to cross.

Peter Finlay.

The reason for the collision between bitcoin and the Cabal, however inevitable it may have been. And he was a Keeper? Agent 21 had reason to be skeptical of the claim, but he would remain silent on the matter. If it were true, what had become of Finlay's password? Memorized and lost to some pathetic icy river in Illinois? Hidden among his estate files and documents already seized and reviewed by the Cabal? Or did Hawke, Finlay's last remaining relative, suddenly have a more important role to play? It would certainly make sense why Shariff was recruiting him.

Agent 21 stirred in his seat and impatiently waited for the light to turn green. "This was unknown at the time of the interrogation."

"Yes, yes it was. And I cannot fault you, my boy. You were just following procedures, if not a bit overzealously," Rickard conceded. "But the landscape has changed since then. We now know gaining control of Satoshi's Fortune is paramount to our success. With that in mind can I assume that, despite your carelessness, you successfully acquired Mr. Shariff's wallet file?"

"You are correct." Agent 21 tapped his pocket slightly and continued his drive through the thickening London traffic. Rain pellets began to smack his windshield and traffic further slowed.

"Excellent, my boy! Now we just need two of the three passwords! Steps have already been taken to ensure Jarvenpaa will be receptive to our forthcoming offer. As I said, Dunwoody is hot on the trail of the unidentified email owner."

"Very good. I'll resume my search for Henry Hawke and Finlay's password."

"You'll do no such thing," Rickard snapped. "You've proven too easily distracted when it comes to that family. If you had properly done your job, you would have immediately known that Hawke was Finlay's nephew and detained him before he knew what hit him. Instead I'm sending you to Sweden to intercept Jarvenpaa and personally deliver our offer. Agent Dunwoody will provide you the details. And don't forget to deal with that abscessed tooth before you leave London; he's giving me troubles."

"What about Hawke?" Agent 21 asked, having no interest in giving up his pursuit.

"The first attempt to lure him in failed," Rickard said. "The Chicago Asset failed. But it did allow us to trace Hawke's phone and determine he was northbound outside of Birmingham. I've taken it upon myself to tap some newly motivated Assets. It's safe to assume they favour the more intense means we wouldn't want to be associated with."

Agent 21 was unaware of any means he wasn't prepared to use. "What Assets?"

"The Bratva," Rickard said, his own self-congratulation apparent. "They've been somehow led to believe that Hawke is responsible for their unfortunate misplacement of bitcoins a few months back. They'll be compelled to find him. To aid them in their little quest, you will provide them with all your intel. Is that understood, my boy?"

The Bratva? Agent 21 immediately questioned the old man's judgment to send Russian gangsters after Hawke. To find him now would require a delicate touch and strategic thinking—not a task suitable for an organization whose first reaction to any obstacle was to bludgeon it to death.

Agent 21's grip on the steering wheel tightened, but his voice did not betray him. "Understood," he replied indifferently.

"One last thing. I know you've continued to press your Boston Asset for more information about who Satoshi is, but believe me that well is now dry. And I can only assume this preoccupation somehow played a role in Shariff getting the best of you. I've been willing to pay the price for your obsession in return for your flawless results, but you've started to test my patience so I'm going to state this once; knowing who Satoshi is does not matter—only finding his fortune does. Am I perfectly clear, *my boy?*"

Agent 21 did not answer.

"Excellent!" Rickard said regardless. "Now finish up your London business and then off to Sweden with you. It's a little chilly there so make sure to dress warm. Oh, and don't forget to provide a copy of the wallet file to Agent Dunwoody. After all, it's Cabal property now."

Rickard ended the call.

Agent 21 continued driving amid the intensifying downpour, and when a sedan made an inadvertent lane change and cut him off, Agent 21 smashed his fist down on the horn as hard as he could.

HAWKE'S MORNING

Deep within the abandoned train station, hidden away from the Cabal's prying electronic eyes and crowbar-wielding Russians, Henry Hawke wanted to do anything but sleep. The room Servo had provided, while never to receive a five-star review, was more comfortable than he expected to find in a cypherpunk's underground sanctuary. The floor still had the odd splintered floorboard to avoid, but it was swept clean of debris. Old pipes rattled unseen behind the walls as water flowed, a noisy reminder that the dwelling did indeed have working plumbing.

After a few hours of tossing and turning, Hawke checked his watch. It read 10:00 a.m.

Too early to rebel, too late to stay in bed.

Hawke rolled off an army cot and stretched his legs. They were stiff, too long unused. His wrists and ankles were a different kind of sore, chafed and red from his capture at Monsef's. He could feel the swelling at the point where Servo's elbow had met his nose, but nothing worse than he'd received during any number of hockey games growing up. A headache from where Servo had hit him with a piece of wood had come and gone, and only a minor cut remained. Hawke sniff-tested his dress shirt.

Passable if he were a freshman in a rush, but not ideal for . . . what was he now? A fortune hunter? A wannabe bitcoiner? Wanted for murder? Unemployed?

After he was done failing to redefine himself, Hawke noticed a cardboard box in the corner, the type a fired employee would fill with pointless knick-knacks and pictures of family. Judging by the layer of dust on the box lid, Hawke figured the owner was long gone. Inside he found a ball cap, a Henley shirt, jeans, and scuffed desert boots that looked to be his size. He went down a different passage off the foyer and found a fully equipped bathroom. Hawke showered and dressed in the commandeered clothes. It was the first time he was outside a suit since this whole bitcoin ordeal began. The only remnant of his old life was the silver watch secure around his wrist.

Hawke looked in the mirror and pronounced himself ready to go rogue.

Now all he needed was to know how.

Hawke checked the kitchen and then the concourse. No sign of the others. Noor was no doubt asleep from the exhaustion of driving all night, and Servo, like many coders, probably kept a vampire's sleeping schedule. Had they been awake, they would most assuredly have told him to err on the side of caution and stay put.

Luckily for Hawke, neither were.

AGENT 21'S LOOSE END

A calmer Agent 21 made his way across London and fired off two text messages. One to Dunwoody for the details for his Stockholm trip. The other to his London Asset to meet not far from the compromised safe house. Agent 21 arrived first and parked by the curb. Knowing the Asset would be late, he called Dunwoody for an update. She happily greeted him on the first ring.

"I have your flight arranged with your backup documentation, *Agent Blankfein*. Hangar 35B at Heathrow. Your standard kit will be available on board. I've confirmed the target has already checked in and his flight will depart London on schedule. Local authorities in Stockholm will hold the target until your arrival."

Agent Dunwoody never failed to have all the pieces in place before they were needed. Agent 21 wondered if she ever admitted to herself just what kind of acts her superb organizational skills had allowed to take place. But then decided it was irrelevant—if she suddenly developed a conscience, then Rickard would have a new agent in her place before the corpse was cold. And the only difference to Agent 21 would be a different voice on the end of the line.

"Anything else?" the current cheery voice asked.

Agent 21 weighed Rickard's direct order to provide the Bratva with intel against his desire to pursue Henry Hawke.

Why exactly had Hawke gone to Monsef's office?

Who had helped him escape from Inspector Smith?

Just how much did Peter Finlay's nephew know?

Did he know who Satoshi Nakamoto was?

The Cabal agent came to the conclusion that it would be unwise to let the Bratva get their hands on Hawke. He asked Dunwoody to cross-reference some specific pieces of data gleaned from his conversation with Rickard that he thought should help answer at least some of his questions.

"That's brilliant, Agent 21!" Dunwoody exclaimed after listening to his request. "I'll do that right away. If you're right, the Bratva will have completed their assignment in no time."

"Agent Dunwoody, I request that you hold off sharing that information. I want to verify its accuracy to be certain, because after last night . . . " Agent 21 hoped he imitated a forlorn individual well enough to gain Dunwoody's sympathy, as she would know he couldn't afford another failure.

"Excellent idea, Agent 21. I'll do the research on my end and keep the results just for you. They should be ready by the time you land in Stockholm."

Agent 21 agreed. With her results in his control, he could dole it out to the Russians as he saw fit, keeping them perpetually one step away from Hawke.

While Agent 21 was considering all the moving parts to his plan, a late model BMW parked down the street. It was in need of a wash and the driver flashed his lights at him, which was unnecessary because Agent 21 knew the licence plate by heart. The action was an annoyance and another symptom of the Asset's inefficiency.

"I have to go." Agent 21 ended the call, hearing Dunwoody's fading question go unanswered, "What about the wallet file . . . "

The Cabal agent unhurriedly approached the BMW, his hair quickly dampened and suit jacket growing heavier with rain. He opened the car door and brushed fast food containers and paper coffee cups aside so he could sit down.

"Tell me everything that happened at Monsef's office," Agent 21 instructed the man sitting behind the wheel.

Inspector Smith puffed on a cigarette already smoked down to the filter. He inched his window down and tossed the butt out. "My head's fine by the way."

Agent 21 didn't blink.

"And I took a big risk for you. I had to dodge and weave a lot of awkward questions with the Chief yesterday. It was an expensive ordeal . . ." Smith combined a raised eyebrow with a nicotine-stained smile. It was the usual song and dance. He regularly wanted more money for his services, which was never a problem. Money was something that the Cabal literally had a licence to print.

"The cost has been added to your next payment. Now tell me, why was Hawke at Monsef's office?"

Smith left the engine running with the heat on, which didn't address the dampness but kept the air heavy with the smell of tobacco and unwashed skin. The wipers made an occasional pass as the rain drummed the windshield.

"I dunno, you heard as much as I did," Smith snarked.

"Who rescued Hawke?" Agent 21 was careful not to ask "Who knocked you out?" as the inspector's weak ego would likely be too offended to continue with the debriefing.

"I dunno, you watched the video as it happened."

Agent 21's expression remained passive, which in turn put Smith on the defensive.

"Learn to fuckin blink, would ya? You're supposed to be some master spy, shouldn't you know all this already?"

The remark shouldn't have generated a reaction from Agent 21, and Smith didn't see one.

"You are correct, Inspector Smith, I should know everything about this assignment. Your debriefing is over."

Before the Metropolitan Police Services inspector could ask about when his payment would be deposited, Agent 21 drove two fingers into his neck, causing an expected choking sound akin to a drowning sack of cats. Satisfied that Smith's voice box was collapsing, Agent 21 then picked up a pen lying in the centre console tray and jabbed it deeply into the middle of the ungrateful inspector's neck and twisted like it was a melon baller, paralyzing him from the neck down. Smith's arms crumpled to his side and his legs flopped apart. His lungs stopped responding to his panicky brain signals and struggled to a halt like a sailboat losing its wind. His only recourse was a pathetic attempt at a scream that failed to even be heard over the raindrops on the windshield.

Agent 21 observed the inspector's insipid final moments with a detached boredom, like watching a movie he had seen so many times he could repeat it from memory; the eyeballs darted about like two caged mice trying to scratch their way out, the silent last words frantically mouthed—transposable pleas for help, prayers for forgiveness, and promises of revenge. None of it mattered to Agent 21. He was simply waiting out Smith's clock.

A stillness began to fall over the inspector; only the sweat dripping from his forehead and minute movements of his tongue told Agent 21 his ghost had not yet departed. Agent 21 mused that perhaps the ghost was waiting for the final payment to be deposited, unaware that money would not help him at his next destination.

The Cabal agent waited another minute, not unaware that Inspector Smith's last act was to waste his time, until Smith's eyes finally glazed over and no whiffs of life remained. His task of tying up the London loose end complete, Agent 21 wiped down any surface he had touched and stepped back out into the rain.

He returned to his car and drove to Heathrow without giving the inspector a second thought. At the airport a private jet awaited him at hangar 35B, and he was welcomed aboard by a flight attendant who knew not to ask too many questions as the twin engines fired up. Within minutes they were in the air and the flight attendant handed him a briefcase as graciously as one would a Fabergé egg.

Inside was his standard kit: a sharpened blade, oiled .22 sidearm with extra clip, stacks of US dollars and euros, a tablet filled with copies of all his dossiers, and a set of IDs in the name of Agent Blankfein of Interpol. Scrolling through his assignment, Agent 21 learned he was investigating the overnight assault of two young women at a downtown London hotel. And in a coincidence that was anything but, the women had identified their attacker as the same man whom Rickard had just discovered was of great interest to the Cabal—Mr. Johan Jarvenpaa.

SERVO'S SONG

"You're a fuckin idiot!" Servo's unruly hair and beard flared out in every direction as he shouted at Hawke. He wore a faded second-hand black T-shirt with THIS T-SHIRT IS A MUNITION stamped across the front in large white text. Printed below the header was the Perl code for RSA algorithm, one of the earliest uses of private-public keys to encrypt messages.

The United States had classified the algorithm as a munition alongside chemical and biological weapons, tanks, and heavy weapons and banned its export, reasoning they didn't want their enemies to be able to encrypt their own communications. Cypherpunks saw it as an attempt to limit an individual's right to privacy from government snooping. The protest T-shirt was a way to point out the impossibility of enforcing the since-lifted ban, as the T-shirt's mere presence in Scotland had proved.

And that threat of government snooping that Hawke may have brought down on Servo was what now had him all riled up. "Fuckin idiot."

Servo and Noor were in the kitchen having breakfast when Hawke returned from his stroll about town. Hawke turned to Noor for sympathy, but the shrug of her shoulders only conveyed an endorsement of Servo's opinion.

"Don't fuckin look to her! I let you into my home, my sanctuary, and you go and parade yourself around Glasgow and all its CCTV cameras like some social media attention whore! Tell me, did you notice a trail of cops following you? Tell me, Suit, did ya?"

" . . . I'm not actually wearing a suit anymore."

"Yeah, I noticed that, too." Servo's anger was compounded by Hawke's borrowing of clothes that did not belong to him. "But anyways, did you even stop to think you might be putting me and Noor at risk? Those CCTV cameras could spot you a mile away!"

"I wore a hat."

Servo turned a fiery red. "Oh, well, you wore a fuckin hat! Fuckin brilliant! Guess the state's billion-dollar surveillance network is useless now that you found its weakness. Just wear a fuckin hat!"

"It was pulled down tight."

"Is he a fuckin idiot?" Servo turned to Noor.

Noor swallowed a bite of her avocado toast. "The jury's still out."

Hawke grew exasperated. "Look, I just went out to look around. And besides, it's me they're looking for. You have nothing to worry about."

Servo only saw an interloper into his world. One who didn't comprehend the risks. "Why the fuck do you think I put that security system in place? To keep Jehovah Witnesses away? No, it's because I'm sure the Cabal has spent months looking for me!"

"Why would they be after you?"

"Because I'm a fucking Keeper of the fucking Fortune!"

Servo's announcement tilted the axis of the room. Hawke felt like he'd been physically knocked off balance. Servo hoped it was dawning on Hawke that he wasn't the only person with a target on his back.

Once the shock faded Hawke had another question for Servo. "Your email is Proverb211@vistomail.com?"

"How the fuck do you know that?"

Hawke searched his pocket and withdrew an orange flash drive.

"The information Aziz wanted me to have. I know the emails of the Keepers of the Fortune."

Servo glanced at Noor, who shrugged.

"It would seem that way," she said.

"Fuck."

"But this is fantastic news!" Hawke said. "We almost have enough to find the fortune! Sara, can you reach out to Johan?"

Noor didn't seem excited, more like inconvenienced by helping Hawke. But she relented. "I don't see why not."

"Great, even without my uncle's password all we need to do is find Aziz."

"Who said I'm going to give you my password?" Servo said, crossing his arms. Here was this Suit barging into his home, throwing private information around, and dictating what was going to happen. *Who the hell put him in charge?*

"We need to find Satoshi's Fortune before the Cabal. This is our chance."

"This is not a good idea." Servo said.

"How can you think that? It's nearly one million bitcoins."

"If you don't believe me or don't get it, I don't have time to try and convince you, sorry." Servo had had enough. He left his unfinished breakfast behind and stomped out of the room, trying to remember why he had opened his door to Noor and Hawke—when he remembered he hadn't. It had literally been kicked in.

Servo was a man who took his ales and his privacy seriously, and had little time for lagers and publicity. And even less for being told what to do. *A Cypherpunk's Manifesto* declared that *Privacy is the power to selectively reveal oneself to the world,* and Servo wasn't ready to reveal himself or his password. He had come to terms with the fact that they would always be after him for something—the fortune, Satoshi himself—but didn't want to make himself a bigger target.

And Servo, like everyone else, didn't know who Satoshi was, but he had little doubt the investor of bitcoin was also a dyed-in-the-wool cypherpunk, and Servo was always secretly pleased when someone in the online communities also referred to Satoshi as one. Cypherpunk was a term first coined in 1992 by a hacker who went by St. Jude at the first meeting of a group of like-minded individuals. They all saw privacy as a pillar of an open digital society and advocated for the use of cryptography to achieve it, resulting in *A Cypherpunk's Manifesto* that outlined these views. And when Servo had read the manifesto as a thirteen-year-old, it spoke to him in ways he understood the Bible spoke to his deeply religious father. The cypherpunks' own holy trinity, however, was more empirical than divine. Anonymous email systems, digital signatures, and, lastly, an electronic currency.

That electronic currency was often discussed in the cypherpunk community—the HTML protocol even had a placeholder for its eventual creation—and attempts were made over the years, such as David Chaum's DigiCash, Nick Szabo's Bit Gold—but none fully realized the goal.

And then, almost casually, definitely surprisingly, like a thirty-year-old carpenter seemingly appearing out of nothingness with a message of love and tolerance that spread faster and was embraced more thoroughly than those in power were comfortable with, Satoshi materialized out of the internet ether with his own message of public-private keys, proof of work, and an immutable public ledger.

The electronic currency was now a reality.

And Servo had ferociously absorbed the bitcoin whitepaper, his new testament, and felt humbled and insignificant before it. Almost immediately he threw himself into the project, writing code, discussing its implications, and arguing about what path bitcoin should take. It brought him into online conversations with Satoshi himself and people who Servo saw as his disciples: Shariff, Jarvenpaa, Noor, and Finlay.

At the same time, his Sanctuary was alive and growing. More anti-establishment individuals unwilling or unable to accept the status quo arrived. Some just passed through and some spoke of making it their home. Servo couldn't have imagined a time in his life when he was so fulfilled.

And then reality set in and the Scriptures of his youth reared their ugly head. *And I looked and behold a pale horse. And the man who sat on him was death. And Hell followed.*

But for Servo it wasn't a horse but a man with no name. It wasn't death but the Cabal. But it most certainly was Hell that followed.

Peter Finlay dead. Andrew Cohen playing Judas. Satoshi gone with only the four Keepers of the Fortune, and an empty digital tomb left in his place.

Servo couldn't tell if the collapse of his Sanctuary was caused by the manifestation of his stress of all things crypto or the attempt at counterculture running its course, but here he was all alone.

The cypherpunk walked through the concourse and arrived at a door that was silhouetted in a soft glow, a familiar angry hum emanating from within. He rattled the century-old door knob to open the door and was hit by the hot breath of a dozen growling computers that made the room feel alive. A former office had been transformed into a space where he did his deepest thinking and most meaningful work, a kind of rectory within his Sanctuary. An L-shaped desk was nested in one corner, equipped with dual monitors and covered in electronic parts and stained coffee mugs. Opposite the desk was a rack of specialized bitcoin mining computers doing their best to secure the network, one block at a time.

Servo sat down and instantly regretted not bringing a fresh mug of coffee. He tapped on a keyboard and brought the screens to life and, in an attempt to escape his unwanted guests, dove headlong into cyberspace. He checked the online forums for any developments, verified that his miners were successfully hashing away, and updated some custom programs that were flying across the blockchain non-stop. He reset his security system as best he could, linking a manual trigger to the sound and light systems to his smartphone until the door could be replaced.

Focusing solely on the digital world, Servo became oblivious to his physical surroundings and failed to hear the approaching footsteps over the drone of his computers. His solitude was shattered when a hand fell on his shoulder. Servo immediately spun in his chair and smashed up against his desk. His fists shot up in preparation to defend himself, and only lowered when he realized who had violated his space, yet again.

"What the fuck are you doin?" Servo cursed.

"I hadn't been sworn at for a few hours so I thought I'd see how you're doing," Hawke said as he kept a steaming mug of coffee from spilling. He kept a mocking smile on his lips that implied he knew something nobody else did, which Servo doubted was true.

"Can't you piss off Sara instead?"

"Oh I tried, but she just looked annoyed and rolled her eyes. You're much more interactive, albeit a bit repetitive."

"Well fuck."

"Exactly. And here, brought this for you." Hawke set the mug down on the desk, which Servo ignored and returned his focus to his screen, hoping the intruder would take the message and leave. The silence rang loud until Hawke cleared his throat, either not noticing or not caring about Servo's desire to be left alone.

"So you're named after electronics or something?" Hawke asked.

"What?" Servo made no effort to hide his irritation.

"Servo . . . servos . . . are you named after electronics?"

"Are you named after a fuckin bird?"

"What?"

"Hawke . . . hawk."

"I just thought Servo was a nickname. Like an anonymous hacker thing."

"No, it's the hand I've been dealt. Servo is my family name." *A strict religious family he hadn't spoken to since he was a teenager.*

"Sorry, I wasn't trying to be smart . . . "

"You were never at risk of that," Servo snapped.

The changes were minute. A hardening of his eyes, a flattening of his smile. Hawke was no longer wearing the public face of an irresponsible smartass banker that everyone assumed him to be. Servo was unexpectedly reminded of the old Blàr boys, three brothers and former SAS soldiers that were common fixtures in his working-class neighbourhood growing up. They could be affable, even charming—he knew his mother always made sure to put on her nicest dress for social events when they were

279

expected to attend—but they each had cold, hard stares that you were always the first to look away from. They also sported the telltale scars of past fights, and what had always confused Servo was how they wore them—not as wounds, but as rewards for a life of adventure and violence. Servo decided Hawke wouldn't look out of place sharing a pint with them.

"If you had one million bitcoins at your fingertips right now, what would you do?" Servo was surprised to hear himself ask the question. He had met many of Hawke's kind since bitcoin had gained traction; if he wasn't in it for the money, it was for the adventure. In all likelihood, next week the Suit would be in a glass office telling his colleagues of the exhilarating time he went slumming outside the fiat banking system and almost got rich.

But Hawke didn't answer straightaway, and Servo witnessed a myriad of conflicting emotions pass through him. Some he expected, a glimmer of greed and maybe— no definitely—some mischief dancing in his eyes. Some he hadn't, self-doubt quickly masked by a thin, cruel smile, indecisiveness obscured by standing tall with his shoulders back. When Hawke finally spoke, he hit all the notes a corporate Suit would: money and value, growth and profit, with lip service to the community, social good, and charity. It could have been pulled from a bank's annual report.

It wasn't so much the content that made Servo want to puke but the banality of it all. He couldn't help but notice that Hawke's expression didn't match his words, as if he were reading the script of a play he knew was shit.

Servo tilted his head. "So make more money, eh, Suit? That's what you'd do with it?"

"Nothing wrong with that," Hawke defended. "You think the infrastructure around bitcoin will just pop up without serious investment? It's going to take a lot of time and money before cryptocurrencies make it out of the people's basement."

"Nobody said there was anything wrong with that. I know bitcoin will only survive if people make money. And Satoshi knew you couldn't build a system that depended on people's charity. He trusted in math to build the system, but trusted in people's own self-interest to make it survive. But at the same time, is money your measure of success?"

Servo was a realist and under no illusions that crypto was a digital gold rush, and he actually welcomed it to a degree. It meant more investment in coders, innovation, and infrastructure. But his own measure of success differed, though was correlated, in that it meant that the general population would be operating outside the fiat system using crypto—without even knowing it. Like the average person sending an email doesn't know they're using TCP/IP, bitcoin and the blockchain would simply be there behind the scenes.

Hawke had his own more personal definition. "Success means I'd know how to go rogue."

Servo erupted in laughter, surprised at such an existential answer from a banker.

"What's so funny?" Hawke's eyes narrowed.

Peter Finlay had surprised him, too, years ago. The older banker had wholeheartedly listened to what Servo had to say, countering with reasonable arguments and helping him understand just how the banking system actually worked. By pointing out how the average person was at a disadvantage, usually without even being aware, Finlay had shown him that the problem with the banks wasn't necessarily the people running them, but the financial system itself.

Now Servo wondered if perhaps he should give Hawke a similar chance to prove himself. He decided he owed Peter Finlay at least that much.

"It wasn't funny, it just reminded me of something your uncle once said. And I don't mean to give you such a hard time. I don't get a lot of visitors down here and don't appreciate when they fuck up."

Hawke was caught off guard by the half-apology and reduced swearing. He stood with his mouth partly open, waiting to defend himself against the expected missing insult. But none came.

"I get it. I didn't mean to put you at risk," Hawke said.

"No problem. Just don't fuckin do it again." Servo picked up the mug and sipped the still-warm coffee, the peace offering accepted. Two sugars, no milk.

The fucker guessed right.

"What are these?" Hawke pointed to the GPUs racked up and mining away.

"Bitcoin mining rigs."

"They put off a lot of heat."

"You know how they work?"

"I'm guessing math is involved."

Servo now understood Noor's habit of rolling her eyes around Hawke. But then the Suit surprised him again.

"They're running the bitcoin code and when a block is released, they're guessing numbers as fast as they can—hence the processors running hot. If they get the number right, they group all the available bitcoin transactions together into a block that gets added to the blockchain."

"Yeah, something like that," Servo said.

Hawke looked at the monitor spitting out line after line of code. "What's going on there?"

Servo swivelled in his seat. "You might like this. Your uncle certainly did."

Hawke pulled up a folding chair and Servo didn't protest. There was something exciting about seeing someone new genuinely interested in bitcoin, a spreading of the gospel to foreign outposts. They both became transfixed by the code flying by on the screen. The text moved fast but the words and sentences could be made out, if only the rhythm could be found.

I have faced it, a life wasted.
I'm never going back again.
I escaped it, a life wasted.
I'm never going back again.
Having tasted, a life wasted.
I'm never going back again.

Time passed with only the hum of the computer fans. Then Hawke asked, "Why are we looking at Pearl Jam lyrics?"

"Because we're keeping the barbarians on the other side of the gate, Henry. I'm processing every lyric, book, quote, popular idiom, and speech ever created."

"Why?"

"Because people are fucking idiots and they need to be protected from themselves. The whole concept of bitcoin relies on cryptography. So not only for mining, but for bitcoin addresses, too. You know how bitcoin addresses are created?"

"That's the math stuff again, right?"

Servo couldn't help himself. He rolled his eyes. "Right. In simplified terms, you start with a private key, which is just a random number between 1 and 10 to the power of 77, which for all intents and purposes is an infinite set of possible numbers. From that private key you derive a public key, a.k.a. a bitcoin address, use a hashing algorithm, and encode it so that it looks something like this: 1PwY98tmZg4g2yB7MdaD5M5fssMPgsrXvV.

"And because hashing is a one-way street, you can share that bitcoin address with anyone and they won't be able to work backwards and find your private key, which is very important," Servo said.

"But if someone did know the private key to that address, then they could just take the coins?"

Servo nodded. "Exactly. Whoever controls the private key to an address, controls the bitcoin within. When you use a software wallet, it automatically generates the private key for any address you create, which is secured by your wallet's password. So don't be a fucking idiot and use something easy to guess like password123."

"Of course not. I capitalize the P and use an exclamation point for the 1, for added security," Hawke said.

Servo nearly ragequit but quickly realized he was being messed with.

Hawke then asked, "So what does Pearl Jam have to do with private keys?"

"Remember when I said your private key was just a random number? Well, you can take any set of data, including song lyrics, and hash them so that it becomes a number and treat that as a private key to create the corresponding bitcoin address. There's no actual software needed for this method of generating an address—so it's known as a brain wallet."

A brain wallet was a powerful concept to Servo. You could have nothing but the clothes on your back and as long as you had the private key memorized, you could have access to all your bitcoins. No one, not even the Cabal, would have any idea that such a wallet even existed. But there was one major flaw with the method.

"People are fucking idiots," he said. "But they also tend to believe they're the smartest person in the room, so when they want to create a brain wallet they'll use their favourite song lyrics or some obscure book passage as the private key. What I've done is created a program that hashes every song lyric, book passage, and whatever other text I can think of and checks the corresponding bitcoin address . . ."

" . . . and if the address has a balance, then you can control those bitcoins."

"You got it. With most lyrics and books digitized, they're all easy to find. This method of creating a brain wallet was more popular at the onset, but it's actually pretty terrible and I wouldn't recommend it. No matter how obscure you think the text you're using is, if it was published and is on the internet, someone is eventually going to guess it. And if it's really obscure, what happens if you die? It's lost forever. So yeah, brain wallets have their uses, but you gotta be careful."

"What do you do when you find a brain wallet?"

Servo scratched his beard. "I take the bitcoins so nobody else does. Then I post the address on the chat forums to try and find the rightful owner. All they have to do is confirm the data set used to generate the private key and I'll return the coins. Usually."

"Usually?"

"Yeah, usually. Not always. Sometimes those people aren't on the chat forums, so they never see my messages. Sometimes they're just jerks. I've been accused of fraud, hacking, and all kinds of unethical behaviour, and it's usually by people who don't know what the hell they're talking about. They got their info from a tweet or blog and instantly they're a cryptography expert. If they're too stupid to realize why their brain wallet wasn't secure, and then hate on me for trying to help, then fuck 'em.

"A fool and his money are easily parted," Hawke quoted.

"It's not even about the money. It's about being responsible for your own security," Servo said. Almost everyone he knew grew up trusting those in positions of authority to keep them safe, whether it was the bank for your life savings, the town company to keep you working, the government to protect your rights, or the Church to save your soul. And he knew first-hand that each trusted authority acted as such on a sliding scale, depending on their own self-interests at that time.

Servo sensed Hawke was starting to realize that bitter truth on his own, based on what he'd been through since the death of his uncle. But instead of growing cynical and withdrawn, as had been Servo's experience, Hawke seemed to want to push back, even if he didn't have the tools.

"What about you, Servo, what would you do if you found Satoshi's Fortune?"

"I never would. I'm not looking for it and don't want it."

"Humour me."

Servo exhaled. He had long ago decided on his answer, but had never shared it with anyone. Partly because of the low probability of finding the fortune, but mostly because nobody had ever asked him.

"If by some remote chance I controlled Satoshi's Fortune, I'd just lock it up and create a new set of Keepers. I don't think anyone should be in control of it; bitcoin was never meant to consolidate so much wealth in the hands of one person."

"Huh. Sounds like something out of a lame Hollywood movie to ensure there's a sequel. But not a terrible idea." Hawke scratched his chin. "Do you mind showing me a bit more about brain wallets?"

"Peter Finlay also had a real interest in brain wallets," Servo said.

"Well, it's all quite interesting—and confusing. And while you're at it, how about a lesson on restoring wallets and how to properly use Linux? Last time I used Linux, I almost brought down an entire network."

"You know just enough to be dangerous, eh? Why am I not surprised."

Hawke laughed. "I'll take that as a yes. Let's grab a few beers and see if I can learn how to be really dangerous," Hawke said, then added, "I bet you like a good ale."

The fucker guessed that right, too.

***

Yuriy Petrovich didn't know how to act intimidating. Luckily for him, the giant tattooed Russian gangster standing behind him filled that role and then some. It was decided during the drive down to London from Liverpool that Petrovich would talk to three entrepreneurs of a bitcoin startup instead of Makarov, as they all spoke the same technical language and were more likely to trust Petrovich than someone clearly more capable of crushing their skulls on a whim.

They had gotten the entrepreneurs' names and London hotel address via text as promised by the Mystery Man. Shortly thereafter he and Makarov packed overnight bags, tossed them into a tinted Range Rover, and made the journey from Liverpool. Petrovich couldn't help but notice that Makarov had also packed a slew of firearms, and his favourite crowbar.

He and Makarov now stood in front of the three entrepreneurs after ambushing them by a white cargo van by the hotel. They had been attempting to load their ATM machine into the back.

"When's the last time you saw Henry Hawke?" Petrovich said, trying to puff out his chest as much as possible to garner their respect, but the three entrepreneurs were fixated on Makarov. They huddled together to discuss their communal answer like they were on a game show and only had one chance to answer right, which, Petrovich thought grimly, wasn't too far off. When they reached a consensus, they spoke in sync, almost comically if not for their trembling voices.

"Here at the hotel. Saturday evening. After the fire alarm."

"Where is he now?"

They huddled again, this time more briefly. "We don't know."

Petrovich felt Makarov's heavy eyes on him. It wasn't a satisfactory answer and still left Petrovich as the most likely person to pay for the lost bitcoins. He didn't have any other questions for the entrepreneurs but, despite himself, was curious about the machine painted orange with a large bitcoin symbol decal. One of the three noticed this and spoke meekly, as if asking a girl out for the first time. "Do . . . do you like it?"

Petrovich remembered he was supposed to be a tough guy and snapped in a harsh voice he had never heard before, "I'd like to know where Henry Hawke is."

Then his smartphone vibrated. A message from the same number that had sent them to the entrepreneurs.

NABEEL MONSEF. QUEEN ELIZABETH HOSPITAL BIRMINGHAM.

Petrovich showed the message to Makarov, who grunted and turned to leave, with Petrovich quickly following. Before they got two feet though, the entrepreneurs loudly cleared their throats.

"What?"

The closest of the three, apparently elected to speak for them, was nudged forward. He held out a business card, which fluttered in his unsteady hand. "Do you want to buy some BTMs?"

Makarov snatched the card and examined it. "What is BTM?"

"Our Bitcoin Teller Machine." The two patted their invention like they were back on the game show, but this time as hosts illustrating the prize.

Makarov looked at the card again and then back at the now hopeful entrepreneurs. "Shouldn't name be Bitcoin ATM?"

NOOR'S ROLE

As the afternoon melted into the evening, Sara Noor left the boys alone to argue or swear or whatever it was they would need to do to mark their territory, and she could occasionally hear shouts and various objects crashing about. If she knew anything about boys, it meant they were now either mortal enemies or best friends.

She sat cross-legged on her bed in another made-up bedroom, refreshed after a shower and a change of clothes. She was pleased to find a pair of jeans and a Colorado Avalanche T-shirt she had left behind from her previous visit to the Sanctuary.

Her laptop was open to her email and she was desperately trying to get ahold of Jarvenpaa. Texts went unacknowledged, his phone went straight to voicemail, and emails went unreturned.

She bit her lip as she read another email that, if true, meant that she would have to make a decision she had hoped to avoid. From friendships to opinions on technical matters, there didn't seem to be any middle ground in this bitcoin world. Everything was binary, especially the bitcoin project itself. Either it was going to revolutionize the world—or be a footnote in economic textbooks.

She wondered if this binary view applied to the people involved as well. She shook her head at the foolishness of such thoughts. People were shades of grey, all capable of acts of kindness and selfishness, of malevolence and altruism. She need look no further than the individuals she now conspired with. Servo, a man who dealt in absolutes when it came to programming and who lived and fought with the hypocrisies of everything else in his life.

Hawke, who if he wasn't a brawler was a banker, who could either play dumb with the best of them or was as idiotic as the rest of them, and who seemed to have a moral compass that couldn't quite stay pointed north.

Noor read yet another email, this one from a contact of hers that had sent four messages since she had arrived at the Sanctuary. The tone had subtly changed from helpful and hopeful to one charged with an undercurrent of threats. Her concentration was suddenly interrupted by a knock on her door, which flew open before she could answer.

"We found Aziz!" Hawke entered, grinning wildly, followed by a more subdued Servo. There was a noticeable lack of animosity between them, which might have been explained by one thing.

"Are you guys drunk?" Noor asked.

"Nope, we've just been drinking for a while." Hawke answered with the slow precision of someone who had been drinking and knew he was being judged.

Noor shook her head, not wanting to get sucked into the semantics. Besides, she had more important issues to deal with. Shariff, if found, now moved to the top of the list.

"How? Is he okay? What happened?" She snapped her laptop shut and spun around.

"It is Aziz," Servo reminded her. "I don't think he's ever been okay. But he's not in the Cabal's hands."

Hawke pulled out a smartphone and summoned a video.

"Where'd you get that?" Noor asked.

"Servo hacked the CCTV network. I watched. Seemed easy—other than getting through the firewall and security stuff," Hawke explained.

"No, the phone. I thought you threw yours onto the highway."

"Yeah, Servo had a drawer full of old ones. He set me up. Helped restore my bitcoin wallet and even installed some hacker software."

Servo grunted approvingly, which was as enthusiastic as Noor had seen him. She wondered how long she had left them alone and what they had talked about—and how much info each had shared with the other.

Hawke handed her the smartphone. "After our second beer, we figured if the Cabal has cameras everywhere, then so do we."

Noor hit play. The low-resolution black-and-white footage was standard CCTV footage, and it began as an ambulance was forced to stop at a busy intersection—and then someone bolted out the back. The fleeing patient frantically looked around so fast he must have gotten whiplash. Even with the grainy footage and the face bloodied and swollen, she could still see into a pair of desperately maniacal eyes. There was no doubt it was Aziz Shariff.

"And that's the only record of him on CCTV cameras. He scampers into an alley and straight up vanishes," Servo said. "God knows where the fuck he is now."

"Maybe he got picked up again by the Cabal?" Hawke offered.

"No, I doubt it. I would know by now," Noor said.

Hawke paused with a question in his raised eyebrow. Noor was thankful Servo kept the focus on the footage.

"Aziz running out of the ambulance raised another question: how did he even end up in an ambulance in the first place? It's not like the Cabal would have let him out of their sight. So we followed the ambulance backwards on the CCTV cameras and saw that he was loaded into the back in a dodgy part of London. All kinds of coppers and emergency crew around. I checked the police logs for that time and location. And there was a kidnapping. And lucky for us, the Specialist Firearms Command in London wears body cameras."

Noor pressed play on the next video. It was the shaky cam footage of a SWAT-like team ascending a flight of stairs. A timestamp ticked away in the corner with yesterday's date. The filming officer kept an overwatch position at the rear of the group as the team took up positions on both sides of an apartment door; and then one cop stepped forward and heaved his foot through the door. The door gave way and the cops filtered in.

"See," Hawke boasted. "I do it as well as the professionals."

Noor didn't take her eyes off the screen as she replied, "Only took them one attempt though."

Hawke mumbled something about just needing more practice.

Noor watched the shaky cam footage jump from eye level to the floor and back again. The muffled audio had cops yelling what sounded like instructions and commands. Then the footage levelled off and showed a man tied to a chair in the middle of an apartment.

"Aziz . . ." Noor whispered. As the officer with the body cam approached Shariff, it became apparent that Shariff was further along in the Cabal's interrogation process than what Noor had last seen from Monsef's. The bruising on his face was palpable and a river of blood flowed out of his mouth. "My god . . ."

"Only time I've seen that much blood leaking was after a fight in my freshman season when a couple teeth got knocked out."

"Did the Cabal knock his teeth out on purpose?" Servo asked.

Noor said nothing.

"Only if they . . ." Servo answered his own question, ". . . that fucking madman actually did it!"

"Did what?" Hawke asked. They were interrupted by the repeated buzzing of Noor's smartphone with incoming text messages. She glanced at the screen and set it face down on her bed.

"Who's that?""

"Ah, Johan, probably," she answered flatly. "Servo, what did Aziz do?"

"The crazy fucker once messaged me some questions, it must have been just after Christmas. Asked about the lifespan of micro-SD cards and conditions they would last in. Moisture, acidity and all that. I joked about shoving a card up his fucking ass to keep it from the cops. Which, of course, Aziz didn't find funny. In fact, he ended the convo right there."

The video continued with the officers circling a man on his knees obediently raising his hands at their shouts. The filming officer circled around until the suspect's face was clearly visible, and the blank eyes stared back at the camera indifferently, as if a parking enforcement officer was giving him a parking ticket and not a SWAT team aggressively arresting him.

"That's the guy from the pub who said he worked for immigration," Hawke pointed out.

Servo huffed. "Immigration, that fucker? That's Agent 21. Far as I know, he's the Cabal's top agent and a soulless bugger. He's been after Satoshi and bitcoin since . . ."

Noor cleared her throat. "Servo, you were saying about the SD card?"

"Right. So a fake tooth would easily fit a micro-SD card. And if that's what Agent 21 ripped from Aziz's mouth, then it would have to have been extremely valuable for Aziz to even put it there and for Agent 21 to want it. I've always assumed Aziz was a Keeper of the Fortune, the fucker would never tell me anything of course, but I'd bet you a bitcoin that SD card holds the wallet file to Satoshi's Fortune."

Noor watched Servo's and Hawke's reaction at learning the Cabal had ripped the most important part of Satoshi's Fortune right out of Shariff's head.

And she feigned her surprise to match theirs.

***

Petrovich hoped the man hadn't died. At least not before he told him what he wanted to hear. He sat on a stool at the man's bedside; the nurse who had checked in earlier saw only a harmless man visiting his recuperating friend. Makarov stayed in the car. Nobody ever considered him harmless and they didn't want the distraction.

"We are not here for you, Mr. Monsef. We only want to find Henry Hawke."

Monsef's breathing was laboured, and he spoke in short gasps that drained him of whatever energy he had left.

"I don't know. Where he. Went."

Petrovich found himself imitating what he thought Makarov would do in his place. He thickened his Russian accent, hopeful it would add a sense of urgency and dread to the Afghani lying vulnerable on the hospital bed before him, one who would have grown up with war stories of the Soviet bogeyman. "Would your wife and child know where he went?"

The heart monitor attached to Monsef spiked and his eyes widened. This pleased Petrovich. His whole time with the Bratva, especially since the hack, he had been the scared one. But now here he was mimicking his organization's innate willingness to do whatever was necessary to survive. Somebody needed to pay for the hack and receive Makarov's punishment. He reached into his coat pocket and felt the cold handle of his black-on-black switchblade.

"Tell me where he is. I don't want anything bad to happen to you, comrade."

But better you than me, comrade.

Before Petrovich could find out just how far from his passive keyboard self he had evolved, and just how far the Bratva's influence had spread within him, his phone vibrated. The new message from the contact read

KELVINBRIDGE TRAIN STATION.

Petrovich got up and left without saying another word.

JARVENPAA'S WHEREABOUTS

With the Sanctuary hidden away from daylight, Hawke had no clear perception of what time it was. The shock at realizing Agent 21 and the Cabal had the wallet file soon faded only to be replaced by a slow burn, pushing Hawke to get out from the underground and take action.

Back in the rectory, Hawke balanced on his folding chair to the mild annoyance of Servo, who had withdrawn back behind a surly disposition. Noor had decided to remain in her room to wrap up a few items and would be along shortly. That was hours ago.

"You think Aziz backed up the wallet file anywhere?" Hawke asked.

"For the tenth time, fuck no. He was as paranoid as they come," Servo muttered.

By Hawke's count it was only the sixth time he had asked but didn't see any value in pointing that out.

Servo intermittently spaced out; his consciousness seemed directly connected to his computer, and he plowed through screens and screens of data that were nonsensical to Hawke's eyes. Now and again he'd mutter something about no new info on Shariff, Agent 21, or whatever else he was searching for. It reminded Hawke of the computer science majors on his floor in freshman year where they would only exit World of Warcraft to mumble something about ordering pizza.

Hawke picked up a laptop that he had borrowed from Servo earlier and tried to look busy. He popped in the orange flash drive to have another look at the list of Keepers. It might be the closest he would ever come to finding Satoshi's Fortune, escaping a life of twenty-five-year mortgages, and selling invented-but-surely-needed financial products to unsuspecting schmucks who were trying to pay down their own twenty-five-year mortgages.

The names associated with the email addresses were now all known, the Keepers of the Fortune identified.

Shariff, his tightly kept wallet file lost to the Cabal, maybe along with his mind.

Servo, disinterested if not repulsed by the idea of the fortune.

Jarvenpaa, Noor said she'd get his advice on the next steps, but so far only silence in response.

And Peter Finlay, a dead man who had likely taken his password to his grave.

Before Servo had withdrawn, he had shown Hawke a few of the tricks of the trade on how to use Linux. He had also helped him create a shell script, a tiny program that would interact with an unlocked bitcoin wallet to create a transaction that would send all its bitcoins to a provably unspendable address, which Servo had created, just in case Hawke found the fortune and wanted to burn it all, as per Shariff's plan.

But with Servo's current mood, he didn't think any other requests for help would result in anything other than cursing. He decided to find out if he knew just enough to be dangerous, or, after Servo's brisk training, was competently dangerous.

He created a duplicate of the burn address script, and while Servo was in one of his one-with-the-Matrix sessions, Hawke deleted the burn address and replaced it with one copied from his own wallet—one only he controlled.

Hawke felt a pang of guilt at this.

Perhaps because of this uncertainty, he created a third script of his own, one he remembered from his college days and hoped, once he showed it to Servo, he might actually acknowledge it was bug-free and something a proper cypherpunk would keep in his arsenal. Hawke copied all three scripts to the flash drive and returned it to his pocket, and went about mindlessly surfing the web.

But as he watched a breaking news video plastered across the top of a news website, Hawke tensed as an influx of adrenalin filled his veins, triggered by the realization that he might have trusted the wrong person.

"Sara!" he shouted. "Sara! Get in here!"

Hawke jumped to his feet and raced back to Noor's room. She still sat on her bed. Her phone was vibrating incessantly beside her.

"Who keeps messaging you?" Hawke asked.

Noor didn't look down at her phone. "Johan. I'll call him back in a minute."

"The hell it is," Hawke snapped.

Servo ambled in. "What's all this yelling about?"

"Are you going to tell us?" Hawke directed the question at Noor.

"Tell, tell you what exactly? You're being paranoid." Noor stuttered briefly, but it was enough to confirm Hawke's suspicions. He snatched the laptop from Noor's hands and smashed a couple keys to bring up the news website so they could all see. There was a book jacket photo of Johan Jarvenpaa presenting the smiling futurist in a warm and optimistic light. The headline below conveyed a much more sinister persona.

Best-Selling Author and Futurist Arrested on Assault Charges.

The program switched to news footage of a dishevelled Jarvenpaa being escorted out of a building in handcuffs, with dour police officers flanking him. His eyes sank to the ground, his shoulders slumped, and his once irrepressible energy was drained from his being. The police escort pushed him through the throng of hungry media, who hurled questions and snapped photos to capture the life-altering moment. The anchor summarized the event. "Jarvenpaa was arrested by Swedish police on an outstanding warrant from London. Two women claimed assault stemming from a rendezvous the night before."

Noor's expression flooded with concern. "They got him," she whispered.

Hawke slammed the laptop shut. "How can Johan have been calling you all day if he was in the Cabal's custody?"

"You wouldn't understand," Noor said.

"Try us."

As if on cue, Noor's phone rang, demanding to be heard.

"I need to take this." She grabbed her phone and pushed past Hawke and Servo, who immediately followed her. She had the phone to her ear, ignoring their calls for an explanation. After no more than thirty seconds, she ended the call and turned to face them. She was a shade paler with fear overtaking her wide, uncertain eyes.

"We have to go. Now."

"What! Why?" Servo asked. He was on the verge of both anger and panic. Anger because this was his sanctuary and panic because he didn't know where else to go.

"Because the Cabal has sent the Russian mob after us. And they're just about here."

Hawke reached out and grabbed her by both shoulders. He spoke in a calm voice that betrayed the simmering anger in his gut. "Sara, how did the Cabal even know we are here?"

Noor swallowed. "Because I told them."

PART 4:

1JKmCwMF8mAXpvjofBta
iFKvNpQhGwkrum

HAWKE'S ESCAPE

It didn't take Hawke long to determine he didn't like getting shot at. The ear-shattering crack, the blinding flash, the mean-spirited piece of metal hoping to gouge a hole in his flesh. It was all very unappealing.

Poised to follow the others to safety through a maintenance tunnel off the concourse that Servo directed them to, Hawke glanced over his shoulder and swore someone had trained a bear to shoot a gun. The beast had to hunch to fit his massive frame though the concourse entrance, and he glared at Hawke with the hungry eyes of a predator. The gun, like a child's toy in his massive paw, was raised and ready to be fired again at Hawke. It was only the shouts in a thick Russian accent of a bespectacled, weasel-faced man that saved Hawke from being riddled with surplus Soviet-era bullets.

"Stop! We need him alive to bring back stolen bitcoins!"

Confusion set in for Hawke, alongside his newfound fear of bears, as he wondered what stolen bitcoins had to do with the Russian mob wanting Satoshi's Fortune. But he pushed the thought aside and threw himself into the tunnel, slammed the door behind him, and engaged the bolt lock to hold off the Russians.

With the door shut it was nearly pitch black. A distant light further down the tunnel called out to him. Hawke's boots splashed in the pools of stagnant water as he ran towards the light—perhaps a bad omen after just being shot at, but it was only the flashlight from Servo's phone.

"Where's Sara?" Hawke asked.

"She went up ahead. Said she needed to get cell reception immediately, so I told her how to get out." Servo's red beard stood out like a flame in the dim light. The laptop he managed to grab at the last minute was stuffed into a backpack.

"We can't let her out of our sight," Hawke insisted.

"Why the hell not?"

Hawke was furious at Noor's deception and felt a fool for trusting her. He had ignored the coincidence of their shared train to Birmingham and her skillful dodging of unwanted questions for too long. Combined with her admission that she had revealed their secret location, it all led to only one possible explanation.

"Because Sara Noor is an agent of the Cabal," Hawke said. Saying the words made him sick, but the facts were clear.

Servo stood in place. "It can't be. I've known her for years."

"Then you've known a Cabal agent for years. How else would she know the Russians were coming?"

Servo didn't have an answer. But he did have one for the Russians invading his Sanctuary and who could now be heard banging on the tunnel door. He fumbled with his smartphone and hit a button on a custom-made app. A moment later the outline of the door was lit up like an alien ship had landed inside the Sanctuary and ear-piercing music blasted nothing but three cords and a feverish drum beat.

"Follow me," Servo yelled over the noise.

The cypherpunk navigated a winding route through the disused maintenance tunnels that snaked all through the underbelly of the abandoned train station. Hawke had lost all sense of direction by the time they arrived at a metal door with EXIT lettering mostly faded away.

"This station was built alongside the river. This door should bring us right to it," Servo said.

Hawke, feeling that breaking down doors was becoming something of his specialty, was about to work his magic when he noticed the latch bolt was out of place.

Someone had recently been through the door.

Noor must have managed to make her way outside. With any luck they would catch up with her before she had a chance to do any more damage.

He leaned into the heavy door and it grinded open. Servo was right. They stepped out onto a rusted maintenance walkway directly above the river. It was low tide and the water had mostly wandered off somewhere downstream, leaving the rotting seaweed and algae-covered rocks to represent the River Kelvin, a tributary off the more popular River Clyde. The mere whiff of the river at ground zero caused Hawke to gag, while clusters of seagulls happily enjoyed their midnight snack on the water's edge and failed to understand his loss of appetite.

A ladder leading upwards hollered at its joints as soon as Servo put his weight on it, with Hawke right behind him. They ascended and found themselves on a pedestrian footpath that mirrored the concrete shore of the inlet until it reached the River Clyde a few miles downstream. They stood in the shadow of the abandoned train station; across the river, in a more civilized part of Glasgow, tall buildings watched over their escape, indifferent to the outcome.

If Servo was right and *Noor the Bitcoiner* just needed to get outside to make an urgent call, then she would be nearby and waiting for them. Otherwise, *Noor the Cabal Agent* had fled what she had set up to be a mauling.

Hawke scanned the pathway.

Sara Noor was nowhere to be seen.

NOOR'S EXPLANATION

"She must have been playing me from the beginning." Hawke cursed Noor's name under his breath. How much more of an obvious cliché could she have been: a beautiful and mysterious woman who had manipulated him into having no choice but to trust her. Hawke felt betrayed, and a little bit flattered. Hawke continued to fume as Servo started back towards the ladder.

"Where are you going?" Hawke asked.

"To find Sara. Maybe she just got lost in the tunnels."

"Someone was already through that door and Sara was the only other person in the tunnels. She's part of the Cabal, Servo."

"Impossible."

"She's been playing me," Hawke repeated.

"You're fucking paranoid."

"An international Cabal that secretly controls the world economy is after me because my dead uncle apparently had a secret password to a fortune in cryptocurrency. I've been framed for murder, beaten, chased, and most recently shot at by the love child of Yogi Bear and Ranger Smith. I think I've passed the point where I can be called paranoid."

"I'll grant you you're popular with the wrong crowd. But Sara ain't one of 'em."

"Then where is she?"

Neither had an answer. The faint sound of punk rock rumbled on amid the squawking of the nearby dining seagulls. A soft breeze carried the scent of the river. And lilacs.

"Trying to save your ass," Noor said. It was as if she had materialized out of thin air. Her arms were crossed in front of a laptop bag strap that ran across her chest and she looked thoroughly unimpressed. In case Hawke and Servo were expecting an immediate explanation, Noor cleared that up by walking away. "We have to go. Follow me."

"Hold on, Sara. Why do you think we're going to blindly follow you now?"

She stopped and thought Hawke couldn't see her expression from behind; he knew from experience it was the posture of a woman deciding on which of a hundred ways she was going to murder him. She turned on her heel and marched back up to Hawke, leaving mere inches between their bodies. Her olive skin radiated warmth and Hawke struggled to maintain eye contact as her body swelled and contracted with each exhale. Soon his breath fell into sync with hers and he could have sworn her lips almost teased a smile.

Which made the quick right hook all the more surprising. The punch landed squarely on his cheek. While it wasn't the hardest hit he'd ever taken, it was perhaps the most confusing. The blow caused Hawke to stumble before he managed to block her subsequent left cross. He grabbed Noor's wrist tightly and could now feel her heart pulsating through skin that was almost hot to the touch.

Noor used her free hand to snatch Hawke's forearm and twist him around, so now both his arm and Noor were behind him. She struggled to hold him in place and eventually relented, as Hawke showed no resistance, slowly letting her fingers uncurl before releasing him altogether. She quickly shoved him to return the distance between them.

Hawke rubbed his cheek. "That's pretty much exactly what I'd expect a Cabal agent to do."

"Jesus Christ, Henry. How many hits to the head did you take playing hockey? If I were a secret agent wouldn't I have successfully seduced you by now to completely gain your trust?"

It was pretty much the exact opposite of what Hawke expected a Cabal agent to say, but he kept that to himself. Instead he just shrugged.

Noor shook her head, annoyed. "The whole purpose of going after the fortune is to keep it from the Cabal."

"Let's clear the air right now. There's been too many coincidences involving you since I met Aziz. How did you know he sent me a message about Satoshi's Fortune?" Hawke tried to read her eyes for signs of deceit, but came away with nothing.

"First, I took an interest in you—professionally— because I knew that Aziz is the most likely person on the planet to be a Keeper. And then I saw him talk to you at the pub. But why? You're a nobody."

"Hey, come on now."

"She's right." Servo had been lurking in the background and now entered the conversation. "From a cryptocurrency perspective anyways. You're not involved in any projects as a developer, you're not part of any of the crypto mailing lists. The only thing that's linked you to bitcoin was your uncle."

Hawke's shoulders deflated—they were right. He hadn't accomplished anything in the bitcoin world. Or in any world for that matter. He was just a nine-to-five lifer with eyes on a fatter pay cheque to buy the stuff he was told he needed. If he had been shot dead what would his obituary say? Henry Hawke: *grew up, went to school, got a cubicle job, pissed off a Russian bear with surprisingly good aim. The end.*

"Anyway," Noor said, forcing Hawke to refocus, "Aziz liked to send messages hidden in bitcoin transactions. It was his way to test your worthiness, to see if you could pull the sword from the stone, so to speak. When I saw him initiate a transaction with you . . . you immediately became a person of interest. Obviously the Cabal thought so too. I bet every message, transaction, and online record of yours was compiled and analyzed the moment Agent 21 met us at the pub."

"All right, but how did you end up on the same train as me?"

"Oh that? I just bribed the overnight guy at the front desk to call me when you checked out so I could follow you."

"So you're a stalker after all."

313

"Better than being a Cabal agent."

"And if she were with the Cabal," Servo asked, "why would she have warned us about the Russians?" The most logical answer was that she wasn't, but Hawke was certain Noor was hiding something. He put the odds at thirty-seventy that she was a Cabal agent and told himself any attempts at seduction would flip the percentages.

"Okay, so I'll buy that you aren't with the Cabal. So what now?"

"I was just on the phone with the contact who warned me we had to leave the Sanctuary. He has a way to get us out of Glasgow and to somewhere safe."

The cool breeze dropped a few more degrees and Hawke shivered. They all became acutely aware that Servo's already faint music had stopped. Noor immediately started walking away before the Russians made their way outside, with Servo following her lead. Somewhat reluctantly, but again without much choice, Hawke followed.

At the late hour there were few people taking the pathway, but still Hawke kept his ears tuned for Russian accents and his eyes on the lookout for bipedal bears. They walked briskly enough to keep warm and arrived at a pedestrian bridge that took them to the southern side of the River Clyde. Hawke had to hustle to walk alongside Noor, who kept a brisk pace.

"So I've been thinking."

"Maybe stick to hockey fights."

"Not enough ice around here. But you said you had to bribe the night clerk to rat me out?"

"That is what I said."

"I'm curious. How much did my loss of privacy cost you?" Her answer made Hawke stop in his tracks as the others carried on. He stood alone at the apex of the bridge, fully exposed to the entirety of the city, and considered how effortlessly Noor had gotten exactly what she wanted, and for so little cost.

Just a smile.

Hawke found himself unsurprised by that.

NOOR'S CONTACT

Hawke, Noor, and Servo trudged along the River Clyde and arrived unharassed at a collection of three futuristic buildings that formed the Glasgow Science Centre. Hawke thought they belonged in an eighties budget sci-fi movie: no straight lines and covered in what looked like tinfoil. The main science mall was crescent shaped and apparently designed to look like the hull of a ship listing to its side, which made Hawke wonder about the judgment of an architect who concluded that the position of a boat worth immortalizing was one where it took on water.

Hawke realized that Noor hadn't elaborated on who her contact was, and wondered why. He had to trust her but found she was purposely misleading.

"Who really messaged you about the Russians? It certainly wasn't Johan since he was in the Cabal's custody," Hawke said.

"No, it wasn't Johan. It was a journalist contact of mine. And he's been providing me information for a day now. That's who I needed to call ASAP. To make sure we have somewhere to go next."

"Who's your contact?" Hawke asked.

Noor flashed apologetic eyes at Servo. "Jack Ka-shing."

"That fucking asshole?!" Servo erupted. "He's the biggest clown in the entire bitcoin space. Has zero knowledge about any of the technical aspects of bitcoin, but he talks out his ass more than anyone."

"Jack Ka-shing . . ." Hawke thought he recognized the name.

"He used to run some hedge fund that made a few hundred million betting that the big investment banks would get bailed out," Noor explained.

Now Hawke remembered the name. With all the big investment firms about to fail and their stocks near worthless, few were confident of their survival. But Jack Ka-shing made the news by buying up as many shares as he could and plastering himself all over TV to boast about the wisdom of his bet. When the first $700 billion bailout was announced, and guaranteed those firms' survival, their shares skyrocketed in value and he made a fortune. He operated the fund for another year without any other big wins and then wound down operations.

"And he's into bitcoin?"

"One of the earliest investors," Noor said. "Also one of its most narcissistic personalities. He claims to be an expert on the minutia of the software, which drives coders like Servo nuts."

Hawke scratched his chin. "You have to give him credit for discovering bitcoin and then doing his research. In hindsight it's easy to say bitcoin would be worth something today. But to invest at the beginning would have taken some courage."

Noor was reluctant to agree. "Regardless, he's hounded me for months about doing an article on him and helping with his marketing. Apparently, he's going to launch the world's first cryptocurrency trading desk. Today he became even more adamant about meeting, saying he had valuable information that he had to share but didn't want to talk over the phone or email. When I asked for a hint, something to ensure an in-person meeting would be worth my while, he said he might have been presented with the opportunity to buy the wallet file."

"*The* wallet file? Stolen from Aziz by Agent 21?"

"The same. It raises a whole other set of questions that we need the answers to, which I think was his point. I reluctantly agreed to meet, after which he warned me about the Russians."

"How did they know to find me at the Sanctuary?" Hawke asked.

"I asked Ka-shing the same thing. The Cabal knew that somebody knocked out Inspector Smith at Monsef's and helped you escape. And they knew your cell signal, obviously. So they just looked for another signal that mirrored your route from Monsef's to when you threw your phone out the window in order to know who was with you." Noor stared at her feet. "And they found mine. That's how they found us at the Sanctuary. I told them, essentially."

Servo's face reddened and he looked like he wanted to invent a new swear word.

"I'm so sorry, Servo. I know how much the Sanctuary meant to you," Noor said.

Servo took a deep breath and exhaled slowly. "Fuck it. Maybe it was time to get some fresh air anyway."

Hawke thought about all the work and sacrifice Servo had invested in the Sanctuary. The cypherpunk's commitment to it, despite the high probability of failure, made Hawke ashamed of the little effort he had put forward to make something of his own life. From a hockey career easily derailed because he couldn't control his temper, to the business ideas that came to life with startling clarity at the pub but went no further, to the desires for a career plucked out of the *Wall Street Journal* stalled because of an unwillingness to play the corporate game. Hawke had so far failed to achieve anything of note.

Now, being presented with an opportunity to forge his own path, to accomplish something of value by keeping Satoshi's Fortune out of the hands of the Cabal, he wondered if he had the inner fortitude to succeed. Hawke wasn't sure if he had ever been less certain about what kind of person he was, or if by standing next to Servo just made it obvious what he wasn't. Hawke was slow to realize, or maybe accept, that this adventure wasn't solely about finding Satoshi's Fortune.

"Where does Ka-shing want to meet us?" Hawke said.

"He owns an estate on the Isle of Man," Noor replied.

"Not exactly walkable. How did he expect us to get there?"

Noor pointed past the museum and onto the river.

Hawke's eyes widened in amazement. Based on the grandeur of what he was taking in, he wondered how much Ka-shing had invested in bitcoin—and just how early he had gotten in.

NOOR'S REASONS

Moored to the pier was an awe-inspiring and stealthy curved yacht, with lines so aggressively sensual it belonged on stage twirling around a pole. It pushed two-hundred feet in length and Hawke appreciated that the hull was facing down. A high-tech tower of bulbs and antennas rotated at its highest point with a sculpted titanium tiger leaping off its bow. The yacht's name was proudly painted in bright orange, which was at odds with the sleek titanium design of the vessel, but its owner had insisted on the colour choice. *Satoshi's Ark*.

Servo opened his mouth to curse something disparaging, but even he had to appreciate the ship's gravitas. "I've never been on a yacht before," he managed to say.

"A *superyacht* actually." A deep voice rang out from the captain's deck. A squarely built man with silver hair that matched the boat's finish appeared by the railing. He was sharply dressed in a white suit with anchors on his shoulder patches and a peaked cap tucked under his arm. He looked like a man always a moment away from a salute. "Ms. Noor? I'm Captain Lee. Please come aboard immediately. We are set to depart."

Noor crossed the gangplank with Servo and Hawke following. Noor and Servo had only their laptop bags while

Hawke travelled with only the contents of his pockets. A smiling crewman in khakis and a tucked-in navy golf shirt with *Ka-shing Investments* embroidered on the breast greeted them. He waited to take their non-existent luggage and looked unsure of what to do when none was presented. Captain Lee descended a circular staircase and waved away the crewman, who looked relieved at having orders he could follow and quickly shrank away.

"Ms. Noor, Mr. Ka-shing has given me precise instructions to make sure your journey is as pleasurable as possible. If there's anything my crew or I can do, please don't hesitate to ask." Lee's deep voice and weathered face gave him an authoritative standing that made his rank of captain a mere formality.

Noor stiffly greeted him back. Hawke was secretly pleased that she could be prickly with someone other than himself. She introduced Hawke and Servo merely as colleagues. Lee gave a conspiratorial wink and ushered them into the main salon. Every door handle, every light fixture, every nut and bolt demanded to be called luxurious. The walls swept by as if pushed by the wind. The plush furnishings stood out like outcroppings from a marble sea floor, which itself was smooth and polished to a golden sparkle. Nature had clearly been the designer's muse.

Lee started into a well-rehearsed pitch about the *super*yacht—he made sure to emphasize the super—almost more salesman than captain. *Satoshi's Ark* could sleep up to twelve guests and another fourteen crew, had its own helipad, swimming pool, jacuzzi, luxury sleeping cabins on multiple decks, and the hull and superstructure were aluminum. If needed, the twin engines could put out over four-thousand horsepower, which they all agreed sounded like a lot. Perhaps Lee expected a more appreciative reaction to his summary as he waited patiently with a half-smile.

"Very impressive," Noor gifted him.

"Excellent. I'll make sure Mr. Ka-shing hears of your compliments," Lee said, reverting to his captain persona. "Now, if you'll excuse me, I'm needed on the bridge. Weather permitting, our voyage will have you in Douglas Harbour by first light where I've been informed a chauffeur will be awaiting to take you to Mr. Ka-shing's estate. So please, make yourselves at home. Do not hesitate to ask for anything while onboard." Lee looked like he desperately wanted to salute but instead turned on his heel and left the three of them alone in the main salon.

Shortly thereafter, the boat began to rock side to side with the twin engines barely audible inside the main salon. With a loud wail of her proud horn and the tiger figurehead lunging westward, *Satoshi's Ark* made sail for the Isle of Man.

Sara Noor wasted no time in taking her laptop up to the second level and situating herself in one of the cabins, closing the door behind her. Hawke and Servo managed to make do without her. Hawke sniffed out the bar and delivered two cans of ale as the pair relaxed on the couches. They debated varying subjects of interest: the future of bitcoin, Ranger's FC table standings, how the Bratva ran their exchange, and whether or not you could actually train a bear to shoot a gun.

By the time the River Clyde gave way to the Irish Sea, they heard a cabin door open and Noor descended the stairs. She didn't say anything as she walked past them and out a sliding door onto the front deck.

"She's struggling with something." Servo noted.

"With what? Trying to figure out another way to hide something from us?"

Servo fumbled with his cross around his neck. "I dunno. We all got our secrets."

"I'm going to go check on her."

Hawke grabbed a fresh beer for himself and, perhaps in a wasted effort, one for Noor. He stepped onto the deck and was greeted by the salty ocean air. The expansive deck was lacquered and furnished with a set of white waterproof couches and loungers ready to seat Ka-shing's dazzled guests. The deck narrowed to a half circle at the bow where he found Noor aimlessly looking at the passing lights of strange ships off in the distance. Her reverie was broken when Hawke rested against the railing alongside her. He offered her the beer and was pleasantly surprised when she accepted.

"Ka-shing is in the bitcoin space for two things. Money and ego," she said.

"Maybe that's what makes the world go round."

Noor scoffed. "I've realized that's what you would think. Make some money and get a little ego boost, all the while enjoying the game?"

"I'm in this game because I didn't have a choice. Remember, it was Aziz who gave me a secret message that I hadn't asked for . . ."

"And you began chasing it immediately," Noor pointed out.

"Yeah, well, who doesn't like a good chase." Hawke wanted to give Noor a sportive wink but decided to be content with her accepting the beer. "And you gotta admit, for all the pain and stress and risks, this is pretty exciting. Right now, I should be finishing up yet another Monday at the office. Filing paperwork and killing time until my boss won't judge me for leaving for the day. But instead here I am, on a superyacht chasing the greatest fortune of the twenty-first century."

"If this is the type of life you wanted, minus the murder charge I assume, why didn't you just quit?"

"If I'm being honest, because I would have just got another job doing the same thing or something similar. I just didn't know how to break the cycle. Work, sleep, repeat. Maybe I'd get ahead, but then what? Buy a house? Settle down and put together an impressive thirty-year retirement plan? It's just not . . ."

" . . . it's just not worth it." Noor finished his thought.

He took a long pull on his beer. "Yeah. Something like that."

"Well, how do you break the cycle?"

It was Hawke's turn to stare aimlessly out across the water. "Go rogue, I'm thinking."

"And how do you do that?"

Hawke smiled and said, "Maybe I'll trust you and see what happens."

Noor nodded and drank her beer. A silence fell between them. Hawke let his eyes drift upwards and watched the crescent moon peak out from behind the clouds and pull at the sea. He and Noor shared an objective, so he chose to believe, and that was to keep Satoshi's Fortune out of the hands of the Cabal. Perhaps that was all they shared. What if by some miracle they managed to gain control of the fortune? Their ideas on wealth differed, not to mention Servo's opinion on the matter. Would they begin to argue, to disagree on what to do with any of the 980,000 bitcoins waiting patiently for a consensus? Would it just be the same game all over again, except instead of being against the Cabal it would be played against each other?

"What's Satoshi's Fortune worth to you?" Hawke asked.

He watched gears whirl behind her wide brown eyes. He didn't know if she was searching for a plausible lie or for enough of the truth to simply pacify him.

"My father was a professor at the University of Tehran. He came from a wealthy family and had all the trappings of a successful life. A nice house, a car, money in the bank to go along with a meaningful career. He and his brothers were active in politics, strictly opposing the religious elements growing inside Iranian society at the time. Then the 1979 Revolution happened and his family was immediately targeted. One brother disappeared in the middle of the night. The other was found dead in his home—suicide by two bullets to the back of the head. Funny that, eh?" Noor was dangerously close to a smile. She continued.

"My father barely escaped with the clothes on his back. He grabbed some gold jewellery and a watch not unlike the one on your wrist and fled just minutes before the new government came knocking. A lifetime of work and effort . . . seized by a group of men with guns because . . . well, they had the guns. So they did. The new government took everything from him because they wanted it. He went into exile and found his way into Canada where he met my mother and rebuilt his career from scratch. He's always told me he's had a blessed life, but after that dreadful night when the men in power took everything from him, his family, his money, he's refused to trust any government. If cryptocurrencies had existed back then, maybe it wouldn't have been so easy for those with guns to steal from those without."

"So you're Canadian? I thought you'd be nicer."

"That's just a myth."

"Any other Canadian myths you want to ruin for me? Maybe not everyone up there is obsessed with hockey?"

"Oh, I love hockey." She leaned her back against the railing, displaying the Colorado Avalanche logo on her T-shirt. "I still say Forsberg was one of the best of all time. If it wasn't for his injuries, *Foppa* would be considered hands down the greatest player of his generation."

Hawke was as big a hockey fan as any and always imagined a career in the game before he realized he didn't like coaches telling him what to do, so he knew that Peter Forsberg's remarkable career was cut short by a slew of injuries. He also realized that Noor still hadn't answered the simple question.

"No more distractions or misdirections. Why are you after Satoshi's Fortune?" Hawke asked.

"Because we need bitcoin to survive. If bitcoin existed when my father was forced to flee his home, he could have kept his money safe from being confiscated."

"That's an extreme case."

"How many people across the globe live under openly hostile regimes? How many have capital controls that dictate where you can and cannot move your own money? But wait—I know what you're going to say—*not in the freedom-loving US of A. We have a constitution.* Yet you have civil forfeiture where the police can seize your money without any due process. The government in the thirties stole from your safety deposit boxes because they wanted your gold. I guess what I'm saying is, you don't need bitcoin if you trust that your government will never abuse its power. Otherwise, bitcoin might be a good plan B."

"So bitcoin is about having control of your wealth?"

"In a free country your thoughts are your own. Why shouldn't your money be as well?"

Hawke listened to Noor, a passion in her voice nearing the surface that was otherwise hidden. A streak of rebellion that hadn't been outwardly evident so far in their travels.

She may not have been a spy, but she certainly had her secrets. And as much as Hawke was at least partially chasing Satoshi's Fortune for his uncle, she seemed to be doing the same for her father. They finished their beers in silence and watched the waves rise and fall, catching the moonlight briefly as the boat crested. She turned and began to leave the deck. Hawke leaned his back against the railing to watch her go, knowing that every answer she provided only gave rise to more questions.

"You said your father was a professor. What was he a professor of?"

Without looking back, Noor answered, "Cryptography."

Hawke found himself unsurprised by that.

KA-SHING'S ESTATE

Satoshi's Ark crept into the port of Douglas under faint grey clouds doing their best to summon enough strength for a morning shower. Failing that, they still managed to overpower the sun's attempt to shine. The superyacht let out two long horn blasts to announce its arrival, as if Captain Lee was expecting a flock of adoring fans or wartime brides cheering its regal entry into port. In reality, it only attracted beleaguered glares from the windburned fishermen making their daily journey out to sea.

Hawke, Noor, and Servo disembarked onto the bustling quay after receiving a well-practiced salute from Captain Lee as a parting gift. They were welcomed by a short servant in a brilliant white porter's uniform with a mandarin collar. He was positively beaming.

"Mr. Ka-shing welcomes you to the Isle of Man," the servant announced before shepherding them to a freshly waxed limousine. There they were greeted a second time by a serious man who looked like an extra in a Scorsese film. His boxy frame reminded Hawke of a Volvo station wagon, and the telltale bulge in the suit jacket under his left armpit reminded him of a Lincoln Continental. The man sat behind the wheel and quickly had them careening through the port city of Douglas with the beaming servant acting as their tour guide.

Hawke learned that the Isle of Man had been dropped into the middle of the Irish Sea without the benefit of arable land or tropical climate. The territory had spent most of its existence as an afterthought to the United Kingdom, acting as a hub for ships the Crown didn't want to be seen in the company of, but with whom she still wanted to maintain a dangerous liaison. When the market for such nefarious seafaring trade began to fade in the twentieth century, the island reinvented itself as an offshore tax haven and gave itself permission to issue those modern-day letters of marque—the state-sponsored banking licence.

The remnants of the old, wayward seaside town could still be seen just beyond the shadows by the port. Women who could be found wherever sailors had shore leave walked home on the boardwalk. Old men broken from a life at sea sat on the porches of bleak boarding homes and cast a suspicious eye on all who passed by. Stately waterfront homes once owned by wealthy landowners now had second chances as bed and breakfasts.

But once they entered downtown, the city transformed itself into something unrecognizable to the previous generation of islanders. An assortment of glass towers imposed themselves upon the skyline. Sharply dressed men and women, indistinguishable from any other metropolitan centre, rushed by on the streets to their office jobs, with a coffee in hand and their eyes glued to their phones. It all announced that financial services were the new dominant industry on the island.

The limousine passed the city limits and headed east up the coast on a winding double-lane road that at times nearly kissed the sea. About the time Hawke grew tired of watching the coast go by, they took a sharp left off the main road and continued on a wide private street, which still smelled of fresh asphalt. They came to a stop at the end of the street before a sweeping golden gate that glittered even under the overcast sky. The driver buzzed the intercom and the gate promptly opened to welcome them inside. There was a half mile of interlocking brick driveway that lacked the sculpted tire grooves of a well-travelled road, and the edges were guarded by young elm trees.

The shingle-style bleach-white colonial home that came into view looked out of place, like the architect had mixed up plans with an old-money client from the Hamptons. They followed the circular driveway and parked under a soaring porte cochere. Before the limousine was in park, the servant was already out of the car and opening the door for Hawke, Noor, and Servo. He didn't so much as offer to take Noor's laptop bag as begged for the privilege. She adamantly refused, which seemed to confuse him. He accepted defeat and ushered the trio into a brightly lit drawing room. The servant offered them something, anything at all, to drink and was again confused when they all declined. He fetched a tray of coffee, nonetheless.

The drawing room had three couches forming a U with the open end facing a fireplace. It had an intricately carved mantel reaching shoulder height and a painting as the centrepiece, which Hawke couldn't name but remembered seeing in poster form in the dorm rooms of the liberal arts girls he used to date. Potted palm trees were spaced evenly around the outside of the room and accentuated how large the room was, which Hawke supposed was the point.

Nobody had said a word since leaving the yacht, and they continued to remain in an uneasy silence. Eventually, the servant stood at the threshold, and with a display that seemed borrowed from a debutante ball gave an exaggerated sweep of his arms as he announced the proprietor of the estate. "Mr. Jack Ka-shing!"

Jack Ka-shing strode into the room. As if it was an unexpected stroke of serendipity that he found Noor in his drawing room, he beamed a wide smile and held out his arms for a joyous greeting. "Sara! So good to see you again." He clamped his hands on her shoulders and kissed both cheeks in a display of his worldliness.

The first thing Hawke noticed about Ka-shing was that he was tall. Very tall. His limbs were stretched out of proportion relative to his torso, as if his adolescent growth spurt had come by way of a torture rack. Only a bespoke suit would fit his frame, one he proudly wore along with fastidiously polished oxfords. His oil black hair was slicked into a perfect wave that crashed just above his forehead, and his tiny eyes remained trained on Noor.

"Jack, thanks for having us." Noor played along with the facade.

"My absolute pleasure, Sara. My absolute pleasure." Ka-shing only released his hands from her shoulders when she motioned to Servo, who sat brooding at the farthest edge of the farthest couch.

"Jack, this is Servo. I believe you've spoken before." Both men muttered a greeting.

"I'm assuming that's a yes?"

"I do seem to recall speaking to a fellow named *Servo* about my plans for bitcoin protocol enhancements on the chat forum," Ka-shing said to Noor as if the cypherpunk wasn't in the room. "I'm disappointed to say I didn't get much buy-in for reasons that still remain unclear. I'm reluctant to say some people don't truly understand the technology and have their own self-interests in mind. I hope that isn't the case, but alas, my proposals always got declined, rather rudely I should say. It's better that we all work together and include at least some of my ideas in order to move the protocol forward. After all, somebody needs the vision to lead bitcoin to the next level."

A vein bulged across Servo's forehead. He sprang to his feet, jabbing a finger at Ka-shing. "All ideas aren't fucking equal. You can't demand an audience for your shitty plans and then claim we aren't being civil when we don't compromise. Half of a shit idea is still a shit idea."

Ka-shing treated the outburst as if he were watching bad television and flicked his bony wrist to change the channel. Noor quickly stepped to Servo's side and put a calming hand on his shoulder. "Jack, I don't believe you've met Henry."

Ka-shing turned his attention to Hawke and waited, as if expecting a magic trick. When none was revealed he put on a business-like expression. "You must be Henry the Hawke. You, sir, are the man of the hour." Ka-shing shook his hand vigorously and gave him an old-boys wink, one of private clubs and insider tips. "We need to talk."

"I'm more of a texter," Hawke replied.

Ka-shing's eyes narrowed, wondering if he had just witnessed the magic trick he was waiting for. "Yes, of course. Very good. Everyone texts these days." He looked Hawke up and down. "I thought you'd be wearing a suit."

"I'm trying out something new."

"I see." Ka-shing considered the answer, then laughed. "Very good indeed. Now, Sara, I've had my servant Xing prepare your accommodations. Three rooms, correct?" He raised an eyebrow at Hawke and let the question linger.

"That will be fine," Noor replied.

"Very good," Ka-shing said, satisfied with the answer. "Now, I have some business to attend to while you freshen up. Xing will show you to your rooms." Xing promptly materialized at Ka-shing's side, smiling through his teeth, and bowed.

Plans were made for a late morning brunch and Ka-shing exited with a ceremonial flourish of his stretched arms. With unrestrained enthusiasm, Xing led Hawke, Noor, and Servo out of the drawing room. In the hallway he was momentarily startled, however, by the unexpected presence of the man who had driven the limousine. He was still very serious and still had the bulge under his armpit.

Xing scuttled by like a mouse past a sleeping house cat and never regained his full-teeth smile as the serious man followed them at a distance. Hawke didn't want to say anything, but a concerned glance from Servo told him they were on the same page.

Once they reached the guest wing, Xing presented them to their individual bedrooms. Hawke was last in line and noticed the serious man take up guard in the hallway. Hawke shut and locked his door and wondered, was a guard needed to keep people out? Or keep people in?

KA-SHING'S OFFICE

Later that morning, it dawned on Hawke what an unusual situation it was that he found himself in. To begin with, the day after squatting in an abandoned train station he was brunching on a patio that overlooked a vast and perfectly manicured green lawn. He was eating his eggs benedict, cantaloupe, and freshly squeezed orange juice in silence beside a woman who had a knack for making him accept half-answers and a practicing cypherpunk who might be the first person to have separation anxiety from a train station. All the while they were being studiously watched over by an eager-to-please servant and by a stone-faced armed guard who was living proof you couldn't overdose on protein shakes.

Jack Ka-shing broke the silence by bursting onto the patio with a pantomime explosion of legs and arms and humble brags. "Sorry I'm late. I was having a Japanese language session and my teacher said she had never seen such amazing progress, so we kept going. That's where I was this morning, by the way. Did you know I can speak Japanese? How is everyone enjoying brunch?"

"It's very pleasant, Jack," Noor said.

Ka-shing noticed Noor's orange juice glass wasn't full, so he snapped his fingers and Xing quickly addressed the situation.

"I'm afraid, Sara, I'm going to have to borrow this gentleman for the afternoon," Ka-shing said and put his hands on Hawke's shoulders, shaking him like an old frat brother.

Noor offered no opposition and Servo didn't look up from his meal.

"I'll have him back in time for dinner." Ka-shing winked.

Hawke got up from the table and followed Ka-shing around the back of the mansion to a detached garage, which was larger than most homes on the island. The floor was coated in epoxy and free of oil spots. Rows of pristine tools were mounted along the back wall and a polished hoist glimmered in the corner. Three cars, each a symbol of wild success, crouched and pointed outwards.

A white 1965 Shelby Mustang GT with dual blue mohawk stripes rushing over its body first caught Hawke's eye. It was raw, angry and impatiently awaited its chance to howl.

Beside the muscle car was a ruby red Ferrari 458 Italia. Low slung, sleek, it looked poised to vanish if you blinked.

And lastly, and most prominently positioned at the centre of the room under a halo of light, sat the jewel of Ka-shing's collection: a Lamborghini Aventador. It was motionless but gave the impression that it was already breaking the sound barrier. The source of wealth behind its purchase was blazoned across every visible inch of its surface with its custom paint job—the bright orange of the bitcoin symbol.

"My babies," Ka-shing gushed. He swept his elongated fingers sensually over the Lambo's roof. "I bought the Mustang after I my made my first million at my hedge fund. The Ferrari after my tenth. I splurged on the Lambo and paint job after bitcoin hit ten dollars a coin. Once you have as much money as I do, you struggle to find objects worthy of your affection."

Ka-shing continued to stroke the Lambo's curves to the point where Hawke hoped he stayed clear of the tailpipe. Ka-shing then turned and winked at him, "What are you going to do once you're a bitcoin millionaire?"

"What do you mean?" Hawke asked.

"Don't worry," Ka-shing said slyly, "I know *all* about Satoshi's Fortune. The wallet file, the two-of-three passwords needed to unlock it . . ."

"Is that so?"

"Noor is a woman who knows a lot about a lot." His hands finally left the edges of the Lambo.

"Huh, she didn't tell me you knew of its existence."

"I'd wager she hasn't told you about quite a bit." Ka-shing let his desired implications take root. "For instance, did you know she's doing a piece on me?"

"Sounds mildly painful."

Ka-shing laughed. "No, not at all. I've been after her for years, for this piece. Why shouldn't one of bitcoin's most successful investors, biggest advocate, and one of the largest known holders get a little media attention?"

Hawke considered the interest the Cabal had shown in other known bitcoiners and thought the answer was self-evident. Ka-shing took his lack of a reply to mean agreement.

"Exactly. With Satoshi gone, somebody needs to promote bitcoin to the masses. And who better than me?" Ka-shing didn't wait for a response and strode to a wall-mounted case. He pulled out a black-and-orange key fob and held it up for Hawke to see. "Now watch this."

With a click of a button, the Lamborghini's scissor doors swung open to the sky, an action that no doubt impressed a great many. Hawke smiled thinly. "I thought you'd just pay somebody to open your doors for you instead of using a key like some sort of plebian."

Ka-shing paid the comment more laughter than it was worth. "Let's go for a drive."

It was cramped in the passenger seat for Hawke. Ka-shing inelegantly positioned himself into the cockpit, almost having to fold his long limbs in half to fit. He flipped open a tab on the middle dashboard to reveal a dangerous looking red button that might have been borrowed from a doomsday device. Ka-shing jabbed it but the world didn't end; the engine just started with an unapologetic explosion.

"I never get tired of that! Don't even need to use a key like a plebian." He eyed Hawke and patted his pocket. "As long as the key fob is nearby, she'll fire right up." Ka-shing paused and then laughed as he said, "Too bad it isn't that easy with women, eh, Henry?"

"Have you tried flowers and candy?"

"Ha! I think a Lamborghini Aventador should work just fine." Ka-shing tapped the gear paddles and jerked the car forward through the open garage door and down the driveway. A black Mercedes sedan was waiting and crept behind them.

"My guard. You met him earlier, I believe. Important people need security," Ka-shing said flatly. He accelerated inconsistently down the driveway and past the open gate, sometimes hammering the gas and sometimes missing a gear shift, making the trip more uneven than the one Hawke had just taken across the Irish Sea. Hawke noticed the sedan was almost right behind them, having no problem keeping up with the Lamborghini despite the disadvantage of not being a supercar.

They eventually reached downtown and parked in front of a ten-story glass tower with *Ka-shing Investments* in thick bold lettering across the facade. They took the elevator to the tenth floor where they were greeted by a sultry young redhead at the front desk, whose day job was apparently that of a receptionist. She smiled at Hawke as if it were last call.

Ka-shing made a show of chatting with her, and she professionally answered all his questions, feigned innocence at each double entendre, and displayed world-class skill at laughing on command. Satisfied with the interaction, Ka-shing moved on.

"I hired her myself," Ka-shing boasted.

"Sometimes resumes are just a formality."

The office encompassed three corners of the floor, with cubicles filling the middle. Each was armed with dual flat screens and a Bluetooth-enabled multiline phone, weapons of war for young men sent off to day trade. The floor-to-ceiling windows allowed in all the natural light the overcast Douglas sky had to offer.

The layout led to Ka-shing's personal corner office whose walls were made of yet more glass—easy for him to observe his troops in battle. A main work desk was fortified with a wall of flat screens, each showing charts of the seductive up-and-down movements of the bitcoin price. A leather couch paired with matching chairs and coffee table adorned one end of the office. A well-used wet bar was stocked with a single malt scotch marketed to affluent stock brokers and lawyers, and a bottle of top-shelf gin sourced from a single orchard in Herefordshire. A bucket of fresh ice cubes and bowls of fresh apples and limes completed the setup.

Ka-shing shut the door behind them and let Hawke, transfixed by the high volatility of the price movements, gravitate towards the monitors. Whereas such volatility was considered an unwelcome risk in traditional asset classes such as bullion and stocks, with bitcoin the rollercoaster ride was part of the allure. It wasn't unheard of to have daily moves of plus or minus fifty percent, which could lead to outsized profits if one had the stomach for it.

"You think you could turn a profit day trading?" Ka-shing said, pointing a long bony finger at the charts. Hawke knew that day trading stocks was largely a fool's

game where you rarely made money over the long term—
and that was with a hundred years' worth of data to
analyze. With something as new and unregulated as
bitcoin, expecting it to end well was akin to letting a blind
man pilot a plane. Sure, he could keep it in the air long
enough for people to think he knew what he was doing,
but eventually he'd fly into the side of a mountain.

Hawke summarized his thoughts by saying, "Maybe."

"Do you know how I became rich? By trusting my gut
and not listening to all those naysayers out there. Did you
know I was a millionaire before I even heard the word
bitcoin?"

"Yeah, you might have mentioned it once or twice on
the ride over."

"And do you know what my gut is telling me now?
That bitcoin is the next big thing." Ka-shing coaxed
Hawke into one of the leather seats and then positioned
himself by the window. He made a show of gazing out past
a hundred miles of unrelenting sea with his hands clasped
behind his back. It was a well-rehearsed pose meant to
convey that the millionaire wore a heavy crown.

"From the moment I was first handed a report on the
technology, I knew that I was going to be *the* bitcoin leader
that everyone would respect. Every new industry has its
titan. Oil had John D. Rockefeller. The automobile had
Henry Ford. The personal computer had Bill Gates. And
cryptocurrency will have Jack Ka-shing. People on social
media the world over follow me and eagerly await my
opinion, my advice, my vision. I'm already trusted and

loved. All those who mocked me will soon beg for a piece of the empire I've built. Do you know what happened when I told my hedge fund golfing buddies my bitcoin dream?" Ka-shing rotated to face Hawke. "They laughed at me."

Hawke didn't know how to respond but had experienced a similar response at his own office at Chicago Mutual. Just the mention of bitcoin brought up sneers and open mockery. Ka-shing moved around the office now, his gangly limbs jutting about like a grown man learning to swim.

"It didn't matter that they laughed. All great men are laughed at when they first present their vision. I had the willpower to ignore them. And the wherewithal to buy every coin I could find until I had amassed what I knew would one day be a fortune. I moved to this welcoming jurisdiction to form my base of operations. I travelled the world speaking at every banking conference I could find, pushing for adoption wherever I went. Did you know I've got two dozen retail stores and restaurants in Douglas alone to accept bitcoin? I've done more for the project than a hundred coders, and you know what thanks I get? Ridicule from those technocrats who act as the gatekeepers to the code. Because I wasn't one of them, my ideas were discarded with contempt. They said I was just another Suit looking to profit, that I wasn't in it for the technology, as if somehow that didn't make me worthy of being involved. Henry, how many times have you been called a Suit by those anti-social geeks as if it were a bad thing?"

Hawke's answer was dangerously close to what Ka-shing wanted to hear, so he kept it to himself. "I think I'm starting to see why you and Servo don't get along."

"Who? Oh, that pudgy dungeon-and-dragons fellow? Yes, I now seem to vaguely recall talking to him about the protocol in the past. People like him will cut off their nose to spite their face. They'd rather their code stayed pure to their ideological view instead of making it more suitable to the real world. Compromise is not a dirty word, Henry. How many legendary leaders of men throughout history found it advantageous to form alliances with groups that they would otherwise scorn?"

Hawke didn't have an answer. But that didn't seem to slow Ka-shing.

"My point is, we need to work together to build my empire. And this empire will come about in two ways. First, bitcoin needs to go mainstream. Everyone needs to start using it and talking about it and wanting to get in. There are twenty-four million millionaires in the world today. There will only ever be twenty-one million bitcoins. That means even the one percenters will be lucky to have even a single bitcoin. Once people open their eyes there will be an epidemic of FOMO unlike any the world has ever seen." He raised his arms to the ceiling for emphasis. "And the second part is I need to control the markets. I need enough bitcoins to dictate which way the markets swing—and how far. I can't buy enough today without unduly pushing the price to the moon. There's only one source that will satisfy my needs." A smirk spread across his thin lips.

Hawke shifted uncomfortably in the leather chair. The blatant and unapologetic talk about bitcoin as a means to great wealth was at odds with the message from Servo and Sara, not to mention Aziz. It was the talk of bankers—bankers that only recently nearly collapsed the world economy with their greed and were rewarded with billions of dollars in taxpayers' money.

But was wealth and the pursuit of it inherently evil? Was Satoshi's Fortune not something to be protected from the world, but something to be used to create more wealth? Hawke's thoughts on the matter were closer in spirit to Ka-shing's than he would care to admit around the others.

Ka-shing seemed to read his thoughts and tried to reassure Hawke. "It's okay to want money, Henry. It's really why most people are into bitcoin, if they're being honest with themselves. It *is* money after all. But I bet none of the other so-called Keepers of the Fortune want you to actually succeed in your quest, do they? Have they made any effort to help you find your uncle's password? A bit hypocritical of them I must say, but not surprising. You're not one of them any more than I am. We look sharp in a suit, for one, and we live in the real world where profit and loss matter, where ideals sometimes have to take a backseat to rent—well, not for me anymore obviously, but the point stands. They won't help you find Satoshi's Fortune because they don't want you to have it.

"Again, I can see that you're pragmatic when it comes to wealth. And I'm not dismissing the paradigm-shifting potential of the bitcoin project. But who says you have to be poor to change the world? Rockefeller, Gates . . . these great men who ruthlessly built their own empires are also some of the greatest philanthropists the world has ever seen. Something that wouldn't have been possible without an empire in the first place. But those technocratic extremists who would prefer to see bitcoin risk death rather than grow in someone else's hands won't openly admit this, but enough money can fix any problem. Even a murder charge . . ."

Hawke grimaced. He wasn't pleased with how much Ka-shing knew about him.

"You can't go back to your old life, though after you hear my proposal I can't imagine why you'd ever want to."

Hawke stood and joined Ka-shing by the window, watching the boats meander in the port and specks of people scatter around below, no apparent rhyme or reason to it all.

"I'm going to build the world's first and greatest cryptocurrency trading desk out of this office. And I want you to join me." Ka-shing jabbed his chest. "Be proud that you look sharp in a suit. I know how to deal with that annoying murder charge. You can easily and very shortly be a free man. A very wealthy free man at that. All I need from you is one thing."

"What's that?" Hawke knew the answer, but he needed to hear it, nonetheless.

Ka-shing eyed him with nervous intensity. "I need you to help me find Satoshi's Fortune."

HAWKE'S SUIT

A fortune for his freedom.

That was Ka-shing's offer. And one Hawke was seriously considering. All he had to do was provide Peter Finlay's password. How and why Ka-shing thought Hawke knew it wasn't clear. Nor was it clear how Ka-shing was poised to come into possession of the wallet file that mere days ago had been ripped from the jaws of its rightful owner. Hawke wagered it had cost him more than money.

There was also the not insignificant fact that a second password would be needed to gain control of the fortune, even with the wallet file. Had Servo provided it? Hawke couldn't believe that was possible. The cypherpunk would rather die than help someone like Ka-shing. That left Johan Jarvenpaa, who was under arrest in Sweden, which reeked of the Cabal.

Back at the mansion there was a call for Ka-shing that he had to take in private. Hawke avoided Noor and Servo but was unable to slip past Xing, who smiled away while informing him that dinner was to be served in one hour and that they had left proper evening wear tailored to his size in his private room, which wasn't creepy at all.

Once in his room, Hawke ignored a very nice suit hanging in his closet and jumped in the shower. He turned the water all the way to hot and when he couldn't stand it any longer, switched to cold to shock himself into an alert state. He dried off and dragged his hand across the steamed mirror.

Many more a man would go rogue if he only knew how.

It seemed like such a simple motto, a call to action that would be easy to live by. But the price for rebellion was apparently to be hunted for murder, forced outside a world you had grown up in and had always assumed would protect you. The life you were told to chase—a career, a nice home, obedience—was no longer realistic.

Yet he was on the cusp of living in an entirely different stratosphere, if Ka-shing was to be believed. He promised to clear his name, provide him with a high-paying job at his burgeoning cryptocurrency firm, and to split Satoshi's Fortune with him. Hawke would be successful, wealthy, and out of jail.

But would he be free?

Hawke couldn't face his reflection any longer and welcomed the distraction of a loud knock at his door. He wrapped himself in a towel and opened the door.

"What the fuck did you do?"

"Used conditioner after shampoo. Supposed to make your hair look better. What'd ya think?"

"I think it's time you got serious, Henry," Noor said, standing aggressively in the doorway.

"In that case, come on in."

The tailored suit hanging in the open closet caught Noor's eye and didn't do anything to lessen her disappointment.

"What exactly did I do?" Hawke asked.

"You made a deal with Jack Ka-shing behind our backs."

"Technically, isn't that what you did to get us here in the first place?" Hawke pointed out.

"I did that to keep us safe."

"Maybe I'm keeping myself safe. Besides, who said I even accepted his offer?"

"Ka-shing did. Said you guys had a great afternoon and were excited to be working together."

"I haven't agreed to anything. He showed me the office where he wants to build his little empire and offered me a job."

"Anything else?"

"He said that he was going to acquire the wallet file and that if I provided him with my uncle's password, he would make me rich and make the murder charge go away."

"But I thought you didn't know Peter's password?"

"Yeah, but Ka-shing doesn't know that."

"Why didn't you reject his offer?"

Hawke's silence was all-encompassing. Noor threw her hands up in disgust. "If you think I'm mad, wait until you see Servo. I thought he was going to have a heart attack."

"Anyone ever point out that you bitcoiners are prone to outrage? Nothing's changed on my part since this morning."

Noor crossed her arms. "Jarvenpaa was released. All charges dropped."

"That's great news!" Hawke said. Maybe the Cabal's power wasn't absolute after all.

"No, it's terrible news," Noor countered. "The official reason for his release was that there was an incorrect identification and the investigators found undeniable proof that Johan was somewhere else at the time of the alleged assault. Both the London and Stockholm police have offered their sincerest apologies for the misunderstanding. The problem is once the Cabal have their claws in you, they don't let go until they've gotten what they want."

"So that means . . ."

"There's little doubt he made a deal with the Cabal. His password for his freedom." The disgust in Noor's voice was palpable, but Hawke could sympathize. It also explained why Ka-shing was so confident he could gain control of Satoshi's Fortune.

Hawke assessed the situation. He was in a luxurious room on a magnificent estate and had access to tailored suits, fine dining, superyachts, and supercars. And now stood a ravishing woman in his bedroom with only a towel and ideology between them.

But in the bitcoin world, Hawke had learned that things weren't always as they seemed.

"What's so funny?" she asked.

"Nothing. Or everything. I haven't decided."

"You care to let me know what you're going to do?"

Hawke imagined Noor smiling. He had to because he hadn't yet seen it.

"First, I'm going to get dressed. And then we're going to go for a nice dinner."

"Fine. But just so you know, I'm going to do what's needed to keep the bitcoin project safe."

Hawke felt she was being a bit overdramatic. "Keep it safe from who exactly?"

Noor matched his gaze. Eventually she relented and walked by his suit dangling from its hanger. She swept her hand across, only to sharply pull her fingers back, as if the material repulsed her. "Keep it safe from people like you."

Hawke smiled after she left. Perhaps cruelly.

He laid the suit on his bed, opposite his jeans and Henley shirt.

Many more a man would go rogue if he only knew how.

He checked his watch.

It was time to make a decision.

KA-SHING'S DINNER

The guard was back in the hallway looking as serious as ever when Hawke exited his room. He went to Noor's room and knocked. She answered the door still wearing her Colorado Avalanche T-shirt.

"A suit, eh?" she said, rolling her eyes.

"I am what I am."

"Servo's not going to be happy."

"I think he'll understand. Didn't Ka-shing provide you with your own evening wear?"

Noor pointed to a dress tossed haphazardly onto a dresser. "I might steal the shoes though."

Servo stepped out of his room still wearing his MUNITIONS T-shirt, and if there had been a suit offered to him, it had probably been tossed out the window. He didn't say anything except grunt at Hawke's attire, which at least meant he wasn't swearing at him.

Xing greeted them and proceeded to lead them in a silent march through the dining room's open doors before leaving them to their fate.

The dining room was a large windowless room with gold trim everywhere. Silk-upholstered chairs sat around a polished table big enough to seat a Catholic royal family.

The only light came from gold candlesticks placed down the middle of the table; they glowered in every direction, causing shadows to dance throughout the room.

Ka-shing stood aside at the far end of the table, a nervous smile on his face, his hands folded in front.

Seated at the head of the table, staring right through them, was a man with the dead eyes of a frozen corpse.

"What the hell is this?" Hawke thundered.

"Please, if everyone would just take a seat. Everything's okay. If you just hear us out you'll understand," Ka-shing pleaded.

The doors slammed shut behind them, courtesy of the guard that had followed them from upstairs.

"Take a seat," Agent 21 directed. The Cabal agent's voice made Hawke's teeth freeze. If he had ideas about making a run for it with Noor and Servo, it evaporated when the guard's hand came to a rest on his shoulder and firmly helped him to a chair directly opposite Agent 21 at the foot of the table.

Noor and Servo followed his lead, sitting on either side.

"Henry, I don't want you to worry. In time, you'll see this is all for the best. *This* is what millionaires do. We make deals. We compromise. My associate here informed me the Russians were after you. He wanted to help you! So I warned Sara. Don't you see it now? I saved you! I saved you all! Just hear us out. I'm confident we can come to a mutually beneficial arrangement." Ka-shing's voice cracked as he spoke.

"And become a Cabal lap dog, like you?"

Ka-shing pounded his fists on the table and attempted indignation as a defence. "Grow up, Henry. You need to play the game, make allies, have insider information. I'm a self-made millionaire, so that is what I did! What I've always done! Now let's be reasonable and make a deal while you still can."

Servo unleashed a torrent of curses. So apoplectic and exhaustive was his rant that his face turned the same shade of red as his beard and his Scottish slang overcame him to the point where nobody knew what he was saying, but there was no doubt it was vile. Breathing heavily, he summarized his thoughts as he inched closer to a heart attack.

"You sell-out! You call yourself a bitcoiner? You're nothing more than a fucking pawn in the Cabal's game! You goddamn fool."

Ka-shing seemed to shrink and wither. He whispered quietly, "I am a bitcoiner. I'm a millionaire. I know what Satoshi would want."

Agent 21 held up his hand, bringing silence to the room. He took a sip of water and chewed on an ice cube. He finally spoke, in an unnervingly calm voice, belying the severity of the situation. "This conversation lost its relevance a long time ago. I am here to secure Satoshi's Fortune and am aware that two of the Keepers are in this room. Provide one of these passwords and you are all free to go. That is my only offer."

Hawke realized with gut-clenching certainty that Noor was right; the Cabal must have broken Jarvenpaa and taken his password. And with the wallet file in his possession, Agent 21 was only one more password away from finding Satoshi's Fortune.

But something didn't make sense to Hawke. Why had Agent 21 gone to all the trouble of using Ka-shing to lure them here when he could have simply let the Russians capture them at the Sanctuary? There was a bigger picture that Hawke couldn't quite see, but it was irrelevant if they couldn't escape Agent 21's trap.

Agent 21 posed a question to the group, "What is your password to Satoshi's Fortune?"

Hawke grinned. "I dunno. Maybe it's something like *we are all Satoshi*."

"Funny," Agent 21 said, but did not laugh, "but coincidentally that was the last thing your uncle ever said to me—so long as you don't count the screams of pain."

Hawke's demeanour changed instantly. His eyes narrowed and his grin devolved into savagery. "You killed him."

Agent 21 didn't blink. "Yes."

If he was going to be charged for murder, Hawke reasoned, he might as well get his money's worth. He was about to lunge across the table and grab the ghost of a man that had murdered his family when Noor leaned forward and put her hand over his, the subtle act shifting his rage into neutral—for the moment at least.

"It was just a big misunderstanding. Really, it was," Ka-shing said, trying to massage the circumstances around Peter Finlay's death. "My associate here just wanted to talk to Peter. He wanted to meet Satoshi. Find out who he was. There wasn't anything sinister about it. Peter just didn't want to play by the rules. If he had just agreed to help the Cabal, things would have gone differently! They would have made him richer than he ever thought possible!"

"Unfortunately for Peter Finlay, it wasn't about the money," Agent 21 said.

"It isn't about money for you either, is it?" Servo said. "It's about knowledge."

Agent 21 cocked his head. "Something like that. For instance, I know why your parents kicked you out ten years ago. I know why you haven't been back to church since. I know your favourite Bible quotes. It all results, Mr. Galahad Servo, in you living a counterculture life and ending up a Keeper. Now tell me, what is your password to Satoshi's Fortune?"

"No idea," Servo said. "Yes, I'm a Keeper of the fuckin Fortune. What a great honour! Chosen! Fuckin great. I don't know why anyone would want control of 980,000 bitcoins at the end of the day. It's potentially worth billions one day—but at the same time, what you build around it would be worth more. Ironic, isn't it? The greatest fortune of the twenty-first century . . . and it was the least valuable part of the project. Well, I wanted no part of that."

Agent 21's eyes narrowed. "What have you done?"

"When Satoshi had me enter my password, I used a randomly generated number, which I never wrote down and don't remember. Fifty characters long. Alphanumeric. If you're lucky, you might be able to brute force it before the sun implodes."

"So your password is lost forever."

"Fuckin right."

Agent 21 was nonplussed. "One last question. Do you know who Satoshi Nakamoto is?"

"You know my answer."

"Yes," Agent 21 acknowledged, "and I've heard it far too many times."

The bullet pierced Servo's skull right between his eyes. A drop of blood emerged from the wound and paused, uncertain of what path it should take, before deciding to slowly trickle down between his eyes, across the bridge of his nose and down his cheek, leaving a crimson trail behind.

Ka-shing's screams filled the air. Agent 21 listened, the silenced pistol smoking in his hand, showing as much shame as a lifelong smoker lighting a cigarette in a crowded restaurant, indifferent to the disgust of others at the act.

"My god! Why did you shoot him?!" Ka-shing cried out.

"He was no longer of any use."

Hawke watched as Servo's lifeless body slumped to one side, blood slowly staining the expensive silk upholstery of his chair. He clenched his fists so tight he felt his knuckles would burst. And then an icy gunmetal object tickled the base of his neck.

"Let's just calm down." The guard pushed his gun firmly into Hawke.

Agent 21 cleared his throat. "Now, let's try this again. Tell me your password to Satoshi's Fortune or I kill your other friend."

"It was my uncle's. What makes you think he even passed it to me? Killing Sara won't change that." It was all Hawke could think of.

Agent 21 gave him a peculiar look. "Whoever said I was talking to you?" His eyes swept across the room and landed on Noor. "I said, tell me your password, Ms. Noor."

NOOR'S SECRET

Hawke was overwhelmed with emotions he couldn't process. Servo's body was still warm and waiting to be grieved, and here was another absolute shock to his system. He felt his self-worth crumble; his only reason for being invited into this bitcoin world was his familiar link to being a Keeper, and now with that broken he was out of place, and out of time. Hawke felt lightheaded and could barely keep his focus on his surroundings.

"Sara is the last Keeper of the Fortune . . ." The words fell out of Hawke's mouth.

"Obviously." Agent 21 kept his eyes locked on Noor, who didn't look away.

"Once I found out you rescued Mr. Hawke, I made a point to know everything about you: high school mathlete, computer science Honours degree with a minor in economics. If you weren't discussing cryptography it was hockey—specifically, and most telling, your advanced statistical analysis on why Peter Forsberg, number 21 of the Colorado Avalanche, was the greatest hockey player of his generation. Since further investigation revealed PeterF21@gmx.com was still actively sending and receiving emails for weeks after Finlay's death, it was easy

to pinpoint you, Ms. Noor, as a Keeper of the Fortune."
Agent 21's gun veered towards Hawke. "So, Mr. Hawke is
clearly worthless and no longer necessary to find Satoshi's
Fortune."

"Wait!" Noor cried out. "Let's make a deal."

Agent 21 remained silent.

"You let Henry go. As you said he's no longer
necessary, so it doesn't matter if he lives or dies . . . "

Hawke felt like that wasn't totally accurate and hoped
Noor would clarify where she was going with this.

" . . . but if you let him live, once the wallet is restored,
I'll give you my password. The blockchain should take
about six hours to download and restore the wallet, so
that'll give him plenty of time to go his own way."

Why should I trust you? Hawke could see the Cabal agent
asking himself that very familiar question. Noor had
somehow, again, positioned herself as indispensable, the
owner of vital information. With Servo dead, she was the
only person left who could find Satoshi's Fortune.

Agent 21 arrived at the same conclusion as Hawke.

Because you have no choice.

"I agree to your terms," Agent 21 said.

The guard moved to Noor and pulled her to her feet.
Hawke stood as well and felt a mixture of anger and
betrayal. Anger that he had been chasing his uncle's ghost
this whole time. Betrayal because she had been lying since
they met.

Noor felt Hawke's burning glare. "You're not expecting
me to say sorry, are you?"

361

How very un-Canadian, Hawke thought.

"Time to go." Agent 21 stood and gently slid the pistol back into an unseen holster.

"Six hours," she whispered as she passed.

It was a message that sent his pulse racing and ushered a new purpose sharply into focus: he had six hours to save her—and bitcoin.

Why wait?

Hawke noticed the guard admiring the cut of Noor's jeans and decided it was now or never. He hurled a fist towards the distracted guard with all his weight and anger and frustration, catching him square on the chin. Hawke leapt forward while the guard was off balance, pulled the guard's suit jacket over his head to blind him, and began feeding him manic punches, the guard unable to defend himself against the strikes.

The crackling of knuckles against skull energized Hawke, but he was caught off guard by a hand on his shoulder. He pivoted just in time to see Agent 21's fingers jabbing towards his neck. He barely slipped past the attack and felt the blow glancing harmlessly off his shoulder.

Countering, he grasped at Agent 21's suit jacket to attempt the same technique that had proven successful on the guard, not to mention countless hockey fights. But Agent 21 deftly avoided Hawke's effort, leaving him only grasping at air. Frustrated, Hawke attempted reckless haymaker after haymaker, but the Cabal agent made him a fool by avoiding each strike with minimal effort, while Hawke began to feel the exertion wear on his muscles.

It was like trying to punch snow, Hawke realized too late. After one last uppercut that flew harmlessly into nothing, Agent 21, seemingly tired of the game, gave two quick jabs flat on Hawke's nose that made stars explode in his vision, and next thing he knew he was being thrown to the ground with unexpected force.

And then he felt cold hands squeezing his throat.

The grip was impossibly strong. All Hawke could do was look up at the Cabal agent, into his lifeless and indifferent expression, as he choked the life out of him. To Agent 21, it would seem, killing Hawke was a mere annoyance, not a passion.

Darkness crept in around the edges of Hawke's vision, punctuated by white specks of stars exploding. In the last moment before it all collapsed around him, Hawke heard Noor shout, "We have a deal, Agent 21. A fortune for Henry's life."

The hands remained tight around his neck for what seemed an eternity. But instead of release, all he felt was more pain, and Hawke was plunged into absolute darkness.

HAWKE'S PURSUIT

There was nothing in the darkness. There was no fortune, bitcoin or otherwise. There was no woman to confuse him, so Noor wasn't there. There was no friendship, as if Servo had never been there. There was no paranoia, so Shariff couldn't have been there.

There was nothing for Hawke in the darkness. So he decided to stop wasting his time and get on with it.

It was as if a switch had been flipped on inside him. His heart thundered so hard the blood stressed the veins and he was jolted upright, sucking in a series of frantic breaths in quick succession.

Hawke was alive.

But Servo wasn't. His body was growing cold mere feet away. A man who had only wanted to create, to make a difference, to push back against the idea that the status quo shouldn't be pushed back against. He was given a key to a fortune and threw it away for the greater good, and died for that sin.

Hawke was pissed off.

He couldn't tell how long he had been unconscious—it could have been a minute or an hour. But Agent 21, Noor, and the guard were nowhere to be seen. Only Ka-shing was still in the dining room with him; the self-made millionaire was huddled in the corner, almost in tears, trying not to cry at the loss of an empire that never was.

Hawke rolled to his side and struggled to his feet. Ka-shing's eyes widened at seeing that he wasn't alone. "You're alive! We can fix this!"

Hawke ignored him and began to search for Noor. He vaguely sensed Ka-shing attempting to keep pace as he raced through the mansion hallways, his pleas echoing loudly throughout. "I was a millionaire before I met the Cabal! I swear! They needed me, not the other way around! I was going to hire you! You can trust me! I'm a self-made millionaire! You have to believe me!"

Hawke found the front doors and readied himself to burst through when they opened automatically before him. Always the dedicated servant, Xing had apparently decided that murder and kidnapping weren't a valid excuse to take the rest of the day off. He held the door open and smiled with maximum effort as Hawke rushed past.

Outside there wasn't a star in the sky, just dark grey clouds heavy with rain. Hawke only caught the briefest glimpse of red tail lights in the distance. The Mercedes sedan was already at the end of the driveway and soon would be beyond his reach. Hawke needed to chase after them.

Hawke's senses were immediately drawn to the bright orange Lamborghini Aventador waiting patiently in the driveway—and he swore the headlights winked at him. He raced forward and opened the door to the sky. Behind the wheel, he was about to try his luck at hotwiring the supercar when Ka-shing threw himself against his prized possession. He leaned into the cockpit and drowned Hawke with his desperate cries.

"Bitcoin is dead, Henry, can't you see that! The Cabal will have control and they'll destroy all trust! Satoshi is dead! But I know what he wanted—we can start our own cryptocurrency! We can make billions! We can be self-made billionaires!"

Hawke reached up and grabbed Ka-shing by the collar with one hand, violently yanking him closer. With his free hand he jabbed the ignition and prayed Ka-shing still had the fob in his pocket. Hawke was flooded with relief as the engine burst into applause and all twelve pistons took turns giving him a standing ovation. He tossed Ka-shing aside and lowered the door, waved goodbye to Xing who waved back, and smashed his foot on the accelerator. Hawke was thrust back into his seat as the Lambo burst out from under the porte cochere, zoomed down the long driveway, and was at the end of the street before he even realized he was white-knuckled and baring his teeth in a grin. He took the turn onto the highway at a speed reckless enough to be worthy of a supercar—the Lamborghini was now on the open highway and out of its cage, stretching its legs and going faster than it ever had before. The butterflies in Hawke's stomach scrambled into the air, but for the moment at least they were flying in formation.

Douglas' tall buildings quickly approached on the horizon, and Hawke spotted the red tail lights far in the distance, the driver still oblivious to being chased. But if they made it into Douglas before Hawke caught up, which at this point seemed a certainty, then the sedan would be lost in the city's traffic and Hawke would never find them again. He needed to use his speed advantage while he still could. With a gear shift, Hawke asked the supercar what it would take to catch the Cabal.

The answer from the roar of the engine was uncompromising.

The Lamborghini demanded madness.

And Hawke readily obliged.

Hawke floored the accelerator and the world outside his headlights ceased to exist. Blackness rounded the edges of his vision, blackness like the one Hawke had just barely escaped. But in the Lamborghini nothing would catch him. He began to sweat and his jaw ached from clenching it so tightly, as if he were physically pushing the car to these unseen speeds. Hawke dared not look at the speedometer for fear of taking his eyes off the road, and then, a split second after he allowed himself to blink, he was right behind the sedan. If the driver of the sedan hadn't heard a sonic boom, he must have noticed the bright orange supercar glowing in his rearview mirror as they reached the city's border. The sedan took evasive action and began weaving through traffic to attempt to shake its pursuer.

To stay on his target, Hawke had no other recourse but to drive like every asshole he had ever met on the road. He ignored traffic lights, raced around slower-moving cars like they were pylons, and drove like he was the utmost priority. Hawke received undignified honks and sharp middle fingers for his troubles, but at these speeds he was out of sight before he could return the favour.

The driver of the sedan was expertly trained and remained evasive. He pulled in front of a city bus just at the moment the oncoming traffic picked up, leaving Hawke unable to pass. Then the sedan slowed at the next set of lights as they turned yellow, forcing the bus and Hawke to stop, while he accelerated through the red light just before opposing traffic crossed the intersection.

Hawke smashed his hand on the steering wheel as he lost sight of the sedan, helpless to do anything about it. Finally, the light turned green and Hawke swerved around the bus and headed in the sedan's last direction.

Where had they gone?

He frantically looked for any sign of the Cabal. Then Hawke saw it. A block ahead was a sign for the airport. He gambled it was their most likely destination and followed the advertised turns. Within minutes the city street widened to double lanes and the buildings grew less frequent as Douglas quickly disappeared behind him.

Blinking lights of landing planes on the horizon told him the airport was a straight shot down the road. And the only vehicle he could see ahead was a black sedan.

Hawke decided to again unleash every one of the Aventador's 691 steroid-infused horses that couldn't pass an East German pee test to save their lives. In a matter of seconds he was red-lining and moving so fast time seemed to stand still. As if teleported, Hawke found himself alongside the Cabal sedan.

And it was at this moment that Hawke realized he didn't have a plan.

If he smashed into the sedan, then everyone, including himself and Noor, would be involved in a reckless and dangerous high-speed accident. But if he did nothing then they would arrive at the airport in the same situation as back at the mansion: Hawke and his fists versus Agent 21 and the guard—both armed.

The driver-side window lowered to reveal Agent 21 with his pistol raised. Hawke quickly discovered that, despite all the engineering prowess that went into the Lamborghini Aventador, they hadn't thought to include bulletproof tires.

Agent 21's pistol spat two bullets into the front wheel. Then Hawke was facing the wrong way, continuing in an uncontrollable spin, deafened by squealing rubber, until he was jarred to a standstill with the fantastic crunch of expensive metals and cracking timber. The Lamborghini's engine, now partially wrapped around a tree, would have to admit that Hawke's mad embrace was, perhaps, a bit more than the supercar had signed up for.

Hawke could do nothing but watch through smoke-filled eyes as Agent 21 carried on to the airport with everything he needed to control Satoshi's Fortune, Hawke's attempt to stop him nothing more than a mere inconvenience.

HAWKE'S FAILURE

Henry Hawke, by all accounts, had failed.

He was on a windswept rock in the middle of the Irish Sea where he had no friends, no money, and no idea what to do next.

He was a toxic asset to those in his past life, and a disappointment to those in his new one.

Shariff was missing. Noor was kidnapped. Servo was dead.

Bitcoin's eulogy was currently being written by Agent 21 and the Cabal.

Many more a man would go rogue if he only knew how.

Hawke laughed bitterly and alone. His uncle's last words came to him now as he sat in the smoking remains of a stolen Lamborghini. Words that Hawke had largely ignored while his uncle was alive, only to take them seriously after he found them engraved on the keepsake his uncle had left behind. As Hawke had thrown himself into the bitcoin world with reckless abandon, he reimagined these words as a call to arms, a way to escape the nine-to-five life, to find adventure and wealth, and, time permitting, maybe even to make a difference in the world. But now it was clear what they really were—cryptic nonsense from a father figure who didn't actually trust him with the truth, a slogan better suited to a teenager's social media post.

Hawke spat blood and extricated himself from the car and took stock of the wreckage. The car was wrapped around an elm tree on the edge of the road and the pinnacle of Italian engineering was now an insurance write-off. The few drivers that pulled over out of morbid fascination barely hid their disappointment at finding Hawke in one piece. No one offered him a ride.

The moon continued to hide under a blanket of dark clouds and Hawke's torn suit jacket offered little defence against the cold winds swirling off the nearby coast. Hawke gathered himself enough to carry on towards the airport. It was a long, cold, demoralizing walk with only the headlights of the occasional passing car lighting the way. He didn't make the walk as a last-ditch effort to rescue Noor, or anything else quite so admirable. He made the walk because he knew that wherever there are airports, there are bars.

Hawke wasn't disappointed as the main drag leading to the airport had three to choose from, mixed in between a convenience store and a car rental business. He chose the first bar, not because its tacky neon lights and blacked-out windows gave the impression it was a fine establishment, but because its empty parking lot meant he could wallow in self-pity alone.

Inside it was dimly lit and smelled of yesterday's potatoes. The bell-shaped bartender wore a frayed white apron and kept a cigarette expertly dangling from his lips.

He sat behind the bar and was so engrossed in reading a newspaper, he was startled to see he had a customer.

"What'll you have?" He put the newspaper down but kept the cigarette in place.

Without any better ideas of what to do next, and without thinking about how he would even pay for it, Hawke sat at the bar and ordered a pint. For Servo, it was an ale. For himself, it wouldn't be just the one.

Hawke downed the first pint before the bartender sat back down and promptly ordered a second. While it was being poured, he noticed a *Bitcoin Accepted Here* sticker by the cash register. Hawke pulled out his phone and checked the balance on his bitcoin wallet. He did a quick currency conversion in his head and determined he had enough money to get blackout drunk and no further. For all the promises cryptocurrency offered, it seemed that all he would be left with was a hangover.

As the bartender slid the second pint in front of him, Hawke asked about the sign.

"Aye, some douchebag kept coming in until we finally agreed to accept them."

"Many people pay with bitcoin?" Hawke asked.

"The odd one here and there. Pretty sure they're all criminals though."

Hawke raised his pint. "Many more a man would go rogue if he only knew how."

The bartender shrugged, coughed a puff of cigarette smoke, and went back to his newspaper.

The second pint brought no more peace of mind than the first. Hawke began to question whether what the bartender had said was true. Are bitcoiners really criminals? In most countries it was illegal to issue a private currency outside of government fiat, so technically the mere act of writing the bitcoin code was a criminal act, which explained a great deal about why Satoshi had chosen anonymity. By all appearances Noor had been above board, but who knew what other secrets she held. Servo argued against privacy infringement and no doubt he ran afoul of any such laws when he deemed it necessary. And if Shariff wasn't breaking any laws in his crusade against anyone who tried to oppress the masses, then Hawke would have been shocked.

His thoughts drifted to the Bratva and their involvement in Satoshi's Fortune. The way he understood it, they were criminals no matter what currency they traded in. But how far were they really from bitcoiners? Their existence came about from the rebellion of peasants against the ruling class—not a stretch to see the parallels. Was the Bratva merely further along the same path, wanting freedom and unwilling to concede it to their oppressors, but perhaps perverted by greed along the way? Again, not something unheard of in the bitcoin world.

But the more Hawke thought about the Bratva's involvement, the less it made sense. Why had the Russian mob pursued Hawke when everyone thought he was one of the Keepers? Why would they work with the Cabal to destroy bitcoin when it was vital to their operations? They would essentially be putting themselves out of business. If Servo was right, their schemes had worked flawlessly until they had been hacked.

The little Russian's words at the Sanctuary came to him now. *He stole from us!*

The Bratva thought he was a thief? *He stole from us!*

They weren't after Hawke because of Satoshi's Fortune—they were after him because they thought he was the hacker! Which meant the Cabal had lied to them!

A plan quickly began swirling in his mind, one that would have gotten a dismissive scoff from Servo and an eye roll from Noor—but one that just might avenge him and save her. But the plan relied on knowing who the real hacker was.

He only knew of one person capable of hacking the mob and crazy enough to do it. He clutched his smartphone and fired off an email, but all he received in return was an out-of-office reply: *"Unfortunately I am unable to reply to your e-mail at the moment. I will answer your e-mail as soon as I return."*

All Hawke could do now was wait and hope its owner monitored the account.

So he waited.

And then waited some more.

Hawke could almost see the bottom of the second pint glass when his phone rang. The voice was raspy, chaotic and its owner fired out his words like a machine gun.

"What da ya know, Suit, you might be ready to lose your barbed wire fences after all."

***

Shariff refused to tell Hawke where he was calling from, how he had gotten there, and if he actually was Aziz Shariff—though his subsequent rant about the Cabal controlling the Metropolitan Police, Jack Ka-shing, and the Bank of England left little doubt. Hawke took his pint to an isolated spot across the empty pub to avoid being overheard while Shariff continued spouting off.

"Suit, your email was vague. No facts that could compromise your next steps. Nothing for an overseeing organization to intercept. I like that. And this call is secure. We can speak freely. Or as freely as one can in this day and age. That is unless the Cabal has succeeded in developing quantum computing. Have I told you I suspect they have an entire team working on that as we speak? Well they do, but that's a battle for another day. What's going on with Satoshi's Fortune?"

"We only have hours before the Cabal destroys bitcoin."

"How is that possible? They would have needed to find two of the three Keepers, and last I knew they were still searching for their identities. And I also sent you to find them first. You gained possession of the flash drive, right?"

"Yup. It's how I got your email."

"Did you find out who Proverb211@vistomail.com was?"

"Yes. It was Servo."

"What do you mean *was*?"

Hawke explained how Servo had died and his password lost, and Shariff lent a modicum of sympathy before demanding to know about the remaining two. Hawke explained what happened to Jarvenpaa at which point Shariff began tossing around accusations of treason and betrayal with his typical resolve.

"Did you find your uncle's password?"

"No," Hawke said.

"Why not?!"

"He wasn't a Keeper."

"What?!"

"PeterF21@gmx.com wasn't Peter Finlay. It was Sara Noor."

Shariff actually remained silent for a brief moment before continuing. "That actually makes a lot more sense. Sara is much brighter than anyone in your family. Where is she now?"

Hawke sighed deeply. "The Cabal has her."

"You let the Cabal take her?!"

"I wouldn't say *let*."

"Goddamnit."

"Yeah. A bad day all around," Hawke lamented.

"So with the wallet file, Johan's password, and Sara poised to deliver hers, the Cabal have everything they need to find Satoshi's Fortune and destroy bitcoin!"

"Like I said, a bad day."

"What are you doing about it right now?"

Hawke examined the remnants of beer in his glass. "Researching."

"Do you even have a plan?"

Hawke did, or at least a reasonable facsimile of one. It depended on his hunch being correct, so he asked Shariff point blank, "Did you steal from the Russian mob?"

"The Bratva's bitcoin exchange? Of course I did! They were faking hacks in order to scam people out of their bitcoins. You think the Cabal is the only risk to the long-term viability of bitcoin? Organized crime and bad-faith actors and hacks and thefts and scams have already sent the public back years in trusting bitcoin. Just more barbed wire fences! People read about an exchange being hacked and the average person will immediately assume it's either a flaw in the bitcoin code or that the entire industry is unscrupulous! Either way trust is eroded. So I had to fight back."

"So . . . you hacked the hackers?"

"I'm not without a sense of irony, Suit."

Hawke couldn't tell if Shariff was joking, or if he even knew how.

"That explains why the Cabal sent the Bratva after me once we escaped Birmingham. The Cabal must have told them I hacked them and they would get their bitcoins back after they found me."

"So your plan involves the Bratva then?" Shariff said. "You fool, they'll make the Cabal's interrogation techniques look tame in comparison!"

"Best we do this right then."

"We?" Shariff asked.

"Yes, we. I'm guessing someone as paranoid as you planned for the worst-case scenario of losing the micro-SD card. I'd wager you put some sort of tracking code in it or something."

"Of course I did, Suit. Do you think I wouldn't be prepared for the entire state-sponsored apparatus to hunt me down? You think the government would really respect property rights if it's something they wanted? No, Suit, they will come for all of us one day. So you'd better be prepared today."

"My thoughts exactly. So you can tell me where the wallet file is right now?"

"Yes." Shariff didn't speak for a moment but Hawke could hear the smashing of his fingers on a keyboard. "Found it. It's been online for an hour now."

"All right. Now, it's time to get it back."

"How, Suit?"

"I've taken a liking to kicking down doors." Hawke proceeded to explain his plan.

And after hearing the plan in its entirety, it was Shariff's turn to wonder, who would be crazy enough to do that?

HAWKE'S FLIGHT

The Isle of Man was an erstwhile pirate's cove whose sons and daughters wanted the world to think it went legit. Thousand-dollar suits may cover up kraken tattoos and legal contracts ostensibly replaced treasure maps, but the jolly roger still flew if you knew where to look. And in the digital age that place was the dark web, an underground network of sites only accessible using specialized anonymity-enabling software.

Servo had equipped Hawke's smartphone with all the tricks of a cypherpunk, including onion VPN software that allowed him to anonymously find an underground digital marketplace where *everything* was for sale and only bitcoin was accepted. Hawke searched the website, navigating past all manner of rebels and criminals offering their goods and services: drugs, guns, stolen merchandise, and, much to his current interest, smuggling.

He found a local pilot specializing in the irregular movement of cargo across borders, and with the correct number of bitcoins sent as payment courtesy of Shariff, they agreed to meet at the airport and fulfill Hawke's travel plans—no questions asked.

The woman who showed up outside the specified airplane hangar looked like a punk rock exile. The sides of her head were shaved with her remaining jet-black hair swept violently sideways. Earrings circled her ears from top to bottom and a bull ring stud dangled from her nose. Tattooed wings spread around her neck and an abused leather bomber jacket covered up the rest of an extensive canvas of ink.

She introduced herself as Lukas. Behind the bloodshot eyes was a woman gathering her second wind. Hawke felt under different circumstances they could have been friends.

"I'm going to England," Hawke handed a bar napkin with the GPS coordinates of Shariff's micro-SD card.

She studied them briefly. "That's the middle of nowhere."

Hawke nodded.

Lukas shrugged. "Whatever, let's get moving."

She took a swig of a mickey and noticed Hawke's concerned expression. "Don't worry, it's only vodka."

"Good thing."

"For sure, you *do not* want to fly with me after I've been drinking tequila. Shit gets wobbly."

Lukas led Hawke to a row of nested planes and pulled the yellow wheel chocks away from the tires of a single-engine Cessna. She hauled herself up into the cabin and barked back at Hawke, "You gonna get in or what?"

Hawke figured he didn't have a choice. Once inside she helped him into a backpack parachute and headset and told him to buckle in. Many of the plane's instrument dials had broken glass, which under normal circumstances might be a problem, but Hawke told himself it just meant Lukas was such a skilled aviator that all she needed to pilot the plane was her gut instinct. Lukas fired up the plane and it slowly coughed to life. Hawke didn't know much about planes, but he knew enough about engines to know that they shouldn't sound like a two-pack-a-day smoker.

"Is that normal?" he yelled through the headset.

"No, usually it sounds terrible. But I've been working on the engine myself."

"You're a mechanic, too?"

"Hell no. But YouTube has videos on everything!" And with that last reassurance, Lukas pushed the plane forward to the unoccupied runway. She spoke to the traffic controller, which sounded less like takeoff instructions and more like a negotiation. With a flick of a switch to kill the radio, she informed Hawke, "We're golden."

He gave his most confident thumbs up, and with a hopeful roar of the engine, the little Cessna managed to get airborne. They quickly left the Isle of Man behind and crossed the Irish Sea. Before he knew it, they were over England, heading straight to where the wallet file, Noor, and Agent 21 were expected to be. He checked his watch. Two hours until the wallet was restored and, assuming Agent 21 succeeded at coercing Noor into giving up her password, Satoshi's Fortune would be in the Cabal's hands.

And Noor would be of no further use to them.

There was the occasional glow of a small town and an even smaller farm, but for the most part the landscape below was a mix of deep blues and blacks in the shape of trees and open fields. After what seemed like an eternity, Lukas shouted, "It's just up ahead. You ready?"

"Don't land nearby. I'm not exactly an expected guest."

Lukas looked sideways and cocked an eyebrow. "Land?"

"Isn't there some old abandoned World War Two airport around here or something?"

"You read too many spy novels."

Hawke didn't argue. The straps of his parachute suddenly weighed heavy around his shoulders. "You expect me to jump?"

"Why else would I have you put on a parachute?"

"I don't know, in case we crashed?"

"What good is a parachute in a crash?" Lukas shook her head as if Hawke was the dumbest man she had ever met. Hawke, quickly pulling up a YouTube video on his smartphone on how to skydive, wasn't so sure she was wrong.

***

Hawke couldn't tell if he was listening to the air screaming by his ears or if it was his own screams. Regardless, he was falling to the earth at over a hundred miles per hour and it was noisy. His eyes watered behind ill-fitting goggles and his heart pumped a deluge of adrenalin through his system, but all he could think about was that he had already paid Lukas in full, so it mattered little to her if the parachute opened or not.

She had flown as high as she could manage with the goal of putting the most distance between Hawke and the earth. If he froze or needed to use the backup chute, it would give him more time to save himself. And gave Lukas more getaway time if he didn't.

After counting off fifteen seconds, as per the YouTube video's clear instructions, Hawke yanked on the ripcord. The thin fabric of the parachute blossomed above him, to his immediate relief, and he managed to steer clear of any trees and land with a roll across a farm field. He dusted himself off and tossed the goggles and helmet aside. He did away with the backpack and watched the parachute drift away until it wrapped itself around the nearest tree.

His phone's GPS pointed him in the right direction. He stuck to the treeline for an easier approach and twenty minutes later could see the outline of an old brick farmhouse standing resolutely against the elements. No other buildings were visible in the surrounding lands. The grass was overgrown and it looked like the owners had simply walked away for better opportunities. The only indications that Shariff's GPS coordinates were correct was a modern satellite dish pointed to the sky and another black Mercedes parked in the driveway.

Hawke stayed concealed among the trees and kept glancing at his watch. Based on when the micro-SD card had first touched the internet and started downloading a copy of the blockchain, Hawke estimated he had just over half an hour before the Cabal gained complete control over Satoshi's Fortune.

Hawke ignored his first instinct, which involved kicking down the Cabal's front door and imposing his will on Agent 21, because it had a close to zero percent chance of success.

Instead, Hawke walked up to the front door.
And knocked.

AGENT 21'S MEETUP

As dawn snuck up on the farmhouse, it was Agent 21 who first heard the unexpected knock. Nobody outside their ranks knew of the Cabal safe house's existence, so he was immediately on alert. The entire farmhouse had remained empty since it had been foreclosed on years earlier, save for a workstation with a wall of monitors mounted against the back of the sizable living room. It was one of these monitors that Agent 21 scrutinized to see who had knocked on their door—and saw Henry Hawke with his hands in his pockets on the front steps, calmly waiting.

Agent 21 had spared him at Ka-shing's, but he deemed this unwelcome appearance a violation of the deal he had made with Noor.

"Kill him," Agent 21 said to the box-shaped guard who had accompanied him from the Isle of Man. The guard didn't flinch at the order. He obediently removed his pistol and lumbered to the front door without question.

Agent 21 expected to watch a quick execution on the monitor, but instead saw an apparent negotiation take place, the results of which entailed the guard returning with Hawke at gunpoint. Hawke stopped in the middle of the room, his hands up in a position of surrender. But his smile told a different story.

"I'm here for the bitcoin meetup," he said.

"The what?" Agent 21 was losing patience.

"You know, everyone gets together and talks bitcoin. Apparently they're all the rage."

"Why is he not neutralized?" Agent 21 asked the guard.

"He said you would want to know what he knows . . . about someone called Nakamoto."

Agent 21's eyes narrowed on Hawke and wondered what game he was playing. The Cabal's priority was Satoshi's Fortune, and to that end he had the wallet file. He had Jarvenpaa's password written down, some nonsensical phrase of numbers, letters, and special characters that was impossible for anyone not a genius to remember. He had Noor bound and ready to deliver her password once the blockchain finished downloading shortly.

He had everything he needed to find Satoshi's Fortune.

But he didn't have Satoshi's identity.

"Tell me what I don't know about Satoshi Nakamoto," Agent 21 demanded.

"You see, this is exactly the sort of thing they talk about at bitcoin meetups."

The audible click from the guard cocking the hammer on his pistol echoed in the living room.

"Okay, okay," Hawke acknowledged the warning. "Here's what I know . . ."

Hawke proceeded to list the various publicly available facts about Satoshi, his birthday, the message in the genesis block, then he moved on to theories about his disappearance, such as he died at Fukushima. He even outlined the case that Satoshi Nakamoto wasn't a person at all, but the name of a secret CIA black project. There was nothing that Agent 21 didn't already have in his dossier and nothing that told him who Satoshi really was. Hawke proceeded to explain the history behind the Cabal and how they had inadvertently created Satoshi as a counterbalance to their power.

The minutes continued to pass and he grew more impatient as Hawke rambled on, as if reciting a poorly memorized presentation.

The Cabal agent glanced at Noor, who looked just as annoyed by Hawke.

"I already know all of that," Agent 21 said sharply.

"I know." Hawke grinned as he checked his watch. "I just needed to kill some time."

Now there was another knock at the door. A much louder one.

Agent 21 shot a look to the monitor but saw only static.

There was a second knock, louder still. It was then Agent 21 realized that it wasn't actually a knock but the powerful attempts of someone trying to kick in the front door.

There was a harsh crack as the hinges were ripped from the door frame and the lock sheared off. The hundred-year-old door fell flat on its face with a detonation of air and dust as two men passed through the threshold. The first man didn't garner a second look, while the other immediately commanded the room due to his towering stature, his menacing growl, and the crowbar firmly in his grip.

"I am Maxim Makarov, Avtoritet of the Bratva. And you—"

"—I know who you are." Agent 21's gun was already pointed at the Russian's chest. "And you have no business here."

Makarov. *The Bratva.* Agent 21 did not like the Bratva. They were sledgehammers where a ball-peen hammer would suffice. Loud, tumultuous bears where a silent owl would catch the prey without alarming the entire forest. Unfortunately, Rickard had involved them in the hunt for Satoshi's Fortune, and despite Agent 21's attempted subterfuge and misdirection, they were clearly still in pursuit and had found the safe house.

But how had they found the safe house?

It was outlandish to think that Rickard would have informed the Russians of their location. Satoshi's Fortune was nearly in the hands of the Cabal and Rickard had never been hesitant to cut ties with anyone he deemed expendable.

Then again, how had Hawke found the safe house?

Agent 21's eyes darted to the micro-SD card adaptor plugged into a computer at the workstation and knew the answer.

Aziz Shariff.

HAWKE'S REBELLION

The Russians had been a bit late arriving, but Hawke had luckily managed to stall for time by repeatedly channelling his inner Shariff. He had mixed feelings about involving them, seeing as Makarov had already tried to shoot him. But once he realized the Cabal had lied to them, they became a weapon—Hawke's only weapon—to use against Agent 21.

Though the farmhouse living room was quite spacious, Hawke felt claustrophobic with all the players present for the end game—two Cabal agents, two Russian gangsters. They all puffed out their chests and readied themselves for the pending battle.

Noor sat uncomfortably in the far corner out of harm's way, at least for now. Hawke fought to avoid her attempts at eye contact and continued to scan the room for an object that was the key to stopping the Cabal. One that he and Shariff prayed was still in Agent 21's possession—and there it was, sitting idly by on the workstation desk, unaware of its importance.

"You are Bird Man?" Makarov grabbed Hawke's attention by jabbing the crowbar at him like a lethal teacher's aide.

The sudden jerking movement caused the guard to grasp his pistol with both hands and spread into a shooter's stance, which Makarov ignored. Even with two guns trained on him, the Avtoritet showed no concern for his safety, as if a mere gun could do no harm to his massive bulk. Seeing as how neither of the Cabal men held an elephant gun, Hawke couldn't really blame him.

"Henry Hawke, yes," he confirmed.

"Very good, Bird Man. Now where are our bitcoins, as Crazy Man on phone promised?"

Hawke grimaced. This is where the plan got a little dicey. In order to get Makarov to come to the safe house, Shariff had promised him bitcoins. The return of his stolen bitcoins, to be precise. And he wouldn't be happy with whoever had held them.

Hawke felt the dampness on his brow. His mouth grew dry. He didn't have the bitcoins.

But he knew who did. Sort of.

Hawke motioned to Agent 21. "This guy has your bitcoins. The Cabal, who I'm sure the Crazy Man told you all about, stole your bitcoins in the first place so you would have the proper motivation to chase me. You think it was just a coincidence you got robbed and then when the time was right, the Mystery Man offers to help you?"

"Mystery Man says you stole them," Makarov said and then smashed the crowbar against the wall. Cracked plaster crumbled to the floor, a sign of things to come for whoever held his bitcoins, if you substituted plaster for bones.

390

"Who do you think was more likely to break through your expert-level security; a dumbass millennial with no formal computer training? Or a powerful international Cabal with all the resources in the world?"

"Yuriy?" Makarov deferred to his weasel-faced partner, obviously the more tech-savvy of them. Yuriy Petrovich had stopped Makarov from potentially killing Hawke in the Sanctuary, and Hawke hoped he would do so again. If he agreed with Hawke, then the plan would at least have a chance of success. If he didn't, then Hawke would walk with a limp for the rest of his life—if he walked at all.

Petrovich pursed his lips as he considered the question. He took his time deciding which of the two options was more likely—and which one was more likely to make him look better in the Bratva's eyes.

With an adjustment of his crooked glasses, his decision was made. He explained something to Makarov in Russian that decided Hawke's—and bitcoin's—fate.

Makarov pulled the crowbar back and roared forward, ready to eviscerate his target.

"Makarov and the Bratva do not like being used!" Makarov shouted into Agent 21's face.

Hawke wanted to hug the little Russki and breathed a sigh of relief. He must have accepted his explanation and now Makarov was Agent 21's problem.

But Agent 21 didn't give an inch to the giant Russian towering over him. The threat hadn't even seemed to raise his pulse. He looked up into the jaws of the bear and said, as calm as ever, "We have not used you in any way. You cannot make such dangerous claims without proof."

Hawke pointed to the workstation and the item he had earlier sought. "His phone. It contains a bitcoin wallet with all your bitcoins."

All eyes turned to a smartphone resting on the workstation—Shariff's smartphone that Agent 21 had taken in Birmingham.

And then, on cue, the smartphone beeped. The cheerful, coin-shaking sound announcing to the room that a bitcoin transaction was received.

Agent 21 reached for the smartphone, but Makarov smashed the crowbar on the table, narrowly missing the phone but destroying the USB card reader that held the micro-SD card in an explosion of plastic shards. Makarov pawed the phone and tossed it to Petrovich.

"It's locked." Petrovich switched to English for Hawke's benefit.

"F@ckTheCabal!" Hawke said. "One word. Ampersand for the a. Exclamation mark. Capital F, T, and C."

Petrovich eyed Hawke, who hoped the Russians cared more about getting the bitcoins than asking why he knew the password to someone else's phone. Petrovich apparently did, and typed in the password.

"His bitcoin wallet just received fifty-thousand bitcoins. The exact amount that was stolen from us!" Petrovich informed Makarov.

Most other men would have attempted to flee before Makarov enacted his revenge, but Agent 21 remained steadfast. "Doesn't mean those were your bitcoins. Could have been from anywhere."

There was no change in his demeanour, but Hawke watched closely for any indication that he realized who had actually hacked the Bratva in the first place, and who could have possibly known an address on that bitcoin wallet to send the fifty-thousand bitcoins to. After a moment, Agent 21's lips twitched into a brief smirk—a bitter one at that—and Hawke knew that he knew.

Aziz Shariff.

"Follow the blockchain," Hawke told Petrovich. The Russian eyed him again but followed the suggestion. With every single bitcoin transaction captured forever on the blockchain, Petrovich already knew the address to which the stolen coins had been moved—he had been watching it obsessively since the hack—and he checked that address now.

It was empty.

The fifty thousand coins had just been moved out in one transaction.

It was the same transaction that appeared in the bitcoin wallet on the phone in hand.

Agent 21's smartphone held the same bitcoins stolen from the Russian mob. His fate had been sealed as soon as the bitcoin transaction was sent and recorded in the blockchain for all to see.

"He stole from the Bratva!" Petrovich exclaimed.

Before Petrovich could finish his sentence, the living room at the quiet abandoned homestead erupted into a warzone.

Makarov jerked his crowbar above his head with two

hands, but before he could smash it down onto Agent 21, he was hit by a flurry of bullets.

The guard's small-calibre pistol knocked Makarov sideways, but only by a step or two. Nothing vital was hit and the half-dozen bullets lodged into his bulk did nothing but further enrage the Avtoritet. The guard ejected the empty magazine and loaded a replacement just as the crowbar smashed down on his right shoulder with a sickening crack of splintering bone. The guard screamed in pain, which was promptly silenced forever when Makarov landed a second strike straight on top of his skull.

Hawke dashed across the room in the commotion to shield Noor, who seemed more annoyed that he was blocking her view of the madness than thankful for his efforts at keeping her safe. Holding her close, he couldn't help but notice she still smelled of lilacs.

"What the hell is going on?" she asked.

"What does it look like? I'm saving you *and* bitcoin. I think it's going pretty well, all things considered."

Hawke didn't wait for her to disagree and looked over his shoulder, just in time to see Makarov twist the crowbar free from the guard's skull. He patted the blood-covered crowbar in his palm while snarling at Agent 21.

And then Makarov pounced. The arc of the crowbar splayed blood across the ceiling and came towards Agent 21 in a grotesquely artistic display. The Cabal agent didn't raise his hands to shield himself from the impending strike, nor did he flinch at all. Just as the steel instrument was poised to meet his skull, he casually sidestepped the incoming blow.

The forward momentum of the missed strike knocked Makarov off balance, opening a window for Agent 21 to counterattack. He quickly dropped the angle of his pistol and fired into Makarov's feet.

The Avtoritet yelped and fell to his knees. Now in a vulnerable position, he found himself at eye level with Agent 21 and, like any wounded beast, lashed out. A wild swipe of the crowbar caught Agent 21 by surprise and clipped the side of his gun, flinging it across the room.

Being unarmed did little to slow Agent 21's methodical attack. He circled around Makarov and having learned his lesson stayed just out of range of the desperate swings of the crowbar. Between each, Agent 21 thrust inwards and jabbed Makarov in the neck before retreating out of range of the follow-up backhand swing.

The strategic strikes to Makarov's windpipe began to pay dividends as he started to noticeably tire. In a last-ditch effort, Makarov hurled the crowbar at Agent 21's head, which he easily avoided. The crowbar clanged harmlessly against the wall and left Makarov exposed.

Agent 21 rushed in and with all his strength jabbed a hooked finger into the Avtoritet's eye socket—and yanked backwards.

Makarov's howling cries rattled the windows and triggered the primal flight response of any living creature within earshot. He flung his hands up to his face to attempt to staunch the blood pouring from the hole where his left eye had been.

Unflustered, Agent 21 circled his prey and calculated the most efficient way to end the Bratva threat. He spotted the discarded crowbar and picked it up, feeling its heft in his hands. He positioned himself squarely behind the once unstoppable force that was Maxim Makarov, Avtoritet of the Bratva, and raised the crowbar for the final blow.

Hawke cringed as he watched Agent 21's victory unfold. In seconds, Makarov would be dead and nothing would stand in the Cabal's way.

Hawke had failed, again.

Agent 21 would not only be free to claim Satoshi's Fortune, but to also deal with himself and Noor. Hawke frantically searched for an idea—anything—to stop the crowbar from striking Makarov's head.

And then he saw it. Agent 21's pistol.

He left Noor and scrambled across the floor and dove after the weapon. He snatched it off the ground and jumped to his feet, immediately training the pistol sights on Agent 21's chest.

Hawke was about to pull the trigger when his stomach sank. The pistol's chamber was collapsed from where it had been struck by the crowbar. The gun would never fire again.

Agent 21 watched Hawke's fruitless effort with a detached curiosity, and maybe, perhaps for the first time, a sense of happiness. He heaved up on the crowbar a bit further to ensure a fatal blow to Makarov's head and was all set to come down—when suddenly he froze.

And his happiness departed as quickly as it had arrived.

It was as if someone had unplugged Agent 21. The crowbar fell from his grasp and rattled harmlessly on the ground. His already pale complexion turned almost translucent. And then, slowly, as if his last act was to fight gravity, he collapsed face down onto the floor.

Protruding from the base of Agent 21's skull was a black-on-black switchblade.

Petrovich stood wide-eyed over his handiwork and looked at his hands as if seeing them for the first time.

Hawke dropped the useless gun and ran to Noor. He untied her arms and was hopeful for a hug but settled for the thank you she quietly offered.

Petrovich left his first kill and went to his Avtoritet. The flow of blood had slowed to a trickle and the cries were staunched by gritted teeth. The little Russian struggled to support Makarov's weight, but he kept at it and both eventually rose to their feet.

"We have what we came for, Henry Hawke. You and your Crazy Man honoured your end of deal and we have our stolen bitcoins back. Now, we go," Petrovich said.

Hawke kept a close eye on them as they hobbled out the front door, with blood trailing behind. Only once he was sure they had left did he exhale.

"It's over," Noor said. She looked at the bodies of the Cabal agents, the latest to pay the price for Satoshi's Fortune.

Hawke eyed the workstation. "No, not yet."

***

Hawke picked up the remains of the USB card reader that Makarov had crushed with his crowbar. The micro-SD card containing the wallet file was cracked into pieces and unusable. The only copy was now on the computer in front of him. He pulled a chair to the workstation and checked on the status of the wallet—the blockchain had finished downloading and it was now fully restored.

The balance screamed at Hawke: 980,000 bitcoins.

All that separated him from the greatest fortune of the twenty-first century were two passwords.

Hawke glanced at Agent 21 staring blankly at him. He must have possessed Jarvenpaa's password. He left the computer and knelt down apprehensively at the Cabal agent's side, not entirely trusting that you could actually kill a ghost. He wasn't surprised the body was already cold. Hawke searched the pockets until he found a small notebook with a leather cover. He flipped it open and found the last entry which was random alphanumeric text.

Jarvenpaa's password.

He returned to the workstation where he typed the password into the wallet. Large green text flashed across the screen: ACCEPTED.

Hawke took a deep breath. Only one more password remained.

As if on cue, Hawke felt a warm set of hands on his shoulders. And smelled lilacs.

"I'm assuming you saved me because I'm a Keeper of the Fortune," Noor said, looking over his shoulder to see the fortune half unlocked.

"I didn't save you *just* because of that," Hawke replied.

"You're such a gentleman."

"A rogue, really."

"Perhaps."

"Do you trust me?"

"Perhaps."

Hawke angled the keyboard slightly to beckon Noor to action.

She paused. "You know what you're doing?"

"As much as I ever do."

His honesty gave her a moment's pause. But Noor didn't withdraw either. She eventually positioned herself in front of the keyboard. Her fingers moved gracefully across the keys and ended the dance by landing on enter.

ACCEPTED.

Hawke now had 980,000 bitcoins at his fingertips, trusted by Noor to make the right decision, whatever that was. With her work done she turned to leave.

"I'm going to see about how we can get out of here," she said.

"Don't you want to find out what I'm going to do with the fortune?"

"No need. I already know."

"Oh yeah? What's that?"

"Something to make me roll my eyes no doubt."

Hawke caught a smile when she looked back at him. And in her eyes he saw a challenge, to both make a decision and live with the consequences. Without another word she left him alone with a fortune to do with as he pleased.

That smile, Hawke mused, it was worth the wait.

He turned his attention back to the computer screen, and the biggest decision of his life.

Many more a man would go rogue if he only knew how.

The words still haunted him, a cryptic riddle, but one that now demanded an answer.

Hawke removed the orange flash drive from his pocket and inserted it into the computer tower. A folder automatically opened displaying the three scripts.

The first script would send the entire balance to Shariff's provably unspendable address, loudly proclaiming to the whole world that Satoshi's Fortune could never be spent.

The second script would send the balance to Hawke's personal address, announcing that Satoshi's Fortune was in play—and possibly destroying all trust the world ever had in the cryptocurrency.

And lastly, the script Hawke created, the result of him knowing just enough to be competently dangerous. Using this script would destroy everything on this computer—including the wallet file—and nobody would ever be able to control Satoshi's Fortune.

Many more a man would go rogue if he only knew how.

Hawke's choices were clear:

Shariff's nuclear option.

Incredible wealth and control of an empire.

Or keep bitcoin and the legend of Satoshi's Fortune alive.

The cursor on the screen blinked patiently, awaiting Hawke's answer.

He typed in his decision and hit enter.

And with that simple act, Henry Hawke went rogue.

EPILOGUE I

John Francis Rickard stood on the steps of the Bank of England and allowed himself a moment to look back over his shoulder. The bank, like its cousin in New York, was a fortress built to withstand a war. Defending three-and-a-half acres of bankers and shaped like a trapezoid, the building was an incongruous mix of unwelcoming designs from three equally gloomy architects over three hundred years.

Rickard had just finished a midnight meeting with the current governor to ensure that, despite the political risk of spending more than a fifth of England's GDP on bailouts, the money would continue to flow unabated from the taxpayers to the United Kingdom's private banks. He smirked at the irony that while the Bank of England continued to advocate the financial soundness of printing money, The Old Lady of Threadneedle Street, as the bank was known, was like any old lady in that she was certain another depression was just around the corner and hid her cash under her mattress. In the case of this Old Lady, however, instead of under a mattress it was under lock and key, guarded by a small regiment. And instead of cash, it was over five thousand tons of gold, or approximately three percent of all the gold ever mined since the beginning of human history.

On top of his delight with the governor's reaction tonight—Rickard loved it when his people attempted even the slightest resistance as it made his power all the more absolute when he tossed aside their notion of independence with a wave of his hand and a bang of his cane—any minute he was expecting a text from Agent 21 confirming that Satoshi's Fortune had been collected and the 980,000 bitcoins had been moved to a new address.

The act would trigger the destruction of the world's trust in bitcoin and initiate its downward spiral and eventual death. Rickard already had his media contacts preparing a flood of *Bitcoin is Dead* stories to fill the morning papers and memorialize the end. He was beginning to get antsy for confirmation from the field.

Rickard slowly descended the bank's steep steps to his awaiting black Mercedes sedan, one hand gripped around the serpent's head and the other clutching his coat drawn against the cold. His square-jawed driver held open the door and helped him into the backseat. Just as he got settled, his phone vibrated. Rickard smiled to himself and began reading the text. The leathery smile quickly vanished when he realized the message wasn't from Agent 21, nor was it something he expected to ever see. He pulled out his reading glasses to ensure he had correctly read the message from the unknown number.

`I hear you've been looking for me.`

A second text quickly followed with an address in London's Balham neighbourhood. Rickard huffed and barked at his driver to head there at once. The traffic was thin and after fifteen minutes of unreturned calls and texts to Agent 21, the Mercedes sedan pulled up to the specified address.

Everything about the semi-detached house politely whispered England: the Victorian design, with bricks old enough to have witnessed the signing of the Magna Carta, and the perfectly coiffed shrubbery joining forces with a knee-high wrought-iron gate that didn't fool anyone into thinking the property was secure. Rickard pushed open the gate with his cane and rapped on the front door. After a disrespectful amount of time with no answer, and the cold beginning to seep into his bones, he was about to announce his arrival again, with more force, when the handle clicked and the door slowly opened.

Rickard was greeted warmly by a man in a crisp sweater with the collar poking out. He was sitting in a wheelchair.

"Mr. Rickard. Pleasure to meet you. Please, do come in and shut the door behind you." The man rolled away, leaving Rickard no choice but to follow his instructions.

"Aren't you going to introduce yourself?" Rickard asked once inside with the door shut. He undid his wool coat and removed his bowler hat.

A warm smile. "Why bother if you already know my name?"

Virgil Pennyworth was right. A quick call to Dunwoody on the drive over had revealed both the phone number and the address were listed to Pennyworth. To Rickard's displeasure they lacked a dossier on him, and he immediately ordered Dunwoody to begin one.

"Yes, I know your name, my new friend," Rickard responded.

"Please, call me Virgil. I shudder to think we're friends, and I'm horrified to think I'm in your possession." Pennyworth wheeled himself down the hallway and left Rickard to follow. They entered the study judiciously warmed by a fire flickering in the hearth, which Pennyworth manoeuvred beside. On the mantel were photographs of a younger, healthier version of the man now warming himself by the burning logs. In one photo, he and a group of unshaved and long-haired college students posed around a computer the size of a fridge. In what might have been the most recent photo, he was standing in nearly the same spot as he was now sitting, holding an orange kitten.

On cue, the adult version of the tabby sauntered in, glanced at Rickard, and seeing nothing of interest, hopped onto Pennyworth's lap, and began purring loudly. Official documents from universities hung above an ancient walnut desk and multiple laptops were set up, with screensavers floating by.

"Tea?" Pennyworth motioned to a silver pot, mugs, and milk on a coffee table centered in front of the fireplace with a matching leather couch and chair. "I apologize. I was feeling a chill and already poured myself a cup." He continued to pet the cat while sipping his tea.

"No thank you. I don't drink dirty pond water."

"Uhh," Pennyworth feigned indignation, "Anarchy in the UK."

"Since I'm still on New York time, a nightcap would be more suitable. Mind if I help myself to a gin?"

"Of course not. However, I'm embarrassed to say I haven't a drop in the house. I'm sure you'll be fine though. I don't see this lasting long."

"No, neither do I." Rickard sat opposite Pennyworth in a leather chair. Its arms were worn and cracked and its seat formed to another man's shape. He rested his hands on the cane straddled between his legs.

"So, you're Satoshi Nakamoto," Rickard said.

The Cabal leader was caught off guard by Pennyworth's hearty laugh. The cat opened its eyes, looked around to see what all the noise was about, and sensing it was nothing that would affect his life went back to sleep.

"I'm very sorry if you've been misled, as I am not Satoshi Nakamoto. I merely wanted to have a chat. I thought all your dossiers and assets would have told you that. You have a dossier on me, I'm sure."

The twinkle in Pennyworth's eye antagonized Rickard like nothing else before it.

"If you're not Satoshi, why did you invite me here?"

"For my own ego, I'm afraid to admit. I wanted to look the head of the Cabal in the eye, while I still had the chance."

"What was your role in the creation of bitcoin?"

Pennyworth considered the question and sipped his tea. "Who I am and what my role was is rather unimportant in the greater scheme of things. Let's just say I am someone interested in the people involved: the cypherpunks, the libertarians, the crypto-anarchists, the bankers. Together they offer an incredible mixture of potential, and together they just might deliver that paradigm shift so many of us want."

"And what paradigm shift is that?"

Pennyworth raised an eyebrow, as if the answer was self-evident. "The personalization of money, obviously. We already achieved the personalization of information with the personal computer and world wide web, and now bitcoin just may lead us on that next step towards true freedom of the individual."

"Bitcoin will never work," Rickard said. "I have an army of economists who agree with me."

"Then this was all much ado about nothing."

"I'm only going to ask you once. Who is Satoshi Nakamoto?"

Pennyworth put aside his tea and held out the palms of his hands. "We all are."

"That is not an acceptable answer."

Pennyworth shrugged. "You can also find it unacceptable that two plus two equals four, but it's a futile endeavour all the same. I should think it's clear by now to a man of your obvious intelligence that Satoshi is not a person."

A wave of irritation swept over Rickard and he punctuated each subsequent statement with a bang of his cane. "I will crush you. I will bankrupt you. I will use all my considerable wealth and power to destroy you."

Pennyworth rubbed the arm of his wheelchair, a slight tremor in his hand. But it wasn't out of fear. "There is absolutely nothing you can threaten me with."

"I've heard more than one man say that before death, only to change his tune. Don't you want to live out the rest of your days spending whatever little fortune you must have? If it's about money, I can handsomely compensate you for whatever information you can provide."

"It's not about the money. It's about leaving this world knowing you were part of something special." Pennyworth smiled. "Besides, no matter how much money you have, you can't take it with you."

"I never quite believed that."

"No. I suppose you wouldn't."

Rickard banged his serpent cane twice more on the floor. "The Cabal will soon have access to Satoshi's Fortune. And then with the simple movement of a few worthless digital coins, the world's trust in bitcoin and Satoshi's credibility, whoever he is, will be destroyed. Bitcoin will end up being nothing more than a cautionary tale mentioned in the same breath as tulip mania and beanie babies."

"You seem to be spending a lot of time and effort trying to destroy something you already consider worthless, don't you think?"

Rickard stood defiantly. "This is not over."

"I don't expect it to be. I expect the death throes from an outdated system where democracy is bought and paid for, manipulated and benefiting only a select few. You and your ilk will come at cryptocurrencies in a variety of attack vectors. As an enemy. As a friend. All kinds of tactics to try and gain control. But your problem is that the code is out there. And knowledge spread among the masses can't be undone."

"Nonsense from a man who refuses to accept how the world truly works."

"When the power is with the people, I tend not to be so pessimistic."

"You're not actually saying you think you're going to win, are you?"

Pennyworth smiled. "No, I'm saying we already have."

The resulting silence spoke volumes.

Eventually the fire crackled to break the impasse.

"Thank you for the chat, Virgil. I won't forget this," Rickard snarled but left it at that.

"It doesn't matter what you do." Pennyworth held his gaze. "Have a safe trip, John."

Pennyworth listened to Rickard walk down the hallway and slam the door behind him. He thought about all those who had declared *We are all Satoshi* before him, how much so many had sacrificed, so much more than him in the end. All the cypherpunks, libertarians, crypto-anarchists, bankers, and ordinary people who had discovered bitcoin, got excited, and contributed in their own way. He returned to the soothing purr of the sleeping cat on his lap and whispered, not wanting to wake him, "We're going to be okay, Satoshi. The project is in good hands."

EPILOGUE II

Henry Hawke ignored the chill in his bones as the cold late autumn Glasgow rain made it clear why Scots spent so much time inside pubs. He stood a distance away from the other men and women wearing their best and blackest Sunday garments, out to impress each other almost as much as the Lord. They listened to every word spoken by the priest, each word more sombre than the last, but not out of place at a funeral for someone who had died so young. And so needlessly.

It was a funeral that could have taken place a hundred years ago—biblical passages of forgiveness and salvation, tears and wails, heavy drinking and simmering anger—not a funeral to be rebranded as a celebration of life; Servo's family was far too religious for such nonsense.

After the casket was lowered and the priest gave his final plea for Servo's soul, Hawke lingered by the grave and avoided the suspicious glares at being the only non-family member to attend. He didn't know if they wanted to blame him, something that Hawke didn't feel was unwarranted, or if they recognized him as a wanted man. Either way they left him alone.

Despite the risk of the police or Cabal appearing, Hawke felt compelled to pay his last respects. He owed it

409

to Servo based on their brief friendship and how much he had learned from the cypherpunk, from how brain wallets worked to what makes a perfect pint.

The rain rolled over the modest tombstone, which seemed obliged to already start crumbling at its edges, and Hawke was forced to smile at the inscription—*Discretion Will Guard You, Understanding Will Watch Over You*—and wondered if the proverb had already been checked to see if it had been turned into a bitcoin address.

Hawke thought of his uncle's own funeral, his own last words not inscribed on granite but engraved on metal by a watchmaker in Chicago.

Hawke was alone in the world, hunted by an international Cabal, never able to return to his old nine-to-five life. It suited him just fine. His thoughts drifted back to his conversation with Servo at his Sanctuary, something said in passing but now, as he stood in a muddy graveyard mourning his dead friend, carried a new meaning.

Peter Finlay also had a real interest in brain wallets.

Hawke looked to the silver watch wrapped around his wrist.

Many more a man would go rogue if he only knew how.

And Hawke smiled.

AFTERWORD

Who is Satoshi Nakamoto? As I write this in January 2019, nobody knows. I suppose it's possible the CIA does, but they're not the most talkative bunch.

To me, the answer to that question is the most remarkable aspect of the entire bitcoin project. It's not the decentralized currency or blockchain tech (though those are quite nice), but it's that Satoshi, after ten years and billions of dollars in wealth creation, hasn't been identified. Hell, we don't even know if Satoshi is a man, a woman, or an infinite number of monkeys bashing away at an infinite number of keyboards.

Think about that.

In the digital age where privacy is routinely invaded by corporations and governments, where individual sovereignty takes a back seat to the greater good (with a moral flexibility to what is both greater and good), where our digital fingerprints are left throughout cyberspace (and backed up on Facebook and NSA servers), Satoshi remains a ghost.

This accomplishment embodies what I believe it means to be a cypherpunk and something they've been trying to tell us is our right—*to selectively reveal oneself to the world.*

If someone can achieve that while being hunted by the most powerful organizations in the history of human civilization (don't kid yourself), then maybe there's hope for the rest of us.

Or maybe Satoshi gets outed the minute I release this book and makes me look like a fool.

Either way, I hope you and Satoshi enjoyed the book. And remember, *We are all Satoshi.*

Alastair Mitchell

ABOUT THE AUTHOR

Alastair Mitchell is the author of Satoshi's Fortune and the
All Jokes Aside series. That's pretty much all there is to
know at this point.

Contact information:
www.alastair-mitchell.com
alastair@alastair-mitchell.com

NEWSLETTER

Don't forget to join to my newsletter for updates and a
FREE copy of All Jokes Aside: What's Wrong with a Little
Destruction

www.alastair-mitchell.com/newsletter

BOOKS BY ALASTAIR MITCHELL

All Jokes Aside: What's Wrong with a Little Destruction

All Jokes Aside Vol.2: Everyone Needs a Hobby

TO LEARN MORE

Bitcoin: A Peer-to-peer Electronic Cash System:
https://bitcoin.org/en/bitcoin-paper

A Cypherpunk's Manifesto:
https://www.activism.net/cypherpunk/manifesto.html

www.ingramcontent.com/pod-product-compliance
Lightning Source LLC
Chambersburg PA
CBHW051208120726
47905CB00004B/1037